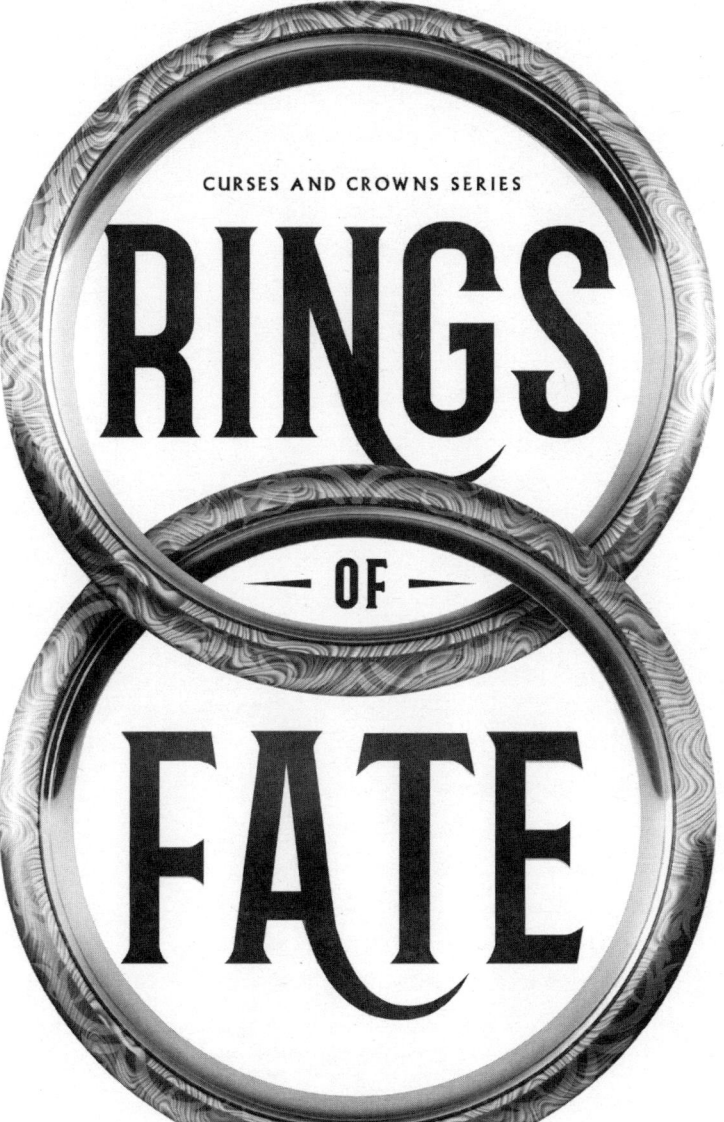

#1 *NEW YORK TIMES* BESTSELLING AUTHOR
MELISSA DE LA CRUZ

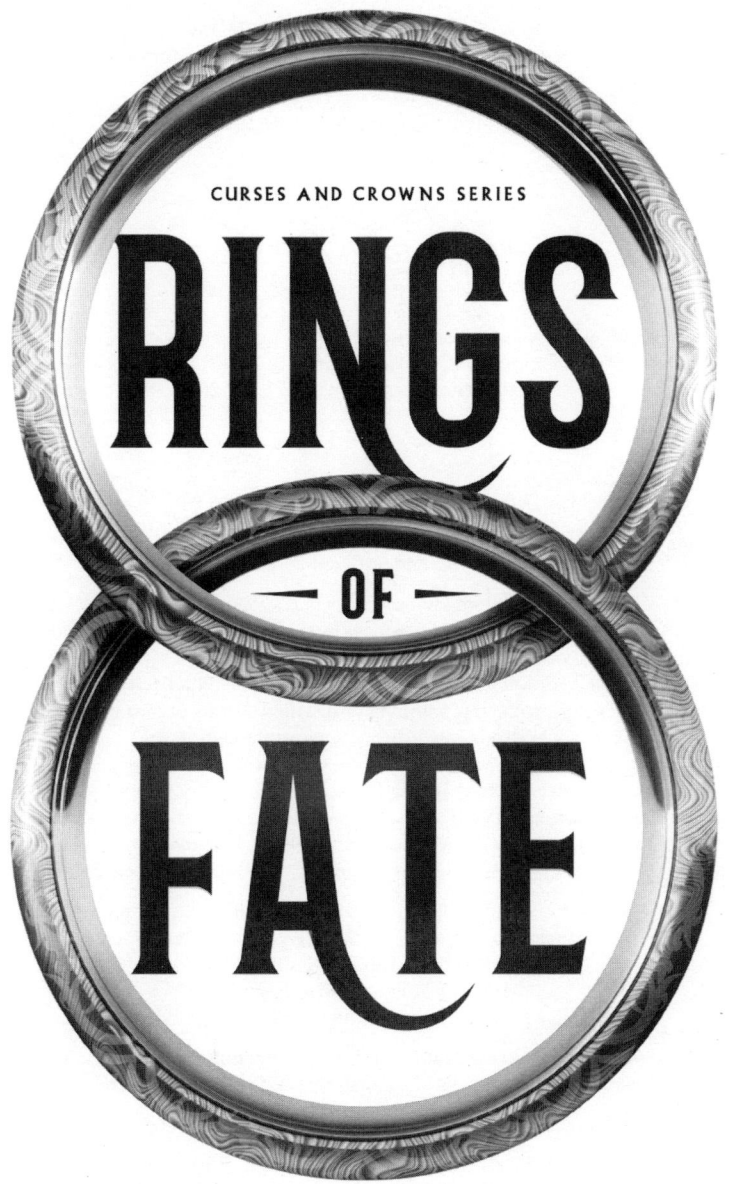

CURSES AND CROWNS SERIES

RINGS
— OF —
FATE

MICHAEL JOSEPH

PENGUIN MICHAEL JOSEPH

UK | USA | Canada | Ireland | Australia
India | New Zealand | South Africa

Penguin Michael Joseph is part of the Penguin Random House group of companies whose addresses can be found at global.penguinrandomhouse.com

Penguin Random House UK,
One Embassy Gardens, 8 Viaduct Gardens, London SW11 7BW

penguin.co.uk

Published by Penguin Michael Joseph, part of the Penguin Random House group of companies, in association with Red Tower Books, part of Entangled Publishing LLC 2026
001

Copyright © Melissa de la Cruz, 2026

The moral right of the author has been asserted

The Red Tower Books name and logo are trademarks of Entangled Publishing LLC and are used here under licence

Penguin Random House values and supports copyright. Copyright fuels creativity, encourages diverse voices, promotes freedom of expression and supports a vibrant culture. Thank you for purchasing an authorized edition of this book and for respecting intellectual property laws by not reproducing, scanning or distributing any part of it by any means without permission. You are supporting authors and enabling Penguin Random House to continue to publish books for everyone. No part of this book may be used or reproduced in any manner for the purpose of training artificial intelligence technologies or systems. In accordance with Article 4(3) of the DSM Directive 2019/790, Penguin Random House expressly reserves this work from the text and data mining exception

Original interior map art by Amy Acosta and Elizabeth Turner Stokes
Interior map frame images by Sinung Wahyono/Shutterstock
and Andrey_Kuzmin/Shutterstock
Interior design by Britt Marczak
Printed and bound in Great Britain by Clays Ltd, Elcograf S.p.A.

The authorized representative in the EEA is Penguin Random House Ireland, Morrison Chambers, 32 Nassau Street, Dublin D02 YH68

A CIP catalogue record for this book is available from the British Library

HARDBACK ISBN: 978-1-911-75008-6
TRADE PAPERBACK ISBN: 978-1-911-75009-3

Penguin Random House is committed to a sustainable future for our business, our readers and our planet. This book is made from Forest Stewardship Council® certified paper.

ALSO BY MELISSA DE LA CRUZ

ALEX & ELIZA TRILOGY

BLUE BLOODS SERIES

DISNEY'S DESCENDANTS SERIES

THE ENCANTO'S DAUGHTER DUOLOGY

HEART OF DREAD TRILOGY (WITH MICHAEL JOHNSTON)

OCTAGON VALLEY SERIES

THE QUEEN'S ASSASSIN DUOLOGY

NEVER AFTER SERIES

WITCHES OF EAST END TRILOGY

Going Dark
Jo & Laurie (with Margaret Stohl)
My Ex-Husband's Ex-Husband (with Rachel Cohn)
The Birthday Girl
The Five Stages of Courting Dalisay Ramos
When Stars Align

For Mike, for everything

and

For Liz, for letting me write it

Rings of Fate is a fun, adventurous new adult romantasy about a sassy barmaid and a cursed prince who team up to save the kingdom. The story contains elements that might not be suitable for all readers, including graphic violence, blood, injury, drugging, attempted assault, kidnapping, imprisonment, torture, whipping, execution, perilous situations, fire, sexual activity, and alcohol use on the page. War and death of family are discussed. Readers who may be sensitive to these elements, please take note.

"Marry the person who picks it up if she's a woman; you shan't marry ME!"

— *The Rose and the Ring*, William Makepeace Thackeray

PART ONE

THE PRINCE AND THE BARMAID

CHAPTER ONE

Aren

When you're a barmaid, marriage proposals are a natural part of the job. A drunkard can find salvation in the bottom of a pint glass as easily as he can find love gazing across a bar. Luckily for me, I'm very good at saying no.

"Still no, Shep," I say firmly. "Don't you remember I turned you down yesterday?"

I set another tankard of ale on the bar and blink at the glassy-eyed farmer who just asked me to marry him for the tenth time this month. Will this jackass ever learn?

"Come on now. I'm serious, Aren," he slurs. His black, beady eyes are unfocused and glassy. "What're you gonna do with your life? Clean mugs all day? You'd be a good wife. You're always a'workin'. It's time you settled down."

This man exhausts me. Or is it all of the men in this town? In fact, I don't think I've ever felt more tired. I'm tired all the way to my bones.

And I'm only twenty-five.

My shoulders sag as I sigh, long and deep. There's no point in letting Shephard Belmis get to me. He's a mouse to be toyed with, and I'm the cat.

His drinking buddy, another ruddy-faced farmer, slaps him hard on the side of his head. "Leave 'er alone, arsehole. You're wasted. Lady's already told you no several times."

"This is your last chance! Marry me, Aren. Ye'd make a good wife and ma. With that sturdy—*hic*—back of yers. Sturdiest back in all of Evandale, and that's saying something!"

The nerve of this bastard. Where's the nearest cliff so I can promptly hurl myself off of it? I would rather die than marry a man who only sees me as a hardworking mule.

Without looking at the geezer, I fold my rag and set it neatly on the bar and prepare to bat around dear ol' Shep. I lean my forearms on the sticky counter, prop my chin on my hands, and flutter my eyelashes.

"A sturdy back! Such a compliment! Please, tell me more!"

"Well, since the wife passed, my kids ain't got no one to look after them," he whines.

"No one? Aren't you sitting right here? Unless you're a…" I pause and then gasp for effect. "…a ghost!"

"Blimey! I'm not a ghost!" But he clearly questions his existence on this corporeal plane because he holds his hands up to hazy eyes to inspect them for a second. Once satisfied that he is, in fact, a *living* old meat suit, he continues. "I just don't have those ca'bilities, you understand. Ain't no one else can cook 'em warm meals or make sure they's clothes is clean—*hic*. A man can't be livin' a life with no woman—*hic*. Ain't natural."

His buddy groans, having more good sense in him than ale, but Shepherd ignores him.

I slap my hand flat against my chest in fake surprise. "My goodness! I never thought of it like that. My heart—it's beating so fast! You really know how to sweet-talk a girl. This is all so…so…unexpected!"

The things I would do for one—just *one*—proposal that doesn't make me feel as sexy as a sack of flour.

Shep wobbles as he stands from his barstool and bows his head in a certain kind of reverence. His friend outright scoffs at this gesture. I can't stifle a laugh.

"So, what do you say, my—*hic*—love? Will you do me the honor of… my wifely honor? My wifely becoming…to me?"

He stopped being totally coherent long ago, but I have to admire his conviction. Shep blinks his droopy eyes as his head bobbles. Sad sack is waiting for an answer.

I've had practice rejecting Shephard Belmis and countless other farmers high on liquid courage, but like I said, I'm fucking tired.

I'm tired of running this bar that I still try to find love for. I'm tired of being on my feet from morning to night. I'm tired of never having any time for myself, not that I ever did anyway. I'm tired of this small-minded town. I'm tired of my regulars. I'm tired of my family, as much as I love them. I'm so tired I could scream.

And Shephard Belmis? I'm most tired of him.

So, I've taken an extra step to fix that tonight. I point to a wooden sign hanging behind me. Painted in neat black lettering, it reads:

BAR RULES

No spitting.
No bare feet.
No gambling.
No poisoning (knives and fists OK).

And last night, I hastily scrawled in one final rule.

No marriage proposals.

**If any of these rules are broken, patron must buy whole bar a round of drinks.*

A sobering shock settles on Shep's face as he reads the sign.
"Rules are rules, Shep," I say with a smirk as I wipe a glass clean.
Vindication.
His drinking buddy nearly doubles over in laughter.
"She's got ya, Shep," he cackles.
"But, but—*hic*—I was serious this time," Shep stutters between hiccups.
"So am I," I reply, elated that I've bested him.
"You'd make a good wife and ma," he rambles as I set down the clean glass and walk toward the end of the bar. "Who'll have you—*hic*—but me!"
He really knows how to woo a woman.
I reach a rope and tug, ringing a heavy brass bell. The sound of it cuts through the noise of the tavern, an alcoholic's dog whistle. The raucous din of the packed tavern quiets for only a moment, heads swiveling toward me.

I give them my best shit-eating grin. "Good news, degenerates! Next round's on Shep!"

Everyone explodes into cheers, so loud it makes the floorboards shake and the glasses on the bar clink together.

I lean over the bar, close to Shep's weathered face. Renewed hope flits in his eyes. He puckers his lips, expecting a kiss.

Instead, I reach into his pocket and pluck out a silver stamped with the crest of Alarice. "That's for the ale." I fish out the remaining three coins. "And the rest is for suggesting the insult of marriage."

His drinking buddy is crying tears of laughter now, and before Shephard can protest, I shove the coins into my apron. They land with a jingle against the rest stored there—just enough noise to remind me the night wasn't a complete waste.

I look out into the crowd. The place is packed. Low benches and long, well-worn tables are crammed with too many bodies. Farmers and laborers sit shoulder to shoulder and knee to knee with merchants and artisans, all of them clinking mugs like they're the best of friends. The Harvest Mother's festival begins tomorrow, so the mood is high. Evandale doesn't get many reasons to celebrate, with a backbreaking workday and the steep cut paid to the marquis, as predictable as the seasons. The very ale they're drinking is the product of the farmers' hard labor. I don't blame them for indulging, even if it does turn the best of men into bumbling idiots.

"Need a six cupper," Bonnie, my junior barmaid, interrupts my musing. She notices Shep, now completely passed out at the bar.

"Another proposal?" Bonnie asks, nodding in his direction. She's a little breathless from running around doling out pints, her cheeks almost as flushed as the patrons'. "How many is that this week?"

"I lost count," I say, pouring another mug. Bonnie stacks them high, like playing cards. She's an expert at this.

"And you'd never consider it?" Bonnie asks.

"Marrying one of these clowns? No fuckin' way. They're not looking for a wife, they're looking for a barmaid at home."

"I heard the marquis himself proposed. Is that true?"

I let out an annoyed sigh. "That old perv asked me to be his mistress, not his wife. Disgusting."

"Can't be that bad, can it? Close your eyes and think of Albion?" Bonnie jokes. "You'd be set for life even without a ring."

A shiver runs down my spine. That slimy lech is literally one of the most repugnant people in town, even if he's by far the richest. But isn't that always the case? The asshole thinks he can buy his way into my pants. Gross.

I step back from the bar and gesture to my tired, formless gown, stained with beer and grease from the roast pork on the spit out back. Standard barmaid uniform. "I'd rather stay here forever than get anywhere near that man. Girl's gotta dream there's something more out there, right?"

The marquis might be chair of the town Chamber of Commerce, but I've kept my books clean and paid our dues on time from the moment my father handed me the keys to the Raven's Beak. He's got nothing on me.

"More? In Evandale?" Bonnie sputters out a laugh as she hefts the tower of mugs, expertly balancing them in her fists. "Good luck with that. And heads up. He's here."

"The marquis?"

"The very same," she says, and I nod, thankful for the warning. She shoots me a meaningful look and heads toward a table of rowdy regulars at the far end of the tavern.

My shoulders relax, and I manage a rueful smile. Good ol' Bonnie. With her pristine complexion and her ready smile, she's all of seventeen and already betrothed to a successful farmer's handsome son. She'll be married soon enough, living a quiet life in a quiet town.

But Bonnie's wrong. There has to be more out there. Is it so terrible to want something bigger out of life? To want the kind of love and adventure bards sing about? I'd never admit it, but Goddess damn it all, I want *more*. I *want* the fairy tale, even if I know I'll probably never get it. Just once, I'd like someone to see me for who I am, even with my smart mouth. More than that, I want to fall in love. Not with a man I can flatten like a rolling pin over biscuit dough. I want a man who will stand up to me sometimes, who's got a backbone and can shoulder some of the weight. Someone I can count on to have *my* back, no matter how sturdy it is.

May as well wish for the moon.

I shake my head. At least I've got the bar to fall back on, even if I'll have to find a new barmaid soon.

Two mugs of ale in hand, I make my way between crowded tables to where I've been flagged by a couple of sellswords, their faces as sharp as their steel. They're not from around here, but that's not unusual. Evandale is at the crossroads of several popular routes, so we're a prime spot for travelers to stop for the night—or longer, as they flee from more dangerous lands.

The sellswords don't look up from their conversation as I serve their drinks. Apparently, the Usurper King of Penrith is hiring anyone who can lift a blade, but neither of these men is convinced the coin is worth the risk. If our King Elgar increases his soldiers' hazard pay as he's been promising, these men would rather sign up to defend Alarice. I've heard others whisper about the Usurper looking to expand his borders and make war against Loegria and Alarice, so there might be some truth to it.

I collect their empty mugs, keeping a mild, disinterested expression on my face, but they don't even acknowledge my existence.

I'm used to being ignored. Patrons talking among themselves, keeping their voices low as I serve their drinks. They don't think I'm listening, or simply don't care if I am, because I'm a nobody. Barmaids couldn't possibly care about the politics of Penrith, a kingdom half a world away. What harm would it do if I were to overhear? I'm used to being invisible, just another set dressing, and I like it that way. It's way better than being proposed to, that's for sure.

They continue their hushed discussion as if I'm not there. Being a nobody has its perks.

I feel someone's gaze at my back, and every hair on my body begins to stand up. I turn to see Lord Breadalbane, Marquis of Evandale, at a table with two of his trusted lackeys. He is almost three times my age, with cold eyes and a lecherous stare that makes me feel as if I'm already standing naked before him.

Ugh. Lord Grabbyhands. That's what the girls call him.

He stares at me like a beast does its dinner as his henchmen bicker amongst themselves. I pretend not to notice him and dodge his gaze.

I walk over to a lone traveler at a table by herself. She doesn't hear me approach, given that a group near her has spontaneously burst out in a harvest shanty. *Four scores of seven whores...*

"What can I get ya?" I ask, hand on my hip.

The woman blinks up at me in surprise and adjusts her spectacles. "Tea, if you please."

"That's all? A tinker doesn't want anything a little stronger?"

The woman gawks. "How'd you know I'm a tinker?"

"You've got a callus on your middle finger," I say. The tinker looks down at her hands. "You hold a tool of some kind, something small, and for long hours. Based on that, you're either a scholar or a tinker, but seeing as you don't have ink stains on your fingers, that's a giveaway."

"I'm impressed."

"Comes with the job," I tell her. Years working at the bar means I'm good at reading people. You can learn more about a person from their body than what comes out of their mouth.

"Where you off to? Back home, is it?" I ask, noting her Loegrian lilt.

The tinker nods. "I'm supposed to meet a friend here and journey together, but he's coming from Penrith, and I've seen neither hide nor hair of him."

Traveling from Penrith has been risky since their rightful king was overthrown a couple of decades ago.

But lately there have been more and more stories of missing travelers who disappear in Estyrion's Great Waste—the land Boreas destroyed. I've never been outside of Evandale to know if these stories are any different from the tall tales the farmers spin during long winter nights to pass the time. But I've seen one too many terrified travelers pass through my doors who whisper about something dark stirring once more in the Great Waste.

I suppress a shudder and maintain the cheerful act; my customers come to the tavern to forget their troubles for a while. "I'm sure he'll be fine," I say, putting on my best smile. "You'll meet your friend, and before you head out on your journey together, you'll bring him back here for a much-needed drink." I hide my creeping sense of unease at the possibility of yet another missing traveler.

I'm making my way back to the bar when the front door bursts open with such force, I'm amazed it's still hanging on its hinges. A dozen soldiers barge into the tavern. They're decked out head to toe in Loegrian blue, with sharp, gleaming swords at their hips. They stand shoulder to shoulder, their massive frames blocking the entrance.

I tuck my rag into my apron pocket and cross my arms over my chest. It isn't every day that soldiers arrive at the Raven's Beak. Even though they're armed, they don't look like they're here to cause trouble.

But what business does the Loegrian royal guard have in Evandale?

Their dramatic entrance clearly didn't have the impact they'd expected because, of course, most of my patrons don't even give them a second glance. Everyone continues to chatter away. The table next to the tinker even starts a new ribald shanty. *When a farmer takes a wife… His balls are set for life…*

The captain—at least I think he's the captain, based on the row of medals gleaming on his chest—steps forward. He looks around and calls out, "Silence!"

No one pays him any mind, save the half-drunk marquis. He starts to make his way toward the guards, likely attracted by the captain's shiny hardware—a magpie drawn to power.

Oh, Goddess, I don't need this tonight.

"Can I help you strapping gents?" I ask, shouldering my way over to the Loegrians. "If you'll kindly pipe down and take a seat…" I motion to a table.

"Thank you, miss," he says politely. "But I must have the floor." He turns back to the tavern. "Silence!" he roars again, but no one listens.

Right. I let out a sharp whistle between my teeth, and the crowd falls silent like dogs called off a hunt. Everyone stares.

"Hey, listen up! It seems we've got an announcement," I say, gesturing to the soldiers.

All eyes turn to the captain, who nods his thanks before he begins. "I am General Marcus Marcellus, and I've come to announce that my lord, the crown prince of Loegria, arrives in two days' time."

Murmurs cut through the tavern. A prince? In Evandale? What the hell for?

The *general*—not captain—continues, "His royal highness is traveling the kingdom in search of his bride."

"Why?" one of the old farmers asks, his words slurring. "He lose her?"

That gets a laugh, but the soldiers are not amused.

"His royal highness has come to collect a bride, perhaps from this very village, on his tour of Alarice."

"You want someone from Evandale?" another red-cheeked farmer croaks. "*I'd* make for a nice bride."

"Me too," another says, laughing. He grabs his neighbor by the face. "Lemme give the prince a big smooch—*mwah!*"

More raucous laughter. If the soldiers had intended to make their announcement to Evandale's most bustling hall of drunks, they've picked well. But my mind whirls and my whole body tingles with what feels suspiciously like hope at this remarkable news.

Despite his bearing and air of competence, Marcus Marcellus looks way too young to be a general. He also looks less than thrilled at his audience. "The prince is coming here in search of a bride per the terms of the treaty of mutual support between the kingdoms of Loegria and Alarice," he declares. He sighs and glances at his men. It's clear he's unimpressed with the pickings so far.

That makes two of us, bud.

Under his breath, the general mumbles, "Dietan has lost his damn mind…" as he looks around. "This is a mistake."

"We can't leave yet, sir," a soldier murmurs.

"I know our orders." He turns back to the tavern, which has settled into its usual hum. Everyone ignores him. Most of them are sloppy drunk, and I doubt they'll remember what happened come morning.

But me? I see opportunity. My brain starts to race.

As the soldiers take a table vacated by farmers who have left to stumble home to their beds, I head back to my place behind the bar.

I'm positively buzzing.

This is what I've been waiting for—a once-in-a-lifetime shot of getting the hell out of this dead-end town.

Shephard raises his head, the bumpy imprint of his wrinkled sleeve in the center of his forehead. "Guess you'll be marrying that prince now instead of me, huh."

Prince?

I almost laugh. "Me? Not a chance," I say.

No way am *I* going to marry the prince… Dear Goddess, what would the prince want with me? I'm…alright-looking, I guess, but rough around the edges, to use a generous term, and the prince won't want a princess with a salty tongue and a sharp wit. "I've got a better idea," I announce a little too loudly.

"Of course she does," a familiar voice says snidely.

As the marquis takes his final strides toward the general, he makes sure his dead eyes are firmly planted on me. I struggle to keep a smile plastered to my face.

The marquis extends a hand to the general, which he takes in a firm grip.

"General Marcellus, is it? Lord Breadalbane. Marquis of Evandale. It is nice to make your acquaintance. I look forward to working together to find the crown prince a bride."

RINGS OF FATE

I see the glint of a gold coin pass from the marquis' sausage-like fingers to the gloved hand of the general. "And make sure you watch out for this one," he says, nodding at me. "She's a wily one."

The general shakes his head and returns the coin with a frown. Then looks to me, puzzled by the marquis' comment, but I know his game—planting seeds of supposed ill repute. I feel utter rage bubble from my toes to the core of my stomach.

Now, I have *two* ideas…

CHAPTER TWO

Aren

"Ow." I suck my pricked finger and taste blood. There isn't enough light where I'm kneeling by my sister's petticoats. I'm working so fast and with such force that the needle went straight through my thumbnail. All I need now is to bleed all over the silk that cost a month's wages.

Yesterday, I managed to get my hands on some rare mulberry silk, and I conjured two dresses for my sisters overnight. I only had enough to buy a precious eight yards, so I had to get creative, embellishing what I could with embroidery and scraps of lace from our mother's trousseau. They look stunning, if I do say so myself.

"You okay?" Sonja asks.

"Yeah, it's fine," I tell her, holding my finger away from the fabric as I finish stitching the hem. "You're going to look perfect, even if I have to lose a thumb."

"Don't even joke," Sonja says, bending down to tie a scrap of cotton around my finger.

My eyes are sore from squinting in candlelight, the tips of my fingers ache, and I've poked more holes in them than a pincushion, but I'm determined to make the two of them shine.

I notice Sonja pout at her reflection in the full-length mirror. As I watch her fluff her hair, it strikes me just how grown up the twins look. So mature, so beautiful. Where did the time go? I blinked and suddenly they're grown women, not snot-nosed kids anymore. Sonja and Ophelia are eighteen now, seven years my junior.

They take after Mother—drop-dead gorgeous, with swanlike necks and golden hair. I often joke I was switched at birth, since I don't look anything like them. I'd believe it if I hadn't inherited Father's striking nose, which suits his weathered face far more than mine.

"The prince of Loegria!" Ophelia sighs from the bed, her gown already perfectly fitted to her body. She cups her chin in her hands as she stares out the window. "Can you imagine? Here in Evandale? What do you think he looks like?"

"Hopefully handsome," says Sonja.

"What kind of prince would he be if he wasn't handsome?" I say mildly, not that I care in the least what he looks like.

"Not any kind of a prince at all," Sonja says.

Either of them would make a fine princess, unlike me. My sisters are everything that a man of royal background would find attractive in a wife—Sonja, a graceful dancer and Ophelia with a gift for watercolors and singing. Me, on the other hand, I can only sing drinking songs and dance the jigs to go with them. It's my job to see my sisters properly settled and looked after. They are my heart's treasures. I raised them, after all.

Our mother died when they had just started walking and I was nine years old. While Father managed the Raven's Beak, I was the one who cooked for the girls, cleaned up after them, nursed them when they were sick, and taught them the best I could. When Father fell ill and I had to take over the tavern as well as care for the twins, I did both without much complaint. I'd give anything for my sisters, even if this isn't the life I imagined for myself.

I turn my eyes back to my work, catching sight of my ragged nails, my hands reddened and rough from years of manual labor. "Done," I say, taking a pin from my teeth and placing it back in the tin. "Phi, come here so I can get a look at the two of you."

Ophelia does as she's told, skipping away from the bed to stand next to Sonja so they can inspect their gowns in the tall mirror.

They both gasp at each other's appearance. My heart pounds with uncontrollable pride.

"Harvest Mother, we look incredible," Sonja says, running her hands up and down her sides.

I stand behind them, admiring my work and my sisters' beauty. A lifetime of caring for them has certainly perfected my talent with a needle and thread. But another type of admiration—bittersweet and nostalgic—stirs within me, and I force back the tears that start to sting the corner of my eyes.

"You'll definitely catch the prince's eye like this," I say, putting an arm around each of them. "One of you has to, or he's mad."

I'm going to win this prince for them, I swear. If he's got to choose a bride from Alarice, here are the loveliest girls in all the land. I pick nervously at the bandages on my fingers.

"Oh, Aren," Ophelia says, eyes shining with unshed tears. "Thank you so much."

Their smiles, bright and dazzling, light up the room.

If the prince falls in love with one of my sisters, then surely the other will capture the attention of some other lord in his retinue. And then, finally, someone other than me will be responsible for them. Two birds, one hefty stone.

As much as I love my girls with all my heart, they're grown now, and I'm ready to take care of just myself for a change—to finally live the life I've dreamed about.

This time last year, Father promised me the Raven's Beak Tavern. He said the day the girls are each well married, he'll give me the deed to the bar and I can do with it as I wish. I can sell the whole thing and leave Evandale for good, travel the world as I dream of doing.

Sometimes, late at night, I imagine the kind of life I could've had if I'd been born far away from Evandale. Maybe I'd be a scholar. Or a sailor. An adventurer who journeys far and wide, sees the world, shapes a life with each passing day, not knowing what the next will bring.

But that's just a fantasy. I'm the responsible daughter, the one who never gets in trouble, who always sets a good example because that's one fewer problem for Father to deal with.

I catch a glimpse of myself standing behind them and sigh. I'm ruining the scene simply by being in the same frame, especially in this drab muslin dress, so I step back and let them have all the glory.

RINGS OF FATE

—

Not even an hour later, commotion erupts outside our window, and we look out to see a gilded carriage rolling past, bobbing slightly on the bumpy dirt road.

"Is it him?" Sonja asks, running to the window. "He's here already?"

"A day early," I note.

"He must really want a bride," Ophelia says, joining us at the window.

The impressive carriage trundles by, flanked by soldiers on horseback, and my heart clenches. A prince such as he would surely appreciate a bride who doesn't have a potty mouth, who takes impeccable care of her hair and clothes, and whose loftiest goal is pleasing her powerful husband.

Sonja and Ophelia are the most perfect choices in Evandale.

CHAPTER THREE

Dietan

I smile and wave to the onlookers as my carriage rolls toward the center of Evandale. "Hello! Hi there!" I call out, flashing my most charming smile.

I am, after all, His Royal Highness, Dietan Cornwallis Arthur William Maximillian Conrad Barclay-Bruce Armandale-Macrae, Crown Prince of Loegria and heir presumptive to Alarice. I have as many names as jewels on my epaulets.

I am their future lord and liege, who will wed some lucky Alarician girl to seal the deal.

The crowd's cheers rise and fall around me, and I try to focus on the variety of faces rather than the monotony of this endless journey.

"Another dead-end town," I mutter under my breath, careful not to let anyone hear. "Who knew there were so many?" Weeks on the road and the repetitiveness of this quest have worn me down. Meet the mayor or local lord, kiss the hand of every unmarried girl of eligible age, feign interest, indicate *nope, not her* as often as necessary, then go on my merry way to do it all over again at the next stop.

At least no one is pelting the carriage with tomatoes this time, but I have the windows up, just in case. I still recall the headache it gave my valet to scrub those red stains out of silk and velvet.

The kingdom of Alarice is tense, accusing my kingdom of Loegria of leaving their borders defenseless. There have been too many bandits, too many marauders on the roads lately. Naturally, they blame my father, King Donnel, for failing to maintain the peace. They are demanding the conditions of the treaty, my marriage, be fulfilled sooner rather than later. So, here I am.

I glance out the window and blink, surprised by Evandale's idyllic charm. Unlike some other shithole Alarician towns I've visited lately, this place is picturesque: golden fields, tall trees, and clear blue skies for miles. The sunlight spills over vibrant wildflowers and grassy meadows, which seem to creep up on everything—houses, roads, even sheep fields and pigpens. It makes me want to breathe deeply, savor the clean air while I'm so far removed from Lundewic's crowded streets and the grime of the previous tour stops. It's…refreshing. Maybe it's a good sign.

Since no one appears inclined to hurl tomatoes, I unlatch the window and lean out, letting the breeze ruffle my hair. Closing my eyes against the bright light, I revel in the warmth on my skin. Sure, my fair complexion will likely burn, but it's worth it. A little sun is good for the soul, and right now, my soul needs all the light it can get.

"Ah, such a lovely tour of the backwater." Jared's voice cuts through my thoughts from the other side of the carriage, where he's draped lazily across the seat, his inky eyes half-lidded with boredom. Lord Jared Gruffudd Mackenzie, eighth Duke of Glamorgan, and one of my oldest friends, rarely holds back his disdain. With his deep umber skin, handsome face, and vast estates that he rarely visits—preferring, as one does, the delights of the capital—Jared could boast he rivals me as the kingdom's most eligible bachelor. But he doesn't because he's also quite humble, actually. It's why we're mates. Except right now he's prickly.

"We're in the middle of nowhere," he continues. "Do you really have to carry on with this charade of marrying some Alarician bumpkin?"

"Don't be a dick," I reply, shooting him a look.

"Aw, fuck off," he retorts, smirking. He always reminds me of a sleek cat—his tendency to melt into seats, like a barn cat on a bale of hay in the sun. He's mostly bored and indifferent, too.

"This whole ruse is ridiculous. Why would a prince search for a bride here," he gestures vaguely out the window, "when you could have your pick of all the ladies at your grandfather's court? Here, she's sure to have four hooves," he adds, shaking his head.

I wave at more villagers, keeping the smile plastered to my face. "According to my mother, apparently my philandering reputation precedes me. So the only Alarician noblewomen who'll have me are the social climbers. And besides, I'm not doing this to actually get married, remember? No one's suspected our true mission yet." I elbow him. "But hey, maybe one of these 'Alarician bumpkins' will catch *your* eye, my friend. And maybe Marcus's, too!"

Jared's laugh fills the carriage. The idea of any of us marrying someone from one of these towns is clearly absurd to him. He's far too busy working his way through the kingdom's married countesses to consider settling down. So many bored, beautiful, married countesses whose husbands are off preparing for or hiding from the impending war effort.

"There's nothing here," he says, gesturing lazily out the window once more. "Fields, fields, and…look, more fields! And so many sheep!"

"Baaaa," I bleat, settling back into my cushioned seat as the carriage rattles onward.

But Jared's in a mood and makes no effort to hide it. "We should just ask around for the information you need and drop all this subterfuge."

"Our official mission is not only to find Loegria's next queen, but also to win the people over and garner the goodwill of my future subjects. And hell, maybe I really will meet someone."

He replies with a grunt.

I give him a playful slap on his chest. "Where's your sense of adventure? A little optimism won't kill you." My attention shifts to a small boy with a runny nose staring open-mouthed at the carriage. I wave at him and then at his squinting grandfather. "Good day, sir!" I call out.

Jared scoffs and rubs at his days-old beard. "My sense of adventure involves hot baths, fine wine, and the company of someone who hasn't lost their mind," he retorts. "The sooner we're back at court in Lundenwic, the better."

I don't bother arguing. We both know we're not going back anytime soon.

Officially, my mission is to strengthen ties between Loegria and Alarice, much like my parents did with their Wedding March years ago. Their marriage is a success on paper even if it is catastrophic in reality.

RINGS OF FATE

My parents despise each other. They've spent just enough time together to produce me and my sister.

But whatever my personal reservations about the institution of marriage, as the heir to both kingdoms, my duty is clear: wed an Alarician girl, fulfill the terms of the treaty, and unite our lands in common defense.

My grandfather, King Elgar of Alarice, named me his heir, upsetting the line of succession for the sake of unity against the growing threat of Penrith—and of the mysterious power stirring in the Great Waste. Elgar's banished brother, Namreth, was supposed to inherit the crown over my mother's line, but no more. In due time, I'll produce some heirs of my own with a nice Alarician girl, and the two kingdoms will become one under my rule.

Of course, my mother wasn't thrilled about me leaving the capital with rumors of war swirling. My father practically forbade it.

Practically.

After Father stormed out of the room, Mother lectured me on how tales of my reputation as a lush and a player had reached King Elgar's court in the capital and ruined any prospect of a suitable match there. I posited that news of my exploits probably hadn't spread to the far ends of Alarice. I told her that my best hope of finding a wife was to fish from a new pond.

That did the trick, and she agreed I should go on this tour to find a wife expediently and unite the kingdoms before the Usurper of Penrith makes good on the looming threat of war. As long as my bride is from Alarice, the treaty doesn't care whether she's of noble blood.

That's not the *real* reason I'm here, though. Unofficially, my mission is much more than just bride-shopping.

Crown Prince is a role I play, like my father's jester performing before the court, and this search for a bride is nothing but a convenient cover for my real reason for being here. I have no true intention of marrying anyone—from this village or anywhere else—before that mission is accomplished. Treaty or not, marriage will have to wait.

Not that I mind putting it off. Marriage only breeds resentment, bickering, and unhappiness, as my parents have demonstrated throughout my life. It's the perfect way to make two people hate each other. Why would I subject myself to that any earlier than I absolutely have to? My life is already a tragedy—I don't need to add a loveless union to my burdens.

At last, the carriage lurches to a stop in Evandale's town square. Before

I can gather my thoughts, Marcus, my ever-loyal general, throws the door open. Taller and broader than me, with tawny skin, a neatly trimmed beard, and a perpetually grim expression, he radiates competence and wariness. Marcus doesn't trust anyone and doesn't try to hide that fact. Subtlety has never been his strong suit. He's always ready for a conflict, a threat, a revolution, an assassination. He'd gladly skewer anyone who even looks at me the wrong way.

"Your Highness," he says, as I step out into the sunlight.

I take in the square, trying to suppress my skepticism. We're in an open area surrounded by a horseshoe of two-story wooden buildings. It's… quaint. Kind of nice, maybe? And busy. We're surrounded by a flurry of activity. Boxes of apples, potatoes, and onions are stacked like pillars, and a humongous pile of logs in the middle is waiting to be set on fire, ready to cook up a large roast. A mound of freshly picked pumpkins stands by a wooden stage, where a great banner proclaims the coming harvest festival.

Clearly, we are just in time for a party.

Marcus has already been here for a day, arranging accommodations for our retinue. His sharp gaze sweeps the gathered crowd, his hand resting instinctively on the hilt of his sword. He doesn't look thrilled, but Marcus never looks thrilled.

"Come on, it can't be that bad," I say lightly, though I know better than to expect enthusiasm from him. Marcus is an excellent general but an absolute killjoy. The latter might be an occupational hazard of the former.

I stretch my legs as I step away from the carriage. It's a relief to escape Jared's constant complaints, even though I, too, long for my suite in the palace after the week we've had. I stifle a sigh and try not to stare at the locals, to search for a particular face that calls to me. I'm not sure who I'm looking for, exactly, but I hope I'll know when I see her. But none of the faces staring back at me are the one.

Might as well get on with it. I raise my voice so it carries over their murmurs. "We're here to find my princess!" I declare with a grin, eliciting a mix of giggles and gasps from the townsfolk. Marcus and Jared's faces don't give anything away, but I can imagine their thoughts: *Here we go again with the bullshit.*

I press on, waving to a group of young women who blush and hide their smiles behind their hands. The townsfolk gather around us, curious but cautious.

Faces peer from windows, and a few young women linger conspicuously near the well. An older man with thinning hair and an obsequious air emerges on the steps of the town hall and scuttles toward me. Given his rich attire, he is clearly nobility. He is alight with the kind of false enthusiasm that makes my skin crawl. He grabs my hand and kisses it with lips that are far too wet. I suppress a shudder.

Even at twenty-two, I hear my mother's voice in my head reminding me of my lessons in etiquette and her stern warnings to never offend the nobility, whose support we need to hold the kingdom together. I force myself to smile.

"Your Highness," the man croaks. "I am Lord Breadalbane, Marquis of Evandale. Your visit honors our humble town. I only received word of your arrival yesterday, or I would have prepared a proper welcome. We are a modest village, but if you have any requests, I will make sure our people do all we can to fulfill them."

I fight the urge to pull my hand away. "Thank you, Lord Breadalbane. But the pleasure is all mine."

What an ass.

Surely, Evandale deserves better leadership than this. The townspeople look like the practical, hardworking sort, and this oily backwater aristocrat wouldn't appear to know a hard day's work if it smacked him across the face.

Still, I must play the part, so I let the marquis escort me into the town hall. It's the grandest building in town, with polished wood floors and hand-painted walls accented with gold foil, mimicking the fields of wheat outdoors. Waiting for us are a handful of local dignitaries standing alongside my councilors. The formality of this bride search is not my style at all.

I gesture to my party. "May I introduce the Duke of Glamorgan…"

Jared makes an exaggerated bow.

"And you've already met General Marcellus, Earl of Coventry…"

Marcus tucks his hat under his arm, his grim demeanor softening just enough to make him look his age, only a few years older than me.

Jared, Marcus, and I go way back to our school days. Before we were handed responsibilities and tasted battle, we raised more than our fair share of hell.

"They are my dear friends and councilors, whose advice has been invaluable as I search for my wife. Imagine—the future queen, born right here in this very town." I stretch my arms wide and grin at the patriotic pride swelling in the room. The royal entourage nods confidently, and I add, "I have a good feeling about Evandale. My future is here!" I've said as much at every town on the route, and every town falls for it.

"Of course, it is a great honor," the marquis replies. He's far older than my father, with a toad-like, grating presence. It's painfully obvious he's foaming at the mouth to marry one of his clan to me, desperate to advance his family's standing. He leads us to a large banquet table festooned with wreaths and fruit.

"I hope you didn't encounter any trouble on your travels," the marquis says as stewards bring out platters of buns slathered with caramelized onions, roast boar, goat cheese with jam, and colorful root vegetables. Peasant food, sure, but this looks divine, and my mouth waters.

"No trouble," I reply reassuringly. "I doubt Penrith would openly attack my caravan. Even if the rumors are true, they're not ready for a war just yet."

Everyone in the room knows the truth: Penrith's forces are testing the borders of Loegria and Alarice. Their army is not exactly subtle.

The marquis sniffs. "Of course not. They're surely no match for King Donnel and his Rings of Fate."

My stomach lurches, but I keep my face neutral, plucking a fresh bun from the table and taking a large bite.

The Rings of Fate are more than just heirlooms; they're powerful weapons from the Second Epoch of ancient Albion. My grandfather gave them to my father as a dowry when my parents married. Meant to tie the two kingdoms' mutual interests together, the silver ring symbolizes Loegria's ores, the gold Alarice's wheat fields. Two kingdoms bound forever, just like the elemental power of the Whisting held inside the interlocking rings.

The Whisting is an ancient magic of the earth—the ability to tame the elemental forces of the ancient wind spirits, the Anemoi. Its masters can level mountains, carve valleys, divert rivers, and forge lakes. At the dawn of time, the earliest kings and sorcerers used the Whisting to turn the deserted, mountainous landscape into a lush country where their people could prosper. The Whisting is the very breath of life. Alas, it can also take life away—if the rumors of a dark magic rising once again are true.

The Rings are our greatest defense against the Usurper.

"Of course, no one would dare challenge the might of the Whisting," the marquis says.

His worshipful tone echoes with the hope that fills every Alarician face in the room, like my father will singlehandedly save them all from the Usurper's wrath.

"The Rings aren't the only reason we're safe in this land," I say, my tone clipped. It's annoying how carelessly the marquis dismisses the bravery of our knights in front of all of Evandale. I'm traveling with a full squadron—plus, Marcus himself is a walking fortress.

The marquis purses his lips. "Perhaps it's easy for the inheritor of such ancient power to speak so lightly, especially when darkness has not touched Lundenwic. The promise of such magic is the only thing keeping the Usurper and his dark creatures at bay."

"That's exactly why I'm here, on the twenty-fifth anniversary of our kingdoms' alliance," I reply, plastering on a reassuring grin. "It's time to find my queen and fulfill the agreement with a wedding, sealing the alliance of Loegria and Alarice just as my father's and mother's marriage united our lands."

That's the cue the marquis is waiting for.

He claps his hands, and a door opens. A long line of girls rushes out, hands clasped tightly in front of them, eyes lowered. They wear ornate dresses that look as if they were ordered straight from the capital, all brocade and heavy velvet and fur. They all have the same coloring as the marquis, save for his white hair—the same ruddy cheeks, the same pointed nose, the same thin lips. If I were a betting man—and I am—I'd say they're all his daughters and nieces. Possibly some granddaughters, too.

"Without further ado, Prince Dietan, may I introduce to you some of the finest ladies in the land: the ladies of House Breadalbane."

Called it.

They line up against the wall, their heads bowed from the weight of their hair piled high on their heads, threaded with jewels and ornaments.

The one at the end can't be older than fourteen. My practiced, perfect smile falters for just a moment. I blanch at the thought of the marquis offering up his own ward so young.

"Oh—meet them so soon? I've barely arrived," I say, feigning surprise.

"We've not a moment to waste," the marquis insists, his enthusiasm unwavering. "The harvest festival begins shortly, and we've arranged the festivities in your honor. It's best to introduce you to our finest now, so you can decide who you'd like to get better acquainted with."

I glance at Jared, silently begging for rescue, but his smirk only deepens.

Marcus remains stoic, offering no help, either.

Great. I'm on my own.

Suppressing a sigh, I step up to the first girl in the line. She curtsies, offering me a demure smile as I kiss the back of her hand. "What a lovely gown," I say, my voice steady, my expression polite. "And your hair—so beautiful."

The platitudes flow effortlessly, practiced over countless encounters like this throughout my youth. I move to the next girl, repeating the process. My smile remains firmly in place, and Jared's smirk and Marcus's stern expression ensure that no one can guess the truth: this entire tour is a farce.

Even if I wanted to marry, no woman in Albion would have me once she learns the truth about me on our wedding night. I carry a dangerous secret that my two closest friends, my father, and I have conspired to keep from the rest of the world—and especially from my mother—for half my life. My father distrusts her still, and our kingdom would be imperiled if I were exposed.

By the time I reach the end of the line of Breadalbane women, I'm struggling to maintain my composure. The youngest girl, the fourteen-year-old, curtsies, and I keep our interaction brief, offering her nothing more than a polite nod. The marquis is beyond disgusting.

"What a warm welcome!" I declare, turning back to the sorry excuse for a man with a broad smile to hide my irritation. "But I must admit, I'm utterly exhausted. I would be eternally grateful if you could show me to our lodgings."

Marcus steps forward, taking over the conversation with his usual efficiency. "This way, sire," he says, gesturing toward the door.

I follow him out of the town hall as quickly as I can without sprinting, trying not to step on his heels. My retinue forms a protective barrier around me as we cross the square, intent on shielding me from the curious stares of the townsfolk, but I motion for them to stand down. Let the people look for a few moments more; that's why I'm here. Faces peer out from windows, and a few onlookers crane their necks, eager to catch a glimpse of the visiting prince, soon to be *their* prince. I keep my head up, face forward. I'm tired. I want this to be clean, simple, and quick.

The inn—a two-story building on the edge of the square—isn't much, but it'll do. Right now, my only concern is getting to my suite, away from the prying eyes of the village. Once safely indoors, I'll be free to focus on what really matters.

RINGS OF FATE

I didn't come here to find a bride. I came here to find a mage.

Her last known whereabouts were reportedly near this town. She's the only one who might be able to help me—not just for my sake but for all of Albion.

For the Rings of Fate are not resting safely behind glass in my father's war room. Gods no. They're buried under my shoulder blades, fused to bone and blood.

My life depends on getting them out of me. And so does the fate of the world.

CHAPTER FOUR

Dietan

At nightfall, I manage to slip out of my room without anyone noticing. Marcus and Jared both pushed to join me for my protection, but I convinced them to stay behind. It's easier for one man to move about without drawing attention than three.

Most of my men have set up in the inn for the night, preparing for my bride search in the morning. To avoid being seen by the guards stationed outside my room, I quietly make my exit out the window, just like we used to in our school days. Even though nobody has the authority to stop me, even a prince is powerless to quell the spread of gossip amongst his men. However, I doubt they would guess that the future king needs to meet with a sorceress.

I creep across the grass, pulling a well-worn cloak around myself, hiding my hair underneath a wide-brimmed felt hat. A neckerchief obscures my face. *That should do it.* I look like a farmer—or at least I hope I do.

Even with the little information my father's spies were able to provide, I need more to find the general location of the sorceress, and I have to start somewhere.

The Raven's Beak Tavern.

I head to Evandale's main social hub to talk to some locals. In front of me, the wooden building sits low and squat, with a thatched roof. From the outside, I'd expect some damp, depressing watering hole, but light and laughter spill out of the open doors, and I'm drawn to it as a bee to a flower.

Once I step inside, I'm greeted by a cozy warmth that's rare in Lundenwic. The tavern is packed, and I feel entirely invisible, which immediately puts me at ease. My shoulders relax as I take in the surroundings: mismatched tables and chairs, the soft glow of lamps overhead.

The air is thick with smoke from tobacco and the roaring fireplace. I grab a table in the far corner, away from most of the other patrons. I don't take off my hat, but I keep a sharp eye on the room, scanning for anyone who might be open to a conversation. Most of the folks here are either deep into their drinks or engrossed in chatter with their companions. I'm the only one sitting alone.

Across the bar, I spot, who I can only assume, is the resident barmaid. I am overcome with an awareness that despite this being my kingdom, this is *her* domain.

She has a mug of ale in one hand and the other on her very lovely hip. She refuses to pass the ale to an inebriated chap who is currently in her crosshairs.

"But I would be good to ya. A good husband. I promise." He pleads.

"I know you're better at talking out your ass than reading signs but Harvest Mother, Aldus, you know the rules." She points, exasperated, to a sign behind the bar that has a litany of rules including one peculiar one—no marriage proposals. I'm struck by the need for this rule.

"But my heart beats for only you," he tries again.

"That's what you said to Julia Falgren just last week." The barmaid retorts.

Some of the patrons around them snicker at this comment and nod their heads. The barb is true.

A point for the barmaid.

He reaches for the beer in her hand. She pulls it away.

The bar roars in laughter. I chuckle as well. This is more entertainment than I was bargaining for.

She squats down to Aldus' level and eyes him long and hard until he looks like a little boy instead of a grown man.

"Next round is on you." She tells him loud enough so the whole bar can hear before reaching into his pocket and taking out a few coins. The man doesn't even flinch. In fact, he acts as if the pleasure is all his.

She turns around to resume her rounds, the bar cheering for the free libations. For good measure, she brings his beer with her.

Touché, barmaid.

But there is a fleeting look of subtle sadness in her eyes, as she takes a sip from the mug. Despite my own distaste for the institution of marriage, a vibrant woman like her deserves more than slurred proposals from the town drunks.

She spots me alone and without a drink, and as if on cue, the feisty barmaid approaches my table.

"What can I get ya?" she asks, thrusting out one hip like she did before. It really is a nice hip.

My eyes lift to meet hers and I notice the light dusting of freckles that grace her cheeks.

She's nothing at all like the wispy, giggling, delicate women paraded in front of me in every town. No, she's striking in every way.

"Ordering something or just gonna waste my time, like old Aldus over there?" She asks.

"I promise I won't propose."

"That's what they all say."

"Do you have a menu?" I ask and I'm met with a blank stare from her piercing dark eyes.

"It's a list of foods on offer, written on a piece of parchment?" I continue, hesitantly.

"I know what a menu is, but this isn't that kind of establishment. You either know what you want, or we don't have it," she says impatiently.

"Do you have ale?" I ask cheekily.

She gives me a long, hard look, and I realize my attempt at a joke didn't land. "We do but I doubt you can handle it," she says flatly.

"We'll just have to see then, won't we? A pint, if you could, kind lady. And what's the specialty of the house?"

"Not sure someone like you would think our offering is good enough."

I raise my eyebrows. "And what type of person am I?"

Her gaze flicks over my hands, my face, and my threadbare cloak. There's no way she can figure out who I really am, but sparring with her sets my blood pumping. "You're someone who's accustomed to tiny delicacies on fancy platters. Things that wobble and take too long to cook," she says, expertly describing the aspic-laden dishes served at court. "We mostly serve salt ham and biscuits here."

"Sorry to disappoint, but I happen to love both of those things," I say smugly.

"Is that so?"

"Can't think of anything better."

One corner of her lip quirks into a half smirk, the first I've seen her smile all night. "Coming right up. Watch you don't choke on our ale, milord."

Yeah, so maybe I'm not fooling anyone with the threadbare cloak. I sigh, watching her as she turns and walks away, a strand of her raven hair falling from her bun. This woman is unlike any other I've met and I need to know more.

Laughter from a nearby table draws my attention. A group of men my age laughs heartily, pounding their fists on the table. Then I see him.

One man's curly hair and loud and braying laugh turn my blood to ice. After a moment, I realize my eyes have played a cruel trick on me. It's not a ghost but a case of mistaken identity. For it can't be Cedric... Cedric is long dead.

The spot between my shoulder blades starts to burn, and I straighten my back to ease the discomfort. *Oh no, not now. Not here.* But the memory is a painful one that I can't escape, as hard as I try. The eerie laughter of two mischievous boys, the war room, the glint of the rings in the moonlight, the look on Cedric's face as I reached for the rings, the darkness. So much darkness. That night my world changed forever.

I shudder at the memory. I try to center myself in my chair, counting my breaths just as my father's witan taught me to all those years ago, to control the Rings' powers within me. I remind myself I'm safe at the tavern and not ten years old anymore.

I jump when the sassy barmaid slams a mug of brown ale on the table along with a plate of biscuits and ham.

"Didn't mean to startle you," she apologizes.

"No, it's all right," I manage to say, coming to myself. "Thank you."

The barmaid's gaze softens, and she looks at me a little longer than necessary. When she turns to go, I reach out to stop her, just short of touching her wrist.

"I was actually wondering..." She looks my way again, and I forget my next words. Her piercing eyes lock directly onto mine, and I struggle for the nonchalance that usually comes naturally. "I, uh, was hoping you could help me locate someone. I heard she might live here."

That piques her curiosity. She raises an eyebrow. "Oh yeah? Who're you looking for?"

"I think she goes by the name Veteria?" It's the only lead I have. I asked the royal councilors in Loegria about the history of the rings and combed through every crumbling, ancient scroll I could find, and that's the one name that keeps coming up.

Supposedly, Veteria is the last surviving Vindar, a band of warrior witches and knights who decades ago kept Alarice safe—until they were disbanded and hunted to all but extinction, along with their magic. But not Veteria. She survived.

Free magic is dangerous magic, my grandfather, King Elgar often says. It's unsurprising that the darkness brewing in the Waste has gained strength in the Vindar's absence; we could sure use them now.

These days, most people who claim to know how to use the Whisting are hacks and charlatans trying to sell something. But lately there has been word of a sorceress who allegedly used the Whisting to hold back a river after a dam burst, saving an entire village from certain destruction. After that feat, she went into hiding, but rumor has it that she settled in Evandale. I would bet my coin that the sorceress in question is Veteria.

The barmaid lifts her chin ever so slightly, peering down at me. "And who wants to know?"

"Forgive my lack of manners. I'm D—" I almost blurt out my real name, forgetting that I'm trying to keep a low profile. "Dario." It's the only name I can think of. Dario? *Really?* I swear I couldn't think of a sillier name if I tried.

"Okay, *Dario*," she says, her tone making it clear she agrees with my own assessment of the name's merits. "Yeah, I know her. She lives in the woods on the outskirts of town just north of here. She's our best healer. Taught most of the wise women here all they know." She tucks a hand in her apron pocket, and I wonder what small healing magics this barmaid might possess.

My heart can't help but leap at the thought.

"Good luck finding her, though," she adds, looking skeptical.

"Why?"

"She's only found if she wants to be. She doesn't like outsiders." Then she bends down and whispers in my ear, "And she certainly doesn't like noblemen who are looking for her."

Her gentle breath in my ear makes the hairs on my neck stand as straight as my guards.

My mind races. I've come too far; I can't give up now. This whole tour of Alarice was routed specifically to get me here so I can speak with Veteria. I'll have to take my chances and seek her in the woods. Failure is not an option. I grit my teeth in determination.

"Thanks for information and the warning, you have my gratitude," I say. "Truly."

The barmaid inspects me again, her arms now crossed over her chest—which I swear I must stop looking at—her brow scrunched as if she's trying to read me like a book in a language she doesn't understand. She only grunts in acknowledgment and then leaves once more.

Left to my own thoughts, I sit in silence. For twelve years, I've carried this burden, the kingdom's greatest weapons hidden uselessly in my flesh. The mere chance that someone could help me return the Rings to their rightful place feels so achingly real that something I barely recognize stirs in my heart: hope.

My gaze drifts back to the man I mistook for my old friend Cedric. If the fates were kinder, perhaps that is what Cedric would have looked like if he'd lived. Smiling, laughing, growing older. I can't bear to look at the stranger anymore.

My curiosity that day cursed not just me but my whole kingdom.

After I accidentally stole the Rings, I did the only thing a frightened ten-year-old boy could think to do: I tried to hide what had happened. I thought my father wouldn't open the box until he needed to defend the kingdom, so I replaced the missing rings with a replica set merchants sell to traveling tourists. I thought no one would notice.

The king noticed, of course. With the war drums sounding from Penrith even then, he had reason to ensure that these great weapons were ready within his reach.

As my father likes to admonish, I got myself into this mess, so I must find a way out of it.

I tried everything in my power to rid myself of the Rings in secret, but they were so thoroughly embedded that removing them would surely kill me.

The few healers who did try did so painfully and unsuccessfully. Every night, I'm plagued with the memories of those torments and visions of my death so real, so terrifying, I wake up in a cold sweat.

The Rings have become a part of me, so I can tap into their power without even thinking about it. My unchecked emotions can summon storms in my room; I call upon hurricanes and tornadoes as easily as breathing. I can destroy my surroundings with a single nightmare—and I have no way of controlling it.

And people have died because of me.

My face pales, and my blood runs cold. I try not to think about it, though it torments me daily.

If I don't complete this dangerous mission my father and his closest advisors have concocted for me, my deadly power, along with my self-loathing, will only spiral further out of my control. The fork in my hands shakes as I bring a bite of ham and biscuit to my mouth. I must look like an idiot.

The great threat to Albion has materialized: the Usurper of Penrith is moving against us. We've known this day would come ever since he killed the rightful king and the rest of Penrith's royal family. He's made no secret of his ambitions to conquer all of Albion.

Soon, my father will have no choice but to use the Rings of Fate to stop the enemies at our gates, and then the whole kingdom—all the kingdoms—will discover the fake rings I left in their place. Without the real Rings, my father will fail, Loegria will fall, and Alarice will follow soon after.

And my parents will have been right about me all along—not only am I an irresponsible loser, but I'm an irresponsible loser not meant for the throne. Certainly not a leader who should be entrusted with *two* kingdoms.

The Rings are a burden I've carried all these years, and if I'm to help defend us all against the Usurper, I need to unbind the Rings from my soul before it's too late.

The sorceress Veteria is real. She will be able to help me. I'm so close I can almost taste it.

Speaking of taste, the biscuits and salt ham are truly the best I've ever eaten. I didn't realize how ravenous I was.

I take a sip of the ale the barmaid gave me. I gasp and cough, pounding my fist into my chest to catch my breath. I'm certainly no stranger to strong drink, but Alarician ale could knock out an ox.

I look at the contents of the mug, bewildered. Did the barmaid play some kind of trick on me? But no, it appears every other patron in the Raven's Beak Tavern is drinking the same brown poison. I turn my gaze to the barmaid, who's watching me from the bar with an amused grin.

She raises a pint of her own, tips it toward me with a wink, and downs it in one.

Despite the burning in my throat, I smile back and match her, lifting the mug to my lips again and finishing it off. Now that I know what to expect, I can prepare for the heat, and the barmaid looks somewhat impressed. Her smile follows me even after I leave the tavern.

The world tips under me as I make my way into the night. The stars are out, bright and twinkling, and despite the heat of late summer, the wind cuts through the open fields, cooling my flushed cheeks and easing my mind.

The Whisting inside me feels at ease, too. Out in the open, I'm lighter than I've ever felt before, like I could spread my arms and fly. With the liquid courage in my gut, my confidence in seeking out the sorceress and persuading her to help me grows tenfold.

The clear, moonlit sky makes my recurring nightmare seem like a distant memory. For weeks, I've dreamed of my kingdom surrounded on all sides by forces so dark and magic so evil that I have no choice but to unleash the unquenchable power sealed in my soul. I can never control it, so each night I destroy *everything*: our enemies, myself, and even the whole world. I wake knowing the magic shows me my future—that I'm going to die.

My people have a saying: *the Winds of Fate blow for all men.* And my own fate has been inextricably linked to the Rings since I was ten years old.

Alone in the town square, I stop, tip my head back, and breathe deeply, letting the wind encircle me. Veteria is here. Now I just have to find this sorceress who hates the aristocracy and can conceal herself with magic to ask her to save the monarchs who erased her order.

She's my only chance escape this fate and be free of the Rings once and for all.

CHAPTER FIVE

Dietan

I wake up in my bed at the inn, panting and flushed. The air in the room swirls around me. Despite the closed window, the fluttering curtains settle down and the vase of flowers stops teetering on the edge of the table. I collect myself, shielding my eyes with my arm, shuddering as another nightmare passes. They seem to be getting worse the closer we near to war. I never get a good night's sleep anymore.

I have a sinking feeling that dark magic is already at Loegria's gates. I've got to speak to the sorceress before my power completely overwhelms me.

At a sharp knock on my door, I leap to my feet. On the other side, I hear Jared's voice. "You in there, bud?"

I grunt as I pull on my clothes, taking a deep breath to calm my nerves.

Jared opens the door and peers at the mess of my room. "Looks like someone had fun last night," he says with a you-dog-you grin.

"Ha, you know it," I say, playing along.

Jared comes in, shuts the door, and wipes the jovial expression from his face. He knows the truth: I haven't slept with a woman in years. The last time I did, it ended in death and disaster—and guilt that's haunted me ever since. I vowed to never share a bed with another person until I get these Rings removed. But of course, a reputation for promiscuity helped stave off marital prospects. More strategically, if anyone noticed the sudden change in the player prince's habits, they'd have asked questions that led straight back to my father...and the Rings. Jared helps me maintain my lie.

At court, I'm still known as a lover of women, parties, fine wine, and a good time. No one would ever guess that I'm celibate, that I only flirt with my so-called conquests but never take them to bed, that I always send them home in a carriage instead of bringing them up to my suite. The women are so insulted by this—rejection from the prince who'll bed anyone with a pulse—that they never reveal they didn't actually sleep with me. Instead, they burnish my reputation even more.

"Bad night?" asks Jared with sympathy. I grimace. I don't want his pity. I pull on my boots, then fling open the door.

I shrug. "Not the worst. I guess it's time to test the waters and meet the lovely ladies."

"You know it, chum," Jared replies, plastering that grin back on. "Get ready for some sharks."

He briefs me on the day's agenda and the latest intelligence reports over breakfast. There have been more sightings of dark magic and strange creatures along Loegria's border with Penrith, but the royal scholars dispatched to investigate didn't find anything—which just means that the Usurper is being subtle, hiding something.

It's too early for bad news. I'm still hungover from last night's ale, blurry and bleary until my first cup of strong, black coffee. I want nothing more than to track down the elusive sorceress so I can give my father his magic back, but first, I've got to act the merry prince of Loegria for all of Evandale to see.

"You know, I'm coming around to this place," Jared says as he spreads butter across his bread. "The ladies here are..." There's a sparkle in his eye as he searches for the word, then emphatically kisses his fingers.

"You've changed your tune since yesterday."

"Well, now I've seen what this town has to offer, and you were right. Fresh-faced country girls are exactly what we need."

I laugh into my plate. Jared's mood is often as capricious as the wind itself, and clearly, my friend is not immune to a pretty face. "Today's a good day, then."

"Just you wait," Jared says.

"Found a bride?"

"Two, in fact."

"Two? I only need the one. I'm not sure Loegria or Alarice would accept a polygamous marriage," I say, amused.

"Sisters. Twins. You'll see."

I laugh again. Jared always has a way of lifting my spirits. "Jared, have you fallen in love again?"

He makes a pained expression, clutching his chest and reeling back dramatically. It's then that General Marcus enters, helping himself to the breakfast spread between Jared and me. "They're already waiting for you," Marcus says around a bite of sausage. "The ladies, I mean."

Based on the way Marcus's eyes sparkle, he, too, is smitten.

"Not you as well," I say.

Marcus lets out a dreamy sigh. "Just you wait…"

The festivities are in full swing when Jared, Marcus, and I step outside. A quartet is playing a jig, and dancers in the square spin with the music. Flags snap in the wind. Ale flows freely. Rosy-cheeked young women in flower crowns clutch one another and laugh, their smiles beaming.

Isn't it a pretty sight? Too bad I'm not going to choose any of them to be my bride. I feel like the worst kind of heel, knowing I'm only going to disappoint all of them, but it's better than the diplomatic fallout that will ensue if I accidentally murder the woman I marry to fulfill our treaty with Alarice. I'll simply continue the charade until I can fix my problem.

Although if Veteria can remove the Rings before I leave Evandale, maybe I *could* find myself a country bride.

In the center of the square, the marquis stands on a stage with some of the other town officials. He spots me moving through the crowd and waves eagerly.

I saunter over, and the marquis pounces on me, gesturing to the line of single ladies beyond the stage, each waiting for their moment in my company. His relatives I met yesterday are at the front, of course.

"Your Highness," says the marquis, "you're just in time."

Jared wasn't lying when he said the maidens of this town were something to behold. Some are fair-haired with locks as straight as wheat stalks, some have brown skin with tight curls, some have sleek and shiny black hair, and others have auburn hair that falls in loose waves. Some are tall and curvy, others small and petite. All are blessed with lovely faces and figures that would make a man weep. Yet there's no sign of the dark-eyed, raven-haired barmaid—not that I'm looking.

"Maidens from the farthest homestead have come to greet you," the marquis says, gesturing to the line stretching from the stage. They look at me expectantly.

One by one, each girl approaches, curtseys, and introduces herself. I charm them with my practiced smile and grace, even as the Rings in my back seem to twitch with every new face.

Soon my cheeks hurt and my lips are dry from kissing so many hands. I'm pretty sure I'm seeing double when two women step forward as one, their beauty eclipsing all those who came before.

These must be the twins Jared was yapping about.

Flaxen hair drapes over the girls' shoulders in delicate curls, shining gold like a wheat field on a summer afternoon. Even to my untrained eye, I can tell their gowns are cut from the finest silk in the region. The fabric clings to their sumptuous frames, hugging every curve and accentuating every asset. Whoever made the gowns is surely an expert tailor. My eyebrows rise. The ladies in the royal court would foam at the mouth in rage if these two ever attended a ball.

How could these country girls afford such luxury? Most of the town, aside from the marquis and his coterie, is humble. My grandfather recently increased taxes to fund the defense effort, and I know the citizenry has felt the pinch. Unless someone sold information to the enemy... But what could anyone in Evandale know that would be useful? The idea seems fanciful.

"Ophelia and Sonja Bellamore, Your Highness," the marquis says with a frown.

I take their hands in turn, pressing my lips to their warm skin. The twins blush and smile sweetly. Off to the side, Jared gives me an encouraging nod.

"Your dresses are as fine as I've ever seen, worthy of a princess," I say, because it's true.

They giggle and glance at each other, excitement sparkling in their violet eyes. They've dusted their cheeks with silver mica powder, bringing out the color of their irises. Truly, their beauty is worthy of songs and poems. Yet I find myself unmoved, as my thoughts linger on the barmaid from last night. Why is she not here? Does she not want to marry a prince? Why didn't I ask her name?

I turn back to the beautiful sisters, their faces alight with hope. I can see why my friends are so smitten, but my false mission feels cruel again. Until I speak with the sorceress, I can't marry any of these women, not even that distracting barmaid. But the marquis, my councilors, the twins—everyone—is watching me expectantly. I swallow the lump in my throat.

"Tell me," I start, scrambling for some further polite conversation, "did you make these dresses yourselves?"

The one on the right—Sonja, with a cheeky smile—shakes her head. "No, Your Highness."

"Our sister did," her twin, Ophelia, says proudly.

"Your sister is a gifted seamstress worthy of a place in my castle."

"Thank you, Dario," a third voice pipes up from the crowd.

The speaker stands not on the stage but next to it. Her dress of linen sackcloth blends in with the bags of onions and potatoes, but I'd know that face anywhere. It's the barmaid from last night. The one I've been looking for.

She lifts her chin, peering at me with a glint in her eye, her hands on her hips. She doesn't look anything like her sisters, and yet I find it hard to look away.

"Show Prince Dietan some respect," snaps the marquis.

"My apologies," she says, bowing deeply, almost mockingly. "It was my mistake. I thought he was someone else."

As intrigued as I am that she's no simpering, giggling maiden—and that she seems utterly uninterested in bagging a prince—I frown. A barmaid makes a good spy, a perfect informant for the enemy. One too many of those strong Alarician ales could loosen the lips of a well-connected merchant or high official passing through. All kinds of secrets could slip from the mouths of travelers from all parts of Alarice and Loegria. Hardly anyone would look twice at a barmaid, not realizing just how much she can overhear. She's the one who told me about the mage, after all. What else does she know? Did she really make her sisters' dresses herself—and if so, who paid for the silk? There are far too many coincidences for her to be anything other than suspicious.

I narrow my eyes and return her forthright gaze.

Who is this woman?

CHAPTER SIX

Aren

I *knew* it. That man from last night is the prince.

I had my suspicions, but I didn't think the prince would be foolish enough to walk around Evandale without protection or to stumble into the Raven's Beak alone. With those polished boots and coiffed hair, I'd assumed he was a member of the prince's entourage, some fancy lord who'd never seen a hard day's work. He had blisters at the thumb like a soldier, but there wasn't a speck of dirt or grime on his hands—the hands of a man used to a life of comfort.

I couldn't help but watch him. His was the only face I hadn't seen before. While he hid his golden hair beneath a cap, silky strands fell on his forehead. He was lean but muscled, so he couldn't be a bureaucrat relegated to hours behind a desk. His blue-green eyes were hooded—haunted, even. I was confused that no one else noticed him. That's when I realized he was good at hiding.

The moment Dietan—*Prince* Dietan—walked in the doors of the Raven's Beak, I knew exactly what he was: a liar. And I don't have time for liars.

I lean a hip against the edge of the stage and force myself not to fidget as he speaks with my sisters again. He's far too annoyingly handsome for his own good. I was right—what kind of prince would he be if he wasn't handsome?

At least he's flirting with my sisters. My plan is working. If either Ophelia or Sonja captures his eye, they'll both be set, and my father, too. My life will finally be my own. But why would a prince hide his identity? Should I be worried for my girls? *Dario, my ass.*

I narrow my eyes. What the hell was he up to, sneaking around last night in that crappy disguise? Why did he ask me about Veteria? A prince seeking a healer so far from court doesn't sit right. Maybe he's sick, or… Maybe he's secretly impotent and is searching for a cure. Maybe that's why he's not courting one of those inbred princesses in the capital. Aren't they all his cousins anyway?

When Sonja finishes whatever she's saying, the prince glances my way, and a zing of excitement shoots through me, like I've been named harvest queen or something equally ridiculous. *What the hell?* Maybe I'm the one who's sick.

Dietan comes to the edge of the stage and addresses me directly. "Your sisters' dresses are beautiful."

I can feel the marquis's unapproving eyes on me. I reel my thoughts back in and force my shoulders to relax as I dip into a stiff curtsy. Dietan didn't say my sisters were beautiful, though—only that their clothes were. *Interesting.*

He raises a golden eyebrow. "And how does a barmaid afford such luxurious material?"

Some compliment, asshole. "Anyone who works hard and budgets well can afford it, Your Highness," I reply.

The crowd inhales collectively. I half expect him to reach down and strike me, like the marquis did once. But to my surprise, the prince only laughs. "I'm afraid you've got me there. I don't know anything about work of any kind."

He keeps his gaze locked on mine as he leaps from the stage and approaches me. He's much taller than I expected, and it's irritatingly gratifying, the way he towers over me. Ugh, why do I feel so *womanly* looking up at him?

"You're not in line to meet me," he says, ignoring the queue of impatient girls glaring at me. "Why didn't you make yourself a beautiful dress as well? Don't you want to be considered for marriage?"

"To you?"

"What's wrong with me?" he asks mildly.

I know I should keep my big mouth shut, but we're already way past any sense of decorum. Besides, he started this. I scowl as I take in his shiny boots, velvet coat, and epaulets—the attire of a proper prince, instead of a shadowy stranger in the night.

Honestly, I like the man from last night much better, but my sisters deserve a prince, and I won't turn them over to the care of a man unworthy of them, no matter how wealthy or titled. The idea of marrying him myself is absurd, but this is a chance to find out what kind of man he is.

"You wanna know what's wrong with you?" I ask. "You're a man."

"Last time I checked."

"Men looking for wives just want a servant they don't have to pay."

"But you would be a princess. I have many servants in my employ."

He's got a point. "Why do you want a wife, then?" I ask.

"The usual reasons princes get married. Unite the kingdoms, guarantee the line of succession, continue the dynasty, that sort of thing."

Right. I suppose a princess could do worse than this stupidly handsome prince—but he's definitely hiding something. "Yeah, except marriage is for chumps," I say.

That turns his smirk into a smile. Huh. I didn't expect that. I thought I'd offend him, as the only girl in town who doesn't want to be a princess. If he's offended, he doesn't look it. Not one bit.

"Funny, that's what I always used to say," he says with a grin. "But one day, perhaps you'll find a man worthy of your talents, my lady." Then he *winks* at me.

The jerk.

Everyone else turns back to the prince as he mounts the stage and sweeps toward the next maiden, without another glance at me.

I don't have time for such nonsense. At least I've determined he has more than a pretty face. He held his temper even when I called him a chump, has a quick wit, and seems to have a sense of humor.

I meet my sisters at the end of the stage, and they step down gracefully, their silk skirts swishing as they whisper and giggle behind their hands. As I follow them across the square, I give the stage one last look over my shoulder and find Prince Dietan staring right at me, a knowing look on his face. I can't manage to pull my gaze from his, but I do conjure an impressive scowl. The very same scowl I use on rowdy tavern patrons that sends them scurrying home before I throw them out.

And Prince Dietan? He doesn't scurry anywhere. He winks. Again! Blasted man, maybe he has a stye in his eye.

With a huff, I spin and haul my stunned ass away.

Thank the goddess, it's the harvest festival. The one night of the year I don't have to work. I sip my mug of mulled wine slowly, determined to enjoy myself for once.

The sunset turns the sky a dusky pink, and a chill sets in. I move closer to the roaring fire in the middle of the town square and watch the dancers skip and spin on the packed dirt. Most have already tossed off their shoes and are dancing barefoot, including Sonja. Sonja knows all the steps and moves so gracefully that people gather around to watch her, clapping along to the drumbeat and cheering her on. Some of the royal guard come over to gawk as well. Even if Sonja's hair is a little disheveled and there's dirt on the hem of her gown, it's hard not to look at her. Getting those mud stains out of the silk is going to be a chore, but I try not to dwell on it too much. I just hope Dietan is watching, too.

Everyone is having a grand old time even though it was a hard summer, with not enough rain and too much sun, a smaller harvest than expected, and the king's defense levies. But soon it'll rain again. Gray skies and mud are a blessing, a gift from the goddess. I can smell the coming storm. It smells like something new.

I pass a table of some of the town's gossipier farmers, a handful of older folks who have seen Evandale spring up from the roots. They like to talk about people, but at least they do it to their faces. I ignore them most of the time but can't help overhearing their conversation tonight.

"That's impossible! The Kilandrar are children's tales! They can't be in Alarice!" Melvin Brody says.

"Unless they crossed the bridge from Penrith—" argues Silas Hong, but Jones Holden speaks over him.

"Ridiculous. The bridge was destroyed. Not even the Kilandrar can fly across that chasm. The only way to Alarice from Penrith is through Loegria."

"Is it so ridiculous? Dark magic is in the air. War is coming."

Children across Albion know the story of Lord Boreas the Unbeliever, who was a disciple of the ancient sorceress Skiron, and how he corrupted the Whisting. He twisted that great gift into the Unseen Death and used it to slaughter his fellow disciples and force the world to submit to his will. Then Boreas created monstrous assassins: the fearsome Kilandrar, foul creatures of wind and hate.

I shake my head. Old-timers. The threat of war is real enough, but there's no way the rest can be true. Children's nightmares walking the earth? It's probably the ale talking.

No one else seems worried. I shrug off the shiver that runs through me. What the hell could shadowy, evil creatures made of magic and created for destruction want from Evandale? Apples? Wheat? Lumber? Ham and ale?

I shake my head. The men are wrong. Definitely the ale talking.

My feet ache. I've been standing all day and desperately want to kick off my shoes and lie down. The wine makes me feel warm and fuzzy. A friend from childhood asks me to dance, but I'm not in the mood.

I find Ophelia sitting at a table near the stage, her chin in her hand as she stares in the prince's direction, her eyes half-lidded, her smile small and hopeful. Dietan and his royal entourage sit at the high table on the stage with the marquis. They're clanking mugs together and laughing, having a grand old time. The prince is supposed to be leaving in a few days, so he must be announcing his choice soon.

I sit next to my sister and take a long, hard swig of my drink. Even the wine in Evandale is strong, but I like the heartiness of it, the taste of home. Maybe that's why I'm in a mood. It's bittersweet knowing that today is a success. My girls have caught the prince's eye. One of them will soon be married, and all our dreams will come true. But damn it, I'll miss them. I don't want them to go. I blink back tears at the thought.

Ophelia sighs dreamily. "Isn't he gorgeous?"

I kick off my shoes. "The prince?" I glare at him over my mug. The firelight catches his golden hair and glints off his blinding-white teeth when he smiles. His changeable blue-green eyes sparkle blue like the sapphire pin at his collar. "I guess he's okay, if blond's your type."

"Not the prince! I meant that Lord Jared…"

"Wait—who?"

"The one next to him."

I look over at the head table. Hmm. This Lord Jared is handsome enough, I suppose, suave and confident like a preening cat. But he's no prince.

"He asked me to save him a dance." Ophelia is staring intently at him, and I doubt she's blinked the whole time, as if a spell has been cast over her. It is so ridiculous; I almost spit out my drink.

"I thought you were hot for the prince."

"He's all right, I suppose," Ophelia says.

"You suppose? I thought you'd be sitting on his lap by now. He's easily the most handsome man here."

Ophelia turns to me with an amused smile on her face. "Oh, so you noticed."

"Noticed what?"

"How handsome Prince Dietan is," she teases.

I groan. "Looks aren't everything." Beautiful people tend to coast through life, vain and shallow, oblivious to the suffering around them. My sisters are the exceptions that prove the rule. "Maybe he's nice to look at, but that's all there is."

"Then why do you want me to marry him if you dislike him so much?" Ophelia asks.

I roll my eyes. "Because once you're a princess—once you're the queen—you'll be safe. You'll have everything you could ever want." *I have many servants in my employ*, the prince said this morning. "You won't have to do a day's work in your life," I say.

"But what if I don't want to be a princess?"

It's hard not to laugh. "Everyone wants to be a princess." I gesture to the crowd. "Didn't you see the line of maidens long enough to reach the capital?"

Ophelia stares at me for a long moment, her eyes hardening and her lips pressing into a flat line. "Harvest Mother, what is it? Do you want me to be happy, or do you think it's a sucker's game to marry a prince?"

"Those two things are not mutually exclusive."

"You know, you're awfully judgmental for someone who pretends not to be."

Her intuition catches me off guard, even if she is wrong. My heart settles, and I take a moment to gather my thoughts. "I just want what's best for you two. I want you and Sonja to find some security. You're the prettiest girls in all of Evandale, and the nicest, and you both deserve the best."

"And Lord Jared is nobody?" Ophelia asks indignantly. "I'd argue Lord Jared could make any girl happy, if not happier than that prince."

I sigh. Ophelia was always the obstinate one.

"You've helped me make up my mind. I'll remind him about that dance now," Ophelia says. She gets to her feet and walks up the stairs to the stage. Dietan and Jared stand and turn to her. I'm too far away to hear what Ophelia says to Jared as she curtsies, but to my supreme surprise, Jared grins, takes her hand, and kisses it. It seems that the prince, too, is taken by surprise, because he glances between the two of them before his eyes find mine.

Caught! I turn away and pretend I wasn't watching, for all the good that'll do me. I try to find Sonja, but Sonja has stopped dancing and is talking with the young general instead. Her hands are clasped in front of her, and she's twisting her hips side to side as she smiles and laughs with him.

Now it's Marcus's turn to grin. It's strange to see the gruff soldier cracking a smile like that. Hold on—is everyone falling for the wrong person? Neither of my sisters are flirting with the prince. This wasn't the plan. I know I shouldn't be upset that they might find happiness elsewhere, especially with lords and generals, but I'm annoyed that I've spent so much time and money making them look like royalty only to watch them settle for less.

Ophelia and Jared leave the stage together, talking and smiling. Jared leans his mouth close to her ear and even puts a hand on her lower back to help her down the steps. The two of them seem totally enamored.

I expect the prince to look shocked or angry, but he's grinning, too, leaning back in his chair and watching them with fondness. Why isn't he jealous? Has a different girl caught his eye? He looks more than happy to let his men entertain the two most beautiful women in town.

The golden prince catches me staring again, and I force my gaze away just as the marquis's red-nosed face invades my personal space. Gross. I turn back to face the stage to dissuade this creep from moving closer.

"Aren," he growls.

"My lord." I sigh. What does this asshole want now? I pick up my drink to take a sip, but the marquis puts a hand over the cup, forcing me to set it back down on the table. His wrinkled hand is pallid, his fingers a sickly blue. I can smell the liquor on him and recoil from the acidic stench.

"What were you doing? With the prince." His eyes are glassy and distant, no doubt thanks to the amount of ale he's drunk, but they remain cold, like a snake's.

"Simply doing my duty by presenting my sisters to the prince," I say, hoping my lips form a smile and not a grimace.

"Not your sisters—you," he spits. "You make a mockery of Evandale by stealing attention from the real candidates."

Now I understand what he really wants. The ale has truly turned the man's brain to rot if he thinks the prince is at all interested in me. I sit up straighter and put my hands on my hips. "Are you truly threatened by *me*?" I press a mocking hand to my chest, forcing a laugh even as heat rises in my cheeks. "Because the prince isn't interested in anyone from your family?" I ask, even as I feel sympathy for those girls. Even if they have little ambition of becoming princesses, marriage to the prince would be their ticket out of the Breadalbane house and far, far away from the marquis. It's common knowledge he beats them with his belt at the tiniest provocation.

"I simply believe the prince deserves finer stock than your family," he sneers. "All you're good for is a roll in the hay."

"Fine," I say, taking the insult and pushing his hand off my cup. I wish I had my frying pan—I'd bash his head in. "I appreciate the reminder, my lord. Don't you have somewhere else to be? More important people to talk to?"

The marquis scowls, as ugly and repugnant as ever, but he skulks away just the same, glaring at me over his shoulder before disappearing into the crowd.

I notice the prince is still watching me. I narrow my eyes at him, and he arches an eyebrow. He is causing more trouble that he's worth. And then, as if the marquis hadn't already put me in a foul enough mood, the prince lifts the corner of his irritatingly attractive mouth in a half smile.

That's enough. I down the rest of my wine in a gulp, scoop up my shoes, and weave my way between tables of noisy revelers. I pass the dancers, the casks of wine, and some children playing swords with wooden sticks, arguing over who gets to act out the role of Prince Dietan next.

As I reach the edge of the square, I stop and lean against the corner of a building, a wave of dizziness rolling through me. *Hold on.* I didn't drink that much.

I push myself off the wall, and black dots flit in front of my eyes. I blink hard and shake my head. *Get it together*, I tell myself, but the world tilts beneath my feet. That wine was too strong. I need to get home and lie down; I can deal with all this matchmaking crap tomorrow. Maybe by then, my sisters and that damn prince will have come to their senses, and he'll choose one of them to be his bride. The marquis is absolutely delusional if he thinks the prince has shown one iota of interest in me.

Something about all this rubs wrong, like a thistle in my shoe. I press a palm to my forehead. The wine is making me confused.

I turn the corner and see the round sign hanging in front of the Raven's Beak at the end of the road. *Almost there.* Head swimming, I brace a hand on the doorframe of a boarding stable. The smell wafting from inside makes my nose burn and clears my mind a bit.

Even drunk like this, I'm certain of one thing: before that prince goes anywhere with one of my girls, he's going to come clean about why he was skulking around in a disguise and asking about a healer. I don't tolerate lies. Even from a prince — even one as enticing as Prince Dietan.

Shit! I shake my head to clear it. *Enticing?* I snort. Yeah, the wine was way too strong.

CHAPTER SEVEN

Aren

I stumble down the darkened street toward the familiar silhouette of the Raven's Beak sign. The music from the revelry fades away; the village is empty, everyone is at the party, and only moonlight illuminates my path. I trip over the cobblestones, cursing every time.

When I finally manage to reach the Raven's Beak, I hold on to a hitching post at the base of the steps for balance. I frown at the darkened door, a reminder of everything at stake. *Fine*, I decide. *As long as my sisters are happy, I suppose marrying a lord and a general is enough.* Once they're married, I can sell this place and get out of here.

I sway and almost fall before I can even take another step. What is wrong with me? I slap my cheeks, willing myself not to pass out, but my vision grows gray and tunnels in.

Something is terribly wrong. The wine at the harvest festival is never this strong. I only had one drink. So why is everything spinning?

Prickly chills crawl up my spine: I'm not drunk. I've been poisoned.

Blue-stained fingers flash in my mind. A hand pressed over my cup.

The marquis' smug face leering.

That lech dosed my drink.

I've studied herbalist remedies with Veteria like my mother before me, and it's becoming clear that the marquis slipped me a dose of devil's breath in my drink, a sweet-smelling, bell-shaped blue flower that can relax a person and aid in sleep—but which in sufficient quantity renders a person unconscious. But why on earth...oh no...

Bile rises up, and I lean over, willing myself to purge the devil's breath still in my stomach. I need to get it out. I'm alone, at night. No one will help if...

The nausea passes, and I blink furiously. I can't faint now. I must get up those steps to safety. I'm not the type to panic, but my breath is coming in shallow gasps and my heart is hammering. Heavy footsteps approach behind me. A shadow creeps closer in the moonlight.

Fuck! My heart slams against my ribs, my pulse a desperate pounding in my ears. My legs feel liquid, but I force myself to move, stumbling forward as dizziness warps the edges of my vision. The air presses down in as if the night itself is smothering me.

The heavy footsteps quicken. Closer. Too close.

I glance up the three steps to the front door of the tavern. I'll never make it. I release the post and stagger toward the dark alley at the side of the building. Not a great plan, but I can't just stand here as the poison overtakes me. Thankfully, I still have enough sense to scoop up my shoe and throw it hard at whoever's following me.

There's a yelp, then a curse.

It's the marquis. Of course it is. He easily ducks out of the way. I'm seeing double, I can barely stand, but I hold up my fists. "Get away from me, asshole!"

The marquis seems to grow larger and smaller. My vision is warping. I shake my head, fighting against the darkness. This is stronger than black market devil's breath; he must have gotten it from some expensive herbalist with more power and knowledge than anyone in Evandale.

"You should have known your place," he sneers. "Get her!"

From the shadows emerges one of his henchmen. I recognize him from the Beak. He grabs me by the waist. I flail, shrieking, and manage to punch him in the ear. Howling in pain, he slams me against the tavern wall. He may be slow, but he's still stronger than I am.

The air rushes from my lungs. He slams my head once more against the hard wooden siding. I scream again as I try to get away, twisting and turning, and pull my arm back to hit him again.

But the asshole catches my hand and clamps down hard on my wrist. I whimper, fearing he might break it.

"Just wait till the prince finds out you've 'left town,'" the marquis muses, an evil grin unfurling across his lips. "Once you're out of the way, he'll have no choice but to pick one of my lovely girls."

This man must be living in a different universe to believe the prince is at all interested in me. But this is the marquis, after all.

The marquis' lackey is taller than me, heavier, and I don't stand a chance to escape, except he's drunk, so I do what's worked for me in past scrapes at the Beak. Mustering the last of my strength, I drive my knee up and kick him straight in the family jewels. He bellows, folding instinctually to protect himself from further assault.

I slip free. *Run, run*, I tell myself, but the darkness creeps in. I can't see, I can't scream, and I can't make my legs move the way I want them to.

"Get her, you idiot!" the marquis squawks.

He's closing in again, and I punch him straight in the chest, but I hit something as hard as iron and my whole hand stings. *Harvest Mother, that hurt.*

"You're wearing armor?" I croak through numbing lips.

This coward is wearing a steel jerkin under his clothes, and I'm only in my thin linen dress. Clarity strikes like a bolt of lightning, and I jab at his face, his eyes, but he turns his head just in time. He smashes a kerchief against my nose and mouth, the sickly scent of the devil's breath searing my throat. He's choking me, his fingers tightening around my windpipe. I can't breathe. Everything's gray again, turning to black. I go limp. I can't fight anymore.

Just then, a strong wind rises out of nowhere. The minion's hand is ripped away, and an invisible force throws him head over heels, slamming him against the wall like he did to me.

I take huge gulps of unnatural, ice-cold air as the sky seems to crackle and hiss, taking on a life of its own. I fall to my knees, coughing and retching. My hands go to my bruised neck. *What was that?*

I check my surroundings to make sure the marquis is not lying in wait, but he's been reduced to a heap of fine fabrics by an overturned cart.

But there's someone else here.

A man pummels his fists into the toppled marquis, hitting him again and again with thunderous blows, illuminated by a flash of otherworldly lightning. The marquis yelps and curses, shouting, "Enough! Enough!"

But the stranger is relentless.

The icy storm howls and turns down the street like Boreas has returned, shaking the trees and rattling the shutters. A vortex of debris barrels toward us.

What the hell is happening?

I struggle to get to my feet, buffeted by the wind. My entire body aches, every move eliciting some fresh pain. I collapse on the cobblestones, but I can't stay here. I want to be as far away from this as possible. Harvest Mother, I just want to go home. But I'm too weak to even crawl up the steps to the door as the storm roars all around me, and the sound of fists striking flesh echoes in the dark.

"Stop! Please! I'm begging you!" the marquis cries.

"If you touch her again, I will have your head!" the stranger roars, punctuated by a gust of freezing wind.

No... It couldn't be...

All I can see is a shadow lifting the marquis by the collar before shoving him forcefully away. The marquis runs off, tripping over the shoe I threw at him earlier. His henchman scampers after him.

A wave of triumph invigorates me for a moment, but I'm still too weak to stand. Everything's gone cold, and I'm shaking.

Now there are strong hands around me, pulling me upright. The stranger. He smells of moss and woodsmoke, of hearth and comfort. The icy wind is gone. He holds me in his arms, and I melt into them. "Hey, it's okay. You're safe now. Come on now, don't fade on me." His voice is warm and kind. Gentle.

Hold on. I know that voice.

I fight to stay awake, but it's no use. I claw at his shirt, but the darkness closes in.

"Third time we've met, and I still don't know your name," he murmurs.

The world goes black before I can give it to him.

CHAPTER EIGHT

Dietan

My entire body throbs with rage, along with a wash of relief that I was here to stop it. The world is an evil place filled with evil men. I must get this woman to safety.

She's easy enough to carry, and I focus on putting one foot in front of the other, holding her tight to ensure she doesn't slide off my back. I've thrown her over my shoulder like a sack of flour, the way we practice in battlefield training. I know how awful this looks, but I can't leave her passed out in an alleyway.

I saw everything. I was watching the barmaid during the festival, and she kept glancing my way as well, both of us making quick eye contact before averting our gazes, pretending as if we hadn't. She wasn't one of the women presented to me, though she doesn't appear to be married. Perhaps she carries a torch for an absent love? The thought sends a flare of power down my spine, so I force my mind to abandon it.

If this woman is a spy, she's a clumsy one, but maybe the best spy is the one you'd least expect. Maybe that's what she wants me to think. Spy or not, I couldn't keep my eyes off her. I was attuned to where she was at all times.

And when her sister came up to my table to remind Jared that he'd asked her to save him a dance, I was looking her way just in time to see that sleazy marquis place his grubby hand over her mug. I noticed just how strangely uncoordinated she became when she left the party. With mounting dread, I watched as the marquis and one of his men followed her.

I didn't know what that sick bastard was up to, but it was nothing good. I was so blinded by anger, I could have reduced the entire town to bits. I had to channel my rage into my fists so the Rings in my back didn't rip Evandale apart and even then, it was close. My knuckles burn hot, still slick with the marquis's blood from where I struck him in the mouth. His teeth took the full brunt of my punch, and I feel some satisfaction that the bastard will eat soup for the rest of his miserable days.

Some of these towns are in serious need of new governance. I'll have Jared put that on the list of reforms I'll enact when I eventually become king in Alarice.

The barmaid groans, and her tears soak through my shirt—or maybe it's drool. At least she seems to be regaining consciousness. She's breathing, but even as she struggles, she's as limp as a wet washcloth. I hold on more tightly. Despite my celibacy, I'm not immune to the pleasant feeling of her chest against my back and the backs of her thighs beneath my hands. I adjust her higher on my shoulder, and she groans.

"Sorry," I mutter.

The whole village is still at the party, but I can't take her back there in this state. After what happened, I'm certain she'd rather go home. She grunts and weakly pounds my lower back with her fists.

"You can't walk," I say. "I'll take you home. Where do you live?"

She moans and points a wavering finger down the street.

I shuffle onward down the main road. "Over here?"

She mumbles an incoherent response, and I think I hear something like "let me go." She shifts again, stubbornly trying to wiggle out of my grasp.

"I'm not letting you down," I say. "Not until you're somewhere safe."

"I fine," she slurs as if she drank her weight in Alarician ale. "Lemme go."

"You can't stand, let alone walk," I say.

"I *fine*," she repeats. At least she's stopped struggling. I sigh in relief.

A minute later, she lets out a soft, "Stop. Here."

The house is, like all the others in Evandale, a pretty little cottage with flowers in boxes on the windows. A single candle flickers dimly inside. I carry her to the doorway but hesitate to enter with an incapacitated woman in my arms. Instead, I knock with a swift tap of my boot.

There's a shuffling from inside, and the door opens, revealing an older man with a prominent nose. He's deeply hunched over a carved wooden cane, with wispy white hair tied in a low tail at the base of his neck. He's already in a nightgown, but he comes alert at the sight of the young woman I'm holding tightly. I'm determined not to drop her now.

"Hello, good sir. May I come in?" I say. "I believe this is your daughter?"

The man nods and doesn't ask questions as he steps aside. He gestures to a small back room.

Inside, there is a single bed. Scraps of fabric hang from a rack, leaning against a table with a sewing station and a sack of straw stuffed in the shape of a woman—more scarecrow than mannequin. So, this is where she made her sisters' gowns.

I carefully lay her down on her bed, atop her patchwork quilt, as her father lights her bedside lamp.

I stand back, watching as her father presses a wrinkled hand to her forehead.

"Aren?" her father asks. "Can you hear me?"

Aren. So that's her name.

She groans and opens her eyes, but they're unfocused. She tries to sit up, but her father puts a hand on her shoulder and pushes her back down.

"What happened?" her father asks, looking at me.

"She needed help," is all I can say, even as the old man takes in my bloody knuckles.

His lips grow thin as he checks Aren, then nods. "We are fortunate you came to her aid. She needs water and rest. She will be all right by the morning." He peers into the empty pitcher by her bed and starts to leave the room, shuffling on heavy feet.

"Please, allow me," I offer, taking the pitcher from his hands.

I move through the dim house and find an ewer of drinking water on the humble kitchen counter.

After I stop pouring, I hear her father say distantly, "There, there. Get it all out," followed by the sound of retching. I wait a moment before re-entering the room, giving Aren some privacy.

When I reappear in the doorway, Aren is coughing into a bucket. She glares up at me under lowered brows. She obviously still feels the same contempt toward me that she's shown all day. *Does saving her from the marquis' attempted kidnapping count for nothing?* She thrusts the bucket toward her father, and he takes it, dutifully.

"I'll be back right quick," he says to me.

I notice an empty washbasin on a small stand in the corner. I grab the washcloth folded over the rim and lean over Aren to wipe a bit of spittle from her mouth. "There you go. Feeling any better?" I ask.

Aren falls back onto her bed, groaning still, and doesn't answer. She pulls the covers up to her chin. I set aside the washcloth and busy myself by looking around her room. The shadows from the lone lamp are long. Her barmaid's apron hangs from a small rack on the wall, a woman's portrait beside it. Her mother, I assume, because she looks remarkably like Aren's twin sisters. But Aren has her eyes, I notice.

I take a seat on the trunk at the foot of her bed, surprising myself with my unwillingness to leave her just yet and tap my fingers on my knees to prevent myself from fussing over her where it's clearly unwelcome. The poison seems to be waning; she gathers up her blankets and curls into herself miserably, with her hair mussed and sweaty. I'm relieved that she seems relatively unharmed.

"Why?" Aren finally asks, half groan and half cry.

"I imagine the marquis will be the only one who can explain himself."

"No—not him. Why you?"

It takes me by surprise. "You mean, why did I help you?"

She stares at me, her eyebrows furrowed, and her lower lip juts out as she frowns, but she doesn't answer.

"Why in Albion wouldn't I?" I ask, shocked. I'm a prince, trained by knights. I would help anyone in the position she found herself in—it's what any gentleman would do.

She doesn't respond but continues to watch me, perhaps too tired to say much more.

She buries her face into the blanket just as the front door opens again, accompanied by her sisters' laughter. I stand as their footsteps near. They come into Aren's bedroom arm in arm, looking happy and gay, but stop short when they see me.

"Oh! Prince Dietan, why are you—" Ophelia starts, but then they see Aren lying in bed, pale and sweating, and rush to her side.

RINGS OF FATE

"What happened?" Sonja asks. Aren wants to rest, but her sisters fuss over her like a pair of hens. Ophelia brushes her hair back from her damp forehead while Sonja smooths the quilt anxiously.

I look back down at the dried blood coating my knuckles, and I scrub it away on my trousers. I won't say anything, not unless Aren says it first.

"Just too much to drink," she mumbles.

Perhaps she fears retribution from the marquis. I will personally see to it that the marquis is severely dealt with. White-hot anger flares inside of me simply remembering the way the marquis's face danced with joy as his man's hands dug into Aren's throat. The Rings in my back make my fingers twitch, and I'm forced to ball them into fists, lest I summon a gale in Aren's bedroom.

"The prince escorted me home," Aren continues.

Her sisters look at me for confirmation.

"Bringing her here was the least I could do," I say, following Aren's lead. It is, after all, half true.

Ophelia and Sonja glance at each other, saying more in a single look than any conversation, but they don't press her further in her current state. Their father returns, carrying a stack of fresh washcloths. I know when my presence might be more distracting than helpful, so I excuse myself.

"Your Highness," Ophelia says. "We are so, so grateful."

"If anything terrible happened to Aren, we would never…" Sonja chokes back her words with tears.

"I'm glad she's all right," I say. "I'll leave her to your capable care."

They curtsy deeply, and I pause in the doorway as they go back to tending to their sister. "Do you need anything? What can we do?" Ophelia frets.

Aren rises on her elbows. "Actually, there is something. Girls, gather some of the herbs from the windowsill—chamomile, lavender. Steep them in water with a slice of ginger. It will help clear my head. And bring me my casket of dried remedies."

I step out into the hallway, and after her sisters scurry past to collect the requested items, I quietly leave the house. I can see the light still emanating from her room, the shadows cast by her family as they tend to her flickering on the walls, and I feel an ache I can't describe—a longing for the return of something that was never mine to begin with.

They love her dearly, unconditionally. I wonder what that's like.

CHAPTER NINE

Aren

The night was shitty, but by morning I've recovered from the effects of the poison, and I'm back at the Raven's Beak by the afternoon. It rains all day, an exhale from the heavens, like a breath that's been held too long gusting from the sky in a great rush. The damp doesn't help with how I ache all over, but I've never been one to take a day off, even when I'm sick. My sisters always tease that the only day I'll rest is the day I die. But they don't know: I'm here today because there's no way in Albion I'm going to let that bastard marquis scare me into hiding at home. He *will* see my face.

I didn't tell my sisters what really happened, though they keep trying to pry more of the story out of me. Of course, they want to know how the damn prince ended up at our house, and they kept teasing me about it, inventing some attraction between us. But I kept telling them it wasn't like that at all. I just had a little too much wine and he walked me home. The prince is a gentleman, right? That's it. End of story.

I don't want to admit that just thinking about what could've happened last night makes me shake. I can still feel the ghost of those fingers choking me. As soon as I can, I'm going to turn that dress I was wearing into rags.

I can't let anyone see the damage, either, so I tied my mother's old kerchief loosely around my neck to hide the bruising. It still smells like Mother, like her homemade perfume of citrus peels and jasmine. Maybe I just imagine it, and it doesn't smell like anything at all. But even after all these years, her scent brings a small measure of comfort as I go about my day, pouring drinks and serving food to those looking for shelter from the rain, wanting a hot meal and to rest their feet by the fire.

At the end of the day, after nightfall, I go out back to feed the pigs, carrying a heavy bucket of scraps. It's still pouring. I freeze when I spy a shadow moving in the alley—the same alley where…

My heart pounds, and I start to tremble all over again, thinking he's come back to finish the job. I want to scream. My blood rushes; rage, hot and fierce, fills me. Before I know it, I'm running after him, my fists clenched. "Hey! Bastard!" I yell, as the rain muffles my voice. "What do you think you're—"

But when he turns around, it's not the marquis, nor one of his men.

"You." I don't know what to say, but my rage is suddenly doused, as if the downpour put it out. My shoulders fall. I'm still shaking, but now from the cold.

"Me," replies the prince. He has a wool hood pulled up, masking most of his features, but the light from the tavern catches his sharp nose and high cheekbones. "I assume you're feeling better today, since you're back to yelling at me." He gives me that charming smile again.

"Oh, about that…" I'm filled with gratitude, relief, and shame that I couldn't fend for myself.

He waves it off as if it were nothing. Maybe it was nothing. *I'm* nothing to him, after all, compared to all the women fawning over him. He was just chivalrous enough to save me.

"I apologize, Your Highness. I didn't know it was you," I finally say.

"Dietan—please, just call me Dietan."

"Not Dario?" I can't help but laugh.

"All in all, I'd prefer my real name." He laughs with me.

It's nice to laugh together after everything. But the rain is falling in torrents on the two of us, and the pigs want their dinner.

"Do you need help with that?" he asks. Without waiting for an answer, he takes the slop bucket out of my hands and sloshes its contents over the low pigsty fence into the trough.

"Thank you, Your Highness," I say as he hands it back to me and our fingers brush.

"Dietan. Please."

I shake my head. As if I'd ever call a prince by his first name. "What are you doing out here?" I ask. He's skulking around alleyways dressed like a thief. I remind myself I can't trust him, even if he did save me last night.

"I mean to take a stroll through the forest," he says casually, as if it isn't storming all around us. A clap of thunder makes us both jump. "So, if you'll excuse me—"

"You'll get lost if you go that way," I tell him, jutting my chin in the direction he was heading.

"Oh, right. I'll go the other way, then." He gives me a wink, just like last night, and heads in the opposite direction.

"You have a funny habit of sneaking around," I say.

That stops him in his tracks again. He turns around, sighing as if I'm keeping him from important business in the woods. "I have to if I'm to get anything done. See, that's the problem with being a prince. I'm recognized wherever I go."

The rain batters harder and soaks into my only pair of leather shoes. "But where in the forest are you going, exactly?" I ask, even if it isn't any of my business.

"Now that is privileged information," he says, wagging a finger.

I scoff. This playful charm of his is starting to grate. Even that annoyingly symmetrical face of his seems a little less handsome. "If you'd tell me where you're going, I could help. Otherwise, you'll get lost out there, I promise you that."

The prince looks at the forest and then turns back to me. He licks his lips, and his eyebrows pull together as he contemplates my offer.

Meanwhile, I'm going to die of a chill. If I'd known he was going to detain me, I'd have put on my cloak.

Finally, he steps closer to me, coming into the glow from the tavern. Rain coats his face, his skin gleaming in the soft light. I stand up a little straighter. Damn if I'm going to look small in front of him. Why is he so irritatingly tall?

But the way he looks at me doesn't make me feel small. His eyes dance merrily as he gazes down at me.

"If I told you, then I'd have to kill you," he whispers.

His tone is playful. It sure doesn't sound like the type of threat he made to the marquis last night. *That*, I believed. But something about him still bothers me.

"No, you won't," I say. "Kill me, I mean."

He laughs again. He has a nice laugh, rich and warm with amusement. "I suppose not."

"Come on, I won't tell anyone. I promise."

He looks me in the eye and holds my gaze. I can't breathe for a moment.

"Right. I think you are quite good at keeping secrets," he says, as if coming to a conclusion.

I wait, but when he says nothing more, I ask instead, "Why did you rescue me last night?"

He could have just walked on by. Princes don't put themselves in danger for other people, especially nobodies like me. For a prince to go out of his way was an act of kindness I would never have expected. He got his knuckles bloody for me; I noticed when he handed me the washcloth. I'm beginning to believe that he wouldn't break my sisters' hearts after all, if that is what they choose.

His eyes gleam, and he clears his throat. "It's a little thing called chivalry. You've heard of it?"

"Yeah, I've heard of it." And there it is. It doesn't have anything to do with me at all. Just duty. Just a man who is *especially good* at being a prince, even when nobody is watching.

I try to thank him but can't form the words. My cheeks burn despite the cool rain against them. "I can take care of myself. I could have handled it." It's a lie, one even I don't believe, but I'd rather throw myself from the roof than admit it to him.

"Obviously. But it's nice to have some help occasionally, no?"

He's still standing way too close, and his singsong Loegrian accent is making my heart race. Maybe it's a good thing he's a gentleman. A chivalrous prince would make a good match for one of my sisters.

Maybe not, if he's fool enough to go tramping into the woods late at night. "You're going to see that sorceress, aren't you?"

He silently raises his eyebrows, hesitating, looking shifty again.

"If you knew anything about Evandale, you'd know it's not a good idea to walk that forest at night. You don't know what's out there, especially these days. You could get eaten by a bear, or something worse. I hear there are all manner of creatures out there."

"Oh, I don't plan to die before my engagement, don't you worry. There'll be an announcement soon," he calls, walking backward.

So, he *has* chosen a bride.

Surely, it's Sonja or Ophelia.

Maybe that's why he came to my rescue, to play the noble hero for them. The thought stings for a moment, but I find my tongue just as he turns forward. "Is this what you'll do to your wife? Sneak away in the night and never tell her what you're really up to?"

That stops him again. He calls back, over his shoulder, and his voice rises above the downpour. "Trust me, Aren Bellamore, if you were my wife, you'd be the first to know my secret."

Huh. He knows my name. Of course he does—my family must have told him who I was. It sounds nice on his lips, like a melody. It fills me with unexpected warmth in this cold rain.

The prince might not be the vain, deceitful man I initially thought he was, but my gut still tells me he's hiding something, something important enough to risk the future king getting eaten by a bear—or worse. The prince is nothing but a liar. Maybe it's better if he leaves this town without a bride at all. I watch him go, all the way until he disappears into the woods.

CHAPTER TEN

Aren

The next evening brings a knock on the door. For a brief, panicked moment I worry that our neighbor, old Mr. Singh, has fallen again, but instead, it's a messenger. A royal one, too—never thought I'd see one of those at my doorstep. Her uniform is immaculate—a pressed jacket and a cap bearing the insignia of the royal brigade of messengers.

"Letters for Miss Ophelia Bellamore and Miss Sonja Bellamore," she says, holding out two identical pieces of parchment, each folded and sealed with wax.

I stare at the letters, numb, before mechanically reaching out for them. They bear the Loegrian royal crest, and delivered at this late hour, they look to be of great consequence. I thank the messenger before turning on one heel to face the girls. Ophelia and Sonja are sitting with Father near the fireplace, curiosity brightening their faces.

"I think these are for you," I say, holding each letter out to its respective recipient. The twins practically leap into the air to grab them.

"Oh!" Sonja cries, staring at the royal seal. "The announcement, it's really happening, isn't it?"

"You don't even know what it says." I stoke the logs in the fireplace, making sure Father is comfortable. He takes my hand and squeezes it. It's hard to believe it could come so easily, our salvation. I'm unsure of how to feel or what to do next, my heart racing and sweat beading on my forehead.

"Remember our plan, Sonja," Olivia says. "Whatever happens, we stay together."

Sonja nods. "There must be a place for both of us at court, or neither of us goes." Then they giggle and hug each other.

I want to be happy for my girls, but at the same time, the weight of those two letters—the heavy parchment, the royal seal, their names gracefully calligraphed on the envelopes—dredges up that familiar feeling of always looking in from the outside.

Ophelia and Sonja look at each other, mustering their courage, before opening the letters together. They both jump up with excitement as they begin to read.

"Well, what does it say?" I feel hope bubbling in my chest, their infectious joy pushing aside my own lingering disappointment.

"We're both invited to an audience with the royal entourage tomorrow afternoon," Ophelia says, handing me her letter while Sonja clutches hers like it's worth its weight in gold. "There's going to be an announcement!"

I didn't expect it to happen so soon, despite what the prince said last night. I thought Dietan hadn't shown any interest in the choices paraded before him. His companions, Jared and Marcus, seemed far more interested in my sisters than he did, but I suppose royals behave differently.

It strikes me as odd that my father and I were not invited to the announcement along with the twins. Surely the family of the prince's soon-to-be betrothed should be invited to witness a prince's proposal. I don't allow myself to think that it's because he chose a different girl.

A sharp pang of regret hits me like cold water, but I push it aside. My sisters' futures and my freedom are the goal. So why am I about to cry, like the feeling of being on the outside is too much this time? I lift my chin. I'm much too sensible for all this. I want to be there to witness the start of my girls' happily ever after, that's all.

"One of you has definitely caught the prince's eye," I say reassuringly, looking to Father, who nods in agreement.

Sonja sniffs. "He's hardly said a word to me except to ask about you, Aren."

"He asked about me? When?"

Ophelia nods. "He came by yesterday afternoon, but you were at the Beak. He wanted to make sure you were fine."

"We told him you're always working," Sonja says. "Did you happen to see him last night?"

I shrug, even as my cheeks heat. The girls don't notice. They've gone back to rereading their letters.

Ophelia smiles dreamily as she always does. Sonja fans herself with the invitation. I feel a rush of protectiveness. They both look so young and innocent, and the world is a cruel place. Hopefully, they will never know exactly how cruel it can be.

I set aside my own strange sadness and embrace them both like I did when they were little, planting kisses on the crowns of their golden heads, where a real crown will soon sit.

"I'm proud of you both," I tell them, a sob in my throat. "Come, let's get to bed so you can look your best for tomorrow."

But long into the night, when the only sounds are my sisters' deep breathing and Father's occasional snore, I lie awake, trying to convince myself that I'll be happy when I'm all alone. I'll have my freedom. Isn't that what I've always wanted? To travel the world, with no responsibilities, no husband, and no one to tell me what to do. So why can't I sleep?

—

In the morning, as the rain hammers against the window, I dress my sisters, putting them in their second-best gowns that I've made for them. When the twins twirl in front of the full-length mirror, gasping over how pretty they look, from their embroidered hoods to the bells at their ankles, I can't help but smile, even though I still wish I'd merited an invitation. Today is all about them, and I make sure my girls feel beautiful, important, and worthy of royalty. No one will be able to take their eyes off the twins from the moment they walk into the room.

Before we leave, Father gathers us to him. He's too weak to join us; his stiff hip throbs even more painfully during rainstorms. The girls kneel before him, smiling with tears in their eyes.

"I give you both my blessing," he says, his voice worn with age. My heart hitches in my throat as he looks at them with adoration. They are, after all, mirror images of Mother. Father is alone, and we are all he has left. He is letting half of his family go, giving them away to an unknown future beyond his protection. But he smiles bravely, and I know he's as proud of them as I am.

"It'll be all right, Aren," he consoles as the twins gather their rain cloaks for the trek to the town square. The bells at their ankles ring out with each step. "Either one would make an excellent princess and will surely bring her sister to court."

"It's a dream come true," I say as my heart seizes with a non-specific sadness.

The three of us start trudging through the downpour. I walk ahead, laying out planks for the girls to step on, to make sure their skirts don't collect mud as they proceed from our house to the center of town. It's easily an hour to the hall at our pace. I strain my back picking up the plank that's left behind and setting it in front of them again.

"Aren, you're soaked. Let us just walk in the mud! No one's going to look at the hems of our skirts," says Ophelia, distressed.

"Yes, or let us help, at least," adds Sonja, reaching down to give me a hand.

I swat it away. "Don't ruin those dresses I made," I tell them, heaving the next plank. "You both must look perfect. That's my job. You do yours, and I'll do mine."

They figure it's worthless to argue. Instead, they take care to lift their skirts a little higher, so that my hard work is worth it. When we arrive at the town hall, I'm soaked to the bone, my back aches, and I have splinters all over my hands. We make it just in time.

I follow as they walk past the armed guards flanking the entrance. My breath comes quicker, my chest tight with anticipation, with the weight of what this moment means for our family.

"I'll watch from the back of the hall," I say. A little thing like not receiving an invitation isn't going to keep me from this important moment in my sisters' lives. "Here, hand me your rain cloaks and umbrellas," I say, leaving the planks outside. I'm as wet as a drowned rat, and my boots are caked in mud, but my girls look as if they floated in on the wind, their dresses pristine and smiles beaming as radiant as the sun.

"You must be the Bellamore twins," greets a man in royal livery with a slight bow. "Please, follow me."

I put my sisters' things away in the cloak closet. Then I kick the mud off my boots as well as I can before slipping into the large room.

I hesitate at the back of the crowd. The marquis will surely be here, and my stomach churns with dread. This is his worst nightmare—a Bellamore twin winning the prince's heart over one of his own flesh and blood.

But the town hall is bustling with so many people, it's easy to disappear into the crowd. In addition to the more prominent citizens of Evandale, including most of the Chamber of Commerce clustered around the marquis, there are courtiers from the Loegrian capital in attendance. The air buzzes with speculation as everyone waits for the prince to arrive.

I look up at the podium, scanning the faces of the dignitaries, but I don't see him anywhere. He's probably planned some grand entrance, in typical royal fashion. My teeth clack and shoulders shiver as the chill of the rain seeps into my boots. I stick to the shadows at the back of the room, embarrassed I'm in such a state compared to everyone else in their lush—and dry—velvets and furs.

At last, the ceremony begins. Lord Jared, the prince's companion, moves into the center of the raised platform at the front of the room, smiling at everyone. I can see why Ophelia is attracted to him. He radiates confidence, smooth and suave. I spot Sonja and Ophelia seated in cushioned chairs on the right side of the room, in front of the stage. There are only the two of them, I notice, and none of the other young ladies who threw their hats into the marry-the-prince ring, which bodes well. The twins lean their heads toward each other.

Hardly better than gossiping schoolgirls.

I stifle a smile. Some things never change.

"Welcome, everyone," Lord Jared begins. "Thank you for joining us on a very special day…" He gestures to the storm outside, and it gets a laugh. I've heard most of Loegria doesn't share the Alarician sentiment about rain, how it brings good luck to people who rely on it. "When we arrived in Evandale to find Prince Dietan a wife, I was skeptical at first. After all, Evandale is far from our court in Lundenwic. But I have come to see the beauty in this land."

There is an appreciative murmur.

"We of Loegria are fortunate to share borders and trade with the kingdom of Alarice, and it is with great pleasure that the prince has gathered you all today to witness this most auspicious announcement."

So, a bride has indeed been chosen.

I steel myself to hear the news while the crowd buzzes with anticipation.

Who will it be? Perhaps it's Sonja, since Lord Jared has been so obviously enamored of Ophelia, and Dietan seems to value his friend enough to stand aside for Jared. Yes, the prince has definitely picked Sonja, who is leaning forward, her lips parted.

Oh, Sonja. I'm happy for her. She'll make a fine Loegrian princess. She is spry and sweet and will make Alarice proud. As promised, I'll dance at her wedding with a happy heart — even as the same ungovernable heart begins to sink into my stomach.

I turn my attention back to Lord Jared, who is scanning the crowd. Where *is* the prince? Why isn't he at the podium? Perhaps Lord Jared will announce the engagement and bring Dietan and Sonja up to the stage together?

Lord Jared suddenly looks apprehensive. He coughs. "Forgive me. I find I am a bit nervous." He looks at his hands, then back up at the crowd, as if he is summoning the right words. "Ophelia Bellamore." Jared extends his hand toward her. "Will you come join me, please?"

A gasp works its way through the room. Oh, it's Ophelia after all. The prince is going to marry Ophelia. Everyone is staring at her, even Sonja, who's helping her unsteady sister to her feet.

But Ophelia soon recovers, especially once she meets Jared's gaze. Her expression relaxes, and she gathers her skirts and approaches, walking as gracefully as if she were floating, her smile blindingly bright. The bells on her ankles ring loudly in a room that has fallen so quiet.

But where is Dietan?

Why isn't he at the podium?

"Today's announcement is not on behalf of Prince Dietan," Jared announces as Ophelia reaches his side.

The room erupts in surprised murmurs, and I hold my breath.

Then, suddenly, Lord Jared lowers himself to one knee. He looks up at Ophelia, who is radiant.

"Unlike the prince, I did not set out to find a bride on this journey. I never thought that anyone could ever bring me such happiness, that there could be someone whose smile makes me believe that the poets and the minstrels are right after all. You, my darling Ophelia, have convinced me that true love does exist in this world. I feel it in every breath I've taken since I've met you."

No one speaks. Like me, everyone assembled assumed that this was a ceremony for Dietan. I knew, of course, that Ophelia fancied Jared, but this is unexpected.

"Ophelia, you have stolen my heart right out of my chest." He lets out a breathless laugh, and I'm struck by wonder. That cocky lord is truly nervous. "The moment I saw you, I knew that you were the only one for me. Will you do me the greatest honor and consent to be my wife?"

Ophelia hardly says "yes" before the room explodes in applause. Jared stands and kisses Ophelia, and she holds his face, kissing him back. I clap as loudly as the rest, even though I don't quite understand. The prince had the invitation sent on Jared's behalf. Dietan hasn't chosen a bride.

Relief washes over me, followed by irritation. Why would I be relieved the prince didn't chose Ophelia? The prince could still choose Sonja. Plus, I'm still sorting out if I trust him.

I try to focus on Ophelia, who looks so happy tears well in my eyes. She's not going to be a princess, but she seems happy with the life of a noble lady. Did she know Lord Jared was going to propose? She must have. She's so graceful, accepting the royal entourage's congratulations, flawless and ready for a life at court.

Ophelia cranes her neck, searching the crowd at the back of the room, where I said I'd be. Her eyes meet mine, and she makes her way toward me. She's as luminous as sunshine. "Oh, Aren! Isn't it divine?" she says, holding her arms out to be hugged and petted despite the mud and rainwater soaking through my clothes.

She'll soon have a hundred dresses grander than anything I can make. I take her in my arms and hold her tight, smearing mud on her skirts. My sister still needs her family. She needs *me*. She's thrilled, but there's terror behind her eyes at the thought of leaving behind everything she's ever known, the kind of fear that only I can quell.

"I am so, so happy for you, my dearest," I whisper fiercely. "You will make a wonderful lady." Soon, Sonja is there, too, and the three of us are crying.

Lord Jared joins us, beaming with pride as he takes his beloved in his arms. I wipe away my tears and gather myself together. Even though I know I look like shit, I put on my best smile to meet one of the great lords of the Loegrian court.

"My lord, you've met Sonja, but may I introduce to you my older sister, Aren," Ophelia says.

Lord Jared bows courteously, and I manage an awkward curtsy in reply. I never know exactly how low to bend my knees.

"Pleased to meet you, my lord," I say. "To say I'm surprised would be an understatement. I didn't expect this."

"Neither did I," he replies, his cheeks flushed. "But I know that this is fate."

"You are a lucky man. Our father is not here, but he gives his blessing," I tell him.

"I am very lucky indeed." He clears his throat and shifts uncomfortably on his feet. "Ophelia tells me you and your father did not receive your invitations. The marquis assured me he'd make certain all relevant citizens of Evandale would be included, especially—"

I hold up my hand. It all makes sense now. The prince didn't intentionally leave me off the list, the marquis did. *The prick*. I lift my chin and smile. "Please, think nothing of it. My father was unable to attend anyway, and I'm here now, my lord."

Jared kisses the back of my hand. "As we will be family, call me Jared. Please apologize on my behalf to your father and tell him that I accept his blessing most gratefully. Ophelia made it very clear to me that she would not accept me unless I agreed Sonja could come with us. Please know I will take care of your sisters; both will want for nothing in Lundenwic."

Ophelia squeezes my hand. "We're both going to move to court, Aren!"

"Oh dear—what are we going to wear?" asks Sonja.

"Aren, you will have to make us a trousseau. We can't show up at court looking like country bumpkins." Ophelia laughs.

Jared smiles. "There is no need to put Aren through that effort. Fear not, you two will have the best of everything." He turns back to Ophelia. "Come, love. There are people you need to meet." Ophelia nods, gathering her skirts as she takes his arm.

"They're lovely together," Sonja says, putting an arm around my shoulders.

I nod in agreement.

"We'll miss you," Sonja says. "You must come and visit us as often as you can."

Then she, too, is whisked away as the young general appears by her side. "Miss Bellamore," Marcus says. "Would you care to partake of the refreshments?"

Sonja smiles and blushes. "I would love to."

I give the general a benevolent smile as she takes his arm. It appears Sonja might not have to wait long for her own proposal. The handsome general can't take his eyes off her.

Then I'm all alone again. My happiness is bittersweet. Ophelia is to be married. Sonja will soon follow. They will both move all the way to the court in Loegria. They've found good men to take care of them, and I'll finally be free. I've done my duty to them, and the Raven's Beak will be mine to do with as I wish. So why does my chest feel so hollow?

Because I'll miss my girls, of course. They will be so far away. Warm tears well up in my eyes, and I wipe them away furiously with my thumb. I'm not going to cry again, not on such a happy occasion.

Jared makes his way back to my side of the room to fetch Ophelia a cup of rose wine and offers me the other cup.

I thank him politely but shake my head. I don't feel like drinking. It's too soon after the harvest festival.

"If I may ask, where is the prince?" I almost say *fool of a prince*, but I catch myself in time. There is no sign of Dietan, not even to congratulate his friend on his engagement. "Is he allergic to happiness, perhaps?"

Jared grimaces and takes a sip from the goblet that I refused. "Ah, Prince Dietan... He's indisposed. He wouldn't have missed this for the world, but between you and me, he hasn't come out of his room all day. He'll be fine, I'm sure. It can take a toll, this much travel and—"

"And disappearing in the middle of the night?"

"You noticed." Jared sighs.

"I notice many things that happen around my tavern. Are you sure he's all right?"

"Positive. He can't get into too much trouble around here, can he?" Jared remarks with a grin.

I shake my head, unconvinced. These fancy aristos really don't have any idea how to survive outside their palaces. After all, Dietan wandered off into the woods in the rain when I expressly told him not to. I'm sure Jared's hiding that Dietan's gotten himself embarrassingly lost.

What an idiot.

CHAPTER ELEVEN

Dietan

"I'm an idiot."

After my foot sinks into what feels like the fiftieth hole I've encountered, drenching me up to the knee in freezing mud, I'm ready to admit that I've made a mistake. Why didn't I listen to Aren? She warned me I'd find my death out here in the forest all alone. But my pride wouldn't let me give up. Desperation, too, if I'm being honest with myself.

Every inch of me is filthy, and the rain hasn't relented. I'm starving and frozen half to death. I curse the heavens as I pull myself out of the hole and curse the barmaid as well. Damn her and her common sense.

Back home in Loegria, rain hardly lasts more than a few minutes at a time, the weather changing almost as quickly as a petulant child's moods. But it's a whole different beast in Alarice—a merciless, endless downpour. That the land hasn't completely flooded by now seems a miracle. After Aren pointed me in the right direction, I consulted the map a helpful townsperson drew for me the day before. "It's on the other side of the wood, just beyond the Halved Hill. Her hut sits overlooking the gully—you can't miss it."

RINGS OF FATE

"Can't miss it, my ass," I grumble to myself. The forest feels unending, densely packed with great oak trees and firs, but it provides little cover. I find shelter under the dripping canopy of a nearby tree and hunker down to gather my strength. I hate the forest. I hate the trees. I hate the mud, and I hate the rain. I hate Evandale. I hate myself.

My teeth chatter as I fumble in my cloak for the map once more, but it, too, is covered in mud. I try to wipe it clean with trembling fingers, but I smear the ink, turning the rivers and borders into one great stain.

I crumple the map and toss it into a puddle. I groan, all caution about kingdom secrets and military espionage washed away by the storm. Surely everyone will start to wonder where I've gone.

My lie about a stomachache will only hold for a day or so. Loyal Jared even volunteered to create a distraction, though I cautioned him not to rush into a *real* proposal for my—and the kingdom's—sake. Somehow, I don't think he listened. Who'd have thought he'd fall so hard so fast?

Jared's engagement celebrations will only keep everyone distracted for so long. Soon, the people of Evandale will notice that no food enters my room, nor chamber pots leave it. The maids will find my room empty, and then the townsfolk will come looking. I shudder at the thought of them finding me lost and shivering in the woods, the truth of my mission exposed. I'd die before I let that happen; although maybe then my father's councilors can dig the Rings out of my corpse.

Come on, man. Get up. You can do this.

The sorceress's cottage must be around here somewhere. Even though I can barely see through the rain, I've got to be heading in the right direction.

I haul myself to my feet, more mud than man, and trudge on, following the gentle downward slope of the forest floor. I tread carefully. One wrong step and I'll end up in another mud hole—or worse, up to my neck in a sinkhole.

I don't see any other creature, animal or human, as I walk. The only company I keep is picturing Aren trudging alongside me.

"I know, I know," I say to my imaginary companion, whose condescending look is more than punishment enough. "I should have listened to you…"

My teeth chatter, and I might truly be going mad, especially if I'm comforting myself imagining Aren keeping me company. The infuriating barmaid clearly finds me ridiculous, and I can't disagree. Most women would leap at the chance to comfort me in this state, but I can't picture

Aren giving me anything but lip. Maybe I'm dying of the chills.

I hear a second set of boots, then the snapping of twigs. I whirl around. But there's nothing—only a thick mist rolling across the ground like a blanket, curling over tree roots and moss.

I must be hearing things. I try to shake it off, try to keep moving. I take another step, but there it is again—the sound of footsteps growing closer.

My heartbeat roars in my ears as I reach for the dagger I always keep on me. I peer into the thickening fog. I can barely see the trees around me now.

"Hello?" I call out. The mist seems to muffle my words.

The skin around the scars on my back tightens painfully. A distinct sense that I'm being watched raises every hair on my body.

Fear grips me, and I take off at a dead sprint, bolting through the trees, my lungs burning, my legs aching with the effort. Whatever is following me dogs my heels. I glance over my shoulder as the sound comes closer and closer, but all I see is fog.

Then I turn—and she's in front of me.

Aren.

I must be hallucinating. The cold has made my fanciful thoughts appear real as day.

"Slow down, you dolt," the vestige admonishes, panting heavy.

My gods, it even sounds like her.

The swirls of her breath curl around her face in the damp air, mesmerizing me further. She looks nothing short of ethereal in the fog. A sorceress, nay, enchantress, all her own.

"You just gonna stand there and look at me like a carp?" She then mumbles something about "idiot men" under her breath, and I begin to suspect this may be the *actual* Aren.

"Aren? Is it really you?"

"Nice to make Your Highness' acquaintance once more," she says, the extra flourish in her curtsey accentuating her sarcasm.

This is definitely real Aren and not some figment of my hungry, delirious imagination.

"I should have listened to you and taken you with me," I blurt.

"Ahh, you've met hindsight and how she's a fickle maiden, huh?"

"What are you doing here?"

"What do you think?"

I was about to ask her if she was lost, too, when I realize. She's here because she was looking for me. She was worried about me. Huh. "So why'd you come find me?"

"When you weren't at the engagement announcement..." So Jared *did* go through with it. "I suspected you were woefully lost. I couldn't very well lose the Crown Prince under my watch, could I? You know—country, duty, honor? I'm told those things matter."

"I'm touched," I say, pressing a hand to my heart. "You actually care."

Aren lets out a huff that blows a stray piece of hair out of her face. Her usual annoyance is clouded with obvious concern, which makes my heart clench in my chest.

"We need to get you back so I can open the pub. People are going to want to celebrate the engagement."

A pit opens in my stomach. But I haven't yet found Veteria. Or better yet, she hasn't found me. Aren's words echo in my head again. It's obvious the sorceress doesn't want to be discovered. Any shred of hope I had vanishes on the back of the fog.

"Come now. Let's get a move on," Aren admonishes, but I can't seem to move my feet. It's not the mud keeping them mired but the disappointment.

"But I still need to see Veteria..." I trail off.

Aren stops and turns toward me, a look akin to pity overtaking her striking features. I must look pathetic.

"I told you—" she starts to say.

"She will only be found if she wants to be. I know," I interrupt, feeling utterly sorry for myself and my doomed situation.

Aren stares unblinking at me until she throws her hands up in the air in frustration.

"Fine!" she says in a huff. "I'm not supposed to do this." She wags a finger at me.

She twirls around, but the bottom of her skirt is so caked in heavy mud that the fabric tangles around her boots. "Veteria! We need your help!" she hollers at the wind. "He might be royalty, but he's not entirely awful!"

What a ringing endorsement.

"Please!" she pleads with the gray sky.

"This is useless." I brush past Aren and begin to walk toward what direction I believe will lead back to town when an old woman draped in animal pelts, her eyes as white as pearls, blocks my path. She holds up her hand, and I'm suddenly thrown backward through the air. I land flat on my back in the mud, and everything goes black.

The first thing I feel is pain. My body aches, my muscles stiff and sore. Light glows through my closed eyelids. As I wake, the pain sets in deeper, rousing me further. Slowly, I crack open my eyes and see a roaring fire. I'm lying on a warm cot, covered in soft furs.

"You're alive," a craggy voice says, and I nearly jump out of my own skin.

"Sadly," says a familiar one.

The old woman from before, her hunched form barely distinguishable from a pile of furs, sits stooped near the fire. Her milky-white eyes peer sightlessly at the flames. Aren is next to her holding a mug of some steaming beverage. Somehow, my clothes are clean and dry instead of wet and covered with mud. Veteria is a small woman, which means that Aren helped disrobe me. I can't help but blush at the thought.

"I don't care for uninvited guests," Veteria says, her head tipped to the side. "I don't know your intentions." She says the second part with an eye toward Aren, who shamefully stares into her mug like she's being chastised by her mother.

"Madam, I mean you no harm, I assure you," I say. I watch her carefully, wondering just how much she can see, whether she's truly blind. She continues to stare, unblinking.

I take a moment to get my bearings. I'm in a one-room cabin, the fire the only source of light. Rain batters the window behind heavy curtains drawn tight against the glass. There are little tables covered in jars and pots. Covered containers of fruits and vegetables line the shelves. Dried herbs hang in bundles from the exposed wooden beams, and a leaning bookcase sags under a wealth of dusty tomes. A fresh loaf of baked bread sits steaming on the table, hot out of a cast-iron skillet. My stomach growls, betraying my hunger.

It's just the three of us except for a black-and-gray cat curled up at my feet. It opens one orange eye, studies me, then closes it again and goes back to sleep. I look again at the great variety of dried herbs. They can't all be local. Someone has spent a great deal of time gathering them and has the resources to procure rarities from afar.

Veteria puts another log into the flame and stirs the fire. Her silence has me on edge.

She finally speaks. "I have seen you in my visions. You are the cursed prince of Loegria. The one who is doomed to death, and all of Albion with him."

CHAPTER TWELVE

Dietan

I draw the blanket tighter around me. The Rings hum at the mention of my curse. "That's why I've come to ask for your help," I say. "I heard you might be able to…" I clear my throat and steal a quick glance toward Aren. "…fix me."

"Fix you?" Veteria laughs, shaking her head.

I visibly pale, like a scolded child. Aren notices immediately. It's bad enough that she knows I'm cursed now, but for her to know the rest? Gods, forbid.

Aren shifts uncomfortably back and forth on her feet. I clear my throat to break the awkward silence—a cue, I hope, for Aren to excuse herself. She looks to Veteria, then to me, and then back to Veteria. Veteria gives her a knowing nod.

Aren pulls her, now dry, cloak from the chair and throws it over her shoulders. "I'll be outside while you talk," she says as she opens the front door and beelines for a wooden rocking chair on the covered porch. Once the door shuts, the tension rachets.

"Why ever would you think that I could *fix you*?" Veteria accuses.

"Because you're a healer, a fabled one," I say, thinking that some brownnosing may help me.

"The curse is entwined with your soul. No one can remove it without killing you as well."

That isn't what I've come all this way to hear. I get to my feet and approach her. "You used the Whisting on me," I say. It knocked me back through the air, the magic coming as easily as a flick of her wrist. "I've heard the stories about who you are and what you did—how you saved Beddlegert last winter during the floods. If you know how to control it—if you truly are the last of the Vindar—you must know how to help me."

"Knowledge of the Whisting is not akin to breaking a curse," she says. "Plus, I removed myself from the concerns of men a long time ago. Too many have used me and my kin for their own purposes. I saved a village once because it was my own, but I will bend to no king any longer."

"But the two are linked, and I humbly ask for your help to save our people."

The old woman turns her milky eyes toward me and scoffs. "How do you claim to have the power of the Whist—"

In answer, I call the power, manifesting a windstorm in the palm of my hand.

Veteria's mouth falls open in surprise as the wind whips against her face. She reels back. "This can't be," she says.

I raise my hands, giving more of myself to the power, but it quickly runs away from me, and I can't control it. The wind fills the tiny cabin, overturning jars, toppling a stool, and sending a table crashing to the ground.

I see Aren's concerned face appear in the window, looking in at the chaos unfolding.

The old woman's face hardens, and she shakes her head as the winds swirl around her, raising whorls of dust. The walls tremble. The cat scurries under the cot.

"That's enough," says Veteria, her voice nearly drowned out by the gale.

I clench my teeth, willing the storm to obey me, but it only grows stronger. I only meant to prove to her what I'm capable of, but the magic has a mind of its own.

"Control it," says Veteria.

"I can't," I grit out, trying not to panic.

RINGS OF FATE

She bares her teeth in frustration, then spreads her arms wide and stomps her foot. The air calms, collected into her outstretched hands. She redirects the wind, thrusting it back into me. I stumble, falling back onto the cot. The Rings in my back settle into a calm hum.

I heave a ragged breath. The cat pokes its head out from under the cot, checking to see if it's safe to come back. The door to the cabin swings open, and Aren appears in the threshold.

"What in the Goddess' name was that?" she asks, her eyes as wide as the cat's milk saucers.

Veteria stares at me with a ferocity that borders on anger, her gaze so intense, I shrink back.

"So, this is the shape of the curse you carry. You did not learn this magic, but somehow, it is a part of you."

An unknowable emotion flits across her face. I wonder if she'll toss me out, or even kill me. I'm too dangerous to allow to live.

But it's not Veteria I'm ultimately concerned about. Aren knows. She hasn't bolted for the door, but she hasn't moved an inch, either.

"I didn't ask for this. I never meant for any of this to happen. I don't know how to wield it or stop it. You're the only one left who can help me. Please." I'm so utterly fraught, my voice catches on the last word. I must make her understand.

That single word—*please*—seems to have an effect. I know how desperate I must sound, and maybe she feels sorry for me. She groans and rubs her temples.

"Tell me, boy," she says. "How did you get this power?"

Though I'm a prince and a leader of men, in front of Veteria, I feel like I'm ten years old again. I feel even more under a looking glass with Aren waiting eagerly for an answer. "When I was young and stupid, I touched the Rings of Fate in my father's war room. When I woke up, the Rings were gone, but I had this." I turn and yank the back of my shirt between my shoulder blades, exposing the interlocking circles scarred into my flesh.

She reaches over and touches them with her papery fingers. Her eyebrows furrow. "The Rings chose you then."

I hear Aren inhale sharply. "Rings?" she murmurs.

"Is that what happened?" I ask Veteria directly, ignoring Aren.

"The wind will go where it finds purpose. Clearly, it found purpose within your soul."

Well, shit, that doesn't sound ominous at all. "The Rings are sentient?" I ask incredulously. What in Albion have I gotten myself into?

"The Whisting is never wrong."

"It's wrong this time. I need to get rid of it, to give the Rings back to my father the king."

Veteria frowns at me. "You come crawling to me for help, yet you question what I tell you?"

I bite back a retort. She's right; she knows more about it than I do—than my father and his advisors, even. She's the only person I've ever met who describes the ancient ways like this. But why did this befall me, when it has never happened to any of my royal ancestors? There must be another explanation.

"You are meant to fulfill a purpose, dear boy," she says. Then, with a sigh, she continues:

"The Rings of Fate were crafted in secret by the Oracle of Alba to contain the power of the wind spirits, the Anemoi, to defeat Lord Boreas. Otherwise Albion would have fallen to the evils of the Unseen Death and the Kilandrar—both born of perverted magic at Boreas' hand. But this dark magic is back. It is in the very air we breathe. Only the bearer of the Rings can defeat it."

"All of Boreas's knowledge of the Unseen Death was supposed to have been destroyed with him, along with the Kilandrar," I say.

"If you actually believe that, I have a bridge to Penrith to sell you," she says, alluding to the broken bridge between Penrith and Alarice that was destroyed in the third epoch. She cackles.

"The Kilandrar are real? Not some child's tale?" Aren asks, clearly just as rattled as I am.

"As real as the very clothes on your back." The old woman pauses. "I'm sorry. I wish I could be of more help to you," Veteria says.

It sounds so final—a dismissal. I have to keep trying to convince her to help me.

"If the Usurper has supposedly reanimated the Kilandrar and is amassing an army of foul creatures, like you're suggesting, and my father marches into battle without the Rings of Fate, he and the army won't survive. Loegria will fall. And if Loegria falls, so will Alarice. I'm alone in this, and I can't save both kingdoms by myself."

She resumes her seat at the fire again. "But he does have the Rings of Fate. You." She points a withered finger in my direction as her gaze roams sightlessly around the room. The look on Aren's face is one I cannot totally discern, but I think she may be concerned. It warms me slightly to think that she may care about me in the slightest.

I try one final plea. "Please. As you can see, I can't control it. I've got to get them out of me." Desperation spills out of me like the magic I can't control. "Is there nothing your magic can do to save my people?"

"What about King Osian?" Aren pipes up. Her look is innocent enough, but Veteria is clearly shaken by the question.

"Don't you speak his name in my home!" she roars. It's almost unbelievable that such a small woman could make such a large, imposing sound. "He is a traitor to the cause. He is no gentleman. He styles himself a king, the Great Waste his dominion, but he is mad and ruthless. Do *not* seek him out."

Aren wrings the corner of her cape uneasily.

"But I've heard travelers whispering about Osian's powerful dark magic. Maybe he could help," Aren adds, trying to defend her suggestion. She really does see and hear everything in that pub.

I have heard the same tales, and to be honest, Osian was on my list if Veteria failed me.

"You are no match for him, young man," Veteria warns me. "You must not seek his counsel."

"But I have no choice if you don't help me."

I can't imagine going back to court and telling my father, his generals, his councilors, and everyone who matters that I failed. My mother already thinks I'm a disgrace, a pitiful excuse for a prince. She more than anyone believes in the mask I wear to keep everyone away and safe from the danger I carry within. My facade as a hapless, immature charmer is an illusion almost as great as the magic trapped in my body.

I can't go running empty-handed back to my father. I can't tell him that multiple kingdoms are in peril because his stupid, selfish son failed at his one assigned task. No, this is my problem to solve. I will do it, or I will die trying and let my friends cut the Rings from my corpse as my last sacrifice for my people.

"I must find this King Osian, and perhaps…" My mind gallops with a half-formed plan, and my breath quickens with desperation. "Osian rules over the Great Waste, does he not?"

"In the city of Engel is what the rumors say," Aren chimes in. Veteria shoots her a look that would kill one of fainter heart—but not Aren.

I've come all this way only to learn I must journey halfway across the world again. So, I need cover. People will wonder what business the Crown Prince of Loegria has in the Great Waste. Word would surely get back to the Usurper.

I came to Evandale pretending to seek a bride in order to seek a mage. Perhaps the solution is simply another charade.

"The Wedding March," I murmur, proud of my own quick thinking. Once I choose a bride, we will have to travel through Alarice and Loegria to seek the blessing of the ancient Oracle of Alba for the union, as royal tradition demands. Alba is close to the fallen kingdom of Estyrion, and once I'm there, I can slip across the border into the Great Waste.

I turn back to the sorceress. "You are certain this King Osian is alive?"

"No good can come of this, dear prince. Go home, find another way to defeat the Usurper, and set yourself free."

But I'm not listening. I'm too distracted by hope, at long last. "Surely, for the good of the entire land…" I begin.

But from her scowl, it's clear Veteria has run out of patience. Her pearly eyes gleam.

"I've told you what I know, so now begone. The both of you," she says, twirling her wrist. A great gust of wind lifts me into the air.

The next moment, I'm standing on solid ground, the wind dissipating to a gentle breeze. Aren is trying to regain her balance on the cobblestones. The sorceress's cottage is gone, and I realize I'm back in Evandale.

It's barely dusk, so it's almost time for Aren to open the Raven's Beak. I'm sure there will be quite the crowd tonight to celebrate the engagement.

"Thank you," I say a little too softly.

"Like I said, it's my duty, I suppose." She turns to look me in the eye, and my cheeks begin to heat from her gaze. I clear my throat, suddenly parched.

"I don't know much you saw, or heard, but please. Do not breathe a word. Many lives are at stake." She must see me entirely different now. Not some spoiled prince but a cursed man, pathetic and doomed.

"Not a soul," she replies. Her lack of barbs gives me a niggling feeling that I'm right. She holds her skirt hem out of the mud as she turns and walks up the front steps of the Beak. I imagine that skirt a fine silk, only the best, like she provided for her sisters. But knowing her a little better now, I bet it's plain cotton. She saves luxuries for those she loves.

Aren silently turns around and gives me a meager smile before disappearing into the tavern.

Laughter pours out of the Raven's Beak, and the sound of it is almost alien to me. I decided to take a walk after we returned to Evandale, conceive of a plan. But now, I'm back among people.

The wind bangs the door open as I step into the tavern, and all heads turn to see who it is before conversation picks up again. No one gives me a second look in my shabby cloak and hat. I'm just another traveler stopping in for a bite. I haven't eaten since I entered the forest, and I'm as ravenous as a bear.

But Aren, behind the bar, doesn't look away. She lifts an eyebrow at me as she pours a mug of ale.

I feel even more unmoored, like I'm adrift at sea. *She knows.* I wave a dazed hand in her direction before heading to the same table I occupied just a few nights prior. I fall into the chair, the fire crackling at my back, lending me comfort I didn't realize I needed.

I ruminate on what the sorceress told me. My quest isn't over—and continuing it might kill more than just me. The road to the lost kingdom of Estyrion is treacherous, especially with the looming threat of war. If the Usurper or his agents found me, I'd make an excellent hostage. I'll need the Wedding March for cover to continue traveling through Alarice and Loegria. It's the only way to hide my true purpose from Penrith's spies. A royal marriage must be blessed by the Oracle of Alba.

"You all right?" Aren asks, approaching with a mug brimming with frothy ale. She sets it down on my table. "You look like you need a drink."

"I do, thank you," I say, then gulp it greedily. It doesn't seem as strong as the ale she served me the first time—or maybe I'm in need of more liquid courage after my meeting with Veteria—so I ask for another, and then another and another as my plan starts to take shape.

It looks like I'll have to choose a bride after all. A bride who is fearless, smart, and capable. Someone who knows the world in ways that can't be taught by scrolls and masters. I'll have to find this person soon.

The last thing I remember before passing out on the table is that it's going to be a long way to the Great Waste if I don't like the person I'm traveling with.

CHAPTER THIRTEEN

Aren

The next morning, sure enough, I find the prince exactly where I left him, slumped over the table, an empty mug still in his hand. His mouth is open, and drool pools under his face. The only way I know he isn't dead is that he's snoring. Loudly.

He drank his weight in Alarician ale last night, and I'm impressed that he's acquired a taste for it so quickly. He had a particularly bad day, and he downed each pint, on an empty stomach, with renewed determination. Before I could cut him off, he laid his head down and didn't move again even after closing time.

I do have a heart. So before closing shop, I draped an old blanket over his shoulders, letting him sleep here overnight.

Now, in the rainy morning, I glance over at him with a new understanding of the man sleeping before me and can't help but crack a smile. Look at him, drunk and passed out like the cursed fool he is. I'll admit he's nice to look at, even in this state. There is a certain boyish vulnerability to the way his golden lashes fall against his cheek. I almost reach out to touch his hair, it looks so soft.

Prince Dietan's snores hitch, and he coughs before snoring again.

I snicker and let him be as I head to the kitchen to prepare food for today. I get the fire going in the stone oven, then work on organizing the pantry, itemizing what's spoiling soon so I can think of what to use first and what else I need to order from the butcher and my favorite farmers.

But the events from Veteria's cottage loop in my head. They're haunting.

The secrecy. The charismatic front. The bride search. All of his aggravating behavior is being painted over with different brushstrokes.

Last night was busy with celebrations of Ophelia's engagement, full of even more drinking and music and food. While orders kept flowing in, I wondered if the prince would attend after the day we had.

Past midnight, I'd all but forgotten about his absence until he showed up looking like he'd been further tormenting himself. I felt for the guy, his face was so drawn and ominous. Who else knows this secret? Does he carry this weight himself? It's a heavy burden.

But now I'm starting to regret letting him stay the night. My pity got the better of me. Is he ever going to get up?

He's still snoring out there, even as I start making breakfast. I fry up some sausages, heaps of whiskey bacon, scrambled eggs and tomatoes with flaky salt, and even whip up my favorite buttermilk biscuits, making even more of a racket with my pots and pans than usual, but nothing seems to wake him. While I wait for the biscuits to finish baking, I open the tavern, bringing down the chairs and stools at all the other tables. I throw a few more logs on the fire. The prince stirs a little when I walk by, muttering something about rings—hopefully dreaming about the one he'll be giving Sonja soon and not the ones that quite literally put the fate of the kingdom on his back.

Should I wake him? Customers will be coming in soon, and I can't have someone—even a prince—passed out in the bar this early in the morning. It's bad for business. I put a firm hand on his shoulder and shake.

He wakes with a jolt, looking bleary under his mussed hair. "What?" he mumbles, confused.

Rough night indeed. "Hungry?"

He blinks at me. "Uh, sure?" He pushes his hand through his hair.

In the kitchen, the biscuits are perfectly buttery and golden brown. I add a few to an already loaded tray, complete with a pot of tea. When I come back to the main room, I find Dietan has roused himself somewhat. His eyes widen as I set everything in front of him. "All for me?" he asks.

I nod, somewhat embarrassed that I've gone to so much trouble.

"It's a lot of food. Won't you join me?" He motions to the feast.

I have to admit he's gracious and charming—for a hungover drunk. I help myself to one of the biscuits before walking back to my place behind the bar. Out of the corner of my eye, I watch him eat like he's never had a meal before.

"I'm surprised you let me stay the night," he says, between a large bite of egg and sip of tea.

"And I'm surprised to find you don't bunk down with a retinue of armed guards. Have you been out this whole time?"

"Pretty much."

"Aren't they in a panic about you?" I ask, wondering why the royal guard hasn't torn Evandale apart looking for their prince.

He waves a piece of bacon to dismiss my question. "Nah, Jared and Marcus will cover for me. I am allowed a little privacy occasionally," he says. "This is incredible, by the way." He stuffs another forkful in his mouth.

"Privacy, huh?" I remember there were rumors about his youthful indiscretions, which seems in keeping with the lifestyle of an entitled prince. But after yesterday, I'm beginning to suspect those rumors are pure fancy.

Dietan wrinkles his nose. "Yeah, my guards were probably relieved to have Marcus cover royal night duty."

"Let me guess—is it the snoring or the drooling that puts them off?" I laugh.

He glances down at the drool still on the table and surreptitiously wipes it clean with his sleeve. "The snoring," he admits.

I allow a pleased smile at that.

Dietan glances around the room while he eats, taking in his surroundings with a curious eye, and I find I don't mind the easy silence between us. It's rare in my experience for a man to not constantly run his mouth. I'm setting up the bar for the day when he lets out a moan that makes me turn around.

He's bitten into one of my buttermilk biscuits. "This might be the best thing I've ever put in my mouth."

"Oh yeah? What else are you putting in your mouth?"

"Wouldn't you like to know?" He grins.

I try not to blush.

Dietan takes another bite. "I'm serious. You, my lady, are great at three things: navigation, swooning in my arms, and biscuits. You know, I may just have fallen in love with you."

I roll my eyes. "Get in line, pal."

"You think I'm joking." He looks wounded.

"About what part?"

Dietan watches me for a moment, twirling his fork. "I'm not joking about the biscuits," he says. "You'd put the palace kitchens to shame."

I know I'm a great cook, but it still warms me to hear that I'm every bit as good as the fancy chefs in the Loegrian capital.

He waggles his eyebrows. "You know, if we get married, you'll need to make me this for breakfast every morning."

"Ha." I shrug, suddenly deflated. *As if.*

"What?" he asks.

I sigh. "You're just another man who's only interested in me for what I can do for you." *But not for who I am.* "Including saving you, I might add." I shoot him a knowing glance, and it's my turn to quirk an eyebrow. All his thoughts are on breakfasts and biscuits. He hasn't even asked about me. He doesn't know a single thing about me and doesn't care to—whether as a man or as my future sovereign. I go back to polishing mugs.

He puts down his fork and clears his throat. I look over to see he's leaning over his plate, his eyebrows scrunched, making his face seem even more youthful. He stares at me like I've said the most absurd thing. "Is that what you think of me? That I just use people? I'm not like that. If you got to know me, you'd see."

I shrug a shoulder like I couldn't care less. "You wanted to use Veteria. And now I bet you're concocting a plan to use King Osian. That'll be ten cobs, by the way."

"A bargain for such a feast," he says, ignoring my jab.

"Twenty, then, including the wakeup call and the blanket," I say flatly, and his eyes narrow. "Surely you of all people can afford such luxury."

His gaze drops to the kerchief at my throat, and I abruptly turn away, focusing on stacking glasses behind the bar. I hear the scrape of a chair and footsteps. Now he's at the bar, right behind me.

"How are you, by the way?" His voice is soft, and I hate how it makes me feel—all soothed and comforted. It's the voice I recognize from that night. Deep. Gentle. *Safe.*

"I'm fine."

"Does it still hurt?"

I pause, gripping a mug. Yes, it still hurts, but it could have been much, much worse had this maddening man not come along and played hero.

"How much would it cost to heal? Because I would give all I have," he whispers.

My breath catches in my throat, and when I glance over my shoulder, I notice the crease between his eyebrows deepening, the corners of his lips falling. That face belongs on a gold coin, just like his grandfather's.

"Don't worry about it," I say at last, bending my head low as if completely absorbed in cleaning this mug. "I'm perfectly capable of taking care of myself. And saving princes from getting lost in forests. I don't need any help."

"Is that why you didn't put yourself on the list of candidates?" he asks suddenly.

"To meet you?"

"Exactly. Not interested in marriage or princes?"

I finally turn around to look him in the eye. "No, thank you. I don't mean to ever marry," I say more forcefully than I'd intended. "I don't look forward to being any man's servant or pack mule. I have enough burdens of my own—I don't aspire to carry anyone else's."

Those words put a momentary chink in his armor as hurt flits across his eyes. He recovers quickly with his usual charm.

"What a terrible assessment of a most venerable institution," says Dietan. He lowers his voice and leans toward me, as if imparting a great secret. "Granted, my parents' marriage is a carnage of bickering and animosity."

"See?"

"But surely there is such a thing as true love," he says, turning up his princely charm. It seems so brittle up close. "There has to be, hasn't there?"

"Not for me." I don't tell him that *of course* I want true love more than anything—to be loved and cherished the way a woman should be loved and cherished. But that's for other girls. Prettier girls. Girls like my sisters. All men ever see in me is a maid they don't have to pay. And this prince is, in the end, a man.

"Not for you?" he asks, seeming genuinely surprised.

"Never," I say, almost believing it. "I don't ever want to marry. I will travel and read books. I am a good navigator, after all."

"Sounds nice," he allows. "But lonely."

"I like my own company," I say pointedly.

He bows his head. "I understand you find my presence distasteful, so I will leave you in peace."

Oh, he looks hurt by that. I didn't think it was possible for a barmaid to hurt a prince. My heart is beating too quickly, and I want to protest: *I didn't mean it so harshly!*

Honestly, I don't know what to think of him. Why does he pay me any mind? Only because I'm useful, I remind myself. I know his secret. He has to be nice to me now—keep me quiet. He's a shameless flirt, and it doesn't mean anything. He's a royal prince, albeit a cursed one, and I'm just a barmaid. I turn away and start folding a pile of dishrags.

Dietan's quiet, but I can tell he's still there. There's a long, heavy moment between us until I hear the stool scrape as he pushes back from the bar and then the heavy clatter of coins on the table.

"Thanks for a royal breakfast," he says.

I can't quite read his tone. Is it sarcastic? Cold? Or downright sincere? I can't tell. It doesn't matter.

Now that my sisters are settled, he'll leave Evandale, and it can't happen soon enough. Even if the thought brings a lump to my throat. Of course, I'll miss my girls. And he must promise not to put them in harm's way.

I look over my shoulder again when I hear his heavy boots heading toward the door. He pulls up the hood of his cloak, pinching it closed at his throat. Before he can go out into the rain, Father ambles up the steps.

Harvest Mother, why is he out in this weather? He must have come to check on me. He's been worried since the night of the harvest festival. Father leans heavily on his cane, watching his feet, and startles when the prince speaks to him.

"Good day, sir," Dietan says, his voice strong. "What a lovely surprise."

I'm tempted to intervene, but to my dismay, Father's smile grows wide. He hasn't smiled like that in a long time.

"Your Highness! What good fortune! I'm surprised to see you here so early."

"Yes, I've heard the most amazing things about this tavern. You own this establishment, correct?"

"I do, but my daughter here runs it. I'm very proud."

"Yes, indeed. I'm so glad I came to Evandale. I know there *must* be a woman here who can keep me on my toes, who deserves to wear only the finest silk!"

He's taunting me. Asshole. Reminding me that he came to find a bride, not a barmaid. I scowl as I furiously wipe down the bar for a third time in lieu of committing regicide.

"Yes, with my daughter Ophelia so happily settled, I do hope her twin Sonja makes a worthy match soon," Father says mildly.

Dietan looks surprised for a moment, as if he hadn't considered the idea, which puzzles me.

"How much longer are you staying, Your Highness?" Father asks.

"I believe we're leaving, weather permitting, at first light tomorrow. I can think of a few reasons to stay a bit longer, if given the opportunity. Alas, perhaps I have overstayed my welcome."

With that, Dietan shakes Father's hand and disappears into the rain, leaving me to fume in silence.

CHAPTER FOURTEEN

Aren

That evening, there is a real engagement party for Ophelia and Jared at the town hall. The prince is hosting, making up for missing his friend's proposal. He evidently wants to put on a grand show, ordering food and drink from the Raven's Beak on a few hours' notice, leaving me scrambling to get everything ready instead of just attending the party as the betrothed's family.

If he thinks he can get under my skin, he's mistaken. I'm more than up to the challenge, and if he's paying for it, then I'll make certain my sister is sent off with the most elaborate feast imaginable.

I spend the better part of the afternoon rolling barrels of ale to the town hall with the help of Bonnie and a handful of royal soldiers, and laying the large table with hearty fare prepared from the freshest bounty of the year's harvest.

All the while, I pretend not to notice the marquis, who stalks around the place barking unnecessary orders. I do, however, note with satisfaction the damage Dietan did to his face. While the very sight of the marquis still makes me shiver, I feel safer with Loegrian soldiers everywhere. The marquis keeps out of my way as well. If I didn't know him better, I'd think he was avoiding me. *Good.*

When the celebration's finally underway, I smile and chat merrily with our guests, accepting congratulations on Father's behalf and ensuring everyone's cups and bellies are full. The hall is full of laughter, and the trill of a flute signals the next dance.

Prince Dietan reigns in all his resplendent glory in the center of the fete, drawing listeners around him as he tells them of his travels. "So, there I was, a plate of oysters in one hand and the duchess's dog in the other, locked on the balcony in a hurricane." He pauses, grinning, for everyone to laugh. He's probably told this story so many times, he knows exactly when to expect it. "As you can imagine, I couldn't exactly go running to the duke now, could I?" More raucous laughter. "So, I'm trying to kick down the door, when who should come to my rescue? The one and only Lord Jared."

Cheers rise as everyone lifts their mugs to the groom-to-be. "Lord Jared!"

Dietan's charisma and his ability to navigate conversations is like watching a skilled swordsman duel. He knows when to make a joke, when to commend someone to make them smile, how to deflect a clumsy remark.

But it all seems so hollow to me, like he's had years to practice putting on the act of the merry prince. I remember his desperation, his pleas, his fear in the healer's cottage. But the night isn't about him. I make a point to always keep at least twenty paces away from him, busying myself in the periphery of his orbit.

Tonight is for Ophelia and Jared.

One of Evandale's many traditions is to personally feed the happy couple, to usher in prosperity and good fortune. The two of them, blushing equally hard, are seated at the high table as they are spoon-fed food by various villagers. No matter which way they turn their heads, they are met with a forkful of pot pie or jam or crumble.

I try to focus on them, but at the same time I can't stop glancing Dietan's way every so often, catching a lift in his voice that unconsciously draws my attention toward him. His very presence annoys me. I still can't shake what he said about hoping to find a woman to keep him on his toes.

With any luck, today will be the last day I'll have to hear that low, baritone voice, and then I'll be free of him once and for all.

Just as I'm cutting up a cake that's been baked into a tower, covered in buttermilk frosting, and decorated with edible wildflowers, I hear that all-too-familiar voice at my shoulder.

"You're keeping busy. Don't you ever take a break?"

My knife hovers above the cake, but I don't turn around. His voice alone makes energy course through my veins. I will my hand not to tremble from adrenaline as I slowly slice the cake and divide the pieces onto plates.

"It's my job, Your Highness."

"I told you, stop calling me that. Just Dietan."

"Nope. Sorry, Your Worship, but we keep to custom here. Just because we're in Nowhereland doesn't mean we don't have manners."

He grins. "Your Worship. I kind of like it. Hey, join the party, will you?"

"Not unless you want to do the dishes." Said dirty dishes are already soaking in a giant tub outside, full of rainwater and suds. If I don't tend to it soon, I'll be up all night after the party.

"Sure, why not?" He shrugs. "I'll help."

"Oh, please. As if you've ever washed a dish in your life!"

He grins wider. "You got me there. I'll have my men do it. Come on, don't you ever take a moment for yourself?"

I laugh as I grab a stack of clean plates. Dietan's leaning against the wall, looking at me, his arms folded across his chest and his long legs crossed at the ankles. Why is he staring? *Infuriating man.* I refuse to meet his eyes.

"Shouldn't you be off finding some woman who will keep you on your toes?" I ask.

"What makes you think I haven't found her already?"

"Well, my other sister seems to be involved with your general Marcus, so I believe she's already taken." I eye the two, who are whispering head-to-head in the corner. I wonder if I shouldn't have said that. Sonja could still be a princess.

Dietan's green-blue eyes sparkle, and it's frustrating how they look exactly like summer sunshine. "I'm not talking about your sister."

I frown. If he's shown any interest in another woman, I haven't noticed it, which means that his intentions are superficial at best and indifferent at worst. Will he tell this mystery woman his secret? Or will she live out her days not knowing who her husband truly is? I feel sorry for whoever he does choose.

Dietan closes the gap between us, and I step back in surprise.

He's so close now, I can smell his cologne, and it makes my head swim. Goddess, why does he smell so good? It's overwhelming, making it impossible to think straight. I'm hit by a flash of memory of when he rescued me from the marquis—how his shoulder felt, pressed against my face, how his scent wrapped around me like a promise of safety. My chest tightens, a confusing mix of longing and regret twisting inside me.

"Hey, uh, don't walk away. I need to ask you something," he says.

"If it's about biscuits—or kings—it can wait until after my sister's party," I snap defensively, continuing to back away. Ophelia doesn't deserve us making a scene tonight.

He takes a couple of steps closer. "No, it's much more important." He bends his head toward mine, whispering, "A business proposition that I hope an adventurous woman like yourself would find amenable." I'm about to ask what he means when we both notice at the same time that the entire room is staring at us. So much for not making a scene.

"Damn," Dietan mutters. He seems to recover smoothly, standing straight and flashing a carefree smile to the crowd. But then, to my utter horror, the prince gets down on one knee and holds up a shiny ring.

What the hell? I feel like I'm dreaming. My jaw drops, and I quickly shut it in embarrassment.

But this is not a dream. It's a damn nightmare. Dietan looks up at me with hope on his handsome face. For the whole hall to hear, he says, "My dearest snarky barmaid, Aren of Evandale, will you do me the honor of becoming my bride?"

It takes a moment for everyone around us to realize what's happening—me, too, for that matter—and a hush falls, grinding the music to a halt with a screech of strings. It's as if everyone has stopped breathing. From the corner of my eye, I catch Ophelia and Sonja grinning.

But Dietan barely moves. He doesn't seem bothered in the slightest. He just gazes up at me with those sea-and-sky eyes. "I realize this is just my signet ring, but I'll make sure you get a real one later."

I can feel heat rising in my cheeks as I look down at him. His face is so handsome—vulnerable, even—as he waits for my answer. My heart beats so fast I can't think.

A prince on his knees is a sight to behold. No one moves. No one breathes. I'm frozen in place. My heart is hammering in my chest, and my hands are cold.

Dietan clears his throat once more. "So, will you? Marry me, I mean?" Then he has the audacity to wink.

The rat bastard. *A business proposition*, he had said. I exhale. This isn't about love. This is some sort of plan he's concocted. I want to slap him. Instead, I clench my fists and reply, "Absolutely not."

CHAPTER FIFTEEN

Dietan

Well, *that's* never happened before.

No one speaks, even as the door slams shut in Aren's wake. All eyes turn to me, and everyone is undoubtedly wondering: has anyone ever declined a prince's marriage proposal?

Someone coughs in the awkward silence.

This is not how I expected things to go. Granted, maybe I should have told Aren about my plan beforehand. But I'd felt such a rush of emotion upon seeing her again after our conversation this morning—and I must get my mission underway.

She's perfect. Despite the smallest of pangs in my heart, I'm sure she'll be relieved that she won't have to marry me after all!

I'll settle her with enough gold that she never has to wait another table in her life, and she can marry whomever she chooses after this adventure. She's clearly made of steel; she can handle anything the mission throws at us. She's good company, too, and would keep me on my toes for the journey.

More than that, I need someone whose heart I can't break. I'm pretty sure Aren despises me.

But my racing thoughts feel hollow like perfectly concocted little lies. Perhaps I'm just as terrible as the men who wanted to use her...but in less dangerous ways.

I scramble to my feet. "Aren, wait!"

I rush after her into the rain, splashing through the streets. She's headed to her tavern, and I catch up just as she disappears through the doorway.

But the moment I step into the Raven's Beak, a mug comes hurtling at my head—

I duck at the last second, and the mug shatters against the wall.

The tavern is empty, since everyone is at the party at the town hall. Aren stands behind the bar, keeping a barrier between us. Even from this distance, I can see how her eyes shine.

Oh, crap.

I drag a hand over my face. *What have I done?*

I didn't mean to hurt her. How could I? She doesn't even like me. Of course, I still assumed she'd say yes to my proposal—or at least hear me out. I'll clarify that I'll pay her for her trouble, and she won't actually have to marry me. The idea came to me after she told me she never wanted to marry anyone—not even a prince. She said she wanted nothing more than to travel, did she not? It's a win-win all around.

"Don't you dare humiliate me," she howls with wild eyes. I've never seen anyone so furious with me.

"What do you mean? I have no intention of humiliating you," I say, holding my hands up, attempting to calm her down. "I honestly didn't expect this reaction. People usually love me. I thought you'd be happy."

"You're playing me for a laugh, and I won't stand for it! Prince or not, you can't treat me like that!"

"It's not a joke, I swear!" I scramble to make her believe me as I approach her. "Anyone would want to marry a woman who makes biscuits like you do—"

She throws another mug at my head, and I duck again, ceramic shards ricocheting off the wall and scattering around me.

"You're just like the rest of them!" she shrieks. "Don't you see that sign? Can't you read?" she screams, pointing to a blackboard with a list of house rules, one of which, apparently is "No Marriage Proposals."

"It's fine, it's fine! I'll buy the next round! I'll buy all the rounds!" I say, trying to placate her.

The next mug lands too close for comfort. *Shit.* "Okay, I surrender—please—just listen for one moment, will you?"

Perhaps Aren's anger is dissipating—or more likely, she's out of mugs, because now she's merely standing there, hands balled into fists at her sides, eyes blazing with fury.

"Thank you," I say, risking standing up straighter. "I meant what I said—you're perfect for me— Just wait!" She moves to grab a plate next but pauses, letting me speak. "You know that I've got my reasons, and I meant that proposal with every fiber of my being. But it's tough to explain with you threatening to bash me in the head every time I open my mouth."

Aren purses her lips as if she's holding back every curse she knows. The heat of her glare could light a bonfire.

"I promise you, my proposal is not a joke. My future—everyone's future—depends on this. Can we at least discuss my proposition?" I ask.

"I will never, ever marry a lousy, spoiled prince like you."

"Great. That's perfect. I don't want to marry you, either. That's exactly why I chose you. Can you sit down and hear me out?" I motion to a nearby table and chairs.

My response must have taken her by surprise, because the murderous look on her face evaporates. "What?"

"I said, I don't really want to marry you, either."

"I knew it." Aren looks as if something large and painful is trying to crawl up her throat. Her face scrunches up, and her eyes turn glassy.

Damn! Every time I open my mouth, I put my foot in it. I realize I might have said something truly heartless, but I didn't mean it that way. I hurry to explain. "You know the real reason I came to Evandale. The Rings I carry. Veteria. The bride search was a ruse. The truth is that I never intended to marry anyone, but I do need your help to pretend that I am."

"That doesn't make any sense."

"I wish you'd said yes so we could have avoided all this." I wipe my brow with my handkerchief. "Now you're really going to have to pretend to be in love with me to make everyone believe it, or I'm toast."

Her forehead scrunches in confusion. It's kind of cute.

"I didn't mean to surprise you, but with everyone watching, it was the first thing I could think of. And I thought it was perfectly romantic," I say. "I really thought I could sell it."

Aren scoffs. "What possessed you to think I would say yes?"

"My wit? My looks?" I laugh. She doesn't. "And my title? I *am* a prince, you know."

Wrong answer. She narrows her eyes and cocks her head, looking at me like I'm a bug she's about to squash. "Tell me the truth. Why did you ask me to marry you?"

I know it's a risk, but I have no other choice. I need a bride to parade through Alarice and Loegria, to fool the Usurper's spies watching my every move. Who else could I ask to do such a thing?

"As you know, I need to go to the Great Waste."

That gets her attention.

"No, you musn't." She shakes her head in worry. "I know I told you about King Osian but Veteria said you shouldn't go."

"Too late. Just hear me out! You'd make a perfect cover for me, to pretend we're going to ask the Oracle of Alba to bless our marriage."

She studies me for a long moment. "That's crazy."

"I know how it sounds…but listen. I need to get to King Osian's castle without tipping off the Usurper's informants. With a bride on my arm, I can travel across borders on a Wedding March and get the Oracle's blessing at Alba, as the unification treaty demands of a royal marriage, without escalating existing tensions into war."

She eyes me with suspicion, hand still at the ready to throw a plate when needed.

"Please. Otherwise Loegria and Alarice are both doomed. And the Kilandrar will find me and kill me."

She's still looking at me, her dark eyes shining with empathy instead of disgust.

An understanding passes between us, and for the first time, I feel seen — honestly seen. This is my chance, and I take it. "I need a cover story for this journey to the Waste, and I humbly request your help. I'll do whatever you ask of me in exchange. This is a business proposition, so name your terms. If you want payment, I will see that it's tripled. You said you want to get out of this town, to travel? You have no obligation to marry me once this is over. It's just for show.

"I left the capital with war looming, and every day I'm away is one my father spends preparing to face the Usurper without me. But this is the final, necessary step. I have the Rings of Fate, and I need to get them out of me before Penrith invades."

RINGS OF FATE

Aren keeps watching me cautiously, as if calculating many things at once. If she says no, I'll need to rethink my whole plan. I'm not sure I'd have a plan at all.

"What will happen to the unification treaty if we don't get married?" she asks. "After we've gotten the blessing from the Oracle?"

"Worried you'll actually have to marry me?" I smile to lighten the mood, but the expression feels tight, like a grimace. I'm getting this all wrong. "Once I deal with the Rings—and pay you handsomely for your help, of course—we can always say that we discovered our insurmountable differences during the Wedding March. They don't tell you this, but that's one of the reasons to have a Wedding March: drag the newly betrothed couple from town to town for weeks on end and see if they kill each other. I'm told my parents almost did, several times."

Aren laughs, a bright and welcome sound, and I'm almost convinced she won't murder me during our journey.

"As long as we part ways before the wedding and there's no divorce, it won't be the worst scandal. The people are on edge because of the Usurper; I say why not give them something harmless to gossip about? I'll go straight to my grandfather's court, offer my profuse apologies, and meet a bevy of noble Alarician ladies who I'm sure will be thrilled I'm available once more." I can't help rolling my eyes. Aren laughs again. But then her eyes flick toward something over my shoulder, widening in alarm.

All at once, I'm ripped backward with such force, the air rushes out of my lungs. I'm briefly airborne before crashing into a nearby table. Pain pops along my back, sending white dots across my vision as I slam into another table, knocking it over.

My ears ring, and pain radiates up my spine. Tears blur my eyes against my will. Dazed, and gasping for breath, I lever myself upright. I come face to face with a creature of darkness. My stomach drops.

They've found me.

It's the monster that haunts my dreams. I can see through its body to the other side of the tavern as it takes solid shape. Gray dust and dirt swirl around it like a humanoid tornado, growing stronger with each passing second. Tentacle-like appendages extend from its form, reaching for me.

Unblinking coal-black eyes stare back at me, strangely still and unchanged, as this creature made of wind raises itself up for another attack.

I sigh.

The Kilandrar are back.

CHAPTER SIXTEEN

Aren

What the hell is that? The creature came from nowhere, melting out of the air like fog, and when it threw Dietan against the wall, all I could do was scramble out of the way. Shaking, I duck behind the bar, peeking over the top of the counter.

This can't be happening.

Kilandrar aren't real. Despite being told the contrary, my brain refuses to believe the truth. And now one of those fuckers is in my bar.

We don't have tornadoes here in the valley. I've only heard of the destruction a tornado leaves in its wake—how it darkens the land, rips through fields and homes alike, tears trees from their roots, shredding everything in its path until there's nothing left. Nothing can be done to stop it.

And that's what's inside the Raven's Beak. A living tornado stands before Dietan, growing darker and larger as it feeds off the air in the room. The fire in the hearth weakens, and the flames lunge outward, sucked into the creature's vortex, before they sputter out.

Everything falls into darkness, but I can still make out its shape, swirling with the embers of the dead fire it consumed. It's stronger now, its winds battering the windows from the inside, shaking the glasses on the shelf above my head and the floorboards beneath my feet. The roof is threatening to tear away like opening a jar of preserved peaches.

Its winds howl like a wild animal, and dear Goddess, that's the Kilandrar speaking. *Prince of Loegria...* it says in a voice akin to screaming, keening gusts cutting through a gap in a window. I clamp my hands over my ears to cover its terrible sound.

Dietan scrambles to his feet and, to my shock, spreads his arms as if to shield me from the Kilandrar—but he looks injured and is moving too slowly.

The Kilandrar grabs Dietan and lifts him up. His feet dangle helplessly as he tries to grapple with the creature, but there's nothing solid for him to grab. The Kilandrar's arm encircles Dietan's throat. There is a horrible noise, like the rushing of wind through a hollow tube.

Dietan's mouth works helplessly, gasping for air that won't come. His eyes bulge; his feet kick. He strains, trying to pull away, desperately pushing against the creature, but he's caught in the air, as helpless as a fly suspended in a spider's web. Baring his teeth, he claws at his own throat.

It's stealing the breath right out of his lungs. It's killing him.

Oh, Harvest Mother, I've got to do something. But my feet are rooted to the ground, paralyzed in terror.

The Kilandrar grows larger as it consumes him. Dietan's face turns pallid, his lips blue. His eyes, bloodshot, roll up. It's choking him—choking the life out of him like the marquis's man once did to me—

Suddenly, I'm full of rage, and without thinking I grab the nearest thing I can find—my iron skillet. I rush out from behind the bar, wielding it high. I lunge forward and swing, aiming for the creature's head, and am taken aback when it doesn't pass through the wind. Instead, the iron skillet makes a sound like a hollow gong as I strike the creature hard.

It drops Dietan. I hit it again, with another satisfactory *gong!*

Dietan coughs, choking on his own breath as it returns to him. He rolls over, eyes closed, and pants as color returns to his face.

I run to stand in front of the fallen prince, holding my frying pan before me like a sword, my entire body trembling as the Kilandrar gathers itself up and turns to face me, its fathomless black eyes glittering.

What in Albion am I doing?

I should run, get the hell out of here. But even though my entire body is vibrating in fear, I can't—I won't—let it harm Dietan again.

I'm standing in front of death itself. It screams at me with the rage of a thousand screeching winds, but I don't dare drop the skillet to cover my ears. I don't understand what it's saying, but I know it's angry.

Well, you know what? I'm angry, too. I'm furious. What the hell is it doing—destroying my bar and attacking my guest?

"Leave him alone!" I shout over its howling. My hair has fallen from my bun in the roaring storm, whipping my cheeks. My eyes water in the wind, but I force myself to keep them open, never taking them off the Kilandrar hissing and circling before me.

I look down at my iron skillet, then back at the Kilandrar, my mind racing. *How did I hit it? Could I hit it again?*

The Kilandrar lunges. I swing the skillet once more, batting its limb away, and the force of the impact reverberates up the frying pan all the way up my hand and arm, making my very bones vibrate like a bell. *That hurts like a bitch.*

It rears back and strikes. I try to deflect it again, but I miss. This time the Kilandrar knocks me down.

I crumple when my shoulder hits the floor of the tavern, screaming at the pain. The Kilandrar twirls, moving as fast as smoke in the wind toward Dietan, but I push through the fire racing through my arm and back. I rush at it again, swinging the skillet into the Kilandrar's head before it can touch Dietan.

The Kilandrar pounces, pinning me to the floor with a furious blast. Its wind-formed mouth opens wide right in front of my face, a tornado of hate and fury, and Harvest Mother, I can feel it sucking the very life right out of my lungs. I drop the frying pan—I can't breathe—I'm going to die—when suddenly the foul creature is the one howling.

A sword point emerges through its dark mass, piercing right through its middle. Dietan's blade.

One slash. Another.

The prince is on his feet, cutting the Kilandrar apart, his blade driving furrows through the elemental, carving it up piece by piece.

The Kilandrar turns its back to me as it bears down on Dietan, lashing him with ferocious wind, but the prince stands his ground. He plants his feet on the tavern floor and wields his sword like a dancer. With each blow, the ferocious winds seem to deflate.

Dietan is relentless, striking one blow after another. His eyes are wide with fury, his brow beading with sweat.

But the Kilandrar raises itself up like a snake and calls forth a screeching, angry gale.

I flatten myself against the floorboards while the windstorm rages around the tavern. All the tables and chairs are upended. Mugs and plates fly through the air, but the winds aren't half as strong as they were a moment ago. Dietan's sword is a blur, a silvery slash of light as he advances relentlessly behind.

With each blow Dietan lands, the creature fades, its power diminishing.

He drives the Kilandrar against a wall, pinning the wind against brick and timber. He leaps on top of the bar and raises the blade high above his head, then strikes the finishing blow. With a great crack, the creature swoops once around the tavern like a ghost before vanishing out the door and into the rain, just one more gust of air that disappears into the howling winds.

Dietan lowers his sword, and his eyes meet mine. "You alright?" he asks.

"I think so," I say.

"Good."

I slump back in relief just as the door to the tavern bursts open again, voices shouting over the storm. Dietan's guards rush in, with Jared and Marcus at the helm.

"What the hell is going on!" Marcus thunders, unsheathing his sword.

"Leave me! Go after it!" Dietan croaks, pointing. He shoves his disheveled blond hair out of his hard, determined eyes.

His men nod and run after the dark spirit, giving chase into the night.

With the Kilandrar gone, the air inside the tavern returns to normal. Even the fire in the hearth catches an ember and reignites. The crackling flames are the only sound aside from our ragged breathing.

I crawl over to him, relieved that he appears recovered and—though I'm reluctant to admit it—impressed by his skill with the blade. He stares at me as well, bewildered but amazed.

"It hurt you, didn't it?" he asks. He holds his head in a trembling hand. "I'm so sorry. This is all my fault."

I don't have the energy to reply. The Raven's Beak is a mess: shattered glass everywhere, mugs and dishes in pieces, and the table Dietan fell into is broken into splinters. But at least the building is still standing. Thank the Goddess for that.

Back on my feet, I reach for my skillet and clutch it tightly against my chest. For some reason, holding it brings me comfort. I take in the damage as realization sets in. I—*we*—just fought an evil elemental spirit and survived.

"You risked your life to save mine," he says. The look of admiration in his eyes is guileless.

"With a skillet," I say, bemused, looking at the pan in my hands.

His laugh is weak. "As good a weapon as any."

"But I thought this would just go through it—not hit it."

Dietan nods. "Yeah. Not sure how my sword could hurt it, either. The scrolls say the Kilandrar cut through armies of men as if they were stalks of wheat." As he gets to his feet, he gasps, teeth bared. He hunches over, reaching his arm behind him. "My back…"

He tries to hobble to a chair, but he can't stand up straight. I rush to support him by the elbow. He inhales sharply, his handsome face lined with agony.

"This way." I guide him into the kitchen, where the oven is still on. I sit him down in one of the extra chairs Bonnie uses as a stepping stool. He sits on it backward, collapsing onto the seatback, his face pressed against its wooden frame.

"Come on." I reach for the hem of his shirt.

"What are you doing?"

"Let's see how bad it is." I tug it up, but he stops me with his hand on mine.

"Just wait—" he says, his breath catching.

"You may need a healer."

He lets out a beleaguered sigh, knowing full well I'm not going to give up. Slowly, I slide his shirt over his head. I try not to linger on the sight of his corded muscles, the sculpted lines of his back. I wince when I see it. A great purple bruise spreads horizontally across his lower back. The edge of the table left an almost perfectly straight line. Several large splinters protrude from his bruised skin. He's lucky he still has use of his legs. I've seen worse, but I know he'll be feeling it for days.

But that isn't the only thing that catches my eye. There are two intersecting ring-shaped white scars between his shoulder blades. The scars are deep, ridged, and thick. They look painful, like the rings were branded on his skin with a hot poker—which I've only ever seen on livestock. My chest tightens. I didn't notice them before at Veteria's.

He truly has the Rings of Fate.

They are a part of him. They look raw, like they haven't fully healed, like they still hurt. He didn't want me to see them.

I tear my eyes away and pretend not to notice. For his sake. For the crown, perhaps.

"Don't move," I tell him. "You'll only make it worse."

Another sigh is all the response he can muster.

I grab a pair of pliers from a drawer, fetch a clean rag from the cupboard, and fill a pitcher from the freshwater basin. I dip the rag in it, then squeeze it out. Dietan sits still, his chest pressed against the back of the chair, but his breathing comes in fits and starts, and his muscles spasm. To his credit, he barely makes a sound. My own shoulder starts to ache from when I was thrown to the floor, but I ignore it.

"Brace yourself," I warn, coming up behind him.

When I remove the first splinter, he sits up straighter and gasps.

I work for several minutes to remove the splinters, then wipe away the blood and press the cool rag to his back to ease the sting. From the cupboard, I retrieve a jar of the salve I make for when Bonnie or I get cuts or burns in the kitchen.

I pull a chair up behind him and open the tin.

"You saved me, even at risk to yourself. Thank you," he says.

"Yeah…you saved me, too, so we're even."

I apply the salve in silence. The rain hammers on the roof, and the fire in the oven crackles, and the only other sound is Dietan's labored breathing. I keep my touch gentle, and I try not to stare. But as my fingers brush his warm skin, I'm acutely aware of how close we are. I could reach up and touch the fine down of hair on his neck.

But I don't. Instead, I study the jars of jam on the shelves, and the apples in a bowl that still need peeling, and… Somehow, my gaze is drawn back to the scarred outline of the rings. Are they really in there, under his skin? Dear goddess, what a burden to carry.

"That feels good. Thanks," he says.

I clear my throat, wiping my fingers on the rag. "Your men will be back any moment," I say, keeping an eye on the door. "So that's what's after you, huh? The Kilandrar?"

"Yep."

"It tried to kill you."

"Yep."

"Has that happened before?"

"Yep."

I frown at his back and roll my eyes even if he can't see it. "That thing might return. Why was it after you?"

He juts his thumb toward his scars, trying not to move too much. The Rings of Fate. How did that wind monster know Dietan has them? It didn't look particularly intelligent. Granted, I don't think Dietan is particularly intelligent, either.

That's mean of me. From what I've seen tonight, he is far from dumb and very brave.

"Does anyone else know about this? Your Rings, I mean?" I ask.

He hesitates. "Not many. Father, Jared, Marcus…that's it. I have to fix this mess I've made, and I don't know if I can."

"I think you need a warm compress now to help the salve work," I say as I stand. I need a moment to think about what this means for me — a country barmaid getting mixed up in dangerous magic and royal secrets.

I return with one of the rags we keep right in front of the oven to wrap warm bread in. He's still hiding his face in his arms, but despite the dim light, I can make out the shape of his lips, the cut of his jaw, and the occasional twitch of the muscle there when pain rolls through him. It's hard not to feel bad for him, prince or not.

I want to touch him — to comfort him — but settle for draping a hot towel across his back as he tells me the whole story, about how he came to bear the Rings of Fate so cruelly under his skin. Two young boys, friends, sneaking into the war room to take a peek at treasure. One touch and then total blackness. Boyish ignorance had condemned him to this doom.

They're the only thing protecting his kingdom and mine.

Which means *he* is the only thing protecting us.

I realize, like a punch to the gut, that this is the first time he's telling me the whole truth — being vulnerable. Unlike when we were at Veteria's cottage when it was clear he didn't want me to know his secret. I don't think he's *supposed* to reveal this much to a random barmaid he's only known for a few days, and I'm warmed by his trust. All the sneaking around, all the secrecy — it's because he carries on his back the burden of trying to prevent a war he might have lost us when he was just a child. I'm sorry I judged him harshly, even if he *is* really irritating.

When he's finished talking, he looks at me with hope and grim resolve warring on his face. I'm not sure what to say.

"And you really think the mad king can help you remove them?" I manage, even though it was my idea in the first place.

"Yeah," he says. "And it's why I asked you to marry me. Will you?"

I throw up my hands. "Are you out of your mind? You nearly died, *I* nearly died, and you still think this is a good idea?"

"You know what's at stake," he says. The weight of his words feels real. I've been marked somehow, like he is, with the burden of knowledge. But I don't want it. I never asked for this—but I suppose neither did he.

Do I have to pretend to be his bride, now that I know? Travel with him to the Great Waste with bells on? I blanch, suddenly relieved that neither of my sisters caught his eye after all. "I'd rather have a healthy tooth pulled with blacksmith's tongs than be paraded from town to town like a prized cow—"

He interrupts me with vehemence. "Look, you're one of four people who knows the truth."

"Five," I interrupt, biting my bottom lip, deep in thought.

"Excuse me?"

"You forgot Veteria," I correct him.

"Okay, one of five people in this entire realm who knows that the truth. The Kilandrar have returned. You've seen what one can do. Imagine hundreds of them. Everyone is in danger, including your sisters, your father, your precious tavern."

"What about what Veteria said? Not to seek out the mad king. Aren't you afraid?"

"The Usurper has shown his hand. All I know is that if I don't return the Rings to my father, there'll be nothing to stop them—all of them. They'll remake the world, just like they did in the age before memory. Everything, everyone, will be destroyed."

I gnaw on my lip some more. It's all true. But...

"I can't help you," I say finally, with a shake of my head. "I'm sorry. I can't marry you, even if it's just pretend. Find another girl who doesn't have responsibilities. I'm needed here. My family needs me. I can't abandon them, even to save them."

He presses his lips together and closes his eyes, pain flitting across his features before subsiding. "Truly? Aren't your sisters off to the capital? Aren't they already taken care of?"

"There's still my father," I say weakly. "I can't leave him. I'm sorry."

"I'm sure Jared would be happy to bring him along, and your sisters and their new staff would take wonderful care of him."

It's tempting, I'll give him that. I imagine my father ensconced in a palace, waited on hand and foot. I imagine him, at his age, plucked away from everyone he's ever known.

"He'd never leave Evandale, and what kind of daughters would force him?"

Dietan continues to look at me, and when I stare right back with no sign of budging, he heaves an enormous sigh.

"All right, then." He groans as he stands, limps to the counter to the right of the wash basin and wraps his hand around a bottle of Alarician ale left over from last night. He swirls the contents and takes a long swill.

I stare at him, aghast. "That's it? That's your answer?"

He lolls his head tiredly toward me, inspecting me with those bright blue-green eyes, like he's surprised I'm still here. He was so adamant earlier about getting me to marry him, going so far as to propose in front of everyone in town—so adamant that the fate of kingdoms depended on my decision—and here he is now, pretending it doesn't matter.

Of course it doesn't matter. I'm just someone for him to use, like all the rest. He'll find another woman.

"After all that, you're just…fine?" I accuse.

He winces as he lowers himself back into the chair. "I'm not going to force you to do anything you don't want to do. I'll just have to find another way to get to the Great Waste by myself… But for now, I'm going to get very, very, very drunk," he says. Then he adds, with a wink that isn't fooling anyone, "For the pain."

I throw the rag down on the counter. "Dumbass." I leave him to his own devices in the kitchen and start sweeping up the ruined dining room.

While Dietan is drinking himself into a stupor instead of plotting his way out of imminent peril, my mind whirs.

Marry him?

No way. Not even as a lie, not even to save the world.

I'll admit it. I'm terrified.

I'm no warrior. I'm not some brash adventurer like in the stories I used to make up for my girls when they were little, dreaming of daring heroics and happy endings. I'm just a plain-faced barmaid in a small town, with no prospects and no great future except for the tavern. But isn't leaving

Evandale and traveling all across the kingdom the very thing I've always dreamed of?

That dang prince doesn't really want to marry me, and that's why I said no in the first place. Plus, why is saving the kingdom *my* problem? Isn't that what kings and princes and armies are for?

And there's still Father to think about. If I'm to travel the world instead of staying in Evandale to take care of him, I could never stray too far. He needs my care. My apron strings will always be tied to the front door.

But I can't stop thinking about what Dietan said. Let my girls take care of Father for a change. They'll have the means.

Like it or not, he was making sense.

What do *I* want, then?

I've stopped sweeping to stare at an empty spot on the floor. I'm bone-tired. My shoulder aches more fiercely than ever, and I want nothing more than to sleep for a full day.

The last thing I hear before leaving is the sound of Dietan opening another bottle in the kitchen.

Royal drunk.

CHAPTER SEVENTEEN

Aren

I find Dietan passed out in the tavern the next morning, just like the day before. Still sound asleep in the kitchen, right where I'd left him, except he's sitting properly in the chair this time, his arms folded over his chest and his head tilted back, neck uncovered and exposed to the air. Way too trusting for a prince to present his exposed neck as an offering like that. Daring a steady blade to finish the job, if you ask me. He's clearly too used to being surrounded by solicitous guards. Or maybe I'm just irritable.

I frown at him as I count all the empty bottles around him. What a mess. I scoop some water from the freshwater basin into a cup and toss it onto his face. *Take that, your royal highness.*

He sputters awake, gasping and coughing, as water drips from his blond locks onto his white shirt. "Whoa, what happened to the sweet wakeup from yesterday?" he whines, wiping the water from his face with his sleeve, looking satisfyingly put-out. "Is there breakfast?" he asks hopefully.

RINGS OF FATE

"You should leave now," I tell him with all the warmth of a winter day. "Your royal entourage is waiting."

It is, after all, the day he said they planned to depart.

He sets his mouth into a thin line as he empties his pockets, placing a thick stack of gold coins on the counter. "For the ale, my sweet maiden," he says. "And to set your tavern to rights."

I manage a smile that feels strained, even to me. I check the stack of coin, which is more than enough for repairs and then some. But is it enough to make up for bringing unnatural terror and destruction to my peaceful town?

In the clarity of daylight, I just want him out of here. The sooner this stupid cursed prince is out of my life, the better.

I walk over to the back door and unlock it, swinging it wide into the rainy morning as Dietan stiffly rises from the chair.

"Your exit, Your Worship," I say.

He nods. "The pleasure is all mine." He's about to step outside but stops, his face turning ashen.

"What? What is it?" I ask warily. My bones feel a thousand years old. My nerves are beyond shot. I don't think I can take any more surprises. *What now?*

Wordlessly, he points to the doorway.

On the ground outside is a man lying face down in a puddle. *Great.* Another drunk.

Except he's not moving, at all.

Cold dread slithers down my spine as I stifle the urge to vomit. Oh, goddess. *No.*

Dietan rushes forward and turns the man over in the mud.

I gasp. He's one of the royal guards; I remember he helped roll the ale barrels to the town hall. His face is still frozen in terror, his eyes bulging, mouth open in a soundless scream. But there's no trace of blood on him, no sign of violence on his person. He just looks…like he had the breath stolen out of him.

Dietan presses his fingers against the man's neck. He shakes his head and then looks up at me, stricken. "The Kilandrar," he says.

My stomach churns with horror and guilt. It must have killed him after we chased it out of the Raven's Beak. He was probably killed by the Kilandrar in this very spot while we were tending to our wounds, and we didn't hear a thing.

We stare at the body.

Then, as if remembering his position in the world, Dietan leans over the man's corpse and recites a hushed prayer. I recognize the Words of the Fallen, asking the spirits to help the man find his way home to the fields of gold. When Dietan's done, his hands are shaking.

"Bless this man and his service to Albion," Dietan whispers. "I thank him for the gift of his life. Blessed travels."

"Blessed travels," I echo.

With a final nod, Dietan sits back on his heels and pushes his hair from his face, rain soaking him to the bone as he looks helplessly to the sky. My dread only compounds the longer I stare at the lifeless body. A man's life was snuffed out by magic as untouchable as the wind. How can anyone stop creatures like the Kilandrar? *How can he ask me to face them again?*

I can feel Dietan staring at me, and when I meet his gaze, I can barely breathe. His eyes are full of conviction; his determination tugs at my heart. Rain and tears roll together down his cheeks. He's angry, and he is brave, and right now, more than ever, he's the prince of Loegria. Noble and proud and carrying the suffering of his people.

Later that morning, the royal carriages are restocked for the road, and their horses stomp in the mud, restless to get back on the road. But my sisters aren't with them. Lord Jared, Ophelia, and Sonja have been ordered to stay behind. Three were lost to the Kilandrar last night, and it is much too dangerous to travel. The prince has instructed his friend and a couple of remaining guards to secure the town and then escort the twins to Lundenwic when it's safe.

All of Evandale has turned out to say goodbye and watch the prince and his entourage leave—except for me. I'm here for a different purpose.

I'm surprised to see Dietan securing the rest of the bags alongside his men when I approach. I'm carrying a rucksack that holds everything I own in this world, including my trusty skillet and pouch of healing herbs.

I've been wrestling with my decision since this morning.

"Fine. I'll do it," I announce without preamble. "I'll marry you." There are rapturous cheers from the onlookers. I see the marquis absolutely seething amongst the happy crowd. I guess he was right to be worried about me after all.

I lower my voice so only Dietan can hear. "I mean, I'll pretend to marry you."

To my surprise, he shakes his head. "No."

"No?" I huff. I want to strangle this annoying man. "Isn't this what you want?" I whisper through a gritted smile. "I thought you'd be ecstatic."

Dear goddess, is he going to make me beg? Some men like that sort of thing. But I'm not going to beg; I'm going to murder him.

He latches the final strap. "After I left the Raven's Beak this morning, I walked the town for hours, thinking over what I'd asked of you, what dangers lie ahead, and I realized I made a mistake."

He leans down and looks me in the eye, and I know we're both remembering the horror we just faced in my tavern. To the town, this must look like a sweet lovers' conversation, not a deep discussion about the future of the kingdom. I can't stop thinking about the guardsman's bulging eyes and pain-stricken face. "I was wrong to even ask. I won't put you in harm's way," he says, looking weary and much older than his twenty-two years. "I can't."

"But if I don't go with you to Alba, it imperils your mission and both kingdoms," I remind him. "You need me." I can't believe I'm trying to talk him into taking me on this death march. So much for not begging.

"I don't. Aren, I've changed my mind. I can't bring you into this. It's just too dangerous. I never should have asked in the first place."

I will not let him break up with me in front of this entire town before we are even fake-married.

"But you did ask, and the answer is yes," I say sternly. "You came to Evandale to find a bride, didn't you? Well, here she is."

When he doesn't reply, I press on. "This is what you planned to do, so let's do it." I silently beseech him to take me at my word before I lose my courage. I could stay—just go home and hide from these living nightmares, under Lord Jared's protection.

Dietan studies me intensely. "Are you sure?"

"You said you'd pay triple, right?" I flash him my best smile, and I name my price. This is a transaction, as he said, nothing more. I can make sure Father's taken care of with or without Lord Jared's charity—and still have my freedom at the end of all this.

If I survive.

Finally, he relents. "If I agree, you must promise me that you will leave with my guards the minute there is trouble. You will come back here or go to court or wherever else you want to go. I can't put you in danger, or I would never be able to live with myself."

"Deal." I shrug as if it's all the same to me, even as my heart seizes at the thought that he might send me away in the future.

I tell myself I'm here for the money, but to be honest, I know I can't let him face those monsters on his own.

"This is what you wanted, right?" I say, as if I don't care what he thinks.

He shrugs an even bigger shrug. "Fine. Have it your way, Aren," he relents. I can see the pain behind his eyes, and I know the road ahead of us will be bumpy.

Dietan turns to the crowd and announces we are officially engaged. The crowd whoops and hollers in joy at the news.

If the people of Evandale are surprised by the swift turn of events, they take it in stride. A royal bride has been found! Right in their own town! There should have been a party to end all parties, but the prince and his betrothed (who would normally be catering any such party) are to leave right away.

The twins are beside themselves with happiness when I find them in the crowd. "Oh, Aren! You'll be a princess!" cries Sonja.

But I can't fool Ophelia. She takes my hands in hers and pulls me close. "But tell me, do you love him? Does he make you happy?" she asks.

"I don't care that he's a prince."

I smile ruefully, hoping that I can still fool my younger sisters. "I'm happy enough. And I can... I can learn to love him, I suppose?"

Ophelia whispers in my ear. "I do hope so, my dear sister. You deserve all the happiness in the world."

"We will see you at court!" Sonja says gaily.

"Take care of yourself, my dearest," says Father, who's leaning on his cane.

Bonnie comes to bid me farewell and promises to take care of the Raven's Beak in my absence. She'll look after the business until my father can find a buyer. I don't trust myself to linger any longer after giving her a swift hug goodbye. If I stay one more minute, I might change my mind. Or cry. Both are bad.

When I hop inside the carriage and shed my cloak, I notice the prince staring at me with a small, pleased smirk. I smirk right back. *Insufferable man.*

"What?" I demand.

"I knew you'd change your mind," he says.

My cheeks heat. "Shut up."

"You're not the type to refuse to come to someone's aid." I'm almost charmed, especially after everything we've already faced together. But then he adds, "Or maybe you just can't resist me." He leans closer in the seat across from me and waggles his eyebrows, and I'm back to being annoyed with him. Does he ever stop flirting?

"I said, shut up." I don't look out the window as the carriage starts moving because I don't want to watch the town disappear behind me. I will not cry in front of Dietan, who is far too smug given the dangers ahead.

I lean against the wall of the carriage so our knees won't touch. "Fiancée in name only, mister."

Dietan raises his hands in supplication. "As my lady commands."

PART TWO

THE WEDDING MARCH

CHAPTER EIGHTEEN

Aren

Our journey begins in silence.

I watch the passing countryside change outside my window as the carriage bounces along the dirt path heading south from Evandale toward Loegria. The landscape is a pleasant distraction while Dietan reads a book on the other side of the carriage. After a few hours, I've already traveled farther than I ever have in my life.

The longer we're on the high road from Evandale, the more the weather clears. Evandale sits in the shadow of a mountain far to the west, which collects rain clouds in its bowl-like valley. As we journey south, the skies turn from dark gray to silver, and then blue peeks out between bursts of sunlight, casting the land of Alarice into the golden beauty it's known for.

Most of eastern Alarice is made of flatlands and fields, but dense forests darken the horizon, broken up here and there by farmland on the outskirts of towns, some of which are large or important enough to warrant a visit from a prince and his betrothed. Dietan has been briefed on the itinerary and tells me a bit about the places we're going: one town is an important hub for fabric dyeing; another one grows a type of fruit that is all the rage in his capital. More than once, the carriage stops to let a herd of sheep pass by, and I throw bits of our snacks out the window to give them treats. Dietan seems amused by this.

I'm nervous about traveling all the way to the Great Waste, but at least I think my family is secure. Ophelia and Sonja's futures are assured, and they, along with all of Evandale, remain under Lord Jared's protection. Dietan left enough soldiers in town to ensure its safety.

"Will the Kilandrar return to Evandale?" I ask, still gazing out the window. Dietan looks up from his book—some kind of historical account of ancient battles—as if surprised I spoke to him at all.

"Only if I'm there. It's me they're after," he says assuredly.

"How can you be certain?" I look straight into his blue-green eyes, searching for the truth.

"I can't be. But I do know that once I left, the town became a whole lot safer." Once the words leave his lips, I know he's not lying. Safer because he's not there to be hunted. Safer because Jared and a small army are standing guard. It's a relief.

I still have to try my hardest not to imagine the Kilandrar bursting into our carriage in pursuit.

As I stare out the window at the endless fields trotting by, I'm still not sure what compelled me to accept his proposal. I certainly didn't imagine in all my dreams that one day I would accompany a prince on a Wedding March through the kingdoms—and certainly not as his *bride*. It's laughable.

But he needs help, that's for certain.

And he's right about me. I'm the kind of person who always comes to someone's aid. Besides, I *do* want an adventure. I want to know what will happen next, and if I remain at the Raven's Beak, I never will.

If I was even remotely worried that I'd miss Dietan when he left, I've buried that feeling deep down. I can't feel anything for the man seated across from me. Nothing at all. We're playing a game for our common enemies to see. He's just pretending, and so am I.

Our traveling party stops once in the late afternoon, purchasing extra provisions from farmers who are eager to sell their goods. Freshly picked mushrooms and potatoes are in high demand, and I can already imagine the stew I'll make with them.

"Oh, look, these are truffles!" I'm delighted. Truffles are rare in Evandale. I hold them up to his nose.

Dietan keeps his eyes on mine as he takes a long sniff. "I've had these," he murmurs. "They're delicious."

"But so expensive," I lament.

"Allow me," he says grandly, paying for the whole lot. "Don't forget, you're to be my princess now."

I refrain from hitting him with my market bag, as I'm too thrilled about the truffles it now contains. "I'll shave them over the potatoes your men got from the other stall."

"Gods, please do" he agrees. "I'm starving."

As we settle back into the carriage, images of last night's attack still haunt my thoughts. Three soldiers killed, the general said, and I know they won't be the last. If the Kilandrar was after Dietan, drawn to the Rings embedded in his skin, then surely they will return. Every time I see a shadow moving on the horizon, I can't help but wonder if it's following us, and I shudder.

"The Kilandrar came from Penrith, right?" I ask Dietan.

He looks up over the top of his book again. I've been silently looking out the window for most of our journey. Without my apron, without my bar, I realize I don't know what to say to a prince who isn't my customer. It's going to be a long journey.

"I can't be sure," he says carefully. "But most likely. That's what my father's spies think."

"So is the Usurper King of Penrith actually Boreas returned, as rumors say?"

"Who knows? Penrith closed its borders when the Usurper killed the rightful king and took the throne. Since then, it's been difficult to gather information either way. The refugees we've questioned hardly know anything." He snaps the book shut and tosses it to the empty seat beside him, perhaps sensing he won't be getting back to his reading any time soon.

He's sitting diagonally from me, leaning against his own window. His long legs take up much of the carriage, leaving me with a quarter of the space for my own muddy boots and hastily packed bag, which I refused to let his men store with the other luggage. I might need my healing herbs or my trusty skillet at hand if the Kilandrar are really following us.

"But if you have the Rings of Fate, you should be able to use the Whisting, right? I saw you wield the power at Veteria's. Why didn't you use it last night against the Kilandrar?" I ask.

Dietan sighs. "I told you. I'm cursed with it, but I can't control it. The Whisting has a mind of its own. It rarely listens to me. Typical of the wind, don't you think?"

"You can't control it at all?"

His eyes harden; he shakes his head.

"But what about the Kilandrar? Are they being controlled?" I ask.

"While it doesn't appear that the Kilandrar are entirely mindless creatures, they're supposedly extensions of Boreas's will. At least, according to the legends. We don't know as much about them as we'd like."

I frown, thinking of what I saw last night. "It could speak, though. It knew who you were by name. It must have been told to find you."

"I'm more concerned that the Kilandrar have crossed the border into Alarice at all. Rumors place them in the south of Loegria for now, but if they're already here… It just means we've got to move faster." Dietan groans and wipes his eyes, his handsome features sagging. The weight of responsibility wears on him. "There was only one this time, but more will come."

That pronouncement chills us into silence again.

When it's time for food, the carriage stops just long enough for one of Dietan's attendants to hand sandwiches and water through the window for us both before heading off again. I'm so hungry, I gobble down the sandwich, and when it's finished, I'm sad I didn't get to savor it. It was some sort of smoked pork with sweet sauce in a sourdough bun. I jot down the flavors in my leather journal so I can recreate it one day when I have a proper kitchen again.

Dietan finishes off the last of his sandwich and licks the sauce from the tips of his fingers, which is…distracting. I hand him a clean napkin.

"Strange that we were both able to hit it. The Kilandrar, I mean," I say. I don't know how we survived the attack.

"You've got quite a swing." He grins.

"A bit of luck and practice breaking up bar fights." I can't help but crack a smile as Dietan chuckles.

He shakes his head. "I think you don't give yourself enough credit. You're kind of a badass."

I flush with pleasure. That's the first compliment he's given me that sounded truly sincere. "Pure luck. But it still doesn't make sense that it worked."

Dietan cocks his head to the side contemplatively and scrunches the sandwich paper in his hands. He leaves the wrapper on the seat next to him, and I scowl at it.

He notices the look on my face. "What?"

I pointedly glance at the crumpled paper beside him and the crumbs littering the carriage floor around his fine, polished boots, and then back at his face. His wide-eyed innocence and handsome confusion are not enough to sway me this time. My lips twist. "Really?"

"What?" he asks again.

"I suppose you grew up so used to everyone picking up after you, you hardly think about it."

Dietan studies me for a moment, his eyebrows slowly rising.

I imagine this is one of the few times anyone, let alone a peasant, has called him out on his privileged upbringing.

"If my lady commands, I'll have someone clean the carriage the next time we stop to rest," he says.

Wait, he's not even going to pick up after himself? I let out a disbelieving grunt and rest my head on the window. "Do you have to be such an asshole?"

"Me? An asshole?" he asks, feigning mock distress. "Look, you're free to do whatever you'd like here, too, fiancée. No one is stopping you. Do I dare suggest that *you* could clean it up? If you wanted to, of course."

I shoot him a look that would freeze even the most powerful Kilandrar in its tracks.

"I rescind the suggestion," he says putting his hands up in the air in surrender.

The urge to pick up the paper, to tidy up after him, is like an itch I can't scratch. My hands clench together in my lap, but I refuse to budge. I do like things tidy. I like organizing the pantry, and I like stacking cups to look nice and orderly, and I like having the floors of the Beak swept and clean, even if the customers leave them dirty every night. But I refuse to be a maid to Dietan, not even for Albion's sake.

We've only been on the road for a day, and I already want to kill him.

With a great stretch that takes up most of the low-roofed carriage, he yawns, and his shirt creeps up above the waist, revealing a flat stomach hardened by lean muscles.

Not that I'm looking.

Not that it makes my own stomach quiver with butterflies. *Get a grip.* He's probably doing it on purpose, to distract me from the mess. And it's totally working.

My boots are still muddy, and I make a point not to look at Dietan as I kick them up on the seat next to him. Goddess bless the poor servant who will have to deal with it later.

"Oh, come on, I was just about to lie down!" he exclaims in annoyance.

It's so immature, but it feels good giving it right back to him. It reminds me of how Ophelia used to tease the blacksmith's son.

"What did you say? That I can do whatever I'd like here? Well, I want to stretch my legs out...like a princess."

He brushes the dirt off the seat with the back of his hand, but the dried mud is too fine and only becomes more ingrained in the fabric. He lets out a huff. "Then I suppose I have no choice but to join you on your side."

This is not at all how I'd planned this to go, especially not when Dietan grunts and settles in beside me. He, too, kicks up his feet, crossing them at the ankles, and grins. "Better." His shoulder presses into mine. *Ugh.*

"How much longer until we reach the next town?" I ask.

"Couple of hours, give or take."

"Hours?" I'm really starting to regret traveling with him in such close quarters for such extended periods of time. He's just so...*close*.

"Unless you want to get out and walk. You'll definitely be able to clear the way with that glare of yours. Everyone will be so afraid of you." Dietan chuckles, folds his arms, tucks his chin toward his chest, and closes his eyes.

I peer over at him. He's not sleeping.

I think he just doesn't want to argue anymore.

The carriage stops suddenly, jolting me awake to find my head is resting on something warm and solid. I lurch upright, pulling myself off Dietan's shoulder, and wipe my face to get rid of the feeling of his soft shirt on my cheek. I must have been lulled into sleep by a full belly and the gentle rocking of the carriage.

"I'm not contagious," he says, watching me with bemusement. "Am I really that awful to be around?"

"Why didn't you push me off you?" I retort.

"Why would I do such a thing? You looked so comfortable," he says. "Besides, it was nice. Cozy."

I don't know what to say to that.

Thankfully, he makes no more mention of it, especially as the door is flung open and he steps out into the warm afternoon sun.

There's murmuring outside, as it seems a dozen or so people have surrounded the carriage. We've reached a town south of Evandale called Elspeth. It's known for its flower fields, which are often used in medicine as well as for decoration. I see rows of beautiful blue flowers off in the distance, and I wonder if the devil's breath the marquis used to drug me was grown here. *The bastard.*

Dietan reappears at the doorway, his hand extended.

I look up from collecting our things from the carriage, since again, he can't be bothered to pick up after himself. I put his book and cloak into his waiting hand.

Turning his face toward me, away from the crowd, he looks like he wants to burst out laughing. I feel I should be offended, but I don't know why. Dietan sets the items down on the carriage seat and holds out his hand again.

I don't move, confused as to what he wants from me.

He clears his throat. "Your adoring subjects await, my love," he says pointedly, and it's only then that I remember: I have a role to play. Princesses don't handle the luggage.

"Don't call me that," I tell him as I finally accept his hand and step out of the carriage.

Cheers and applause wash over us, and I'm taken aback by the enthusiasm all around as Dietan presents me to the village. His hand is warm in mine as he raises it above his head, like we are victors coming home from battle. I look out at all the faces of people who could have been from Evandale—rough, bronzed, and worn but smiling. They cheer and clap.

Dietan lowers our hands and squeezes my fingers, drawing my attention.

I widen my eyes in question.

"Don't hit me," he murmurs out of the corner of his mouth.

Before I can ask why, he sweeps me into his arms, into a close embrace. One hand is still clasped around mine, while the other is gently but firmly on the small of my back. No one has ever touched me there, and I freeze.

"*Try* to look like you want me," he says, again talking out of the corner of his mouth.

"What?"

He leans in close and looks like he's about to plant a kiss on my lips, except I turn my head at the last minute, and his lips land on my cheek instead. If he's surprised, he doesn't show it, placing a gentlemanly peck there as if that's what he meant to do all along.

Oh.

The crowd roars with approval, but I don't hear any of it. It's as if every nerve in my body is suddenly turned toward the sun. I'm acutely aware of every place his body touches mine.

His lips are warm and soft. His stubble scratches against my skin like sandpaper, in a strangely pleasant way. His breath tickles my neck while his fingers curl slightly on my back. His other hand engulfs mine like a glove. He's so close to me that I can see the beginnings of his beard, every smile line, every lash touching the soft skin under his eyes. He's beautiful. A true prince.

Thankfully, he doesn't linger, though the brief moment his soft lips touch my cheek feels like an eternity.

When he opens his eyes—blue today like the deep, summer sky—they twinkle when he smiles.

"Good job," he whispers.

As he pulls away, I feel like I've been thrust into a blizzard after sitting by the hearth. If not for his steadying hand on my back, I would have stumbled. Is this what women mean by swooning? Goddess damn it all. I can't feel this way about him. This is all just pretend.

I stand still, trying to collect my thoughts and not blush, hardly aware of what's happening all around me. Dietan greets the mayor of the town and introduces me and his entourage. He thanks the village for their hospitality on the grand tour with his chosen bride.

Little girls lay bundles of pink-and-blue flowers at our feet. Old women place wreaths on our shoulders, draping them so high that I can barely see over the stacks of greenery and blooms. My nose is full of their heady scent, making my head swim. All the while, Dietan's hand is clasped tightly in mine, as if he knows I'm overwhelmed. And I am, because my skin is still tingling where he kissed me.

I'm thankful that the wreaths hide my face, because otherwise everyone would notice that I'm completely stunned. What the hell is happening? I hate this guy. Well, maybe I don't hate him—but I don't think much of him. He's just some dumb prince. Plus, that wasn't even a proper first kiss.

But I feel like I'm floating on a cloud, and I let myself be led inside the inn. It's a relief; I immediately feel right at home. Inns are the same everywhere: a tavern occupies the ground level, and a staircase at the back leads to the rooms on the upper floors.

I follow Dietan up the steps into the finest suite in the inn. Of course, this is a small town like Evandale, rather than the lap of luxury Dietan's probably used to, but the room is clean, the bed has new sheets, and there are fresh flowers in a vase on the nightstand.

The bed.

Oh.

We're supposed to be getting married. We're supposed to be in love.

There's only one bed.

Does he expect me to sleep in here—with him? In Evandale, brides and grooms don't share a bed until their wedding night, but maybe Loegrians do things differently. My body begins to buzz like a wasp's nest, but before I can ask, we're brought to a small foot-bathing station: two chairs in front of a steaming tub of water, with oils, sponges, and towels. Candles have been lit all around the room, despite the warmth of the sun pouring through the windows. It lends the room a distinctly romantic quality.

An older woman, old enough to be my mother, is already kneeling on a cushion near the bath, smiling and waiting for us both. Thinking of my mother makes my eyes tear up a bit. What would she think if she saw me here, a bride to a prince? Would she be proud? Or would she be worried about me, if I told her the truth of our arrangement? Would she have told me to go or stay?

After we're seated, two girls remove our flower wreaths, then begin removing the petals from them and mashing them with a mortar and pestle. I'm unaware of the customs in this town, and I've never been a guest of honor, but I assume it's all part of the ceremony. Dietan looks so at ease, giving me a reassuring smile that only awakens more butterflies in my stomach, so I just follow his lead.

The girls sprinkle the ground-up petals in the water, and the woman says a blessing over it. Dietan bows his head, so I do the same, watching him out of the corner of my eye. The woman dips her hand in the water and places her wet thumbs on both of our foreheads.

"It's a ritual for safe travels," Dietan whispers. I'm reluctantly impressed that he's so well educated about customs from all over Alarice. "It's supposed to give your feet the ability to always find the path you need."

"And your head the sense to know when you find it," the woman adds, pointing to her own forehead. She smiles and then leaves.

"Go ahead," Dietan says when we are finally left alone.

I put my feet in the bath and sigh in pleasure.

"Not so bad being royal, huh?" he asks, soaking his own feet. "Perks of the job."

"For us? Oh, it's great. But those poor women probably wasted the whole day preparing for our arrival. Ever think of that?"

"Well, not really," he replies offhandedly.

"Not really? Don't you think she has other duties? Work that'll put food on the table? Work she ought to be doing instead of…this?" I wave a hand toward the foot bath.

"I guess I hadn't thought of it that way," says Dietan.

"Perhaps you ought to. Are we even paying for this little blessing?"

Dietan comes up short, scratching his jaw. "I'll see that everyone is well compensated."

"You do that."

When we're done, Dietan hands me a towel. I dry my feet and stand up. The suite is easily bigger than my bedroom and the twins' combined. A spread of food has been laid on a table against the far wall. Dried meats, cheese, and fruit. I'm surprised; I thought there would be a banquet like the one in Evandale, where we'd have to put on a show. I'm grateful to eat in privacy. There's no kitchen or time for me to make a proper warm meal, so the truffles will have to wait for later.

I notice the bed again and feel my cheeks flush as hot as the bathwater. Is Dietan going to be sleeping here? Does he expect us to carry on the charade even in private? What exactly did I sign up for?

Dietan is finishing drying his own feet when he notices I'm just standing there like a pile of rocks. A curtain of blond hair falls into his eyes, making him look even more boyish. "If I'd known kissing you was all it would take to shut you up, I might have done it sooner."

"Ha," is all I say, fiddling with a lock of hair that's fallen from my bun.

Knowing he noticed just how I froze under his touch leaves me doubly flustered.

Dietan screws up his eyebrows. "Do you really hate me so much that you can't even pretend to kiss me?"

I clench my fists in annoyance.

His smile falls.

"I just didn't expect it, that's all," I say. "You took me by surprise."

Dietan holds up his hands, placating, as he's now used to doing with me. "It's not my fault. The crowd expects a kiss or two. It's a Wedding March, after all. We need to give them something to talk about, and it's only a kiss. I mean, it's not like it's your *first* kiss or anything."

I know I'm turning as red as the flowers in the vase because he suddenly looks away. "Oh no— Don't tell me you've never— Not that I think you're some kind of—" He must sense he's treading into dangerous territory, because he interrupts himself. "You knew we had to pretend to be engaged. I assumed you'd had some experience, especially with a thing as small as a kiss."

What did he think? Just because I'm a barmaid, I must've fooled around with every farmhand and apprentice in town? I'm as embarrassed as I am frustrated.

All my life, I've been looking after my sisters. All my life, I've been taking care of Father, and the house, and the Beak. All my life, I've never had time to make myself pretty or moon over some boy. Never once did I ever have time to sneak away in the night to do something "as small as a kiss." I was more likely to wait at the window for a hopeful young man to walk one of my sisters home after a stroll through the town square.

A kiss isn't a small thing. It's not something to do just for the sake of doing it.

Who cares that I'm a quarter of a century old and I've never been kissed?

"Wait, you haven't…kissed anyone?" he asks.

"No," I say, my face burning hot and my jaw set tight. "I haven't." I didn't think this far in advance. I didn't consider that I would need to kiss him at all—don't princesses just smile and wave?

When I kiss someone, I plan to mean it. As the years passed and no kisses came, I just thought maybe no one wanted to kiss me.

"Oh," is all he says. He must sense that it's a topic of personal conflict, because to my great surprise, he doesn't laugh or make a joke. "I'm sorry.

RINGS OF FATE

I should have accounted for your feelings..."

His words seem sincere. But why would he ever care about my feelings? That's not part of the deal. I don't know how to respond when he's being so...nice.

"Um, and just in case you were worried, we're not sleeping here together. I wouldn't ask you to do that," Dietan says, breaking the silence. He opens the door I'd assumed led to a closet, revealing a connected bedroom with its own bed. "I didn't want you to think you would have to sleep with me at night. I mean— You know, sleep *next* to me, not..." Now he's the one furiously blushing.

My stomach twists. "Right. Wonderful. On that, we can agree." I'm relieved but also disappointed, and I'm not sure why. Harvest Mother, did I *want* to sleep here with him? The thought makes me flushed; it feels wonderful and awful at the same time.

He studies me, hand flexing thoughtfully on the doorknob to the other room. There are some stray flower petals from the wreaths left in his hair, and I want to reach up to pluck them out, but I don't. I keep my distance.

He opens his mouth, then stops himself from saying whatever he originally intended. After a beat, he says, "Look, I'm sorry that I upset you. I'll do better next time. Your first kiss should be special. I'm a jerk. I'm sorry."

A prince. Apologizing. That's a new one, and it feels real. But then I remember him on one knee, asking for my hand, when it was just a ruse, just a way to fix the problem he carries between his shoulder blades. That looked awfully real to everyone else in Evandale, too. Do princes even apologize to commoners?

I lift my chin. "It's all right."

He tilts his head in a slight nod and leaves, closing his door behind him.

I wait, listening to him moving about in the adjoining room, my heart pulsing rapidly. I hear his feet moving across the hardwood floor, the soft thud of a wardrobe door closing, the thump of the mattress as he throws himself down on top of it. Then there's silence.

Meanwhile, I sit on the corner of my own bed, allowing the day's events to catch up to me. Thoughts of my sisters, my father, of leaving Evandale all flit through my mind.

But really all I can think about is Dietan on the other side of the wall. He's so close but separated by what feels like an entire world. The gentle breeze blows the lace curtains apart, revealing a glimpse of flower fields in the light of the setting sun. I'm going to be traveling with him for a long time, and it will feel even longer if I continue this vendetta to annoy him simply for being who he is.

I need to apologize, don't I? I've been hard on him, and he apologized first. It's only fair.

I walk over to his door, raising my hand to knock, then hesitate. We're engaged in name only. We are business partners mutually invested in the success of this mission. I need to establish boundaries and make sure no lines are crossed, but…I must admit I enjoyed his kiss on my cheek, even if I didn't show it.

At last, I knock.

"Yeah?" he calls.

"I'm sorry, too," I say, loudly enough that he'll hear me through the door. "I'll be more prepared when you kiss me next time."

When he doesn't reply, I think he might have fallen asleep, but after a moment I hear his familiar baritone and a smile in his voice. "I look forward to it."

CHAPTER NINETEEN

Aren

The sound of footsteps wakes me from my sleep. I'm still half dreaming, the early-morning sunlight dim behind my closed lids. I feel a presence pass above me. It must be one of my sisters. I wonder if I'm late to open the Raven's Beak, but then I remember I'm far from home, and the hand on my shoulder is unfamiliar. I jump awake, only to find a young woman looming above me. She jumps, too.

"Who are you? What are you doing here?" I wildly assume the worst, even though some part of me wonders why an assassin is dressed like a lady's maid.

"Oh! I'm so sorry, my lady. I'm Lydia. I'm your bridal attendant."

"My bridal…what?"

Lydia looks a bit like me—the same coloring, about the same height, with dark hair and eyes. She wears ribbons in her hair, woven into her braids. Her accent is Loegrian. She's broad-shouldered with defined muscles in her forearms. Her hands, now clasped at her waist, are callused, like any working woman's hands.

"I'm your bridal attendant," she repeats. "I'm here to see to your every need while you journey with the prince. I thought you knew…" She looks worried, as if she did something wrong.

I let out a ragged sigh and glare at the wall separating me from Dietan. Did he even think to mention Lydia to me?

Annoyance snaps me fully awake. If I'd known about having a lady's maid, I wouldn't have jumped down the poor girl's throat. A week ago, I'd more likely have been in her position than mine.

I can only guess what else Dietan has failed to inform me about.

"No, I'm sorry," I say. "You just startled me. You move quietly."

The girl bows and accepts my apology. She hurries about my room, dutifully preparing a morning routine more elaborate than what I'm used to at home, as I throw the covers off and stretch. My back aches from sitting in the carriage all of yesterday, and my spine cracks wonderfully.

Lydia presents a small basin with a towel for me to wash while she lays out my clothes.

The water is cold, briskly waking me up for more hours on the road. I'm patting my face dry when I notice the garments Lydia set out. One is a traveler's coat unlike any I've seen. It's made of a heavy wool, dyed Loegrian blue, with a large hood to keep out the rain and sun. Ornate embroidery and beading run down the front. It'll easily go past my knees, and the cut is meant to flare out at the waist, the silhouette of the latest city fashion. It isn't ostentatious, but it also isn't plain, and it's exactly the type of coat I always wanted to wear but could never justify making for myself. Practical but stylish. I'm amazed. I run my hands over each bit of the coat, luxuriating in every detail.

"The seamstress's stitchwork is of the Loegrian variety, with crystal and pearls in each loop, but I added the Alarician knots in the buttons to make it feel more like home for you," Lydia says proudly.

I look up at her, stunned. "Thank you."

Lydia nods, her smile small but demure. "It was an honor."

A yearning homesickness washes over me as I blink away tears. These little touches of home are reminders of why I'm doing what I'm doing.

"Prince Dietan had it made especially for you," she says. "He hopes you like it."

"I love it," I tell her, feeling warm all over. Somehow the idea that he thinks of me at all makes me sweat, even though I know it's not personal—I need nice clothes to look the part of a princess-to-be.

Lydia helps me into the coat, securing each button with a twist of her fingers. It's a perfect fit. I look at myself in the mirror as she starts fixing my hair, and for a moment I don't see a barmaid, but the royal bride that the people expect me to be. A future queen. For a moment, I believe it, too.

When I meet Dietan downstairs for breakfast, his eyes light up when he sees me wearing the coat. "You look ready to handle anything this journey throws at you," he says.

"Well, as long as it can be met with a deadly frying pan." I can't help but grin, and Dietan's smile deepens.

We depart from Elspeth at first light, making good time as we rejoin the high road south. With our supplies restocked and spirits high, the hours pass quickly.

When we stop again in Port Tyralis to feed and water the horses, Dietan informs me that the small town is important for regional trade. This time, I'm prepared for what comes after Dietan helps me out of the carriage. All eyes are on me, Dietan's bride-to-be. The prince holds my hand steadily while he addresses the crowd, but I don't hear a word of it. My heart is beating so hard that he must feel it through my skin. My lips tingle with anticipation.

Dietan looks at me, eyebrow raised, asking if I'm ready. I nod, as ready as I'll ever be. My heart is galloping like a horse, but when he leans in, he merely brushes his lips on my cheek once more.

Oh.

That's nice. I can feel his stubble against my skin and his breath on my neck, a moment's respite, a brief second where the rest of the world melts away, and it's only the place where he touches that exists.

Then it's over.

But I prepared for a kiss, a real kiss. I feel let down somehow. Does he not want to kiss me anymore after yesterday? Soon, he pulls his hand away, too, and doesn't stand so close, and the moment ends. I try to blink away the strange ache in my heart.

Then his face melts into my blurry vision, his eyes soft, his lips slightly quirked. "Everything okay?" he asks.

"Totally fine."

"You look disappointed."

"Not a bit."

"Not even a tiny bit? Now I'm the one who's disappointed."

I bite my lip. I want to put my hands around his neck and choke him, but I don't. That's not what a princess would do.

Before I know it, we're back on the road again. Every time we stop in a new town, I take his hand, and I know what's coming next. A kiss on the cheek. That's all.

Still, the crowds seem satisfied with our performance.

The people cheer, and after a few more towns, we decide to put on a real show. I relax in his arms, letting him dip me lower as my hand wanders around his back to pull him closer. I'm starting to appreciate how Dietan holds me, firmly but gently. And I look forward to the way he nuzzles my neck, sending tingles up and down my spine. His lips press against my skin. Once, he even lingers and drags his lips down against my jaw, almost to my neck. I can't help but gasp a little.

"Oops, got carried away that time," he murmurs afterward.

I'm sure he knows exactly what he's doing. He never tries to kiss me on the lips again, and every time he doesn't, I die a little inside.

Do I really want to kiss him? *Him?* Ugh. But what if I do?

The next several days pass much the same way. The weather is the only thing that varies. One day we're caught in a rainstorm and the carriage wheels get stuck in the mud, and it takes everyone's effort to get it out. Dietan and I even help push, slipping and sliding in cold mud nearly up to our knees. I end up soaked to the skin, because I refuse to risk soiling my new coat.

We sit on a several daises for celebratory banquets in the larger towns and share private meals in smaller ones. Each inn is warmer and cozier than the next, every room with separate beds—always separate. Whenever possible, Dietan keeps to his own private quarters, which doesn't go unnoticed by his guards, who keep watch in front of our rooms through the night. He never lingers to dine with his men, which I gather is unusual, and he always closes the door between our rooms when it's time to rest.

I'll admit that traveling with the prince has become slightly less annoying, especially since I pointed out his bad habits. He makes attempts at cleaning up after himself, and I make a point not to nag him about it.

Lydia and I grow closer, sharing my bed because I can't imagine my bridal attendant, this young woman barely older than my sisters, sleeping in a tent like Dietan's men.

One night between cities, we arrive in yet another small town, barely a village. There is only one inn, which has only one room, which goes to me and Lydia, leaving the rest of the traveling party to set up tents under the night sky.

At least the inn has a proper kitchen I can use, and I'm finally able to serve the truffles we picked up with roast pork and potatoes. I even have time to bake a side of garlic bread. That night, I serve up a hearty meal for everyone in the entourage around a fire in the innyard.

"That was the best damn meal I've ever had," Dietan says happily when he's finished eating.

"Hear, hear," agrees Marcus. The soldiers raise their goblets — and some even clank their swords, which are never far from their hands — in appreciation.

"Ah, we're all just tired of dried meat and old bread," I dismiss with a blush.

"No, seriously, best meal ever," says Dietan.

"You said that about breakfast at the Raven's Beak," I remind him.

"Because that breakfast was also the best damn meal I've ever had. Can you make biscuits again?" he asks.

"Maybe." I shrug. Then I add, in a lower voice, "But I don't think you deserve them."

He laughs. "Don't be harsh."

"Spoiled prince."

"Snarky barmaid."

"You think that hurts? Try harder, Your Worship."

He looks serious for a moment, even slightly wounded. "Aren, I don't have it in me to argue tonight."

"Fine, me neither." I sigh. Truly, I don't know why I'm so mean to him. I tell myself it's because *somebody* needs to keep his princely ego in check.

I leave him alone and walk over to where Marcus is sitting by himself on the other side of the campfire, writing on parchment, a ledger in his lap and a sheaf of papers at his side.

He looks up when I take a seat on a log nearby. "Bickering like an old married couple again," Marcus says, returning his gaze to his paper. "Why don't you invite him to your room one evening? Maybe he'll be less grumpy. You, too."

"Excuse me?" I gaze across the innyard at Dietan, who is helping get the horses settled. His laughter easily carries on the slight evening breeze. He jokes that one of the horses is giving him an attitude, and so he feeds it an apple from his palm. I pull my coat tighter around me, suddenly cold and grateful for the heat of the fire.

"The two of you, keeping separate quarters. You don't have to. This isn't the second epoch anymore. Nobody expects you to, *ahem*...wait until marriage, so don't be concerned about keeping up appearances of propriety. No one really does that anymore, at least not in Loegria," Marcus says.

"It's not— He's arranged it that way." I feel embarrassed about the situation. The men must think Dietan doesn't really want me, that he's just marrying a pliable country bumpkin to fulfill the treaty. *Then he can get back to being a man-whore*, I overheard one of them saying. I don't think they know we're keeping separate rooms because this is all a farce, a charade. But surely Marcus must know that our relationship isn't real.

"That's what I meant about issuing him an invitation," Marcus says meaningfully. "I know he has quite the reputation, but at heart, he's a gentleman."

"Oh...I don't know..." I say, feeling hot at the thought.

"Well, I for one am glad the prince has decided to settle down," he says, giving me a pointed look I can't quite understand. "Between us, I thought he'd never find the one."

"I find that hard to believe," I say. "He likes everyone. He's such a flirt."

Marcus shakes his head. "That's all an act. I've known him since we were kids. Trust me. He's not like *this* with any woman. He's usually not interested enough to spar. I suppose that's why he chose you."

I fall silent, glancing around at the others, a couple of whom are looking our way. I've come to trust the gentle giant. He's keeping us all safe. So what on earth does he mean?

"How much do you know about..." I trail off as I try to recall what Dietan said about who he's told about the Rings of Fate. Marcus is just pretending for his men, right? I shouldn't say anything. But why is he giving me romantic advice?

"How much do I know about Dietan?" Marcus prompts. "I know he can be pig-headed, but I can also tell when he's truly happy." His smile is soft, and for a moment, it irons out the hard, focused lines on his young face. "He hasn't been happy in a while. We're all worried about war."

So, Marcus has noticed Dietan's worry. *How much does he know about Dietan's plan?* I don't respond, especially not when Dietan plops himself down on the other side of the fire, his elbows on his knees as he tears off a chunk of the garlic bread.

Marcus goes back to his paper, as if he, too, doesn't want to reveal that we were talking about him. Dietan smirks like he knows, and it looks like it gives him immense satisfaction to be the subject of conversation. The man sure does love attention.

I refuse to give him any. I turn toward the fire, stoking it with a stick. The logs pop and crackle, sending wisps of embers up into the dark sky, joining the stars that glitter overhead in the moonless night.

Marcus scribbles away with a quill, his brow furrowed in concentration. I'd assumed he was working, attending to whatever important correspondence occupies a general's evenings. The paper at the top of the stack next to him looks like a military briefing, and an alarming one at that, reminding me that our peaceful Wedding March is just a lovely illusion in more ways than one. It's meant to reassure the people in dangerous times.

But then I glance at his ledger and notice the name at the top of the page.

"Are you writing a letter to Sonja?" I ask.

Marcus plants his hand over the paper, but even the great width of his palm can't hide it. "Pardon?" he says innocently.

"You *are* writing to my sister!"

Even Dietan seems amused. His smile grows broad. "Romantic bastard," he says with the teasing tone that only comes with a decade or two of friendship.

"It's nothing, really," Marcus says. "I've just been thinking about her, and…" His eyes soften as he gazes into the fire. "Jared better make sure the girls and all of Evandale are safe."

"He will," Dietan says, his chin wrinkling when he frowns. "If there's anyone I trust with my life, after you, it's him."

"Thank goodness for that," I say, offering a silent prayer to the goddess.

A moment later, Marcus groans. "This is a disaster! I'm not a poet." He holds the paper at arm's length, as if distance will improve it. "It sounds like a field report."

I laugh, which makes Marcus smile, despite his frustration.

"Would you like me to help you?" I ask. "Write the letter?"

"Really?" He looks up at me hopefully.

"If I know my sister, a letter coming from you would make her year."

Marcus passes me the letter. I try not to laugh; it does sound like a report. It's an oddly clinical itinerary of his day.

"It's awful," he says, seeing the look on my face.

"No, it's not that bad!" I say, lying through my teeth. Dietan laughs into his hands, and I shush him.

"Marcus is much better at expressing how much he likes someone *without* words," Dietan says, waggling his eyebrows.

Men. I press my lips into a thin line. "Not a detail I needed to know."

Now they're both laughing at me, and I laugh, too, more comfortable around them than ever. Since the journey began, I've felt like a fraud, like I don't belong here. But in this moment, we're all friends.

Marcus holds out his hand, and I give the letter back. He crumples it up defeatedly and tosses it into the fire. I realize there's a smoldering pile of letters at the bottom of the pit. He's been at this for some time.

"Let's start over," I tell him. "If it feels awkward talking about yourself, talk about her."

"What would I say?"

"She likes to dance, so maybe write about how you would want to dance with her the next time you see her, and how you want to see her smile, and how you want to take her in your arms… How you dream of the rhythm of her heart like a song. Does that help?"

Marcus nods. "Okay, I can do that. Thank you. It's still harder than letters to the families of the fallen, and that's saying something." He starts scribbling on a fresh sheet of paper.

When I smile encouragingly at the general, I notice Dietan watching me over the flames. His lips curl up when I meet his bemused gaze. I abruptly look away, suddenly feeling like the fire is too close to my face. I don't know what to think when he looks at me like that. I try to imagine him writing a letter like that to me, and I can't.

"Sewing, cooking, and now poetry… Is there nothing you can't do?" Dietan asks.

I don't glance back at him, especially since I can hear the smirk in his voice. I stoke the fire again. "One thing I'm not good at is putting up with people who annoy me, actually."

"Well then, I've met my match," he says.

"You're putting up with me, are you?"

"Same as you are with me. And we're not good at it, are we? Putting up with each other?"

I glare at him, but he only smiles wider. Why do I find him so annoying… so annoyingly attractive? *I know where this leads*, I tell myself, *and I'm not going there.*

With a great rush of air between his teeth, Marcus hides his laugh behind his ledger, like he knows something we don't.

"Don't worry, Aren, I *am* enjoying your company," Dietan says.

Unable to come up with a suitably snarky retort, I bid them both goodnight.

Some things never change. The man is still a liar.

CHAPTER TWENTY

Aren

We arrive at last in Fawnsreach, a town two days' journey from the very southern border of Alarice. The bridge between the kingdoms means the large town is only a day's journey from Loegria. It's a popular destination for travelers and merchants offloading their wares and resupplying their packs. The buildings, painted in bright blue and red, encircle a well-worn market square where the crier announces the royal entourage's arrival, his voice carrying over the busy chatter of the crowd and the calls of the merchants hawking fresh fish from the day's catch.

The air smells different here, salty from the sea, and cold. I've never seen the ocean, but even that novelty leaves me feeling bitterly homesick. My new coat keeps me warm enough, but it doesn't stamp out the ache deep inside. Lately I've seen the inside of a carriage more than I've seen the world.

I didn't know that pretending to be in love with the prince and watching him pretend to be in love with me would make me feel even lonelier. I didn't know how hard it would be to live a lie.

RINGS OF FATE

Is it a lie, though? I turn Marcus's words over and over in my head. *He's not like this with any woman. I can also tell when he's truly happy.*

The prince, happy with me? I'm not sure what to think.

We settle into yet another inn, and after a cold meal of cheese and bread, I go up to the room I'll share with Lydia. This time tomorrow, we'll be in Loegria. Before these few weeks, I'd never even traveled beyond Evandale, and now I'm going to see a whole different kingdom. *Dietan's* kingdom. I'm nervous. It's one thing for the villages all around Alarice to welcome me as their future princess; it's another to pretend to be a princess in his actual kingdom. Loegria is rich and cosmopolitan. Surely, the court will not be pleased he's chosen a lowly barmaid.

Midnight. I can't sleep, with my thoughts all jumbled up, so I decide to take a walk. With an early start scheduled for the morning, it might be my only chance to see the town and feel the ocean breeze on my face, even if only in the dark.

Under Marcus's orders, the guards have been especially vigilant of late, accompanying me and Dietan absolutely everywhere, so I swap my fancy coat for Lydia's plain wool one. I move carefully so I don't wake her, shifting my weight without disturbing the mattress just as I did when my sisters were little and slept on either side of me. I turn the doorknob carefully and put on my shoes only once I'm outside the room. There's a guard at the end of the hallway, and his partner is probably at the bottom of the stairs, so I head in the other direction, down the hidden service stairs that lead directly to the kitchen.

It's the first time I've been alone since I first agreed to accompany Dietan on this journey, and the solitude is a welcome balm. With my hood up, I look just like any other traveler passing through. I don't have to worry about being recognized because the streets are mostly empty. I wander through the buildings, the glow and laughter from nearby taverns pouring out onto the streets—like evenings at the Beak. As I crisscross my way through town, I don't see a single other soul except for a lone cat that comes trotting out of the darkness to weave between my legs. I scratch it behind the ears before it bounds away. As I arrive at the sandy dunes of the shore, the cold sea breeze hits my face, invigorating me. The night is calm, and without the moon, only a curtain of stars overhead reflects off the dark water. When the sunrise begins to peak above the blue horizon, I return to the inn before anyone notices I'm gone.

I slip off my shoes before entering the room. But I pause as I step through the doorway, my hand on the doorknob. There's a chill in the air that wasn't there before. The room is dark, but it feels different from when I left. There's a sound from the window—the curtain, rustling in the breeze—while the rest of the room is eerily still, setting me on edge.

Something's wrong.

I run to light a candle and gasp at the scene.

The bed is empty; sheets and blankets pool on the floor. A picture frame on the wall has been knocked askew, its glass broken. A chair lies on its side, one of its legs broken. My coat lies rumpled on the floor. The curtain is half-torn from its hooks, billowing like a ghost in the open window.

I run over to Dietan's adjoining room and don't bother knocking. I fling the door open—his bed is empty as well.

Oh dear goddess. Ice-cold dread washes over me. I bound down the stairs of the inn, shouting. One by one, Dietan's men poke their heads out from the other rooms, confused but alert. When I make it to the tavern on the ground floor of the inn, Marcus is there, sword already in hand.

"Aren, what's wrong?" Marcus asks.

"Where's Dietan?" I cry, fearing the worst. *Did the Kilandrar get him?* I can already see his pale, lifeless face frozen in a scream, blue lips that will never feel warm again. A shudder racks me, terror tightening in my chest like a vice. My breaths are coming too fast, too shallow, as if the air itself is turning to stone in my lungs.

From behind comes a familiar baritone. "I'm here! Aren?"

At the sound of his voice, a wave of relief crashes over me. My chest heaves as the crushing weight of fear lifts, leaving me lightheaded with the sheer, desperate gratitude that he's here—that he's alive.

Dietan comes through the front doors of the inn, having just been from outside. He is unhurt but tired. He likely didn't go to bed at all, either.

I run toward him before my mind can tell me to stop. I throw my arms around him in a wave of relief. He stiffens, surprised, but then his body begins to melt into mine as he wraps his arms around me in return. He releases me and braces his hands on the outside of my arms, studying me with intense worry.

His face is tight, concern pinching his features. "What's the matter? You're shaking."

My relief is short-lived when I remember why I ran downstairs in the first place. "Lydia. She's gone! She's—"

Dietan doesn't wait for me to finish. He pushes past the crowd drawn by my screams and bounds up the stairs to see for himself. I run after him as Marcus starts yelling orders to his men.

Inside the room, Dietan grows preternaturally still. His eyes are focused, narrowed to slits as he takes in the scene. He barely moves a muscle, save for the ridgeline of his jaw.

Marcus arrives shortly on our heels. "We've secured the perimeter but…" The general looks into the room and curses. "You're sure she was here?"

"Yes, when I left her, she was right there." I point to the now-empty bed and the pile of sheets on the floor.

"You left the room?" Dietan asks, rounding toward me, suddenly very angry. "On your own? Without telling anyone?"

"I wanted to take a walk—" I don't finish my sentence because Dietan starts shouting over me.

"Promise me you'll never do that again! Not without me or one of the guards!" he yells, his face turning red.

"Dietan, I'm all right," I say, instinctively putting a hand on his arm to calm him. It's the first time I've called him by his first name. The first time I call him by his name rather than "your worship" or "my lord."

He takes a deep breath. His emotion subsides as he stares at me intently. "But you could have been hurt."

"I'm perfectly fine."

He nods, looking relieved, then turns to Marcus. "Is it the Kilandrar?"

"No…" Marcus kneels down, inspecting a scuff mark on the windowsill. He traces the outline of a boot. He then notices a small amount of blood on floor below the window that looks like it was deliberately used to draw a symbol—a line with three triangles under it. Maybe Lydia was trying to tell us something. "This is the work of men," Marcus concludes.

My mind races. Someone snuck in through the window? I'm scrambling for answers. "Why would someone kidnap Lydia?"

"She's no ordinary bridal attendant." Marcus's expression is grave. He and Dietan exchange a look I can't interpret, then Dietan nods and he continues. "She's your body double. Every member of the royal family has one for their protection." He shoots a dark look at Dietan. "Some are too foolhardy to use them."

"You know why I can't," Dietan says.

I suspect I know why, too. His secret is too great to let anyone get that close.

My skin pricks with gooseflesh. *A body double.* I should have suspected there was another reason for Lydia's solicitousness. I bought the explanation of a bridal attendant too easily, caught up in my own lie about being engaged to Dietan. Lydia was not just a lady's maid; she was my shadow. Whenever I wasn't with Dietan, she hardly left my side for a moment. And now she's missing.

"You're saying that someone was trying to kidnap *me*? But why?" *Oh, right.* It's because I'm supposedly going to be a princess. Someone of worth. Someone to ransom or take hostage.

Marcus exchanges a glance with Dietan, who looks distressed, pale, and weary.

"What are we doing? We've got to find her," I say. It's infuriating that they're all just standing there. "They can't have gone too far!"

"We'll send a team to find her," Marcus says. "But for now, we must get you and Dietan as far away from this place as possible."

I hate that he makes sense, that he must put the prince's safety above all else. "We can't just leave her," I insist, but I'm swimming against the current.

Dietan turns to me, anguished. "I didn't want to frighten you. But we had to take certain precautions. We've had word that the Usurper's agents—and not only the Kilandrar—have been more active lately."

"But we can't just leave. This isn't fair—they wanted me, not her."

"Lydia's a brave girl. She knew what she was signing up for," Marcus says grimly. "She is a trained warrior, not just a lady's maid. All royal body doubles are. If it hadn't been her, it would have been *you*."

I feel numb all over, even as Dietan puts a comforting arm around my shoulders. "Don't blame yourself," he says sincerely.

But I do blame myself. If only I hadn't left the room. Maybe the two of us together could have fended off the kidnappers. Lydia might be dead now, and it's all my fault.

CHAPTER TWENTY-ONE

Dietan

I'm glad for the distraction of having to pack quickly. I clench my jaw and hope Lydia was able to fight them off. She didn't deserve this. I say a prayer for her safe return, even though I know it's unlikely. She's either dead or had to avail herself of the hemlock all royal guards carry in case the worst should happen. Aren mentioned that there were less painful options when I informed her of this policy, but Marcus prioritizes speed and efficacy over comfort. Maybe Aren and I will implement some changes when this is all over.

But of course, there is no Aren and I once this is over. Again, I have to remind myself that this is purely a business deal.

Marcus sent two of his best soldiers to look for Lydia, but the rest of the company must be on our way. Getting Aren away from danger as fast as we can is priority. We make quick work of stuffing our sundries and supplies into satchels and sling them onto the carriage. As dawn breaks, we water the horses and load our gear. By the time the sun creeps above the distant hills, our royal caravan is back on the road.

Instead of traveling as a pack as we have done so far, Marcus has set up a perimeter around our convoy. A handful of men scout ahead and few guards bring up the rear to alert us to any signs of trouble.

I climb into the carriage and take a seat across from Aren, who's turned toward the window, her pale face contrasting with the glow of the morning light. She's staring at the landscape, but it's clear her thoughts are elsewhere. Her eyes, reflected in the glass, are glazed, her stare a thousand miles away.

Of course, she blames herself for Lydia's kidnapping. No matter how many times I assure her it wasn't her fault—that she could be dead if she were in Lydia's place—it doesn't help. I'm grateful Aren snuck out and wasn't asleep in her bed last night. The thought of something happening to her—I don't think I could bear it.

I can't keep doing this.

Marcus is worried that whoever did this will soon figure out they've captured the wrong person and return to finish the job. Not to mention the Kilandrar are still prowling the land, hunting for me.

I take in Aren's thick, wavy black hair, the gentle slope of her cheek in profile, her slender fingers propping up her chin. I lean over and clear my throat.

She looks up, tears in her eyes.

"Look, I've made a decision," I say. "This situation has become too dangerous for you. I can't let you continue to do this. It was selfish and stupid of me," I tell her, feeling awful. I'm the worst sort of heel. Why did I ever allow her to come with me in the first place?

Aren stares at me in a daze.

"What I'm trying to say is… You can't stay with me. You need to go, for your own safety." I see now that my plan was utter madness from the beginning but I feel compelled to explain myself.

"With war on the horizon, I'd forgotten that I have more enemies than merely the Usurper and the Kilandrar. I know from years of briefings that, in addition to those who would take royals hostage for ransom, there are also those who would like to see the treaty between Alarice and Loegria collapse, who do not want to accept me as my grandfather's heir and their future king. My cousin, the Duke of Lancaster for one, and my own granduncle, Prince Namreth, to name another.

"Namreth has been sending assassins to murder me since I was named heir to the throne instead of him.

"Really, I come from a lovely family. So many relatives who want to see me dead.

"But Namreth is one of the staunchest traditionalists when it comes to male-line inheritance, primarily because it benefits himself. He's gone missing since his banishment, his last known whereabouts somewhere in Penrith, but there the trail goes cold though my father's spies keep trying to find him in order to fend off his troublemaking."

I shake my head, trying not to picture what would happen if the kidnappers are successful in capturing Aren. They're no real threat to my riches or my birthright, but they can hurt me. They can take away the one thing that supposedly matters the most to me: my beautiful, innocent bride. Dear gods, what have I done? What was I thinking? Why did I put a target on her back?

"You're sending me away?" she asks incredulously. "After all this? What about your…problem?"

"I'll figure it out, but you have to go," I say, feeling utterly wretched. My mother is right, after all; I'm a coward and a fool.

"You don't want me here, do you? I'm just dead weight. I can swing a frying pan, but I'm no warrior, no Lydia."

I shake my head vehemently. "No…this is just too much to ask of anyone. Of you. I should have found another way. I should never have let you leave Evandale with me."

"Well, it's too late. I'm here, and I'm not going anywhere," she says, sitting ramrod straight, her eyes flashing with annoyance.

My words were meant to comfort her, but instead, I've upset her.

"Tell the truth. You can't abide my company, I've cost you a valuable warrior, and you're trying to get rid of me so no one else in your entourage dies protecting me," she accuses.

"No, that's not it at all! It's just too dangerous." Trying to get rid of her? I'm trying to save her life. Why can't she see that?

Her eyes narrow as she says, "You knew it would be dangerous when you asked me. And we fought the Kilandrar together, remember? I know it's dangerous."

"But it's even more dangerous than our intelligence reports predicted," I say, more and more desperate to make her understand.

"Too bad. I'm not going anywhere. I have people I need to protect from the Usurper, too."

I exhale in annoyance, reluctantly impressed by her spirit. "Please don't make this harder than it already is."

"I'm not leaving. End of discussion." She huffs and folds her arms across her chest.

I tear my eyes away and resolve not to press the issue for now. But doesn't she want to live to attend her sister's wedding? Why won't she listen to reason?

I wish I knew how to make her feel better, even if I can't make her understand why she must go home. A man of worth should be able to muster the courage to reach out and hold her hand. I want to touch her simply so she won't feel so alone, so abandoned. But my hands remain firmly wedged under my armpits. I've grown used to holding Aren in public, but it's always been a staged performance…

That embrace at the inn earlier, though. That wasn't for show.

Regardless of the performance we put on for the world, the truth is that we're business partners, not intimate ones. To touch her now, in the privacy of the carriage, would feel like overstepping.

I could ask if she wants to be comforted, but I'm not sure I want to hear her reply. What if she says no? The rejection alone would make the rest of the carriage ride unbearable. She's already made it clear she thinks I'm nothing more than an arrogant oaf on the best of days, despite this morning's display of concern.

So, I keep my hands where they are.

She doesn't say a word.

Her silence is slowly driving me mad. I want to lift her spirits, distract her, maybe make a terrible joke that she can roll her eyes at. I can't think of a joke that feels right for the moment.

The landscape rolls past, the air heavy with tension. When I can't bear it anymore, I cross the carriage and take a seat beside her. We don't touch. I just want to show her that I'm here.

She glances at me briefly, and to my relief, she doesn't move. She resumes staring out the window. I gaze up toward the ceiling, searching for the right words. I know I'm not good at comforting others.

"You're beating yourself up about this," I say.

"It's my fault, isn't it? For sneaking out?"

For a moment, this strong, stubborn woman sounds so uncharacteristically childlike that I have to suppress a completely inappropriate smile. "It's not. Trust me, I would know. People have been trying to assassinate me for as long as I can remember. Blaming yourself for the collateral damage is never the answer."

She remains unmoved, except for the fist in her lap, which tightens around the hem of the lovely coat I had made for her.

"I'm not like you," she says, her voice hoarse. "I'm not really a princess. I don't want to be the reason people get hurt."

Her words sting. I didn't ask for this life. But then, she didn't, either. She's not used to it like I am. The pressure, the expectation, the attention—good and bad.

"I agree. To tell you the truth, I've always hated the job," I say. It's such a relief to admit it aloud.

How much better to be like my fourth cousin once removed, a contented baronet in the countryside, whose only responsibilities are his sheep and keeping his wife and children happy—probably in that order. He was even allowed to choose his own bride: no treaties to consider, no kingdoms to unify.

More than ever, I'm glad I chose Aren. She's been unflagging through this whole thing.

But I must let her go. It's the only way to keep her safe.

She scoffs. "No way."

"It's true," I add. "Being a prince is a burden."

"Liar," she says, but at least there's a ghost of a smile on her face. "You? Give up your valet and your fancy clothes? Please."

I frown. I can't tell if she's teasing. Is that all she thinks of me? I'd hoped I'd risen a little in her estimation. I forge on anyway. "I know you don't believe me, but it's true. I'd give it all up so I don't have to live with the fact that there are so many people in the world who could die because of me or want me dead. And they haven't even gotten to know me first."

"You think getting to know you first would stop someone from wanting to kill you?" she asks with a straight face.

I hesitate to reply, and then Aren snort-laughs. "I was kidding." She chuckles.

I laugh, too, relieved it's a joke—relieved she's in good enough spirits to make jokes at my expense. I feel a sliver of accomplishment. "You have a point there."

But the moment of levity ends, and I gesture around us—at the carriage, at myself. "Being a prince means people want to hurt me and anyone I love." I wince at my choice of words. I don't *love* her, right? I forge on. "That's just how it goes. I've come to terms with it because I can't change who I am."

She looks at me, her eyes glassy again. My stomach clenches when I see the pain there, and I look away. "It never gets easier," I say, "knowing that people can get hurt simply by being around me, simply because it's their job to protect me. It never feels fair, and nothing I ever do can repay them for it."

She sheds a solitary tear. I pretend I don't notice and squirm in my seat, my mouth suddenly dry.

It's a great comfort to share my heartbreak and guilt, but I can't bear to talk about it further nor add to her distress. I want to share everything with her, but I can't.

"I'm telling you, from firsthand experience, that you're allowed to mourn—but you're also allowed to live."

My words hang in the air between us, our bodies swaying in tandem with the movement of the carriage.

For a long while, Aren doesn't say anything, and I don't expect her to. She gazes back out the window at the rolling fields. I don't know if what I've said helped, but I hope I've invited her inside, into my confidence. It's been too long since I've been honest with anyone, even myself. Just talking about it feels like a weight's been lifted from my chest.

As the hours pass, to my surprise Aren leans against me and rests her head on my shoulder. She's warm and soft, and I dare not move. I hardly take a breath as she settles against me and eventually falls asleep, her breathing softening around the edges. She's exhausted. We're both exhausted, but I don't sleep.

Her hair smells like orange blossoms, and I'm reminded of that first time I tried to kiss her, that day in Elspeth, the first time I touched her skin, and it makes me smile because it's a good memory.

Aren sleeps for most of the journey, her head heavy on my shoulder. Only when the carriage slows does she stir. She blinks her eyes open, stretches, and yawns as she wakes. I haven't moved for hours. My shoulder aches a little, so I wriggle it softly to relieve the tenderness in the muscles. Aren looks around, as if confused about where she is, before glancing out the window again.

Outside, travelers pass by the carriage, walking in the opposite direction. They are hunched over, weighed down by heavy bags; many pull carts behind them or lead horses on foot. Most look to be refugees from Penrith. Many have fled since the Usurper took charge, threatening to overwhelm the resettlement program my grandfather's administrators set up.

"Are we almost to the bridge to Loegria?" she asks, turning her head to look at the people walking by.

"I think so." I roll my shoulder. The scent of her still lingers on my shirt, and I like it. It feels like I'm not alone.

The road grows increasingly crowded, and the carriage slows to a crawl in the traffic. Some curious eyes turn our way, but most people keep their heads down, uninterested in the royal carriage and entourage. Something more than the usual snarl of traffic is going on. I reflexively bring my hand to the knife I always carry sheathed at my hip.

We finally arrive at North Dunston, the Alarician outpost closest to the Loegrian border. The city sprang up generations ago at the foot of the bridge connecting the two kingdoms. Its grandeur is a welcome distraction that catches Aren's attention. She peers out the window at the vast cityscape before us. As we crest a hill, I signal for the carriage to stop before we descend the gentle slope into the city, so Aren can take in the view.

She leans halfway out the carriage window, her eyes wide with wonder. A grin spreads across her face. I'm glad to see her smiling again.

North Dunston looks as if it has grown out of the ground itself, towers jutting into the bright blue sky like gray blades of grass. Wind cuts through the city; colorful flags flutter in the breeze. The cold air pricks my skin.

The city started as a tiny outpost for travelers passing between the two kingdoms. It quickly expanded as the years passed. Lean-tos and dirt roads gave way to buildings of brick and cobblestone streets. North Dunston became a real city, with all the latest modern marvels from the capital.

Outside the carriage, an Alarician soldier shouts, "Bridge delays expected due to closure. Unnecessary travel is discouraged."

Tell us something we don't know.

To call it a bridge would be like calling a log a toothpick. The word doesn't capture the enormity of the massive thoroughfare justice. The Bandai Bridge spans across a vast, empty canyon between the two continents and is as wide as the metropolis at its feet. The bridge is a relic of the first epoch, a structure made of stone and magic, a testament to the sorceress Skiron's power. She controlled the winds, bending the earth to her will. It was her vast power that Boreas the Unbeliever studied and inherited.

Traffic jams are common on the bridge, but I've never seen such crowds. There are twice as many people as when we passed through at the start of my bridal search. I open the other window as Marcus walks up, matching the carriage's slow pace.

"I don't like the look of this," Marcus says. "Some of the guards are hearing that changes to the refugee resettlement program are causing unrest. There's a pileup at the border as people scramble to get across before the new laws take effect. You know better than me, though. I'm not in those meetings."

I glance over at Aren, who looks away but is clearly listening with interest. "Some of my father's advisors have been urging greater caution, believing that the Usurper might have placed spies and saboteurs among true refugees. Before we left, the king was in favor of maintaining the current level of resettlement, albeit far from the border. I've not had news that he's changed his mind."

Marcus looks grim. "Some of the vendors on the road are reporting attacks on southern Loegrian villages. And there was an attack on the bridge itself not two days ago. Bandits raided and killed a couple of travelers. The whole city is on high alert until they can figure out what happened. If it's Penrith's doing, which seems likely, I'm not surprised by the change in policy."

If Penrith is already attacking Loegrian villages, then outright war is close at hand.

Marcus interrupts my thoughts with his usual common sense. "For now, let's get you and Aren into less recognizable clothing. There's nothing to be done about the carriage itself, but we're taking down the banner and throwing some plain cloth over the top."

RINGS OF FATE

My valet comes up to the window with a beat-up leather jacket and cap for me to wear. "Sit tight. Stay here with the men," Marcus says. "A few of us are just going to check out what's happening. We'll be back before sundown."

A ren looks a little sorrowful as she shrugs off the coat I had made for her and sets it on the seat between us. My valet hands her one of my leather coats. She dons it without complaint and tucks her hair up under a cap. She looks just like any other traveler making their way through the city. She doesn't look like a princess. If the kidnappers from Port Tyralis are still on our trail, they'll have a harder time picking her out of a crowd. She'll blend in with everyone else. But those striking eyes of hers would stand out anywhere.

It strikes me that I would know Aren in a crowd no matter what she's wearing. I'm attuned to her now in a way I've never been with a woman.

"You look good in my jacket," I say, feeling warm all over at the sight of her in my clothes. She looks tiny inside the large garment. I imagine removing it with my own hands and feel a hitch in my trousers.

Aren touches her cap, smiling. "You don't look so bad yourself, for a scruffy peasant." I can tell she's scared, making the best of a dangerous situation. On a whim, I take her hand and give it a squeeze.

She squeezes back and doesn't let go. Warmth runs within me.

"I'm sorry that this isn't quite the world tour you were hoping for," I say.

"We're farther from Evandale than I've ever been," she replies.

"With any luck, you'll make it all the way to Lundenwic."

She drops my hand as I realize what I've said. In the enclosed safety of the carriage, I got carried away for a moment and imagined her as a real princess in Lundenwic. I forgot she's just in this for adventure and gold and to help me save the kingdom. She doesn't actually want to marry me.

"There's no other path to Loegria, is there?" she asks, changing the subject.

"There isn't." The rocks in the canyon below are as sharp as razors, and the wind down there could shred skin from bone. That's why the bandits attacked the bridge. It's a lifeline between the two kingdoms.

This isn't just the work of thieves, which is what the local authorities continue to tell people to stave off panic. This reeks of Penrith plotting. The Usurper is cutting Alarice off from Loegria, dividing the two kingdoms as the first step of his conquest. "If we can't cross, we're trapped here, like everyone else," I say, balling my hands into fists.

"What do we do?" Aren asks.

"We find a way across that damn bridge."

CHAPTER TWENTY-TWO

Aren

Marcus tries to deter us from crossing the bridge. He wants us have more guards for protection, but Dietan refuses. That man is as stubborn as an ass, but I know he only has imminent war on his mind. We must have no time to waste.

Marcus has no choice but to follow Dietan's order. Together, they determine it will be safer to send the carriage and horses back to Evandale with some of the entourage while we walk across the bridge under the cover of night. Travelers on foot will surely attract less unwelcome attention than the target a royal cavalcade would create. Not to mention, in case there's trouble, the heavy caravan won't slow us down.

When the sundown bell rings, I throw my rucksack onto my back. I notice Dietan slips his signet ring into an inner pocket for safekeeping. We mustn't display anything worth stealing—or killing for.

I'm nervous, but I try my hardest not to show it. This is an adventure, and I'm going to treat it like one. I tuck my hair up under my cap and roll my sleeves up and walk toward the outskirts of the city with the party.

Marcus instructs his men to keep their weapons tucked into their waistbands and under their shirts, so the glint of metal won't be visible in the starlight. Dietan tucks his sword under his coat and sheathes his knife against the small of his back. My only weapon is my frying pan, which is nestled safely in my pack.

Even without the driver, valet, and aides, our party is larger than most here—ten in total. But we move quickly and quietly in the darkness.

"Let me take that," Dietan says, reaching over to hoist my pack off my back.

"Thank you, kind prince, but I'd rather keep it on me," I say as I pull it away from him.

"I hate when you call me that."

"I apologize, *Your Worship*," I tease.

He rolls my eyes. "I have a name, you know."

"Yeah, you keep reminding me."

But at least we're bantering again. It feels...right. I've been so upset with him. How can he leave Lydia out there to fend for herself? We should be out there looking for her. I know he says that my safety is his priority, but doesn't he care at all?

I knew the risks would be great when I agreed to this journey, but it feels even more dangerous now that we're tiptoeing across the Alarician border in the dark. There's still a large crowd jostling their way toward the bridge. If years at the Beak taught me anything, it's that desperation makes people do dangerous things.

My heart pounds as we march up to the city gates that lead out to the bridge. They aren't guarded, which feels wrong. A large wrought iron fence blocks the way. Signs hang askew over the gates, warning of the bridge closure, telling all who enter that they do so at their own risk. I follow Dietan, squeezing through one of the gaps in the fence. The others follow suit, and we step onto the bridge.

On Marcus's orders, no one speaks as we join the line of people shuffling out of the city. *Heads down, but stay alert*, the general warned.

I watch the stream of travelers move around us. As the lights from the city gates fade, the shadows on the bridge lengthen. I can't help but imagine Kilandrar everywhere, and fear settles in the pit of my stomach. Soon, there will only be darkness and the occasional flicker of torchlight thrown by the lanterns held aloft by fellow travelers. I urge my feet to keep moving.

RINGS OF FATE

The bridge is easily the largest thoroughfare I have ever encountered, yet claustrophobia is a heavy weight against my chest as the buildings on either side of the path loom three stories high, casting deep shadows onto our path. All of the windows are dark, the merchant stalls shuttered, and the only sound is the eerie howl of the wind.

The Bandai Bridge is legendary—a marvel of science and magic. But it now feels like a crowded artery of human suffering. We are swept up alongside desperate souls fleeing a war that a week ago, I barely knew existed.

My breathing becomes short and labored. I can feel Dietan walking a few paces behind me, and I desperately need his reassurance. Without thinking, I reach my hand back to touch his. His fingers ever so lightly grace mine, confirming he is, indeed, here for me.

We set a brisk pace, keeping to the periphery of the road as best we can to minimize our visibility. My heart gallops as I scan the bridge, studying every traveler and shadow. I listen for trouble, but all I hear is our own footsteps and the chatter of the crowd.

Minutes turn to hours. The crowd thins as a shadow looms in the road ahead. A toppled wooden cart sits upended in the path. It's surrounded by boxes and luggage as if it was hastily abandoned.

A voice in my head screams at me that this isn't what it seems.

I think it might be a deliberate roadblock—meant to slow us down and make us easy targets.

Most of the other travelers turn around when they see the overturned cart, making their way back to Alarice. The few who carry on give the cart a wide berth, as if it might come to life and attack them.

Marcus and his soldiers keep their eyes on the shadows, where bandits might hide within the barricade. We skirt the edges of the roadblock without incident.

Anxiety tastes like iron on the back of my tongue.

Or that could just be the fact that I'm gnawing nervously on my cheek.

"Halfway there," Marcus says, suddenly appearing at my side.

I jump. He moves as quietly as a cat.

"Stay alert," he adds.

"Do I look like I'm not?" I attempt a grin.

"It's my job to keep you on your toes. Keep an eye out."

I glance behind me at Dietan. He simply nods, reassuring me that everything will be all right. At least we've made it this far.

We pause for brief break. A few loaves of bread and waterskins are passed around. The things I would do for my kitchen and a hot meal right now.

None of us bother sitting. We huddle together on the side of the road, our bags secure between our feet as we stand in a tight circle.

Dietan breaks his loaf in half and hands a piece to me. I muster a smile and thank him.

"Here. Come see," he says, pointing to a gap in the buildings, where there's a narrow view of the canyon below us.

Dawn breaks over the canyon. In the night, it looked like a river of shadow, but in the brightening daybreak, the canyon is a muted ribbon of pink and gold. The rocks below gleam like starlight, their faces as sharp and beautiful as diamonds. The wind strikes the canyon at an angle and sends eerie music up the rock walls, like blowing on the lip of a bottle, like the world itself is singing.

The sunrise warms my face, and I can't help but let out a tiny gasp as I take in the view.

It's the most beautiful thing I have ever seen.

"Not bad for a death-defying journey," Dietan says, glancing at me with a soft smile that makes my heart skip a beat. The brilliant light of the sunrise reflects off of the prince's perfect features, illuminating him in an ethereal light. It's maddening how handsome this man is.

The wind blows a strand of my hair free from my cap and into my face. He reaches out to brush it away when a woman's voice cries out from ahead. "Pickpockets! My coin purse is gone!"

Instinctively, his hand goes to the small of his back where his knife rests, and disappointment washes over me.

"We shouldn't stay here any longer than we have to," Marcus says, striding over to us. "Get ready to move."

I steal one last look at the view. I'm transfixed by the combined beauty of the canyon and Dietan. I make myself a silent promise: when times are better, I'll come back here to see sunrise again. Possibly with Dietan by my side...

But then I remember that I mustn't feel hope where he is concerned. He's just pretending to care about me. That was the deal.

After several uninterrupted hours, something strikes me in the back of my shins.

It's a child's red ball.

Two floppy-haired boys in ragged clothes chase after it through the crowd. They laugh and weave between the travelers. Even here, with war looming, these kids have found a moment of joy—a chance to just be children.

Dietan picks up the ball and holds it out to the smallest boy, who laughs behind gapped teeth. I don't remember a time where I was ever that carefree.

"Thanks, sir," the boy says, running a quick lap around Dietan.

A flash of movement catches my eye—the boy's hand reaching for his dagger, slipping it from its sheath. But Dietan is too fast. He spins, quick as lightning, gripping the boy's wrist and retrieving the blade. "Good try."

"Don't know what you mean, sir." The boy sniffs.

"You'll need to be faster if you want to rob me." Dietan releases him, and the boy bolts.

"Slick," I say, genuinely impressed by his cat-like reflexes. "He had fast fingers. But you were faster."

"I'm not completely useless." He smiles back, tucking the dagger back into its sheath.

Marcus steps up beside us, glancing at our entourage. "I reckon that boy isn't the only thief around here."

Everything we own is strapped to our backs or slung over our shoulders.

The soldiers form a loose blockade around me and Dietan, with guards behind us pressed two deep. It'll be harder for thieves to target us if we move quickly. Marcus leads, parting the crowd with his elbows and his commanding presence.

The sun arcs across the sky. The massive bridge stretches endlessly into the mist.

The fog thickens, obscuring everything beyond the soldier in front of me. For an instant, I lose track of our party, and my heart begins to race. When the fog clears, they're right by my side, and relief washes over me.

We walk for another day as the sky turns purple once more. The crowds slow, choking the walkway. "People are setting up for the night," I observe. My feet hurt, and I am more tired than Shepard Belmis ever made me feel.

Indeed, travelers pitch tents in the road and throw tarps over carts to create shelter. As we weave through the masses, we find ourselves pressing up against the others who have given up for the night, claiming spots to camp.

"Should we stop?" Marcus asks. "Draw our men into a circle and fortify for the night?"

"No," Dietan says firmly. "Not yet. It's too crowded. There are too many eyes looking in our direction." He points out an emptier patch of the bridge far in the distance. I hope my legs don't give out before we get there.

Marcus issues orders, and the soldiers reluctantly keep moving.

As the sky deepens, makeshift shelters and sleeping bodies on the walkway slow us to a crawl. Only a sliver of the moon lights our way and more fog rolls in. We can barely see in front of our noses.

Rough-looking men linger at the edge of the road, watching travelers pass. I point them out to Marcus. "Spies?" I quietly ask. "Or lookouts?"

"Probably both," Marcus says. "Best to double our pace and move onward."

He signals to the soldiers to pick up speed, but it's nearly impossible.

The road is clogged with campfires, tents, and carts. We pick our way through groups of travelers huddled around their flames, their hoods pulled low. We tread carefully around others who are fast asleep.

We're making our way through a dense cluster of encampments when several travelers suddenly rise to their feet.

"I'm so sorry to have disturbed—" I begin, but then I see a flash of metal.

These men are armed.

It's an ambush.

CHAPTER TWENTY-THREE

Dietan

The ragged men draw knives from cloaks, streaks of silver glistening in the faint moonlight. Before our soldiers can even drop their packs and arm themselves, they rush toward us.

One of the bandits forces his way between Aren and me. He grabs Aren's pack, dragging it from her shoulders. She screams, but his grip is too strong. He pulls her away with it.

My heart lurches. I lunge, chasing after them, my sword drawn. My own pack has already been stolen. "Aren, let them have it!" I yell, but she shakes her head and holds on to her rucksack even as she's dragged backward, her heels skidding against the bridge.

Stubborn woman! Let go!

I curse the gods as I run after her.

The bridge erupts into chaos. Surrounded, Marcus shouts orders. Blades clash as my soldiers battle the bandits. One of the thieves blocks my path, so I knock him in the face with the pommel of my sword. I sprint after Aren, my heart thumping.

I find her struggling to keep hold of her rucksack. She fights the thieves tugging at it. "Aren, give them the damn bag!" I call, slicing my way toward her. I reluctantly admire her courage but wish she'd relent before they hurt her.

A blade kisses my shoulder, drawing blood. I whirl, my sword raised. Instantly, it clashes against my attacker's blade. I push against him with all my strength, forcing him backward until he stumbles and falls. Leaping over him, I chase after Aren, who's being hauled backward to the edge of the bridge.

The thieves struggle against her stubborn will. The only thing that separates them from the limitless depths of the canyon is a low wall. One misplaced foot, one push, and she's gone. But she's too far—I'll never reach her in time. I can't think. I can barely breathe. Then I remember I'm not alone.

"Marcus! Aren's at the ridge!" I shout. A nearby soldier hears me and runs toward her. Amid the chaos, I realize my company is winning. Our attackers may have the numbers, but they are no match for my seasoned knights who've spent their lives with a blades in hand.

"No you don't!" Aren cries. She's freed her skillet from her bag and is swinging it wildly at the thieves. Teetering at the edge, she manages to fend one off. Another ducks under her arm and yanks the strap of her rucksack from her shoulder.

As the strap slips, Aren grabs the pack before it hits the ground. The thief shoves her closer to the edge, trying to wrench the bag from her grip. One more push and she'll fall.

My heart races at the thought of Aren falling. I hack through my opponents with a fury unbound. I push forward, redoubling my efforts, but I can see I won't make it in time. Neither will the soldier rushing to help her.

Dear gods. I'm going to lose her.

Something rises deep within me. Every nerve tingles as the Whisting comes alive. The power inside my soul surges outward, a force I can neither control nor stop.

Like a bullwhip, it cracks across the bridge, upending carts and sending plumes of dust into the sky. The storm lashes the thief grappling with Aren, wrapping around his torso and flinging him over the edge of the bridge. The man vanishes into the mist below, his screams echoing in the dark, then fading into nothing.

Aren stumbles forward onto the walkway. She collapses to her knees, clutching her skillet in one hand and her rucksack in the other. But the soldier who ran toward her isn't so lucky. He's still caught in the Whisting's storm, limbs flailing like he's a spinning top. His sword wedges into the parapet. His body twists at an unnatural angle. His arm snaps, and he screams in agony. Before the Whisting finally slams back into me, the storm has his feet dangling over the edge of the wall.

I run to him, grabbing his uninjured arm and hauling him back from the ledge. A second pair of hands latches onto him. It's Aren, seemingly unharmed except for a dash of blood on her brow.

Relief floods through me, my knees threatening to collapse, but there's no time to rest. Together, we pull the man to safety, leaning him against the low wall. His arm is mangled, his breastplate badly dented.

"What was that, Your Highness?" he asks.

"Looks like a strong wind whipped up," I say, guilt weighing heavily on my chest. I caused his injuries. "How bad is it?" This is not how I wanted to send him back to his family.

"Probably broke a rib or two. Definitely his arm," Aren says.

"I'll be back to form once I find a healer. Don't worry about me, sir," he says through gritted teeth

"And you?" I ask Aren, noticing she's still gripping the frying pan.

"I'm all right," she says quietly. She glances over the edge at the void below. "Thanks for saving me." She pauses. "I guess I should have let go of the bag."

I'm about to agree when my knees buckle. Aren catches me before I collapse. "It's the Whisting," I explain quietly, my head spinning. "Takes a lot out of me."

Marcus and the rest of the company arrive.

"Strange how that gale came out of nowhere, sir," a soldier comments. "Fortunate, though."

"Fortunate indeed, probably just the unpredictable winds from the canyon," I say, sharing a knowing look with Aren.

"They won't pull that trick again anytime soon," Marcus says. "But it cost us. Most of the thieves were easily vanquished. But the rest vanished, taking all our provisions with them."

"It cost us more than that," Aren says, looking at the soldier's broken arm.

She kneels beside me. She doesn't think twice when she starts to massage my aching shoulder with one hand, her touch strong yet comforting. She steadies my head with her other hand, and a shiver runs down my spine. I need to escape her touch or I fear this business arrangement will never work.

"It's all right. We don't need supplies," I say, rising to my feet. I point at the path ahead. "Look. We're almost to Loegria. We're nearly home."

CHAPTER TWENTY-FOUR

Dietan

Crossing the bridge is a small victory.

It'll be more difficult for my enemies to follow us past the more heavily fortified Loegrian border. The more distance I put between Aren and her attackers, the better.

The Loegrian guards at the gate watch as we approach, naturally curious to see what brave or foolish souls have dared undertake the journey. As word of its danger has spread, only a handful of people have made it this far across the bridge. But I feel far from a homecoming hero.

I'm troubled by how easily I was able to call the Whisting—and how I was so close to hurting Aren. The Whisting killed that bandit with ease. My soul is hollow with fear. The sooner I remove the Rings, the better off everyone will be.

South Dunston lies before us. The city is flanked by gentle hills covered in lush trees and moss-covered stones. Its sprawl winds like a river through the mountains, carving itself to match the flow of the valleys. Pulleys powered by horses and oxen stretch like spiderwebs across the cityscape, carrying trolleys and carts high above the roofs of buildings. Shadows from these contraptions move across the streets like giant clouds.

I hope Aren finds the city beautiful. I'm too exhausted to appreciate it right now.

Guards stop us at the gate. "Papers," the one closest says, holding out his hand in a carelessly imperious gesture.

"Watch your tone," Marcus snaps, his temper worn thin by the long night. "This is the Loegrian royal caravan."

Nonetheless, he gestures toward one of our aides, who clumsily shuffles through papers, trying to find something with the royal seal.

"Royal caravan, is it? Where's the prince's carriage, then? The banners, the horses?" the guard says, unsmiling. "Papers."

Marcus looks ready to punch the guy, but I stop him with a shake of my head. I doff my cap, and the guards' eyes widen. I look remarkably like my father did thirty years ago, and they've never updated his likeness on the coinage.

"Your Highness," he stammers, bowing low. Others nearby overhear and quickly follow suit. I remember my task and extend my hand to Aren. She takes it, confusion written across her face.

"May I present Loegria's future queen, Aren of Alarice," I say, raising her hand for the crowd.

Aren stands up straighter, plastering on a gracious smile, and waves shyly at my subjects. If I hadn't endured the same ordeal, I wouldn't be able to tell how tired she was.

Their response is muted, half-hearted applause and weary murmurs instead of cheers.

I don't blame them.

"If you would be so kind as to show us to the nearest inn—"

"Of course, sire. Please forgive us, sire, but His Majesty, your father, was the one who ordered us not to let anyone in without proper traveling papers, sire," says the now-apologetic guard.

"Understood," I say, as the rest of the guards leap to action. They guide us into the city, apologizing profusely for their lack of preparedness and insisting we'll be given the best rooms in South Dunston. Aren thanks them on behalf of our whole party. I'm proud of how far she's come. She may be a natural princess, after all.

Gasps and murmurs follow us through the streets. I smile and greet my people as best I can, but exhaustion blurs the edges of my vision.

The guards bring us to a large inn, and I stop the overeager cohort before they leave. "If you'd be so kind, we'll need some horses, supplies, and anything you can spare for our journey south."

"Of course, Your Highness," says the captain. "Though supplies are running low, we'll do our best to accommodate."

It's as I feared. The brewing hostility is already consuming resources.

"Whatever you can spare," I say. "We must make it to the Oracle of Alba as soon as we can."

The words feel hollow on my lips. Despite the reassurance any mention of the Oracle seems to give my people, I wonder if it's worth continuing this lie about a wedding when the shadow of war is already upon us.

Once the captain and his men have left, we can't make it to our rooms fast enough. Aren's smile gives way to weariness. She barely says anything as she sees herself to her room. Marcus refuses to rest until he's established a security perimeter. Everyone needs a fresh start.

Tomorrow can't come soon enough.

Despite the ache seeping into my bones, I can't fall asleep. Instead, I sit at the window, staring out across the city—south, toward Estyrion and the Great Waste. The darkening sky that looms on the horizon is like a great shroud shadowing the land.

We're on the road before anyone has truly gotten a good night's rest. We set out with a horse, a simple wooden carriage, and humble supplies. Breakfast was sparse, though the innkeepers assured us that the next village on the road south would have more provisions. South Dunston has been overwhelmed too quickly by refugees from Penrith to feed everyone.

I don't complain, though my stomach does.

I march for hours behind the cart with my men, letting Aren sleep in the back of the open carriage, curled under a pile of blankets. We can't overburden our only horse.

The rhythmic impact of my boots on the dirt road sends occasional shooting pains up my spine. I'm still sore from the battle with the Kilandrar as well as the bandits on the bridge. But I can't stop. The faster we reach the Great Waste, the faster I can put an end to this misery.

Marcus walks beside me, scowling. He's giving me the silent treatment, his head held high and shoulders back. I hate awkward silences, especially from one of my oldest friends.

"I know it was foolish of us to cross when we did," I say. "You can be angry with me. That's fine."

"I'm not angry," Marcus replies, his voice icy. "You gave an order, and we saw it through."

I sigh, pushing my hair from my forehead. "You know I had to. I hoped you, of all people, would understand. We couldn't afford to linger."

"I'm well aware that leadership means making difficult decisions, but I also hoped you'd have some common sense when it comes to your own safety. I promised your father I'd bring you back alive. Although your mother favors the Princess Royal, she's no Namreth. Your sister would much rather have a life of horses and balls than the weight of the crown someday."

His sensibility and knack for calling out my flaws rivals Aren's. "I know, I'm an idiot."

"Far be it from me to question orders," Marcus says, "but you know what I think of this whole charade. A mission to the Great Waste is a death wish, no matter what your father says. And you're marching your new fiancée straight into it." His eyes remain fixed on the horizon, but his words carry a twinge of pain.

He's probably picturing how devastated Sonja would be if harm came to Aren.

I swallow the lump in my throat. "You've seen the torture my father's surgeons and councilors put me through trying to fix this, without any success. This is the only way."

"I saw what you did on the bridge," he says. "Perhaps you need practice, rather than"—he waves a hand at the cart—"all this. We're men now, not boys in our fathers' shadows anymore."

I wish I had half his confidence. Marcus is already a fine general at our age, already a veteran and a leader, not a fuckup like me. When the Usurper attacks, my father needs to be the one wielding the Rings, not me. Even though he's never used them, since he's never had reason to, until now. The skirmishes and battles we've had in the past against ruffians and local warlords have been easily won by our armies alone.

I keep my eyes on Aren's sleeping form in the cart ahead of us. Focusing on her helps ease the tightness in my back.

Marcus sighs. "Fine, I may not know anything about magic, but I'll tell you what you should do as your general. Return to Lundenwic posthaste. The king needs you. There's no safer place for you and Aren."

I shake my head, noticing that the men are starting to look our way. They can't hear us, but they can tell we're at odds. They assume it's regarding our next stop—so I speak up loud enough for them to hear. "Court is a fortnight's journey. No. We will proceed to Alba for the Oracle's blessing, as planned."

The men nod and resume their low chatter among themselves. Marcus, however, stiffens. "There's something you're not telling me."

He knows me too well.

The gulf between us widens, and I struggle with how much to reveal. "You're right. I'm hiding something," I admit. "I plan to go to Estyrion, to the Great Waste, *alone*. But I need you to make sure Aren gets to safety. Take her where she wants to go—back to Evandale or to court."

Marcus rounds on me. "Alone? That was never the plan. Are you so eager to jump feet-first into the Abyss to meet your ancestors?"

I close my eyes. "I need to do this alone. You just have to stop asking questions."

"Fallen Estyrion is cursed. You can't face that madman, that King of the Waste, by yourself!"

Fear holds my tongue. I've seen Marcus dead before me in my nightmares—dead by my own hand, the power of the Whisting ripping him apart.

"You're one of my oldest friends. Don't you trust me?"

Marcus lowers his head and takes a step back. "I swore an oath to protect you, and the king's orders supersede your own. If you're going to the Waste, I'm coming with you, Your Highness."

The title strikes a vulnerable spot in my heart. Marcus never uses it when we're alone.

Fine. If I can't convince him, I'll simply sneak off.

I've gotten good at that.

As we round the hill, everyone stops in their tracks. The cart screeches to a halt, and Aren, bleary-eyed, sits up from her blankets.

The village below us is a picture of devastation, every building reduced to smoking ruins. The ground is as black as charcoal, and the unmistakable shapes of bodies litter the grass—corpses charred beyond recognition.

I don't need anyone to tell me who or why. This is the work of raiders from Penrith. The Usurper's shadow army is here, inside the borders of Loegria.

War has arrived in my kingdom.

CHAPTER TWENTY-FIVE

Dietan

A pit of dread like an icy maw swallows my heart.

Marcus swears. Aren leaps down from the cart and grabs her rucksack, as if she means to rush in to help. "What happened here?" she asks, her voice small.

"Nothing good," I say as I lead the way toward the village. "Get back in the wagon," I add.

She doesn't.

We search for survivors, but all is deathly quiet except for the occasional sound of popping wood. Embers glow beneath piles of rubble. Smoke lingers in the air, and the stench of burned flesh turns my stomach. I clamp my mouth shut.

Marcus kneels in the soft earth, one hand on his blade as he studies a set of boot marks in the mud. He locks eyes with me, and a quick nod tells me all I need to know. We can't stay here long—the prints are fresh.

Whoever did this is still around.

But we can't leave until I'm sure there's no one alive who needs help.

We stumble through the ruins, upending fallen carts and charred barrels. Warehouses of wattle and daub have collapsed. My men thrust logs beneath fallen rafters, lifting what they can to crawl under the wreckage, searching for survivors.

Where the streets narrow to the width of a man, a large house has toppled over onto the smaller one next to it. Marcus and I slip through an open doorway. Aren follows close behind instead of remaining with soldiers standing guard outside.

Inside, the air is thick with dust. Shafts of sunlight pierce through a jagged hole in the ceiling. My boot comes down hard on a charred beam, splitting it in two.

A rattle echoes from the back of the room. Whispers drift through the air.

I stiffen, my hand reaching for my sword, ready for an attack. But then I see a family—a woman and her children—huddled in the dark.

"Please, come out. You're safe now," I say, lowering my blade. "We are Loegrian soldiers, not raiders from Penrith."

From the shadows, the woman stumbles forward, her face caked in ash, eyes wide. She gasps when she sees me, flanked by Marcus in his well-worn uniform. "Are you...?"

"Prince Dietan," I say with a dip of my head.

She curtsies as her children hide behind her legs.

"What happened here?" I ask.

The woman shudders. "They came without warning—so many of them, in black armor, wearing the Usurper's emblem. Our village tried to fight back, but any man who survived was rounded up and herded into the woods. You could hear their screams. I think—I think they burned them alive." She starts sobbing but wipes her eyes and forges on. "Then they— they took the remaining women and children. My children and I hid in a secret compartment in the wall that was built during the wars between the four kingdoms."

I think fast. "My soldiers will take you and any other survivors to Lundenwic, where you'll be safe," I say, nodding to Marcus. "Is there anyone else left?"

She shakes her head. "It's been quiet. I went out—I tried to find others. There's no one. We were going to leave, but..."

"But?" I press.

RINGS OF FATE

"But it wasn't just the Usurper's raiders who did this, Your Highness," she whispers. "There was something else."

"Tell me."

She trembles, terror etched into her face. "It wasn't... It wasn't human."

"Kilandrar," I say softly. "You saw one?"

"Many, Your Highness." Her voice drops to a whisper, as if she's afraid she might summon them. "I think...they're still here."

A great whirlwind roars through the narrow street outside, tearing apart the remains of the wrecked houses, sending debris hurtling through the air.

The woman screams and gathers her children back into their hiding place. I pull Aren behind the smoldering remains of the hearth. Marcus and the rest of the company fall back and take cover.

I press a finger to my lips at a low hiss outside the crevice concealing me and Aren. She clutches my arm in frozen silence. The Kilandrar passes within arm's reach. I will myself to remain deathly still, even as the Rings vibrate in recognition, as if calling to the dark creature.

I know it senses me nearby.

I can't be fearful. If I am, the Whisting will rise and the Kilandrar will see us. But if I stay quiet and calm the Rings, it might go away—just as it has before. *Be still*, I warn, grasping for control, but the Rings writhe inside me, reaching for the Kilandrar's magic, itching to be free.

If it senses the Rings and calls them, will the Kilandrar tear them straight out of my body and deliver them into the Usurper's hands?

But I can't do anything but hide this power and hope the Kilandrar passes us by.

Aren presses closer, the wall behind us growing hotter by the second as the Kilandrar's wind stokes the embers. The crackle of fire reverberates through the plaster. We should move, but we can't. Any sound would draw the Kilandrar's attention.

We hold our breath, and for a heartbeat, it's as if time itself freezes. The Kilandrar prowls outside the ruined home. Its presence is a storm of malice, reaching for the Rings with its dark power.

Smoke chokes the air as the Kilandrar whirls through the broken windows. My eyes burn, and I close them.

The Whisting threatens to rise within me, but then Aren suddenly takes my hand. In the darkness, she's my only link to the world.

"It's okay," she whispers. Sweat beads on my forehead, and my hand is clammy in the warmth of hers.

At the sound of her voice, the Rings stop humming. The Whisting is calm inside me, and I can breathe again.

Slowly, the thick smoke dissipates, the hissing sound recedes, and after an excruciatingly long time, there is silence at last. The Kilandrar is gone.

"Thank you," I whisper.

"For what?" she whispers back. "I didn't do anything."

I shake my head, unable to explain my gratitude. I needed her calm presence today, but I can't let the Kilandrar get this close to her again.

I send the mother and her children off to the safety of South Dunston with a couple of my men. I send my fastest rider to Lundenwic with a dispatch of the highest priority for my father and his council. They must know that the Usurper's army has breached our borders.

We are at war, at last.

I am out of time. My father needs the Rings. *Now.*

The rest of the company presses onward to Alba, putting as much road as we can between ourselves and the burning carnage. Marcus and I agree it's too risky to travel past sundown. Now that we're weeks away from the closest village or outpost, we'll have to make camp.

We find a spot near the river large enough to accommodate a circle of tents. The soldiers race to set them all up before nightfall. I get the fire going in record time, my anger and frustration feeding the flames.

Marcus remains silent. I look at the men and wish I could tell them about my curse, about the true danger of our mission. They all think that if we keep moving, the Usurper's dark creatures won't find us again. They don't know that I stole the kingdom's most precious treasure, and the Kilandrar will keep pursuing me until I'm no longer in possession of the Rings.

I drag my tent farther away to separate myself from the rest of the party. I crawl inside and fall into a fitful sleep.

Alone.

My dream is not like the others, yet it feels exactly the same.

It begins with shadows and whispers, with movement out of the corner of my eye. Something calls to me. It's not a mortal language, but the sounds of life itself: the rustling of leaves in the wind, laughter bursting from healthy lungs, a gasp of pleasure from a lover's touch, a whistle to call cattle home, the final exhale of a soldier on the battlefield. It's life, and it's death. It's the Whisting.

My kingdom of shining white stone high upon the mountain is surrounded by dark clouds. A power—evil, wild, and ancient—churns like a boiling cauldron, consuming all in its path.

It knows me.

It sees into my soul.

The storm howls like hungry wolves. Bodies are strewn in the open fields, fallen men at the feet of the once-great city. I stand over them—over my dying friends. Marcus and Jared lie prostrate, their open eyes clouded and skin gray with death.

In the dream, I know that using the Rings will kill me—and I don't care. There's nothing left for me.

I see Aren sprawled in the grass, her eyes sightless and her dark hair a cloud around her head.

Everyone I care for is dead.

And that emptiness, that hollow in my heart, fills with the Whisting.

In the nightmare, as always, I raise my arms, and the storm surges. The power within me finds a home in the whirlwind. The darkness roars like a great beast as the world around me explodes.

At dawn, I pack up my tent alone. We walk most of the morning with our bellies still empty, our feet still sore. After my restless night, the nightmare still has its claws in me.

Aren's hand brushes mine with infinite gentleness. It's like she senses my dark thoughts, and I nearly jump out of my skin.

"Sorry," she says softly.

The moment it takes me to settle my heart back into my chest is excruciating, but I manage a smile.

"You okay?" she asks. She regards me so sweetly, with such genuine concern, that for a moment, I forget we aren't actually betrothed. I almost kiss her then and there. And not on the cheek, either.

Can I claim that we need to keep up appearances for Marcus's men?

I wave a hand with studied carelessness. "Yeah, nothing to worry about."

She doesn't press, and I wonder if she believes me. Instead, she pulls an apple from her pack, tosses it into the air, and flicks it off the end of her elbow. I catch it deftly.

"You need it more than I do," she quips, grinning. "You're all skin and bones. Losing your vaunted good looks a bit, and I know you pride yourself on that."

My feet trail to a stop, and a smile tugs at my lips as I watch Aren walk ahead. The way she looks at me over her shoulder, with a glint in her eye that wasn't there before, makes the heat rise inside my skin. With a delicate hand, she tucks a lock of hair that's fallen from her bun behind her ear, and I can't take my eyes off her.

Still smiling, I take a large bite of my apple, wiping the juice off my chin with the back of my wrist, then catch up to her. I walk close enough behind her that I can smell the warm scent of her hair. Somehow, she knows how to make me feel better.

But my loneliness follows me like a shadow. Even if Aren seems to be warming to me, I can't let her get too close—not until these cursed Rings are out of my life.

My nightmares are a constant reminder that I'm on the road toward a lonely end. Maybe this does end with Marcus digging the Rings out of my corpse for my father to wield.

Maybe that's the fate I deserve.

The path winds over hills, cutting across the field like a snake. I nearly walk into Aren when she suddenly stops, just around the bend.

She's stock-still, frozen, her hands clenched into fists at her sides. The abject terror on her face stops me cold.

I follow her gaze to a body in the middle of the road. A body with wavy, black hair, sightless brown eyes, and blood trickling from the corner of her mouth. Her hand is outstretched toward us like an eerie warning.

The corpse is that of Aren's kidnapped body double, Lydia.

I haven't escaped danger by simply braving the Bandai Bridge and crossing the border or even by evading the Kilandrar.

The enemy is here, and they're close.

If the burned city wasn't warning enough, this is their war cry.

CHAPTER TWENTY-SIX

Aren

I can't sleep.

All I can see is her sallow, sunken face. I'm so upset I can't think straight.

Before I can stop myself, I fold up my bedroll and walk through the darkness of camp. I'm so angry, I don't even announce myself when I push open the flap of Dietan's tent.

"Hey, you—" I'm about to unleash a torrent of curses, but then I see him.

He's bathed, his hair still damp, lounging on his bedroll reading. He's wearing a silk nightshirt open to the waist, his burnished skin made even more golden from the candlelight.

Oh.

It didn't occur to me that he would look…like *that*.

He jumps when I enter. But when he realizes it's just me, he relaxes a bit. "What's up?" he asks, propping himself up on one elbow and putting down his book.

I try not to look at the muscles peeking out from his shirt and focus on his face—which really isn't making things better. The man's as handsome as he is confusing, and he's damned confusing, especially right now. I take a deep breath.

"Marcus said you're sending me away tomorrow. Is that true?" I try to keep my voice steady. I can't have him thinking I'm weak. Especially after everything we've already gone through.

Dietan looks at me coolly, like I'm interrupting his rest. "That is correct. You both leave at dawn."

"But you need me," I choke out. Anguish claws my throat raw. I drop the bedroll I'm holding. "You can't just send me away. We had a deal." My chest tightens with a painful ache, as if my heart is fracturing.

He looks bleak. "We've been set upon by bandits and the Kilandrar, and the Usurper's troops are sure to follow. You saw what my enemies did to Lydia."

I nod. I overheard Marcus talking to his men. She'd been interrogated, tortured, and then her throat had been slit. I shudder remembering that sweet, brave girl, and feel helpless with grief and rage.

"I can't let it happen to you, too, Aren. I wouldn't be able to live with myself, deal or no deal." He smiles grimly. "Don't worry, I'll make sure you get your gold."

Does he really think that all I care about is the gold? Does he take me to be that greedy? That shallow? I begin to protest.

He holds up a hand. "I know we planned for you to leave after we made it to Alba, but we've taken this farce as far as it can go. I need to make sure you're safe. Tomorrow, Marcus will escort you back to Evandale. I'll continue on with the rest of my men."

The word "farce" feels like a slap in the face. My stomach sinks. "You're sending me home?" I've missed my family, but the thought of going back now is no comfort.

"Or wherever you want to go. But you can't stay."

You can't stay with me, is what he's saying. *You're no longer useful*. My heart twists.

"No," I say, exasperated. "I'm not going anywhere."

It's like he hasn't learned anything about me. I don't give up.

"That was our agreement," he says tightly. "At the first sign of danger, you'll go with my guards somewhere secure. There have already been too many close calls." More softly, placatingly, he adds, "You needn't worry. Marcus will keep you safe. He's the best there is."

"But I—" *I feel safe with you,* I want to say. *I want to be with you,* I want to say. But I don't. For a moment, Dietan looks like there's more he wants to say, too, but then he pointedly picks up his book.

I remain standing there with my mouth still open, even as no words form.

"Yes? You have something else to discuss?" He sounds annoyed from behind the pages.

He looks up at me with his eyes narrowed, and I don't care for that look one bit.

"I don't remember agreeing to that," I snap, crossing my arms. "And I'm not going anywhere!"

"Look, let's talk about it in the morning, okay? Go to bed. We're both exhausted. And you should…" He gestures at my chest. "Your wrap is…"

I look down. In my rush to shout at him, I hastily threw a shawl over my dress, and in my anger, it's slipped off my shoulders, pulling the neckline of my dress down with it.

He's blushing as he turns away, and I feel hot—with more than mere anger—as my chest heaves.

I wrap the shawl tightly around me, even more annoyed with both Dietan and myself. He probably thinks I'm a mess, nothing like the princesses he's used to who wouldn't have a hair out of place.

He can't even look at me.

But I'm not leaving. He'll be just as stubborn in the morning. Two can play that game.

My tent is on the opposite side of camp, and the walk feels like an eternity. Even though we're hidden in a forest, with guardsmen on watch, it's too isolated. Goddess damn it all… After what they did to Lydia… I don't want to be alone tonight.

"My tent doesn't feel safe," I blurt.

"Marcus and the men will protect you. It's everyone's sworn duty," he says, looking everywhere else in the tent but at me.

"It's their sworn duty to protect *you*," I point out.

Dietan's face softens, but he doesn't argue. He told me it never gets any easier when people who swore oaths to protect him get hurt. It's just part of being royal.

I don't think I'll ever get used to it.

But I have to keep reminding myself that none of this is real. I'm never going to be his princess. I can't forget that I'm not worth anyone's sacrifice.

"Look, can't I just stay here tonight?" I ask, trying not to sound pathetic. Now he'll definitely send me away in the morning, but at least I'll be able to sleep tonight.

Dietan looks momentarily confused, then stands up. "Ah…yeah, of course you can stay here," he says, softening slightly. "This tent isn't any safer than yours, but…whatever you prefer. Yours is near the fire, right?"

He walks toward the tent flap. The dumbass thinks I asked him if we could switch. That is not at all what I meant.

"No, I want to stay here," I say, putting a hand on his arm, "with you."

Dietan freezes as if I've turned him to stone. The tension in his shoulders could shatter bricks. I can't see his face from this angle, though I can see his jaw muscle twitch.

"No," he says sharply and shakes me off.

The rejection stings like a slap. "Why?" I ask, trying to hide the tears in my voice. "I'm supposed to be your fiancée, right? I've heard about your reputation; I doubt your men would care. I promise you won't even know I'm here."

"You don't understand," he says roughly.

"Don't understand what?"

Dietan finally looks me in the eye. As if he's admitting something shameful, he says, "Aren, I don't share a bed with anyone."

Oh, *please*. From what I've overheard of his guards' conversations, he has quite the reputation at court as a philanderer whose bed is warmed by a steady rotation of willing ladies.

Right?

Unless…the rumors are deliberately untrue? I examine him carefully. He's hidden one secret for half his life; he must have more.

"I just don't want to be alone tonight," I say, hoping to put him at ease.

"Alone," he echoes softly.

His eyes bore into mine, his gaze so intense, I take a step back. My wrap falls off one shoulder.

He looks at my exposed skin like it's burning him alive. I shrug the shawl back up, but he stops me with a hand on my bare skin. I think he's going to pull it up, but his hand just remains there, holding me, touching me.

I gaze up at him, at his half-lidded eyes. My body is on fire with the heat between us. His hand trembles on my skin.

"Dietan…" I whisper.

He's so close. I turn my chin up toward him. My head is spinning, and my insides are twisted up and melting. We lean toward each other. The air between us crackles.

But then he closes his eyes and groans, his shoulders sinking. He yanks my wrap back up over my shoulder and releases me, like he can't stand to touch me.

I read that totally wrong. He doesn't want me at all.

"You really don't like me, do you?" I say, trying to tamp down the hurt in my voice.

When he opens his eyes again, his irises blaze green in the firelight. He drags a hand through his golden hair and shakes his head. "I just—I don't want to share a tent with anyone, all right?"

"With anyone, or with me?" This time, I can't hide the ache in my voice. See, I've noticed that he's started to act differently toward me after being on the road together for so long. The aggressive charm he uses on everyone else has disappeared. I can tell he's himself around me. He seeks me out. We've walked together for hours, sometimes just sharing a comfortable silence, our hands finding each other for small caresses.

Maybe none of that matters now.

"Just admit it. You regret asking someone as common as me to be your fake bride. You asked me because no one else would be stupid enough to go on this dangerous Wedding March with you with war coming, but I thought..." I falter when I glance up at him; he looks wild, angrier than I've ever seen him. His lips are pressed into a thin line, but still he says nothing, and I'm desperate to fill this terrible silence, to change that look on his face, so I keep talking.

"You're the only one here I can talk to, but every night you hide yourself away." I exhale, feeling more vulnerable than I've ever been. But I can't stop the words from flowing out of my lips. "I know I'm not really your bride, that I volunteered to be part of this lie so you can save the kingdoms. But after all the awful things that've happened, I just want to feel like we're on the same mission, together. I feel so lost some days. I just need... I need..."

I need you.

I wish he'd say something—anything. I can't read him. If I knew him better, I'd swear he looks anguished, like he wants to speak, but then the pain in his eyes disappears as if it was never there in the first place.

Screw it. I point at the hard ground between us. "I just want to sleep here. Is that so much to ask?" I point to my bedroll lying next to his, like

I'm planting a flag, staking my claim on land that belongs to him.

Finally, Dietan raises his chin and looks down at me, a prince again, unmovable. "Yes, you signed up for this," he says, his voice low. "I told you it would be a hard journey. I told you not to come. I'm sorry, but I can't give you more than was agreed. And you can't stay here."

I'm sure as hell not going to make this easy for him. We both know what's out there. He'll have to throw me out himself. I step so close to him that I can smell the soap he used. I look up at him, once again irritated by how stupidly tall he is. I could slap him—I *should*.

Instead, shocking even myself with my boldness, I put my hands on his face and force him to look me in the eye. My anger dissipates, leaving only pain and fear. "I'm scared, okay? After what happened to Lydia, what we saw in that village, I just want to sleep somewhere I feel safe." Though it kills me to admit it, I finally add, "I feel safe with you."

He puts his hands on mine and wrenches them away, but I fight him. We stand there, locked in place. His eyes are filled with ice and fire.

His hold on my wrists is tight. His pupils dilate, and his nostrils flare.

"It's for your own safety. Why won't you listen?" he says. And then, as if he can't help himself, he pulls me tightly against him.

He's holding me so closely I can feel his entire body against mine. He's all muscle pressing against my softest parts. I can't breathe. He feels so good. He bends down, nuzzling into the crook of my neck, and groans. "Gods, why are you so infuriating?"

"I could say the same about you," I murmur, breathing against his warm, bare chest. "Let me stay here, just for tonight."

"I wish I could. I really wish I could," he says raggedly, "but I can't." He tears himself away and practically pushes me away from him, still holding the book he was reading.

I stumble, catching my footing at the last minute before I fall. Harvest Mother, what is wrong with him? He's hot and cold, and cold again.

"You asked me to help you, to come on this quest with you. I know when we're in public—when you kiss my cheek and hold me for everyone to see—it's all an act. But you know what I think?" Dietan lifts an eyebrow. He looks almost as indifferent as a statue. He's so beautiful in the firelight, but now I can see the turmoil behind his eyes. "I think you're afraid to admit that you have feelings for me. Real feelings—as much as you pretend you don't. And that's the true reason you're sending me away—because you can't stand to think you might like some peasant barmaid for more than just a roll in the hay!"

He has a scary smile on his face. I know I'm right, so I continue.

"That's the truth, isn't it? You hate me, but you hate yourself more because you want me! And I *know* you want me!" I wave a hand at my body. "Even if you act like a cold, indifferent prince, I *know* you! So just admit it!"

Dietan smiles like he's gotten caught. He drags his tongue against his bottom teeth. Neither of us moves, until he throws his book across the tent in a fit of temper. A forceful gale suddenly blows all around, headed toward me.

I almost laugh, but I don't, because Dietan suddenly collapses. He falls to the floor, his hands at his throat. The wind dies before it can hurt me.

I drop to my knees next to him. "Dietan! What's happening? Dietan!"

"I can't—I can't breathe…"

An otherworldly breeze fills the tent once more.

But this time, the Whisting is killing him from the inside. The fire in the lanterns starts to flicker and dim as Dietan is smothered by an invisible force.

"Dietan, no!" I scream at him. "Make it stop!" I cradle him in my arms as he fights for his life. "Breathe! Breathe!"

Tears burn his eyes as he thrashes. He can't break free. My terror brings everything into focus. I feel his hands struggle, feel his magic sucking the life out of him.

Harvest Mother, he's going to die.

And I killed him.

CHAPTER TWENTY-SEVEN

Aren

Dietan motions frantically toward his bedroll at the other end of the space, his arms flailing and his face turning blue.

"What do you need?" I ask, just as panicked as he is.

"The knife..." he gurgles.

I immediately dive for the knife by his bedside. In one swift move, he slices the blade across his palm, blood rising in its wake, and instantly, air rushes back into his lungs. With a horrible, ragged gasp, his body convulses and he curls into himself.

But he's breathing. The relief I feel is unlike anything I've ever felt before—so intense, I fall to my knees beside him again, unable to stand. He's alive.

"Dietan..." I say gently, touching his shoulder.

He lifts his head and gives me a weak smile as he holds his fist clenched tight to his chest, blood seeping from between his closed fingers. He takes several labored breaths. "I'm all right. It's all right."

I pull him to my chest tightly, holding him as he continues to cough and wheeze. I have no doubt that if it had gone on a second longer, he'd be dead.

"It's okay," I whisper, quivering as I run a soothing hand through his hair. He clings to me like I'm a life raft and he's adrift at sea. I can tell he's forcing himself to remain calm as he leans his trembling body against mine. I reach down to take his hand and notice he's bleeding profusely from the fist clenched at his chest.

"Oh shit!" He allows me to pry his fingers open. The knife wound went deep. His hand is drenched in blood like a red glove.

I rip a long strip of ragged fabric off the hem of my dress.

"What are you doing?" he asks.

"I'm helping you, you dummy."

"But your dress."

"Forget my fucking dress!" I wrap the cloth tightly across his palm, the blood already soaking through the fabric. I keep going, winding it tighter and tighter.

"You don't have to do that," he says. It's clear he didn't expect me to come to his aid after our argument.

"I'll fix it later," I say. "It doesn't matter."

"I'm sorry. I didn't mean to..."

I scowl at him, but there's no heat behind it. He just looks back at me, ashamed. "I'm sorry," he says again. "I'm a mess."

Somehow, it takes all the wind out of my sails, and I sigh. It's one of those dramatic, long-suffering sighs. His face twitches into a smile, and he looks away, covering his mouth with his other hand, holding in a laugh.

Ridiculous man.

I tie the fabric off tightly, cinching the knot in the middle of his palm. He hisses, taking in a breath between his teeth. "I have some dried Feverfew petals from Elspeth," I say, tying off my makeshift bandage. "It'll numb the pain and keep your wound from festering."

He nods, his face drawn with pain. Then, all of a sudden, he presses his uninjured hand firmly against his mouth. He's laughing.

I can't believe it. "What the hell is so funny?"

He's laughing so hard he's crying. I watch him, unsure what to do as he's overcome with hysteria. He's probably in shock.

"You accused me of having feelings for you, and I almost died," he chokes out. "You almost killed me."

At least his color is back. I raise an eyebrow. "And?"

He wipes his tears with the back of his wrist. "This is exactly what I was trying to tell you. You'll be the death of me." He tries to stifle his laughs.

"All this because you can't face your feelings. Just like a man," I harrumph.

He bows his head in what looks like shame, then starts to chuckle again.

I frown at him. "It's fine," I continue. "We'll…talk about it later. Just—sit there and let me get the medicine."

Feeling more determined than scared, I leave his tent and return quickly as I can with my rucksack. As I pull out the tin of Feverfew petals, Dietan crawls to sit on his bedroll. He props his elbows on his knees and lowers his head in fatigue.

I kneel next to him, grinding the dried petals to powder between my fingers. "I'm warning you, this is going to sting. But you're welcome in advance."

Without asking, I take his wounded hand and unwrap my makeshift bandage. To my relief, the bleeding has mostly stopped. I sprinkle the ground petals onto the cut, and he doesn't flinch, even though I know it stings like crazy.

I wrap the cut again, this time with the ever-clean gauze I purchased from the apothecary along with the herbs.

He flexes his fingers when I'm done, and I'm relieved he still has use of his hand. "Tingles," he says.

"That's good. It means it's working." I pull his hand back toward me and examine it closely as he flexes it. Even now, I can't help but admire the strength in his hand, how beautiful his fingers are—like every part of him—and I start to blush, thinking about how he had pressed himself against me, the heat between us…

"What's the verdict?" he asks.

I snort as I tidy up and close my rucksack. "You'll be right as rain soon. You're lucky I thought to buy supplies. Helps to be prepared on the road."

"That's why I asked you to come with me," he points out.

"Yeah, so you've said. You just want me here because I'm useful, practical," I say, trying to keep the disappointment from my voice.

"But you *are* useful and practical. Is that such a bad thing?" he asks.

I shrug. I'm so tired of being seen as nothing more than a convenience.

After a moment, his shoulders slump. "I'm sorry," he says. "I didn't mean to scare you." He's apologizing for the wrong thing, but I let it go.

RINGS OF FATE

"I wasn't scared," I lie. I was terrified. Seeing him so close to death shook me to my core, and I still feel faint. "What happened just now—when you couldn't breathe. That was the Rings calling the Whisting, right?" I ask.

He sighs and drags his other hand down his face. He looks as if he's trying to smile, but he can't quite meet my eyes. "Yeah. Since I don't know how to control the power inside me, I can't risk being with anyone because I..." He trails off as if choosing his next words carefully. "You saw what happened on the bridge. That soldier is lucky he only broke a few bones. In the past...I've killed people. Accidentally. I never mean to. But they died because of me."

I freeze, like an icy hand suddenly gripping my heart.

Died because of him?

I'm not naive. I've seen Dietan use his sword to protect me. He's about to ride to war at his father's side, and bards will sing of his bravery and strength. Of course, he's probably killed people...he's a prince who has been called to battle, but by using *that power*?

He's hanging his head, picking at the gauze around his hand. He stops when he senses me watching him.

I recall my almost kidnapping in Evandale and the attack on the bridge, where I was saved by a sudden gust of wind. "Then what happened to you just now—when the Whisting attacked you—you've used it to do *that* to others?" I ask.

Dietan exhales. "It's always been an accident, I swear. I can't control when the Whisting rises or what it does..."

I can't imagine him choking someone to death with magic. "But maybe...you killed them because...it was self-defense?" It had to be. He's not a cold-blooded murderer. He's no Boreas.

He shakes his head, and I can feel the blood draining from my face.

"No," he says quickly. "They didn't attack me. Or at least Cedric—my best friend—he wasn't doing it on purpose. I accidentally killed him in the practice ring. He's the last person I ever sparred with." His lower lip trembles, and he works his jaw side to side before taking a deep, ragged breath. "The other was the only woman I ever loved."

"Oh," I say softly. I feel a flicker of jealousy at his admission that he was once in love, but it's quickly doused as I realize the magnitude of his confession.

He's killed two people.

Two people, the ones closest to him, killed by his own hand due to the Whisting inside of him.

The truth is like a struck match in the darkness. It changes everything. He's carried this secret for so long, it's rotted him from the inside. It must be a relief to finally admit it to someone—to me.

"So, you can't control your magic?" I ask.

He looks like he's done talking about his feelings and seizes the topic gratefully. "That's right. I can't summon it or bend it to my will like my father did. It just...happens. If this King Osian can get the Rings out of me, then I can finally be at peace." Shadows catch in his deep-set eyes, lending his expression haunted, hollow weariness.

"I'm sorry," I whisper. "I know you're a prince and I'm just a barmaid, but I understand."

His eyes light with hope as he finally meets my gaze. "You do?"

"When my mother died, it was as if my family died with her. And she died...because of me." I close my eyes and take a deep breath. "I caught the red fever after playing with some kids she told me to keep away from. She got it from me, and she died."

"It wasn't your fault," Dietan says, shaking his head. "Red fever is highly contagious."

"Everyone says that, but it doesn't change what happened or how I feel about it."

He reaches for my hand with his good one and squeezes. "I'm sorry."

"Thank you." I nod and squeeze back. "Tell me about them, your friend Cedric and your..." I hesitate. "Your lover."

Dietan sighs. "Cedric... He was a good mate. He was the one who snuck in to see the Rings with me that night. I was the one who always got us in trouble, and he loyally followed my lead. Cedric was the best friend anyone could have."

"As for her... Her name was Liesl. She was a lady of the court of Alarice. I've never told anyone how she died."

"What happened?"

"We went to bed, and I woke up the next morning—and—she was lying next to me, but she wasn't breathing. The healers said she stopped breathing in the middle of the night. 'How strange,' they said. 'A tragedy.' Nobody suspected—not her family, not the Alarician court. But I knew. I knew what happened."

"The Whisting," I whisper.

He clears his throat and continues. "The Whisting responds to heightened emotions, like anger or pleasure or pain or fear. I've been plagued by the same horrible nightmare every night ever since the Rings bonded to my soul. The Whisting must have sensed my fear during the dream. I must have—*it* must have killed her in my sleep, and I didn't even know."

Harvest Mother, he's carried this guilt inside him ever since? "That's terrible. I'm so sorry." He can't look me in the eye, so I dip my face to peer into his anguished eyes. "But just as you told me, you mustn't blame yourself. It was an accident."

"It doesn't change what happened." He shrugs. "Accident or not, they're both dead because of me."

He looks so miserable that tears spring to my own eyes in sympathy. I was right about his talent at hiding—he's spent his whole life perfecting it. "They say you're incorrigible. That you've slept with every maiden from here to Penrith, but none of it is true, is it?"

He nods. "It was just a cover so no one would guess my secret. Our enemies have spies everywhere, especially at court."

"And you're not just some spoiled prince, either, are you?" I bump him gently on the shoulder.

"Well, I hope not." He grins, at last, and I smile back at him.

We sit next to each other in silence for a while. I'm acutely aware of the warmth seeping through my sleeve where his arm touches mine, and I know he's aware of it, too, but neither of us pulls away. Something between us has shifted. The enormity of his secret weighs on me, as does the fact he trusted me enough to share it. "What are your nightmares about?" I finally ask.

Dietan sucks in a deep breath, mustering his courage. "The end of the world. My own death. The death of everyone I love. My kingdom covered in shadow, and me at the center of it all. The cause of all that destruction."

"They're just dreams," I say stoutly. "They're not real."

"Right."

"I mean, they're not prophecies."

"But they're not *not* prophecies, either," he says, and I realize I don't know the half of how the Whisting works. Maybe he doesn't, either.

I don't argue—for now.

"There were past kings who could wear the Rings and call forth visions of the future," he continues. "My father could sometimes intuit which general was going to win a battle, or whether the harvest would be bountiful that year. I just...*know*, once in a while. I sometimes get a feeling. Maybe about a person or a place. But it's the same way I know that the Kilandrar are close. The Rings connect me to them."

"Well, thank the goddess you did, or we'd be dead by now. Do you think they're still nearby?"

"They're not far. I know the Kilandrar are waiting to strike. Probably under the same command of whoever kidnapped and killed Lydia."

"The Usurper of Penrith?" Chills run down my spine just saying his name. In Evandale, we say it's bad luck to talk of evil things.

"That's the only answer that makes sense. Dark forces are growing, so my father has been preparing for this."

"They say the Usurper..."

"Is Boreas returned, I know," he finishes.

I wrap my arms around myself. "Do you think he is? Boreas the Unbeliever?"

"I don't know. But the Usurper has the same ambition to conquer the free kingdoms of Albion."

I shiver, even though it's warm in Dietan's tent.

"They undoubtedly had to regroup when they realized their mistake in capturing Lydia, but that's little reprieve. No matter what I do, wherever I go, people will get hurt."

"Like you said, I know what I signed up for. I knew the risks," I say, looking him squarely in the eye.

Dietan tilts his head to the side, looking grave and like he thinks I'm being dense. "It will only get worse. I've dragged you into a battle you're unprepared to face, and I knew that the moment I asked you to come with me. It was selfish—"

"It was to save our countries!" I interject, but he plows on.

"—and I've put you in danger. And now that you know the whole truth about me, you should see that you need to leave, for your own sake."

"Are you trying to scare me away?"

"I have been since the beginning. I told you not to come with me." He sighs. "I should have forbidden you."

I raise an eyebrow. "Forbidden me? You think you can order me around just like that?"

He shrugs. "I'm a prince, aren't I? I can order you to do things..." He grins, back to being a terrible flirt.

I snort, mollified despite how annoyed I just was. "What things?"

"Oh…I can imagine all sorts." His grin grows wider. "Make you tear off more of your dress, maybe. I think my hand needs another bandage."

I laugh and toss a pillow at his face.

He bats it away and stares at me so intently that for a moment, the heat between us rises again. I can feel myself melting at my core, certain that he can see it all on my face. But then he looks away, and the moment is lost.

I swallow my disappointment.

"It's late, and you're hurt," I tell him softly.

"I'm fine," he says, "thanks to you. But the Kilandrar can sense the Whisting. They're surely on our trail. And next time, we might not evade them."

"Then we'd best be prepared and get a good night's rest." I walk over to the bedroll I brought with me and arrange it next to his, along with the pillow I threw at him.

"You still want to stay here?" He sounds surprised. "After everything I've told you?"

"I know how to stop you from hurting yourself or anyone else now." I point to the knife by his side. "Blood magic. It released the Whisting's hold on you. And now we know how to fight the Kilandrar, too." I begin to unbutton the fastenings on my dress.

His entire body tenses. "What are you doing?" he demands.

"What does it look like I'm doing? Getting ready for bed. Be a gentleman and turn around."

Dietan falls silent and faces the other way as ordered. I quickly remove my outer garments so I'm wearing only my smallclothes and a modest linen shift. "You can turn around now," I tell him. "Did you peek?"

"Of course I did." He grins. "With a beautiful woman undressing in his tent, what man could help himself…"

I blush. I've only ever heard such praise from drunk farmers hunting for another pair of hands to cook their meals or care for their motherless children. And yet, coming from this prince who commands servants aplenty, who has greater need of a friend than a maid, those words feel sincere for the first time in my life. Still, I don't want to fall for it. "I'm nothing and nobody," I say.

"Aren Bellamore, that could not be further from the truth," he says solemnly.

"Shut your trap."

"I can't win with you, can I? You accuse me of being cold, but when I'm nice, you don't like it, either," he says, exasperated.

I shake my head and cluck my tongue, even though I'm still blushing furiously. "When we were fighting. When I accused you of—having feelings for me…" I start. Now he's the one blushing. "You turned the Whisting on yourself rather than let it hurt me."

He starts getting into his bedroll and sighs. "I don't know if I did."

"You were able to control it. You directed it toward yourself. Dietan, you'd rather kill yourself than anyone you care for," I say with a small smile on my face.

He notices. "What?"

"You care for me."

"I never said I didn't," he says. "Of course I care for your well-being."

Fine. Be that way, arrogant man.

Still, when we look at each other, an understanding passes between us. Something delicate, so fragile and tender that we both leave it unsaid. Neither of us speaks for a long moment.

"We don't have to talk about that anymore," I say with a yawn as I slip underneath the blankets. "I don't want to cause you any more distress. I don't want that to happen again. I now understand why you didn't want me to sleep in your tent."

"But you still mean to stay?"

"Yes."

He frowns. "You're risking your life, you know."

I turn on my side so I'm facing him. The lamplight casts shadows on the planes of his troubled face. "Dietan, I'm not afraid of you. You would never hurt me, ever," I whisper, and I believe it with my whole heart. Then I roll over and drift off to sleep, secure by his side.

He cares about me.

CHAPTER TWENTY-EIGHT

Aren

Dietan tells me he tossed and turned all night and didn't sleep a wink. Regardless, in the morning, there is no more talk of sending me away. Maybe he changed his mind or maybe he's just tired of arguing.

I know *I* am.

Our caravan continues through the outskirts of Loegria. But now, there are no more stops for the Wedding March, no more announcements and cheek kisses.

There's a war on.

Marcus is surly and quiet, and the soldiers are nervous as well.

The closer to old Estyrion we travel, the grayer the sky becomes. The sun has retreated and is merely a hazy disk behind the clouds.

But even with the sun hiding behind cloud cover, it's hot here. I take off Dietan's leather jacket and wipe sweat from my brow.

I wrinkle my nose at the scent of smoke so acrid I can taste it on the back of my tongue. It doesn't smell like the comforting warm hearths of Evandale. It's thicker, more acidic, and stings my eyes.

Father used to tell us stories of the Great Waste and how nothing could grow there—a land decimated by Boreas's magic. When I was a child, it was difficult for me to imagine such a place. I grew up surrounded by lush fields, rolling meadows, and streams full of frogs and fish. It doesn't feel real until I can see it, and smell it, for myself.

The Great Waste is nothing but desolation.

When we finally arrive in Alba, the westernmost Loegrian city bordering Estyrion, the clouds are thick. The air itself seems to hold its breath, waiting for the release of rain that never comes. It doesn't look like it's rained here in centuries. The ground is as cracked as a dry riverbed, and dust settles on every surface. Our hair and clothes are covered, the grit invading every pore.

For a moment, I just take it in.

Alba is eerily quiet for a city. Even the wind doesn't walk its deserted streets.

It's almost like a dream—a surreal one.

It's difficult to discern where the horizon ends and the city begins. Heavy fog blankets most of city, strangling the sunlight. Alba appears to be made of limestone, but now it's turned a dull gray, mirroring the sky. I can barely make out a few towers beyond the rooftops. In the distance, I can see the shadow of the great bridge is a menacing specter, haunting the road already traveled.

Perhaps at one time, the city was beautiful. Now it's as still as a graveyard.

Where South Dunston was bustling, Alba is a ghost town. Successive generations of inhabitants must have fled from the Usurper's troops near Penrith's border and then from the Mad King in the Waste that used to be Estyrion. The innocents still here are either stubborn, apathetic, or have given up entirely.

The few souls we pass don't acknowledge us. Their gazes are on their hands as they sharpen their swords, weave grass into rope, or cook small game over open fires. Tears prick the corners of my eyes when I see small faces peer out from dirty windows covered in soot and grime.

Hacking coughs come from behind closed doors, and I wonder if the smoky air will make us all sick, too. I don't have anything in my healing kit of herbs that can ward off this strange miasma.

Dietan's dour expression tightens with tension as we walk among these people—his subjects. Does he feel responsible for their well-being, as their prince? Is he witnessing the reality of life in one dark corner of his kingdom, or a portent of what is to come for all of Loegria if we fail?

When he meets my eyes, I can see the despair in his, and I know he's tearing himself up inside seeing the state of his people, his kingdom.

No one speaks as we walk through the city. The despair is too vast to ignore.

Carts full of belongings have been left abandoned in the streets. Those who fled must have left these behind mid-flight, taking with them only what was necessary for survival. What happened here? How much of a hurry were they in for them to leave their possessions?

What were they running from?

I can tell by the ransacked contents of the carts that they've been picked over by those who remained. Nonessentials like vases and some broken children's toys are all that remain in the overturned crates.

A craggy voice barks down at us from above. "Go! Shoo! Go!"

An old woman waves at us from her balcony, where her clothes are hanging to dry. They are already covered in a fine film of dust.

She throws her arms out, as if trying to scare a rat out of her pantry, but someone from inside grabs her and guides her back in before closing the door. "Leave this accursed place while you still can!" she shouts from inside.

Dietan sighs and keeps walking, but I have a bad feeling about this place.

"All right," says Marcus. "The temple is this way."

It's easy to forget in this desolation that we are here to receive the traditional blessing for our supposed upcoming nuptials. We need to keep up the charade until we disappear into the Waste. Both Loegria and Penrith need to ready troops for war. Which buys us a few weeks, possibly, to solve Dietan's problem.

The temple of the great Oracle of Alba looms above the city, tall and proud. Unlike the other buildings that surround us, its limestone exterior is clean and gleaming. Gold inlays in the stone glint in the rogue rays of the sun. It's nothing short of breathtaking—clearly cared for lovingly.

In the beginning of the third epoch, the Rings of Fate were crafted here. It was once filled with mages, Vindar, and a host of holy leaders who held services and tended to citizens in need.

Now, for all its beauty, it is desolate.

We walk over the threshold of the temple's wide, bronze double doors.

In the dimly lit antechamber, a man in cream-colored robes sweeps under a row of hanging braziers.

"Greetings, Father," says Dietan.

"Prince Dietan," the priest gasps, dropping his broom. "Your Highness, what brings you here?"

"I've come to seek the Oracle's blessing for our engagement." He smiles, putting an arm around my waist. "This is my intended, Aren of Evandale."

"Dear me, I wish we had been more prepared," the priest says. "Was there no messenger?"

"It appears our messengers have been delayed," says Marcus, coughing.

The priest looks around at the depleted temple, at the desolation of the city behind us, and smiles sadly. "That's not unusual these days, I'm afraid."

"It's all right," says Dietan. "We're, um, pressed for time."

"I'm sure you are needed back in Lundenwic," the priest says. "Well, come into the house of the Oracle, my children, and we will bless you with the waters of Alba." He leads us inside.

It's cool and dark in the temple, and I'm relieved to find it doesn't smell like the smoke outside. Instead, it's peaceful and clean. Stone pillars line the vestibule, and the domed ceiling has a singular skylight. Diffused light washes the room in an ethereal light. It's a sanctuary awash in gentle healing magic.

The priest stands before us at an enormous marble basin filled with water on a smooth stone pedestal. In a place of honor at the far end of the room is a large statue of a woman, with one hand outstretched and an inscrutable expression on her face. She is watching over us—the Oracle, the revered emissary of the Anemoi. Her presence looms large but is a calming balm. It's a nice reprieve from recent events.

The priest dips a scepter into the basin and recites a few lines of prayer in a tongue I don't understand. Without further ceremony, he flicks the water at Dietan and then at me. I blink in surprise as the water splashes into my eyes. I didn't expect that. As we bow our heads, I share a small smile with Dietan, who discreetly wipes his face.

The priest puts one hand on Dietan's head, but when he places the other on mine, he gasps. I feel a tiny shock—like static in a winter knit—pass between his palm and my head. He looks at me intensely. "Aren of Evandale, yes?"

"Yes," I reply, suddenly nervous.

RINGS OF FATE

The priest murmurs to himself. His eyes roll back in his head ever so slightly.

"What's wrong, Father?" Dietan asks.

The priest locks eyes with me once more. "It's been a long time since the Oracle has spoken. She has sent me a vision."

Dietan raises his eyebrows.

"You must never leave his side, my daughter," the priest says, his hand heavy on my head.

"What?" I question, startled.

The priest saw me in a vision?

I would have expected a more dramatic display when the Oracle spoke—but I'm no expert on holy things.

"What did you see?" Dietan asks. "Please enlighten us, Father."

But the priest only shakes his head, distressed. "If you continue on by yourself, my son, there is only darkness and death." The priest turns to me. "I implore you—do not leave him," he repeats, looking meaningfully at me. "Never. For the good of all Albion. Promise that."

Sweat forms on my brow at the priest's conviction, and I nod my head. "I won't leave him. I would never," I breathe.

Next to me, Dietan squirms.

Yeah, he still wants to get rid of me, after everything. Asshole.

I bet he wishes we'd left the Oracle off the itinerary.

The priest clears his throat. "May the sacred waters of the Oracle bless the coming marriage of Prince Dietan of Loegria, heir to the throne of Alarice, and Aren of Evandale," he intones. "May your union bring peace to both kingdoms and strength to our people for centuries to come."

"Goddess willing," I say, which is what we say back home.

"May the wind be ever at our back," Dietan murmurs, which is the Loegrian way. He takes my hand and squeezes it, and when our gazes meet, his eyes are soft. I know what comes next to conclude this kind of rite. My whole body begins to hum like a beehive.

He draws me closer, and I can't stop my heart from galloping out of my chest, because now he's lowering his head as I raise my own. He murmurs, too softly for the priest to hear, "Don't hit me, okay?"

"Okay," I breathe.

Then he kisses me. His lips touch mine. They flutter as if asking a question. For a split second, I think he's about to pull away because this is just pretend. We're fooling Dietan's soldiers and the priest—even the Oracle.

But then his arms encircle my waist, and he draws me even closer. I wrap my arms around his neck, and we're pressed against each other, and everything around us melts away. He opens his mouth to mine, and I do the same, breathing him in. The press of his tongue against my own sends fire racing to every inch of my body. He nibbles on my bottom lip, and now every part of me is burning.

His body is all heat and muscle against mine. I tilt my hips a little, which makes him groan. My fingers weave through his silky hair, and he draws me tighter against him. For all his secrets and denial, this man wants me, and that alone makes me want to give him everything.

Then Marcus coughs.

Shit. I blink my eyes open, and my cheeks burn hot. *Shit, shit, shit.*

Dietan chuckles. "I forgot where we are," he murmurs, still holding me in his arms. Then he releases me, and my body is numb everywhere we touched.

I blush and smooth the front of my dress. I can hardly look at the priest. I enjoyed that so much, I damn near forgot everything, including my own name. I wonder how much of it was just for show. Based on Dietan's quick breaths and flushed cheeks, maybe none of it…

Dietan grins at me, and I grin back. I got what I wanted. I've waited all my life for a kiss, and that was one for the ages.

CHAPTER TWENTY-NINE

Aren

At last, we've arrived at the bridge between Loegria and the Great Waste of Estyrion.

If the royal soldiers are surprised that we aren't making our way back to the capital, they don't show it. Perhaps they simply follow Marcus wherever he leads.

Like the bridge connecting Loegria and Alarice, it's a massive thoroughfare. But where that bridge was teeming with travelers, this one is eerily empty. The stores lining the bridge are shuttered, the houses dark. Our party is the only one that dares cross into the fallen kingdom.

"Dietan?" I ask, and he understands my silent question.

"I know," he answers. He, too, is taking in the charred trusswork and support beams overhead. Not only is the bridge empty—it's cloaked in smoke.

I can't bring myself to go further than the beginning brickwork as I peer into the haze. I'm covered in gooseflesh, and I clutch my pack so tightly, my fingers start to go numb. I feel Dietan come up to my side, also stopping just short of stepping onto the bridge. His eyes narrow as he looks down its length. Crossing the bridge means we'll be exposed once more, but it's the only way into Estyrion.

The bridge looks passable, but portions of it are damaged by some kind of explosion. It looks like a battle happened here recently, yet there are no bodies, no injured soldiers, no other evidence of human passage.

"The Usurper's work?" I ask.

Marcus joins us, taking in the damage with a keen strategist's eye. He kneels and scrapes a long finger in the ash smeared on the railing. Nodding, he rubs it between his fingers and smells it. "Alchemist's powder."

"What's that?" I ask.

Dietan looks gray when he replies, "It's an explosive powder ground from highly volatile stones, mined deep in Estyrion. It's one of the only resources of value left there. It can create fire on impact. Devastating if deployed in large quantities."

I don't like the sound of that at all. "But they left the bridge intact?"

"Whoever was here would be foolish to demolish the only passage between Loegria and Estyrion. They need it as much as we do," Dietan explains.

Dietan looks past Marcus to his men, who are waiting patiently for the signal to advance. "You two should turn back now. I wish you would listen to me. Marcus, take some of the men and get her out of here and keep her safe."

"You can't be serious. I'm not leaving you," I tell him, hiking my rucksack higher on my shoulders. "Didn't you hear the priest?"

Dietan sighs.

"What she said," adds Marcus.

Arguing with both of us is a losing battle, and Dietan knows it.

"Fine. You're free to make your own decisions—I won't issue an order—but this is a bad choice."

"The same one you're making," I shoot back.

With a resigned sigh, he nods to the men, turns on his heel, and strikes out to cross the bridge.

My skin feels tight all over my body, like it's being tugged in different directions. Every instinct in me screams to turn back, but I push down my fear and put one foot in front of the other, following Dietan into the acrid haze. The buildings on either side are empty; some doors are cracked open, but I don't see any movement in the dark behind them, as if the people who lived here left in a hurry.

Loose scraps of parchment blow down the empty street. Window shutters clack against their siding, sounding a rhythmic *rat-tat-tat* sound that echoes my pounding heart. I would swallow my fear, but my mouth is too dry.

The trusses overhead creak and groan in the wind, secured by ropes stretched above us like a spider's web. Ragged Loegrian flags flap on their poles. Everything about this place sets me on edge. It feels like we're being watched, and I want to believe that it's just my imagination, but I can't shake the dread creeping down my spine.

Marcus's bootsteps are quiet, as if he, too, senses that something is wrong. The wind barely helps clear the smoke and visibility is low. Even Dietan, who walks a few paces ahead, is merely a shadow.

I look up and spy fabric whipping around one of the rooftops. I freeze, staring at it. Was it just another flag? Or is someone—or something—up there? Blood roars in my ears, and I try desperately to listen for any movement, but the wind drowns out all else.

I try not to panic as I catch up to Dietan. "It feels like we're walking right into a trap," I whisper, leaning in close to his ear.

He nods, his eyes still ahead. "I know. I feel it, too."

My stomach twists as we pass under a large arch festooned in tattered pennants and broken wind chimes. It's the halfway point. Now we've crossed onto Estyrion's side of the bridge.

I look over my shoulder, at the path leading back to Loegria. Marcus and his men are a good distance behind me. Marcus catches my eye and nods. He's frowning, focused, and never takes his hand off the sword at his side. He gestures to his men to speed up, to draw even with me and Dietan.

But it's too late.

I hear it first—the distinct sound of rope sliding against the metal above us.

I hurl myself onto Dietan's back, shoving him forward. We fall to the ground just as the archway collapses behind us in a great cloud of dust and debris.

The sound is explosive, like a whip cracking. My ears ring loudly. I can't stop gagging on the dust, and I'm shaking uncontrollably.

Dietan's hand finds mine, and his tight grasp helps me up. We're both unhurt, but his beautiful face is pale and smeared with dirt.

I can hear Dietan's men shouting from the other side of the rubble. The arch that marked the border between kingdoms has been reduced to a tangled mess of support beams and stone.

We've been completely cut off from the others.

Marcus's face appears in a gap in the debris. He reaches his arm through an opening barely wide enough for a person to slip through. He beckons me to grab his hand and climb through the opening.

"Quickly! Now!" Marcus shouts.

Heavy footsteps hammer on the beams above us, surrounding us on all sides. From below comes the sound of wood splintering and stone cracking. The ground beneath our feet starts to crumble. The impact is tearing the fragile bridge apart.

Dietan shoves me forward, and Marcus grabs my arm and begins pulling me through the opening. Then I turn and reach for Dietan, but my hand grabs nothing but air.

"Dietan!" I cry.

"Don't worry, I'm right behind you!" he shouts even though I can't see him in the dust and haze.

Marcus pulls hard as I wriggle through the gap, struggling for purchase. The support beams scrape against the side of my head. It's such a tight squeeze that I have to close my eyes so I don't panic. Splinters scratch my cheeks, and I cry out, but Marcus keeps pulling, pulling, pulling until I emerge on the other side of the bridge.

I rush to look through the hole, but I can't see Dietan because standing in the middle of the bridge is a Kilandrar. Its black winds form what appears to be a cloak and hood.

There is nowhere to hide. It's found us.

To my utter horror, Dietan comes into view walking toward it, his hands flexing at his sides. I can feel the wind pulsating each time he flexes his fingers. The Whisting.

"Dietan! No!" I scream as Marcus tries to pull me back.

"*Go!*" Dietan shouts, the wind already drowning out his voice. "Marcus, take Aren and *go!*"

The Kilandrar watches him carefully, waiting to see what he'll do. Out of the haze, another shadow appears behind it—a second Kilandrar. Then another one. And another.

So many. Too many.

A gale rises in their presence. A whirlwind swirls around them, kicking up dust and debris that stings my skin like needles.

Dietan stands before them, his feet planted firmly, raising his hands in front of him. He is going to face them on his own using a power he can't control.

He looks over his shoulder at me and salutes.

A defiant goodbye.

I scream his name one last time before Marcus pulls me away.

CHAPTER THIRTY

Dietan

The sound of her voice shouting my name gives me something to fight for.

I need to face the Kilandrar alone. *She'll be safer with Marcus*, I try to tell myself. They'll all get back to Loegria. They'll survive this, and if I don't... I don't want to think about that. For once, I actually have something to live for.

But the look of betrayal on Aren's face when she realized I wasn't behind her will haunt me. I broke her trust, and if I live, earning it back will be a top priority, right behind saving the realm. But like I told her in my tent the other night, I can never be with anyone.

Not when this curse is embedded in me.

It's too dangerous to love anyone. It's too dangerous for her to love *me*. If I die, at least I'll die knowing I saved her life.

The Kilandrar encircle me, calling for the Rings, which vibrate in recognition. The sensation snakes down my spine with eerie intensity.

Dietan of Loegria. So-called heir to Alarice. You have taken what is not yours. Thief of breath. Brigand of the zephyr. We shall return the Whisting to its true master.

Sure, I think. *Whoever the fuck that is.*

"Oh yeah? Why don't you come and try, you assholes!" I shout.

The Whisting swells inside me, filling me like the deepest breath, and I exhale. The Rings on my back come to life. I try to focus the magic, to wield it like I would a sword in my hand, but the power bursts out of me like a tempest.

Buildings on either side of the bridge crumble as a sphere of pure energy explodes outward from my body. The ground beneath my feet, already weak and crumbling, starts to give way. Cobblestones drop into the chasm below, leaving gaping holes in the road. The stones don't fall straight down. No, instead, they are borne away in the gales whipping between the two kingdoms.

I struggle to maintain a grasp on my power, but it's like trying to hold on to your cloak in a hurricane. I have no control; I'm at its mercy. It's wild, untamed…

And it strikes me that I can use that to my advantage.

I raise my hands, like I saw Veteria do in her cottage. The storm whips around, now emanating from my body. The force dispels the smoke, letting me see the Kilandrar clearly.

None of them move. They aren't afraid of me.

They're testing me.

Let them.

Sheer ignorance and desperation spur me forward. I'm not afraid of them, either.

I focus on breathing in through my nose and out through my mouth. I feel strong—stronger than ever before. Wind courses through my fingers, tearing the roofs off the nearby buildings like they're paper.

Dietan of Loegria. We will destroy you and everyone you love.

I glance behind me at the gap in the rubble where Marcus and Aren watch, faces etched with fear for me. Aren shakes her head and screams something I can't hear over the roaring wind. The Kilandrar turn toward them, hissing, rising into the air—about to attack.

"No!" I shout, facing down the Kilandrar. "You will not touch them!"

I summon a gale so powerful, my feet begin to slide along the cobblestones. The Whisting encircles the Kilandrar. I trap them in the eye of my storm despite their attempts to push back with their own squall.

Pieces of buildings tear away, and the air explodes with the sound of beams snapping and stone falling. The wall of debris behind me starts to blow away, large pieces breaking off and tumbling backward toward Loegria.

All I feel is the magic rushing out of me. It's unlike anything I've ever experienced before, except in my dreams. It's pure, raw, elemental power—and I want more of it.

I let go. I give myself over to the Whisting inside me. My feet lift off the ground.

The Kilandrar fight furiously against the tornado entrapping them. They howl, growing more frenzied. They'll break through soon—I can feel it.

But they won't get past me.

Two rings of light appear on the bridge, circling the Kilandrar in thin, glowing lines. The wind carves a clean line around them. Then, with a high-pitched screech, the wind slices all the way through the cobblestones like a knife through butter.

With a groan, the entire section of the bridge falls into the chasm below. The Kilandrar plunge through the gap, followed by a wave of rubble. They screech and flail, cursing my name as the winds of the canyon engulf them, and they vanish from sight.

My vision goes dark.

In one breath, I'm floating above the bridge. The next, I'm on the battlefield, surrounded by corpses.

Then I'm back on the bridge again, my tempest ripping the overpass to pieces beneath my feet.

I'm consumed by a vision of the entire kingdom engulfed in shadow.

Back on the bridge where I'm losing control of the Whisting. *It was never yours to control*, screams a voice in my head. The bridge is crumbling. Soldiers are yelling. A voice cuts through the chaos.

The battlefield. Everyone I care about is dead on the ground.

"Dietan!"

My name—someone is calling my name. I almost forgot I have a name. *Is Dietan my name?*

I turn toward the sound. A figure braces against the wind, arms up, shielding their face.

Her face.

Her beautiful face.

I know that face.

She's on my side of the expanse, running toward me.

"Dietan!"

She's so small, an insignificant speck compared to the power roaring around us—the power that is me.

Her voice is pleading, and the look in her eyes—

My feet hit the ground, and I take a faltering step, catching myself. She looks so scared. Why is she scared of this glorious tempest—of me?

She's scared of me.

I try to call the cyclone back into myself, commanding it back into my body. Then I'm choking, just as I did the night she visited me—

Aren. I remember.

Her warmth, her touch, the prophecy.

The Whisting surges through me, greedy and grasping, leaving me empty. I've used up all the air around me, and now I have none left to breathe.

I created a vacuum. An abyss. My knees hit the stone, and I clutch at my throat, desperate for a breath that refuses to come.

The knife. I remember the knife. I reach for it at the small of my back, but my fingers are numb, and I fumble for the hilt, struggling to pull it from its sheath. When I finally plunge it into my healing hand, nothing happens.

I still can't breathe. The blood magic doesn't stop the Whisting this time.

I close my eyes and turn inward. I'm so cold. Everything inside me is frozen. I gasp and choke. The Rings are the only thing humming hot and strong as they unleash their power and drain me of life.

I'm going to die.

Then something hits me square on the side of the head.

A skillet?

I tumble forward, but Aren catches me before I fall.

I'm so shocked, I take a deep, dizzying breath.

A breath!

Aren is holding on to me with one hand, clutching the skillet in the other. Her face is scratched, her clothes torn and dirty, hanging off her like rags.

"Breathe!" she screams at me.

It's an order.

But I am breathing, I want to tell her as I fall forward into her arms with a huge, gasping wheeze.

"Harvest Mother!" Aren cries, gripping me tightly. "Don't die on me!"

I cough so hard I taste copper, burying my face into her chest. She's the only thing keeping me from falling over. She grabs my head, her fingers pressing into my face as she looks me over. I can barely keep my eyes open, I'm so drained. Her expression is racked with worry and anger, but mostly relief. I crack a smile as my head lolls on my neck.

Everything goes black, and then Aren is shaking me by the shoulders, as if she can rattle some life into me. "Dietan!" she cries, her beautiful eyes shining with tears. "Come back to me! Dietan!"

I can't speak.

I saved everyone from the Kilandrar, but if I hadn't stopped when I did, I would've brought the whole bridge down. I would have killed everyone anyway. I would've killed myself, too, if it weren't for Aren's skillet.

"Yes?" I croak. "What is it?"

She clamps her lips tightly together, glaring at me like she wants to hit me again. Her chin trembles. I must still be dizzy, because I could swear she holds me a little tighter, a blush rising in her cheeks. I want to run my fingers through her thick hair, to wrap my body around hers. How delicious it was to kiss her at the temple. I could've kissed her for days. Even when she's furious with me, she still takes my breath away—in the good way.

"You're really pretty," I murmur weakly. "Shall we have that talk now? About our feelings?"

"You've lost your damn mind." She can't help but laugh through her tears.

"Where is everyone?" I ask.

"On the other side of the bridge," she says. "I made it to you before you completely blew the bridge in half."

I peer down into the gap I created. The Whisting sliced clean through the stone. I can't spot the Kilandrar below. All I can see is the canyon, blanketed in rolling clouds.

I shake my head to clear it of the remnants of my perennial nightmare and the Kilandrar's dark whispers.

Who is this master of the Whisting?

Marcus is shouting to us from the other side of the gap, but I can't hear what he's saying. Aren and I stand in Estyrion, but Marcus and his men are trapped on the other side in Loegria...and boy, he is not happy about it.

I ignore Marcus and focus on the beautiful woman standing next to me.

"You should have stayed with them," I say, weakly, wheezing. I still can't fill my lungs.

"What, and miss all this?" she says, gesturing to the blackened ruins around us.

I collapse against her shoulder, utterly exhausted.

"You brave idiot," she grumbles, holding me close. Her embrace warms me inside and out.

Just before I give in to the hypnotic allure of unconsciousness, I realize Aren got what she wanted after all. It's just the two of us for the rest of this journey.

PART THREE

THE GREAT WASTE

CHAPTER THIRTY-ONE

Dietan

My head still throbs where Aren smacked me with her skillet. One thing's for certain: the woman has good aim. It's a bearable pain—familiar, even. The fear and dread are much harder to shake.

I almost lost myself to the Whisting. If Aren hadn't intervened, I don't know what would've become of me.

"You okay?" she asks, her voice soft and hesitant. She's been silent by my side as we walk across the rest of the bridge. It's just the two of us now. Marcus tried to make us come back, to find a way across the gap in the bridge, but it was futile. So, we just kept walking.

I wonder what my men think of what happened. They all know now. They saw the power I hold in me. Did they connect it with the Rings of Fate? I just have to trust that Marcus can keep them from figuring it out.

"I'm okay," I assure her, rubbing my head. "You really do have quite the swing," I add with a half-hearted grin, trying to make light of it, since it's clear we're both still shaken.

My usual charm doesn't work on her, or maybe my heart's not in it. "You?"

RINGS OF FATE

"I'm all right," she says tightly.

I know those words are masking a world of emotion. If she hadn't blatantly ignored me, I'd be dead—or worse. Thank gods for her stubborn streak.

I know we've made it to the other end of the bridge when my boots suddenly hit soft sand instead of brick. The gray smoke starts to clear, and I squint at the sun breaking through the clouds. I didn't realize how much I missed sunlight until now.

Aren blinks up at the suddenly blue sky, shielding her eyes. "That's weird. I thought Estyrion is supposed to be all gray skies and blackened ruins."

I nod. That was certainly the case on the other side, in Alba. But here, the smoke and acrid stench have vanished.

"Is that... Is that real?" Aren asks, her voice full of wonder as she stares at the city that rises up in front of us.

Glittering crystalline towers reflect the sunlight. Mirrored structures stretch out, expanding across the canyon cliff and out of sight. Glass statues of ancient kings stand on either side of the city's entrance, draped in lifelike flowing robes, their hands raised in welcome.

"I thought everything in Estyrion was destroyed when Boreas fell," she murmurs in awe.

"I don't know," I say, shading my eyes as I look around.

The city looks intact and dazzlingly beautiful. Before it fell, Estyrion was the most powerful of the four kingdoms. As I look more closely, I realize why it looks so strange.

The city is empty.

There's no one here at all. It's as if Aren and I are the only two people left in the world—something I wouldn't mind one bit.

Aren cranes her neck gazing up at the distant glass towers cutting through the clouds in the too-bright sky. Her lips part slightly in amazement.

But the city is lifeless. It's as still and silent as the paintings depicting its grandeur that hang in the palace in Lundenwic.

As we approach the entrance to the city, it feels frozen in time—a relic of an age-long past. There's no sound except for the howl of the wind through the empty streets. The hairs on my arms stand on end.

"What is that?" Aren asks, pointing.

I follow her gaze to rippling in the air around the glass structures. The mirrored surfaces appear to bend. It's like a distortion in a pond.

I take a curious step toward it, and as I draw closer, understanding dawns on me. "It's a mirage," I say. Suddenly, the confused and conflicting intelligence reports about the region make more sense. "It's just an illusion. This is what Estyrion City must have looked like before it fell. It isn't real."

"I wonder what is real, then," Aren says. "The smoke and the ruins—and now this? What does the real Estyrion City look like?"

"We'll find out soon enough," I say as we walk toward what looks like a wavy curtain hanging between us and the beautiful architecture. When we reach it, I hear the faint, high-pitched buzzing of a spell, like a gnat near our ears.

Aren hikes her rucksack higher on her shoulder and gestures determinedly ahead. "Together, then?"

I nod. Side by side, we step through the rippling wall of the mirage.

The moment we do, everything changes.

Instead of a glittering city, a vast desert stretches before us. It's blindingly bright and impossibly hot. A gust of wind held back by the mirage rushes past us, blowing sand and dust into our faces. I close my eyes a second too late. The sand fills my lungs and leaves me blinded for a moment.

All around us, mounds of sand, shifting in the wind, stand where the shining buildings were a moment ago. Now that I'm no longer dazzled by the illusion of the crystal city, I remember where I am.

The Great Waste. This is what remains after Boreas's destruction. He killed everyone and everything in the kingdom and turned it all to dust.

I know the history. This was once the greatest of Albion's kingdoms, the most beautiful of the First Epoch. But now it's just an endless desert. No wonder we call it the Great Waste.

All those lives, gone.

I glance at Aren, who is trying to shield her eyes from the sun. Already, I can feel my scalp starting to burn. I pull on my cap for protection, but the heat immediately makes my head sweat.

It's going to be a long walk to Engel, where the mad king resides.

We begin our trek, climbing tall dunes. We slide on the soft sand beneath our feet. Each stride feels like walking through molasses. The ground gives way beneath each precarious step, sometimes sinking us into deep drifts that rise to our thighs.

Walking through the desert saps most of our energy. What strength the sand doesn't take the sun drains, forcing us to pause frequently to rest and drink. There is little room for conversation. We wordlessly scan the horizon for any sign of sanctuary. I worry that we'll run out of water. Marcus and the men have most of our supplies. We can't die before completing our mission. We've come too far.

On one of the highest dunes, we stop to get our bearings. There's nothing but rolling sand as far as the eye can see. No shadows, no clouds, no reprieve from the relentless sun and the endlessness of the Great Waste. My compass is useless, spinning aimlessly amid the Waste's destructive power. But something out there calls to the Rings within me, so we set out in that direction.

It becomes clear that traveling during the day is a mistake. When the sun reaches its zenith, the air itself burns our lungs. Aren and I are relieved to find the ruined shell of a building. Even in its shade, the oppressive desert air settles like hot breath on our skin. We sweat through our clothes, losing what precious little water we've consumed.

The sand burns anything it touches. My leather shoes can stave off the heat for only so long before it feels as if I've stepped onto Aren's frying pan. But the heat isn't the only problem.

At night, the temperature drops so low that my fingers and toes go numb. No matter how much I breathe warmth into my hands or tuck them deep into the folds of my clothes, I can't escape the cold. We huddle together as we walk, but the freezing temperature robs me of any enjoyment at Aren's closeness. We must once again seek shelter from the punishing sun.

It's nearly impossible to sleep, no matter where the sun is in the sky. When we rest, my thoughts flit from one anxiety to the next while Aren attempts to nap.

When I finally drift off from sheer exhaustion, I'm too tired to dream of anything but endless sand and sun, and empty crystal streets.

Marcus was right—I've stepped into a hellhole. Worse, I've brought Aren with me. She doesn't deserve any of this suffering.

How many days have we been walking? Time plays tricks with your mind in the desert.

"You don't look good," Aren says one morning, studying my face.

I snort.

"And don't say 'speak for yourself,'" she adds with a weak chuckle.

"You always look good," I blurt out. I'm half-delirious, and I don't intend to flirt, but she smiles, and that's enough to get me back on my feet.

I can't imagine surviving this torturous trek on my own. Her presence is the only thing keeping me going. I need to survive for Aren; I can't leave her alone here. Before I met her, I had come to terms with my inevitable demise. But now, with her by my side, she gives me newfound hope for survival. Just when I want to start living, I can't very well die. The irony is too grand.

We come upon no village, no outpost, nor even an abandoned hut, and the supplies in our backpacks dwindle with each passing day. We'll need to further ration our food and water.

"Here," I say, offering Aren my waterskin. I pretended to drink my share so she can have more.

"You didn't have any." It's not the first time she's noticed, but her protests grow softer each time.

I shake my head. "Take it."

Too weak to argue, she does as I say, and I'm relieved to see a bit more color in her cheeks.

There's no life here at all. Sand gets everywhere: between my teeth, under my eyelids, beneath my fingernails. The dry heat ripples across the horizon, warping the land and creating more illusions. I know they aren't real, especially when they show me my white city in Loegria, with its lush pools and verdant gardens.

When we rest, wasting precious hours, she lies on her back at my side, her face twisted up in agony. In her dreams, she cries out for someone, though I can't tell if the name on her lips is mine. Her sleep is always fitful. Her lips are cracked and bleeding, her cheeks burning red, her skin peeling. Her eyes are sunken, her gaze distant, and I know I don't look any better. We save what little food and water we have for when we must walk another step.

I know I'm dying. More importantly, Aren is, too.

I have no idea how much farther we need to go. We follow the sun. All I know is that we need to keep moving east.

We come upon the head of a large statue that is buried in the sand. As we lie in its shade, I think the illusions on the horizon are playing another cruel trick on me. But as I stare, an image comes into focus, and I hear the sound of a wagon.

Despite my aching muscles, fear jolts me into action. I scramble to sit up, my heart racing. I reach over to Aren and touch her shoulder. She lurches awake, and I press a finger to my cracked lips, then cup my ear, urging her to listen. Her eyes widen when she hears it, too. It's not a mirage after all.

RINGS OF FATE

We stare at each other. Whoever comes our way could cut our throats as easily as rescue us. Fearing the worst, we tuck ourselves deep into the statue's shadow, pressing against the hot stone to stay out of sight.

Why is there a wagon in the ruins? How?

I lean low, just enough to see the hooves of a horse and four wheels rolling through the sand. Is it the Usurper's scouts? Is Penrith's army here? Or has some other enemy—perhaps the ones who kidnapped and killed Lydia—found us?

But I can't let our potential saviors slip away. We're going to die if we keep going the way we are.

Nodding at Aren, I slip out from the statue's cover, and she follows. Together, we approach the wagon as it passes. It's a covered sleigh pulled by a single horse, its wheels wide enough to glide over the sand. The linen canopy conceals the driver, but there has to be someone inside.

"Wait," I whisper. My voice cracks, dry as a piece of toast. Straining, I raise my voice. "Wait!"

The wagon stops right in front of us.

There's a rustling sound, and then the back door opens. A veiled figure emerges, their face and body obscured entirely by flowing white cotton.

Aren stiffens beside me. She's seen it, too: the glint of metal in the stranger's hand. A sword.

Instinctively, I move in front of her as the figure jumps from the wagon, sword pointed directly at my chest.

I raise my hands, which takes more effort than I thought possible. The sun beats down on my face, and I can barely keep my eyes open. I'm teetering on my feet. "Please," I croak. "We don't mean any harm."

Through half-closed eyes, I see the stranger stop two sword lengths away, their gaze fixed on us, unblinking.

"My wife and I," I manage, tipping my head toward Aren, "we need help."

Calling Aren my wife feels good. It's also a gamble—I hope it makes us seem less threatening. If Aren wasn't as desperate and dying as I am, she'd probably give me a withering look right now. I keep my hands raised, surrendering to whatever fate has in store for us.

I'm not sure if the stranger understands me. They stand still as a statue, watching us. Then, finally, they gesture toward the wagon with their sword. A clear signal: *get in*.

I don't care where we're going or if we're going to be killed. We just need to be out of the sun. Aren and I waste no time scrambling into the wagon and find that it's full of woven cloth and bolts of fabric. A merchant, then. The stranger, still silent, climbs into the driver's compartment, and Aren and I collapse into each other in the darkness of the wagon. Even though it moves slowly, the cart kicks up a slight breeze that immediately cools the sweat on my skin. I close my eyes and let my head fall back, grateful for the relief. Aren melts with exhaustion on the floor beside me, against the hard wagon wall.

"Where are we going?" she whispers.

I shrug my shoulders, too tired to say anything more.

We follow some unseen path, in roughly the direction of the Whisting's call. I'm lulled into a hypnotic trance as the wagon sways, losing all sense of time and space. I come back to myself only when the wagon stops.

Before I can react, the wagon door is thrown open, and someone reaches in and yanks me out by the front of my shirt. I land hard in the sand, too weak to stop my face from hitting the ground. I hear Aren shriek as she, too, is forcefully pulled from the wagon and slammed down somewhere behind me.

"Leave her alone!" I try to scream, but a gag is put in my mouth, wrapped around my head, and tied with a knot tight against the back of my skull. My hands are bound behind my back, straining the muscles in my shoulders tightly enough to pop.

Aren thrashes and fights as her own cries of fury are muffled, but strong hands prevent me from turning toward her. I struggle, but there are too many people holding me down.

They search me, under my clothes, checking me for weapons. Someone upends my bag, sending my empty waterskin flying into the sand. They confiscate my royal knife, and my blood pumps in fury. They rifle through Aren's pack as well, checking for weapons or valuables. There's just her skillet, a second empty waterskin, and some dried, unappetizing plants.

"Clear," a man's gruff voice says, out of sight.

A pair of boots steps in front of me. I raise my head as high as I can, straining my neck to peer up at my captor. She looks to be middle-aged, weathered, with sharp eyes. She carries a gold knife in her holster and wears an embroidered sash.

She looks down at me and tongues the inside of her cheek, clearly unimpressed. At last, it appears she's decided our fate. "Get them inside."

CHAPTER THIRTY-TWO

Dietan

Aren and I are carried, bound, into a small dwelling. The space is a modest living room, with pillows and blankets surrounding a small hearth. A fire crackles despite the heat of the day. Even with the hearth, it's much cooler inside. The stone walls keep the outdoor heat where it belongs.

We are both shoved onto the pillows, and the woman walks around us. Pacing the room, she empties her pockets and unties her sword belt. Her weaponry looks familiar, but my dry eyes could be deceiving me.

"You can leave us," she says to the others who brought us here so roughly. I scowl as they make their exit.

Aren seems unhurt but frightened. She's breathing hard around her gag. I wish desperately that I could touch her, comfort her, but I can hardly move an inch.

My arms ache, my head still hurts, and my legs are throbbing. I try to shrug my shoulders to loosen my bindings, but the ropes around my wrists dig in even more tightly with every small movement. I want to assure Aren that we'll survive this, but all I can do is meet her gaze and plead for her not to panic.

Casually, the woman pours two meager cups of water and places them on a small table beside us. It's barely a sip, but even that small amount is the equivalent of gold right now. Aren stays still, waiting, and so do I.

The woman watches us for a moment, seemingly satisfied. She moves behind us and unties our hands. Aren and I rip the gags out of our mouths, and we nearly knock over the cups in our haste to drink.

I wonder if water always tasted this sweet. I close my eyes and swallow it all.

"Slowly," the woman says. "Or it'll come back up."

I try to obey, but it's difficult. I want more. The water is cool all the way down to my stomach.

"Please, we mean no harm," I finally say.

"So you claim," the woman replies matter-of-factly. She takes a seat on the floor across from us, peering over the crackling flames.

Everything about her screams *warrior*—the broad shoulders, the muscular forearms, the steady gaze. Now that I'm no longer quite as parched, I can feel my wits returning, and with it some recognition of who this woman might be. There have been rumors of her over the years. Most assumed she died.

Is that the same nose, the same jawline from the portraits? I study her face with watering eyes, just as she inspects us both.

"Who are you?" she finally asks.

"Dietan Cornwallis Arthur William Maximillian Conrad Barclay-Bruce Armandale-Macrae, Crown Prince of Loegria and heir presumptive to Alarice." The truth spills out of me before I can stop it. I don't even realize what I've said until Aren glares at me, her eyes wide.

"And you?" the woman asks Aren.

"Aren Bellamore of Evandale," she answers dutifully.

Her reply surprises the woman. She raises a curious eyebrow and then turns back to me. "Are you two really married?"

"Engaged but not really," I admit, unable to stop the truth from slipping off my tongue.

"We're only pretending," Aren says. She looks surprised at her own honesty and clamps her mouth shut to stop herself from saying more.

My eyes flick to the cup. Whatever the woman gave us wasn't just water.

"So, a prince and a…" she starts.

"Barmaid," Aren supplies.

"A prince and a barmaid. How curious. And not a married couple as you claimed to be."

"We didn't mean to deceive you," I say quickly. "We were desperate for help. We didn't want to look suspicious."

"Heh. A Loegrian prince wandering the Great Waste, suspicious?" The woman chuckles. "Can't be. So, what business do you have here? What brings you to the remains of Estyrion?"

I try to come up with a lie—something easy. That we got lost, that we were kidnapped and abandoned, that we were separated from our party. But the words refuse to form. I try to say anything but the truth, and my tongue feels like cement in my mouth. I fight desperately for control over my own mind, closing my eyes, focusing like I've practiced for years to quell the Rings, but the impulse to tell the truth is still overwhelming.

"We're here to solve my problem," I finally blurt out. My heart thunders in my chest. I know that if she asks, I'll tell her the entire truth—and I can't. "Don't ask me to reveal any more than that, I beg you."

She raises her eyebrows, then looks at Aren, who's fighting so hard against her own honesty that her whole body is shaking.

"Please," I say, to draw her attention back to me and spare Aren. "It's my problem, not hers."

"What problem?" she asks.

Of course she would.

Anyone would, after hearing my answer.

I wince as I am compelled to speak. "I seek help from the one who calls himself King Osian of Engel."

At that, her eyes darken. "What for?"

I clench my fists, fighting my own tongue. The longer I remain silent, the more it feels as if my mind is melting. I can't stop myself. I answer, practically gasping as the pain disappears the moment I spit out, "To stop the coming war."

The woman smiles. "That may be your truth, but no one can stop the Usurper of Penrith from marching on the rest of Albion. And I doubt Osian wants to stop him. The King of the Waste is in league with the Usurper."

Well, this is…terrible news.

I meet Aren's frightened gaze, and it takes everything in me not to reach over and take her hand.

"Now tell me the truth," the woman says. "Why are you here?"

This time, the words tumble out immediately, as if pulled by a string. "Because I have the Rings of Fate."

The woman goes very still.

She watches me with a look I can't decipher, as if she's peeling back my skin with her eyes, examining my insides and finding me wanting. "Tell me everything," she says.

No. I won't. I fight against the magic, sweat pricking at my forehead, my whole body trembling as pain grips my head like a vice—but in the end, the poison wins. I tell her everything she wants to know. I tell her about the Whisting, about the Rings in my back, about my fear that Loegria will march against Penrith without them, and about how I need to find a way to remove them before I kill everyone. About how Engel is our only hope, as I've been told Osian has arcane knowledge of the Whisting.

"We've been wandering the desert for days," I say, finishing my story. "No food. No water. Until you found us."

"Please," Aren says to the woman. "We're just trying to save him and everyone else in Albion. Just let us go. The less you know, the safer you'll be."

"The Kilandrar are after us—after me," I correct. "The sooner I find Osian and get the Rings removed, the sooner I can stop the war. I can stop everything."

No one speaks again for a long while.

The woman rubs her jaw, her eyes fixed on the fire, her gaze distant as she contemplates all I've told her. I clench my fists on my lap, praying I haven't gotten us into even more trouble. Oddly enough, though, her wariness has started to ebb. I relax my hands as she lets the silence stretch on.

Like any diplomat, she's waiting for us to fill it, to offer more information unasked. I keep my mouth shut and let my eyes wander to the sword and belt on the table. I wonder if it was her birthright or if she has a collection of stolen treasures to which she will soon add my royal knife.

"You've gotten our names," Aren says. "Now tell us yours."

"I know her name," I say. It's a gamble.

Aren starts, looking at me in confusion.

The woman's eyes meet mine, and I don't shy away. After a moment, her gaze softens, and she relaxes back into a pillow, propping herself up on her elbow. "Who am I, Prince Dietan of Loegria?" she asks.

I cough. "You are Princess Katharine of Penrith, daughter of the last true king and ruler-in-exile of that kingdom." I think for a second. "And my second cousin once removed, I believe."

Aren's eyes grow wide.

"I know my history," I say with a proud smile. "I saw your sword and the sash you wear. There were reports that you might have escaped. That you were in exile amassing a small army. My father sent emissaries to find you after the Usurper first took your father's throne. We've been looking for you for a long time. I'm glad to discover you're still alive."

"Good work, cousin. Yes, we fled Penrith and settled here, in the Waste, for our safety. Not that we've been at all safe, and to be honest, both of you should probably go back where you came from."

"You survived," Aren says, ignoring Katharine's warning. "Everyone said you were killed when the Usurper took the throne."

"I had to let the world believe I was dead so I could live. I thought to make a stand from here to retake Penrith, until this Osian fellow came and claimed the Waste for himself. Ruined my plans."

Another woman enters the room and nods a greeting. "She's right, you know. You both should go back to wherever you came from." She's smaller and gentler-looking than Katharine, though she's dressed in the same fine linens as Katharine.

"This is my wife, Jingu," says Katharine.

"Trust me," I say, "I would rather not be here, either. But I have no choice."

Katharine sighs. "The land itself is hostile and unfit for even the most prepared travelers, which is exactly how Osian wants it. He may not have created this environment, but he has taken advantage of his kingdom's isolation to exert unnatural control over his people. I doubt he will help you. You are a fool to seek his counsel. He cannot be trusted."

This is exactly what Veteria said, lifetimes ago, but neither she nor Katharine seem to have a better solution.

"Perhaps not, but I don't know how else to get the Rings of Fate back in the hands where they belong. I'm running out of time. Please, let us go so I can see this through."

"And let you die out in the desert? I think not. Jingu's people have learned how to survive in the Waste, and even we know we can't outsmart the land. Believe me when I tell you, you won't discover any solutions in Engel. Go back to Loegria while you still have the chance and find another way."

She picks up a larger ceramic pitcher and refills our cups. When she notices us watching her warily, she adds, "Trust me, it's just water this time."

I can't afford to doubt her, so I drink some more. It's just as delicious as the first cup, but I hope it's untainted.

"Slowly," Katharine reminds me just as my stomach cramps.

Aren and I drink quietly, slowly. Jingu sets food on the table beside us—a small platter of fresh fruits carved into exquisite shapes. She pushes the plate toward me. "One bite at a time."

Immediately, I start to feel better. I'm able to restrain myself and savor each bite as instructed, and my stomach settles with each passing moment.

"What did you dose us with?" Aren asks.

"Water from the henbane cactus. It forces the drinker to only tell the truth—to their fullest knowledge, of course. The effects should have worn off by now." Katharine looks at me. "Do you want to try to lie?"

I believe her. I don't feel that strange itch in my mind that forced me to answer truthfully.

It's a relief.

"I needed to keep my secret. I don't mean to be untrustworthy."

"Leaders make difficult choices, and I see that your intentions are pure. But you can understand why we've needed to use the cactus more frequently."

"Osian?" Aren asks, reaching for another slice of the beautifully carved fruit.

Katharine nods. "It's difficult to trust anyone in this blighted land. Apologies that the lack of trust extended to you, cousin."

I choose not to hold it against her. I'm trespassing on this land under false pretenses, and with war looming, it's difficult to tell friend from foe. If I were in her position—a princess in exile, hunted and in hiding—I'd be equally wary of anyone crossing this border under mysterious circumstances.

"The world is on the precipice of war. I must try to get to Osian, even if my mission is sure to fail."

Katharine looks solemn. "Then you're going to your doom. He is intent on building a new kingdom from the ashes of Estyrion. Anyone who sets foot in Engel is forced into service. People in the Great Waste don't have much, and what we have dwindles every day. This so-called 'king' promises a solution for those in desperate need, but it comes at a terrible price. He's building an indentured army, and no one can escape."

My father's spies have heard rumors of such an army, but it chills me to hear this from a trustworthy source. "How do you know?"

Katharine's lip twitches. Pain. It flickers across her eyes, and she shifts uncomfortably on her pillow. Jingu takes her hand and massages it.

"We've lost many to the false promises of this so-called king. Our eldest son, Arnfried, for one. We haven't heard from him in months since he went to Engel for supplies against our admonishments. He joins many who have gone before him and disappeared," Katharine tells us.

I see a mother's distress in her eyes. My stomach lurches. I feel for her—the terrible weight of being unable to save a loved one. And worse? Not even knowing if they are alive to save.

"The few resources Estyrion holds Osian has harnessed into building Engel and its dreadful army, with none to spare for the rest of us. The city is a cursed place, sucking the marrow from this already barren land and leaving nothing behind."

"But what else am I to do?" I ask. "You know I spoke the truth, and you know I can't stop until I've exhausted all my options. This is the only way our kingdoms can defend themselves against the Usurper and the Kilandrar's dark powers without exorbitant loss of life—well, other than perhaps my own." I try to sound flippant, but Aren looks alarmed—stricken even.

I hope it reflects a depth of feeling for me that she hasn't shown before. I turn back to Katharine. "I wish you'd join us when the time comes."

Katharine's gaze shifts to Aren. "Like you've convinced a barmaid from Alarice to join you on your impossible mission?"

"Aren is one of the most loyal people I've ever met," I say, feeling the need to defend her. "If you can't trust me to see this through, you can trust her."

The exiled princess of Penrith huffs loudly through her nose, amused. Aren flushes deeply and averts her gaze, but I mean every word. I wouldn't have gotten this far without her.

Katharine seems satisfied. My conviction seems to sway her, or at least the understanding that I cannot be stopped.

"You two are braver than most. I'll give you that. Not smarter, but definitely braver."

"I still have hope that I can persuade Osian to see reason. Perhaps we can even get your son back. Katharine, if I succeed, I can save *everyone*. Even return you to Penrith." I may have taken that a bit too far, but I hope Katharine finds it compelling.

She smiles at me like I'm an innocent child. Like she thinks it's a fool's hope. "Eat," she says, gesturing to the fruit before us. "You'll need your strength."

While Aren and I eat and drink what we can, Katharine readies precious new supplies for us. We finish the fruit and some hot porridge, and she gives us a healing salve that must have some magical properties, because within moments, my lips are no longer cracked and split. The painful sunburn on my face and neck disappears. My head and legs have stopped hurting, too.

Aren looks much better as well. Especially after Katharine presents us with fresh clothes and tells her the village has public baths.

It's then that I realize I haven't seen Aren smile in days.

Katharine and Jingu are more than generous, offering aid despite having so little to spare in their ramshackle village. I owe them more than my promise to find their son.

"Since you have the means to travel across the desert," I tell her, "go across the bridge to Alba. A general by the name of Marcus and a handful of Loegria's finest are likely securing the town and waiting for me there. If you need anything, tell them I sent you." I twist one of the buttons of my coat until the frayed thread gives way. I drop the button into her open hand. "He'll recognize this."

Katharine closes her fist and smiles inscrutably. "I appreciate the fine offer, cousin." She insists on telling the other villagers that Aren and I are merely hapless explorers in need of help. Even if the people don't believe the lie, no one challenges her.

Aren leaves to go to the women's baths and I to the men's, where the cool waters soothe my skin. Travel, and the harsh conditions of the Waste, have taken a toll on my body. I hope Aren has fared better, and I worry about the toll this journey must be taking on her mind, as it has mine.

I think about Marcus and Jared. I know how much I asked of them, two men trained for leadership and war. But Aren? She's gone the farthest and the longest, and my stomach hollows out when I think about the many injuries that must now scar her body, too.

She's a civilian, a barmaid who deserves to be a princess. I feel unbearably selfish for asking her to do any of this, but especially now that we're heading to such a dangerous, dreaded city.

When I return, dressed in clean clothes, my mind is made up.

"Don't you dare," Aren says as if she's read my mind.

"Don't what?"

"Don't try to leave me here, or send me away again, or whatever bullshit you're thinking this time."

"You know what I'm thinking?" I ask, a glimmer of a smile on my lips. She's wonderfully annoyed with me again, and the fire in her eyes makes me want to cheer.

She huffs and blows at a lock of hair that's fallen across her face. Then she haughtily lifts her chin, puffs out her chest, and deepens her voice to do her best impression of me. "'Don't come with me to Engel. You won't be safe. You, a weak woman, should go back home and let me, a big, strong man, handle it.'" Her eyes narrow. "Well, face it, mister. We're in this together."

"I could order you to go," I rumble. "You are, after all, my subject."

"According to the unification treaty, I'm really not until you marry an Alarician girl. And"—she holds up her left hand gasps in feigned surprise—"I don't see a ring."

For a moment, all I want to do is to get on one knee and offer her my mother's opal ring. There's a yearning in me to prove my troth, to make our pretend engagement real. I wonder if it would make her nicer to me.

Probably not.

And I wouldn't have it any other way.

That kiss at the temple felt so real. The memory makes me want to relive the moment now, to see if it feels just as authentic.

"Hey, if you want to foolishly put your life in danger, I can't stop you," I say, holding up my hands in surrender.

She crosses her arms and smirks. "Exactly."

"That isn't the victory you think it is," I reply.

"What else could possibly happen?" she asks airily. "We've already been robbed by bandits, hunted by raiders, attacked by Kilandrar, almost died from dehydration—I think things are looking up from here."

She looks so fierce and fearless in this moment, I need to kiss her again. Now.

"What?" she snaps, and I realize I've been staring at her mouth for longer than is normal. "Do I have something in my teeth?"

I cough. "No…"

"Oh," she says, her voice suddenly low and husky. "Because I thought…"

I lean forward. "You thought?"

She looks deep into my eyes, and I lean in even closer. I can see every freckle on her nose and cheeks, the dimple when she smiles. I close my eyes, and our lips meet. Her mouth is as warm and inviting as I remember, despite the dry desert heat. I put my arms around her, can feel her fingers digging into my shoulders. I run my hands down her back, then lower still to cup her—

Someone behind me clears their throat.

"Oh!" Aren jumps back, blushing furiously. "Katharine!"

Damn.

"Sorry for interrupting," Katharine says, stepping into the room.

"I'll, um… I'll go see Jingu about our rations," Aren says, rushing from the room. Maybe she's embarrassed. Maybe she doesn't want to be seen kissing me.

That's a possibility.

I've made it quite clear how I feel about her. I almost killed myself with my own power rather than admit my feelings. But now I realize I have absolutely no idea how she feels about me, beyond the undeniable spark between us.

Maybe she's just on this journey for that pot of gold and to save her people, like she said at the outset. Then she'll walk out of my life forever.

"She feels so much for you, that one," Katharine says, as if reading my mind.

I don't know what to say. I wish she were right, but I'm pretty certain what she sees is just a physical connection. Aren ran away, embarrassed to be caught kissing me, after all.

Katharine clicks her tongue, muttering something about "young love" before handing me a pair of goggles. "These will help protect against the sun's rays and from any illusions, natural or otherwise. You'll need them in Osian's territory. Your horses are ready. Are you?"

"As I'll ever be," I allow.

Even a well-deserved rest and a meal of healing herbs and fruit can't change my trepidation.

"Travel at night," she says. "It's too hot during the day without proper shade. We've packed some more provisions for you and Aren to help stave off the worst of the dehydration, but take care. You will be at the whims of the winds. Boreas's wrath inflicted on this land was unflinching, and nothing can save you. Do not hold out hope that nature will be merciful."

"I won't." I look at her keenly. "I wish you would join us in our fight against the coming darkness. It's already on your doorstep. We can stand together, cousin," I say. "Like the three kingdoms did in the old days."

Katharine holds my gaze like she's deciding what to reveal and how much she trusts me still. Finally, she sighs. "We've survived this long after getting chased out of Penrith by keeping our heads down. I will not put my people in even greater danger." She reaches into her pocket and hands me a small vial. Inside is a clear liquid, slightly thicker than water. "Take this with you. You might need it where you're going. Tread carefully and trust your instincts."

"What is it?" I ask.

"A precaution. To protect the thing that matters most."

She tells me how to use it, and I don't hesitate to tuck it into the folds of my new jacket.

CHAPTER THIRTY-THREE

Dietan

At sundown, I find Aren outside the stables, petting a majestic white mare with unusual flat hooves wider than dinner plates. The horses here have adapted to enable them to trek across the soft sand without sinking. The horse beside it, also white, is already loaded with our packs and eagerly stamps its hooves.

Aren is dressed as I am, in long, draping white linen. While mine is a loose tunic and trousers, hers has clasps that secure it close to her body, cinching her waist and complimenting her figure. I've never seen her wear such a fitted outfit, defining her every curve.

I'm staring so intently that when she turns around, I almost drop the goggles I'm holding. I hand them to her, attempting to be smooth. *This isn't the time or the place*, I remind myself, trying to assume a nonchalant air, even though every nerve in my body comes alive in her presence.

"Thanks," she says, looking at me curiously as she takes the goggles and rests them on the crown of her head.

RINGS OF FATE

"You look ready for the desert," I say, trying to regain my cool. *Stop wanting what you can't have*, I tell myself. *She likes kissing you, but that's all she'll ever want from you. She thinks you're spoiled and stupid.*

"Pretty great, right?" she says with a smile, as if the earlier awkwardness of our interrupted kiss never happened. "This side protects me from the heat, while the other side"—she shows me the black lining of her coat—"protects from the cold."

I nod, trying to focus on her words instead of how good she looks. I've been given a coat like it, too. The fabric is handwoven, the hood large and sturdy, sheltering me no matter the temperature outside.

"I meant what I said back there," I tell her. "About you being the most loyal person I know."

We can be friends. I can do that—be the bigger man. Try not to murder anyone who looks at her the way I look at her. I can let her go...after a few more of those kisses.

Aren looks at me from beneath her lashes before tearing her gaze away and smiling. "Yeah, yeah. Don't get all sappy on me."

Definitely friends. Or? This woman confounds me.

Before we leave, Katharine, Jingu, and their daughter come to wish us goodbye. The girl, who can't be more than eight, stares at Aren and me, her awed expression making me smile.

"Engel lies west of here," Katharine says. "Follow the brightest star, the Lady of the Lost, and she will guide you through the night. In three nights' time, you'll see the city."

"Thank you," I say. "Truly. I vow, as prince of Loegria, you have an ally in me."

I hold out my hand, and Katharine takes it, her grip strong. We shake firmly.

"Go, cousin," she says. "Since I cannot dissuade you, I hope you find what you seek."

Without further delay, Aren and I leave the village, riding west, taking a barely visible path toward the fading red-orange sunset. Already, I'm feeling more confident than ever.

Now that I'm not freezing during the night, I'm better able to appreciate the stars that glimmer overhead. The heat of the desert warps their light, making them undulate in blue and orange hues. It's as if some godly hand spilled diamonds across the sky, so vast and so deep. When

I tear my gaze away and look at Aren, I find that she, too, is enraptured by the light above.

"There she is," she says, pointing at one that shines more than the others. "Right on time. The Lady of the Lost, the brightest star in the sky, to guide us on."

But I find it hard to look away from Aren. I allow my smile to answer her own.

When we stop just before daybreak after our third night of travel, we make camp on top of a sand dune so high, I might have believed it was a mountain. In the distance, I can just make out a flicker of light on the horizon. The sun is rising behind us, so we're facing directly west. That light ahead can only mean one thing.

"Engel," Aren says. "We're almost there."

I look at her, a spark of hope blooming in my chest. Her bright eyes fill me with a lightness I haven't felt in so long.

Maybe I'm not the greatest fool in Albion for embarking on this quest. After all, if I had done things differently, I would never have met Aren, and that thought is too much to bear.

Maybe all will be well in the end. The Rings of Fate removed from my body, returned to my father, and the Usurper defeated. Aren makes me feel like I can conquer the world.

"Let's make a break for it," she says, with a naughty smile unfurling across her face.

"Now? It's almost dawn."

"All the more reason to make haste," she says. She smiles at me, mounts her horse, and adds, "The sooner you remove the Rings, the sooner your real life can begin. We are so close."

It's hard to argue with her, especially when she has that gleam in her eye like she's challenging me. I mount my horse, and together, we make for the shining city rising from the desert waste.

Several hours later, we pause at the top of a dune. The horses huff and paw at the sand restlessly. "What is that?" Aren asks. "It doesn't look like a cloud."

I squint into the bright daylight through my goggles, which Katharine said would lay bare any illusions. But the midday sun is high in the sky, and we still haven't reached the city. If it's not another mirage, Engel is farther than I anticipated.

Is the Great Waste nothing but mirages and magic?

Because now, a great cloud suddenly blocks our path. It looms like a monumental wall, so thick even the ferocious desert sun can't pierce it. Sand churns within it. Where we stand, everything has gone unnaturally still, as if the land itself is holding its breath, waiting for impact.

The ground trembles, and there's a rumble that grows louder and more menacing with every pounding heartbeat.

"It's not a cloud," I say, dread filling my veins as the wall plummets toward us. "It's a sandstorm."

My horse rears up, almost bucking me off. I grip the reins, trying my best not to panic, because if the horse is worried, then I should be, too. "Get to cover!" I shout.

Aren doesn't need to be told twice. She kicks her horse into a gallop toward the wall of sand. I almost cry out for her to stop, to turn around, but then I see where she's headed. There are ruins half buried in the dune just ahead of us. Shelter.

I give chase, kicking my heels into my horse's sides as hard as I can, desperate to catch up to her. My breath comes in sharp, shallow bursts, and my chest tightens as the storm looms high ahead, swallowing half the sky in darkness.

The ground trembles beneath us, a deep rumble vibrating through my bones. The storm is alive, a monstrous, growling beast bearing down on us.

It swallows us whole in an instant.

It's as if we've crossed into another world. Grains of sand slice into my skin like a thousand tiny daggers, stinging every exposed inch. My goggles fog up and scratch against my face. I have to close my eyes, trusting my horse to follow Aren's. My heart pounds so violently in my chest it feels like it might burst. I grit my teeth and forge on.

The sand deepens.

My horse slows, snorting and stamping as massive drifts block our path. The wind howls, drowning out my own panicked thoughts. As the sand shifts beneath us, the horse rears with a desperate scream, and I'm thrown violently from the saddle.

I hit the ground hard, the impact rattling my teeth and sending a sharp pain through my shoulder. Sand engulfs me, dragging me into the suffocating darkness as I claw and kick to keep my head above the rising tide.

"Aren!" I scream, but the wind rips her name from my throat and scatters it into the void.

I kick my legs, forcing my body to move through the heavy sand. My limbs feel like lead, my muscles scream in protest, and my lungs burn with every breath. The horses' cries pierce the storm. They're sinking fast. The sand has buried their legs up to their bellies. They thrash and kick, but it only pulls them deeper. The sand is relentless, swallowing everything.

I can't find her.

She's gone.

The realization slams into me like a fist to the gut. A cold, sickening dread grips me, hollowing out my chest. My breath hitches as images of Aren buried alive, suffocating under the sand, flash behind my eyes.

No. No, no. I can't lose her. I can't.

The Rings in my back stir. They feed on my fear like a parasite. Their hum grows louder, vibrating through my spine, taunting me. They want to help.

Use us, they whisper.

The temptation claws at the edges of my mind. I could stop the storm—I *should* stop it. But I don't trust them. I don't trust myself.

What if I make it worse? She's out there, somewhere.

What if I kill her?

I clench my fists so hard my nails dig into my palms, the sting grounding me. The Whisting's wild power churns inside me, feeding on my desperation, begging to be unleashed. My entire body shakes. My head pounds with the effort of holding it back. I feel tears streaking down my face, mixing with the grit of sand.

I have to find her.

"Aren!" I scream again, my voice cracking with anguish, but the storm consumes her name like it consumes everything else. My throat is raw, my voice lost. I stagger forward, nearly blinded by the sand that slips beneath my goggles and stings my eyes.

Then I see it. A shadow, crawling beneath a collapsed wall.

Aren.

I drag my body through the unrelenting storm. The sand presses against me, pushing me backward, but I don't stop. My knees buckle, and I slam into the ground. I claw my way forward, ignoring the searing pain in my hands and the sharp sting of tears streaming down my scratched cheeks.

When I reach her, she's pressed against the wall, her arms covering her head, trembling as the storm rages around her. Relief washes over me so fiercely it nearly steals the breath from my lungs. I throw myself on top of her, wrapping my arms around her as tightly as I can, shielding her with my body.

"You're okay!" I yell, though I don't know if she can hear me over the roaring storm. She clutches at me, her fingers digging into my back as she hides her face in my chest. Sand pours over the wall, piling around us, burying us inch by inch. I kick at it, trying to keep it at bay, but it's too fast. Too much. It's going to bury us alive.

The Rings grow louder now, a steady, insistent thrum that radiates through every nerve in my body. They mock my fear, my weakness.

Use us. Stop this. Save her. Save yourself.

"No!" I scream, my voice raw, throat burning. "No, I won't! I can't!" What if I make it worse? What if instead of saving us, I doom us? I can't give in.

My chest tightens, the anguish suffocating me as much as the sand and the wind. I futilely try to push us both above the rising tide. Pain rips through my shoulder like fire, but it's nothing compared to the fear. The fear of losing her.

I close my eyes, my forehead pressing against hers. "Please," I whisper, not even sure who I'm begging—her, myself, the gods. "Please don't let me lose her."

The sand is at our chests now. My magic rears up inside me as it senses the deadly weight crushing in on all sides. My fingers twitch of their own accord, and I clench my fists tight, fighting it.

I can't—not when Aren is right here. Not if I might hurt her instead of helping her. Each breath I take is shallower, sharper, the weight of the sand squeezing the air out of my lungs.

The Whisting screams to be used.

I don't think I can hold it back anymore.

A furious scream tears from my throat, a sound born of desperation and fury. The sand starts to overwhelm us, rising over our heads.

The storm rages above us, violent and all-encompassing, and then—suddenly—there's only silence.

The world is still.

I kick furiously, pulling Aren with me by the arm. My head breaks the surface of the sand, and I gasp for air. Sand covers every inch of me—my ears, my nose, my mouth. I cough and spit, shaking out my hair, clawing at my face to free myself from its suffocating grip. Beside me, Aren takes a ragged breath, choking on sand as we swim up through the loose grains, freeing ourselves inch by inch.

The storm hasn't vanished. It's all around us, but it's...frozen. Suspended in time. Sand particles hang in midair, shimmering and still, as if caught in some unseen web. Everything is silent, the unnatural stillness broken only by our retching and coughing.

"You did it," Aren says, her voice hoarse as she stares wide-eyed at the frozen storm.

"It's not me," I say, barely above a whisper.

"What?" She looks at me in confusion.

"I didn't do this." I look around, awe and dread twisting in my chest as I take in the surreal scene. Through the suspended storm, a figure emerges, walking toward us with deliberate, measured steps. The sand shifts away from him. The Whisting clears a path, blowing the grains aside like a gentle breeze.

It's a young man, probably a few years younger than me. His skin is pale, his tall nose sharp and angular. His dark hair is smooth and brushed back from his face, not a single strand out of place. He walks with his hands clasped behind his back, as if he's taking a casual stroll in a pleasant garden. His expression is flat, bored, utterly indifferent to the storm around us.

He could be handsome, I think distantly, if he didn't look so unimpressed by everything.

I struggle to get to my feet, sand pouring off me. My body is heavy and sluggish with exhaustion as I offer Aren a hand. She takes it, and manages to rise as well, though the sand clings to her. She is still buried up to her knees. She braces herself, her breathing shallow, her gaze fixed on the stranger.

The man stops several paces away. He's cool and calculating as he peers down his nose at us. We're insects he's discovered crawling in the dirt.

RINGS OF FATE

His posture has gone from casual to rigid, his presence unnervingly commanding. For a long, agonizing moment, he says nothing, letting the silence stretch. Then he snaps his fingers, and the frozen particles are released from their paralysis, but instead of resuming the storm, the sand falls gently back to earth.

Finally, in a voice as smooth and cold as the edge of a blade, the stranger says, "Prince Dietan, I presume?"

CHAPTER THIRTY-FOUR

Aren

Just when I think our luck has finally turned, here comes *this* prick.

I've always prided myself on reading people as soon as they sit down at my bar, and there's something unsettling about this haughty stranger. His face is too perfect and his voice too smooth. "Smug" sums him up.

I dislike him immediately.

And then, of course, there's this whole business of how he stopped the storm with his immaculate control of the Whisting. At least that's what I assume happened, since Dietan says he didn't do it. I'm grateful this stranger saved us, but his attitude I could do without.

"Do you know this guy?" I ask Dietan.

Dietan doesn't get a chance to answer as the stranger speaks for him. "I believe Prince Dietan and I have yet to be introduced. However, we know all who enter our domain, barmaid."

Talk about an arrogant bastard. Even more annoying is that whoever this guy is, he doesn't even think I'm worthy of a name.

"And you are?" Dietan asks.

"King Osian's emissary." He bows elegantly.

Why does he look familiar? I squint in the bright sunshine and study his face, but I can't place him. Maybe he traveled through Evandale? I'm good at remembering faces, even ones who only passed through the Raven's Beak.

But I'm coming up short.

He looks to be about twenty years old, with thin lips and striking blue eyes. He carries himself with a grace that gives the impression that he's floating.

Dietan raises his eyebrows, and I know he's thinking what I'm thinking: *something's off about this so-called emissary.*

"I am indeed Prince Dietan of Loegria," Dietan says imperiously. "I wish to speak with your lord."

"Of course. He is expecting you. Word of your engagement has reached our ears, and the king himself would like to congratulate you on your upcoming nuptials."

The emissary turns his gaze to the mound of sand nearby, then narrows his eyes. A stiff wind cuts through the sand, revealing the horses trapped underneath.

I gasp at the amount of control this man has over the Whisting, so unlike Dietan's chaotic outbursts.

The emissary smiles, and it brightens his whole face, making him look even younger. "There you are."

The horses are unhurt but dazed, and they stand up on jittery legs. They shake out their manes and stamp their hooves, clearly frightened by what happened. With high-pitched whinnies, they rear up on their hind legs, kicking out, and take off east, toward home.

I watch them until they disappear into the horizon, wishing Dietan and I were dashing away with them. If this emissary has such abilities, I shudder to think what powers Osian himself might wield. If Katharine is to be believed, fear twists my insides when I consider what he could be using that magic for.

What possessed me to insist on coming with Dietan all the way here? My heart squeezes uncomfortably, and I place a hand over my chest. I know the answer to that but don't allow myself to dwell on it. There's a lot more at stake than my silly feelings.

"You stopped that storm with the power of the Whisting," Dietan says.

The emissary bows his head modestly.

"How?" Dietan asks, and I can hear the desperation in his voice.

"The King of Estyrion is quite powerful," the emissary replies. "He is very generous with his gift and will teach any who seek the knowledge of the Whisting, unlike those outside our borders. Now," he studies us with a baleful eye, "I must request that you surrender your weapons to me before we proceed into the city."

"May I ask why?" Annoyance is clear in Dietan's voice. He probably doesn't want to part with that knife he always carries with him. Harvest Mother, I'll be dead before I give up my frying pan, though it's not a weapon—in most hands, anyway.

"Everyone is most welcome in Engel, but those who seek our protection must surrender any instruments of violence. We are a peaceful people."

Dietan looks wary as he hands over his royal knife and sheath.

I clutch my weathered rucksack close, and when the emissary gives it a pointed stare, I lift the flap so he can see inside. "It's just a pan," I say. "It's for cooking."

The emissary looks thoughtful. "I suppose if we are to be fearful of a skillet, we are not much of a people."

Thank the goddess that worked.

Dietan straightens, standing tall like the real prince he is. "Lead the way," he commands.

This is it, then. It's time to meet the mad King Osian of Engel.

Instead of leading, the emissary walks by Dietan's side. I follow, with only a skillet to protect us, hoping it's enough.

I fall back a few steps, assuming the role of dutiful woman—not a role I usually play. But by letting the men walk ahead, I have a chance to finally breathe. Knowing the emissary isn't watching my every move like a snake ready to strike gives me cover to observe.

But my relief is only momentary. As I trail behind these two men, it occurs to me that I don't belong here. I don't mean *here* as in this hellscape; nobody belongs *here*. I mean I have no business consorting with royalty.

My eyes begin to water, and I blink to clear my vision.

Must be the sand.

I study the two figures proudly striding ahead of me. It feels strange to see Dietan acting all official. I haven't thought of him as royal for some time now.

He's just Dietan.

I only call him "my prince" or "your worship" to get under his skin because it's fun to annoy him.

As we follow the emissary out of the sand dunes, my thoughts wander back to that kiss at Katharine's.

It felt so real…

Well, the one at the blessing ceremony seemed real, too, but he *had* to kiss me then. At Katharine's, it felt like he kissed me because he *wanted* to—because he *needed* to. But what do I know? Despite all of the conversations I've had at the Beak with all manner of men, I don't have any *firsthand* knowledge of romantic relationships. Though my gut tells me that Dietan has feelings for me, I'm having a hard time trusting that intuition.

I tug my rucksack higher on my shoulder. How far would that kiss have gone if Katharine hadn't interrupted us? I try not to wonder, but it's all I can think about. Heat rises in my cheeks, and this time it's not from the desert.

What will happen when this journey is over?

If we both live, that is.

When we get our first look at the shining city, I feel more like a peasant than ever.

The city of Engel is made almost entirely of gold. Under the bright light of the desert sun, everything—from the towers to the streets—shines tenfold. Walking up to the front gates would make anyone feel insignificant. Especially someone like me who has never seen this much gold in my life.

When the solid gold doors open, I hesitate. Dietan glances over his shoulder at me. For a fleeting moment, I glimpse the concern in his expression before he resumes his royal facade for the emissary's benefit.

All I want to do is run in the other direction.

Katharine warned us that anyone who sets foot within these gates never leaves. If I enter this city, I might never see my sisters or father again. Even if Dietan succeeds in solving his problem, *I* may never be allowed to leave.

Dietan is a prince. He is trained to maneuver through the intricacies of court politics. He belongs with people of power, and there is an entire government ready to swing into action to negotiate his release. I'm nothing, no one, compared to him. I'm not even his bride.

I'm just part of a lie.

I hold myself tightly as I follow Dietan and the emissary, willing my knees not to give out.

Goddess, why can't I just go home—and take Dietan with me?

That's where he belongs. In Evandale. At the Raven's Beak tavern, with a mug of ale and a plate of my biscuits. He looked so happy there. We'd have a good laugh together. I'd call him names and order him around. He'd laugh and help me clean up, learn to do the dishes.

We'd be happy.

We could find another way to remove the Rings in his back. I'm sure there's something his father's advisors missed.

"Dietan," I whisper.

The emissary continues walking as Dietan stops and turns to me. "Yeah?"

Let's leave this place. I don't have a good feeling about this. We'll find another way to fix you. I think we're going to die in here.

But I can't.

But I don't say any of that. What was I thinking? He chose to be here. He's a prince. He can't live at the Raven's Beak. War has arrived in his kingdom, and his father needs the Rings of Fate.

I must not be thinking straight because of the heat.

Ahead, the emissary has stopped, waiting for us.

I meet Dietan's blue-green eyes, and my breath escapes me. This man has given me so many chances to back out. He's even tried to force me to leave, yet here I am. I *can't* leave. Not without him. Asking him to leave when we are so close to his goal would be unfair.

The weight of kingdoms rests on those broad shoulders.

"Nothing," I say, shaking my head.

"Are you sure?" he whispers back.

No, I'm not sure, but we've come this far, and we can't turn back now. This is why we're here: to remove the Rings, to change the course of the war, to return to Loegria and save everyone in Albion.

Dietan waits patiently, standing tall and confident and regal, like the prince he is. "Come on," he says, trying to reassure me with a nod, and I attempt a smile, but it feels tight and unconvincing, as if I'm pulling the corners of my lips up with my fingers.

"It'll be okay," he says, taking my hand and looping it through the crook of his arm. He places his free hand over mine, and I feel steadier at his touch. "I promise I won't let anything happen to you," he adds. "And if we're lucky, maybe I can convince King Osian to become an ally in our cause. Whatever Katharine's experience, there may still be a way to get him on our side."

I'm pretty sure luck has nothing to do with it.

I swallow the anxiety bubbling up my throat and nod. I don't trust this King Osian, and I wish I'd never mentioned the mad king all the way back in Veteria's hut, but I do trust Dietan, and that's worth more than a city made of gold. He gives my fingers a reassuring squeeze before we walk side-by-side through the gates.

"Welcome, Prince Dietan of Loegria and Aren of Evandale," the emissary says, smiling so wide, his teeth look like fangs. "To Engel. The last free city in Albion."

CHAPTER THIRTY-FIVE

Dietan

The gold is a little much, if you ask me.

Castle Engel is situated high on a hill in the middle of the walled city. I keep Aren close as we walk up the steep, sloped streets paved with more gold. As the emissary guides us through narrow alleyways, I can feel Aren's fingers trembling in the crook of my arm. I place my hand over hers again, stroking her knuckles with my thumb.

I want to assure her that whatever occurs, I'm going to make certain nothing happens to her. I, too, feel deeply uneasy walking the streets of Engel. A golden city hidden in the Waste, resplendent and clean, a shining example of the ingenuity of mankind—but I see hardly any evidence that people actually live here.

Most shops are closed, homes shuttered, and schools quiet. Flags with the king's crest, a sun on the horizon opposite a three-peaked mountain, flap in the oppressive desert breeze. We pass by parks and squares, where a handful of people walk quickly. No one lingers near the pools or misting gardens to stave off the desert heat. In a city as grand and beautiful as this,

I expect to see its people thriving. This is more of a ghost town than Alba.

Aren's hand tightens on my arm, and I know she's noticed the oddity as well. A cold knot forms in my stomach. I force myself to breathe evenly, to keep my shoulders relaxed, though the tension mounts beneath my skin. My calm demeanor and perfectly practiced smile never crack, especially when the emissary glances back at us every now and again.

"Beautiful, absolutely gorgeous," I say, my voice smooth, even as that knot in my stomach twists.

"Thank you. We're very happy here. King Osian takes excellent care of his citizens."

All five of them...

I refrain from saying anything further, instead turning my attention to Aren. "It's marvelous, isn't it, my love?"

"Yes," she agrees, a little breathless. She isn't quite as convincing as I am. "Is this the kind of city we'll be living in once we're married?"

"You haven't shown your blushing bride the pride and joy of Loegria yet?" the emissary asks, a teasing glint in his eye.

"Saving the best for last. No offense," I say with a casual laugh, though my shoulders feel stiff under the weight of his scrutiny.

"Indeed, Your Highness. I have no doubt that Aren of Evandale would feel right at home in Loegria. But a woman from Alarice must be feeling far too flush in our climate."

Aren is caught fanning herself, and I can tell it isn't an act. The heat has us both on edge. "I'm sorry. I'm not used to the heat. I deeply apologize for my obvious discomfort," she says.

"Not at all. All who come to Engel are welcome. We shall see to your every need."

His hollow hospitality makes the tension knot in my shoulders. I try to keep my expression neutral as we follow our guide up and up the sloped streets all the way to the palace entrance. I can't help but feel exposed without my knife.

Stone-faced servants are already waiting for us at the front doors, dressed in uniforms embroidered with gold thread. It's the most people we've seen all day.

The castle is grand, with its many towers and parapets ascending toward the bright-blue sky. The glare from the sun is blinding. I avert my eyes, afraid I might lose my vision if I stare too long.

Inside the castle, the relentless heat finally abates. I feel a wave of relief as we step into the grand entrance hall. The painted ceiling above us depicts a starry night sky that contrasts with the golden walls and pink marble floor. It's supposed to feel majestic, I'm sure, but all I can think is how tacky it looks.

Too much gold. Too much pink marble. Just…too much.

Oil paintings of the historical kings of Estyrion line the walls, their stern gazes seeming to follow us as we pass. Sheer curtains frame doorways leading to rooms that branch out of view. A grand double staircase stretches toward the second floor. Sunlight pours through open windows, illuminating every inch of the castle with an unnatural brightness. Servants in pristine white-and-gold embroidered uniforms stand at attention by every door, their eyes fixed straight ahead, ready to spring into action at a moment's notice.

"Welcome," the emissary says. "The king is occupied at the moment, so please allow our staff to guide you to your quarters."

He smiles warmly, but I don't trust it.

Servants step to our sides and relieve us of our rucksacks. Aren resists for a moment, hanging onto her precious skillet and herbs, before relinquishing her pack when I put a hand on her elbow. We're outnumbered. We must trust in Osian's eerie hospitality if we're to ask anything of him.

The servants abruptly lead us to one of the nearby wings and down a flight of stairs. The castle is so vast that I have trouble getting my bearings. It's larger than my family's in Loegria, that's for certain. Every room we're whisked through feels like another turn in a labyrinth. One could easily get lost in its endless hallways of pink marble and gold.

Aren leans in close, her breath hot against my ear, and whispers, "I don't like this place." To anyone watching, it looks like she's murmuring sweet nothings to her fiancé. My hand reflexively wraps around her waist, playing into the act. She doesn't flinch away, thank the gods, and for a fleeting moment, the feel of her by my side eases the tension gripping my chest.

I dip my head low, whispering against her hair. "I know. Me too."

In response, Aren puts her arm around my waist also. We are the very picture of a couple in love. I secure her to my side, trying to draw strength from her presence and enjoying the steady feel of her body against mine as we follow the servants leading us to our quarters. My stomach twists in quiet unease, but I keep my steps steady and my breathing even.

"This way, if you please," the servant walking ahead of us says, leading us through endless receiving halls, reception rooms, and what I can only assume is the king's throne room. A massive golden chair hulks in the middle of the grand space, gaudy and overwhelming.

We walk together, clutching each other, as the servants guide us to a staircase spiraling downward into the deeper levels of the castle. My unease sharpens with every step. The air feels heavier, thicker, the lower we go. I tighten my arm around Aren's waist as if I can shield her from whatever waits below.

I think about turning back. About sprinting up the stairs. But such foolish notions will surely get us killed.

When we enter a dark hallway, my suspicions are confirmed. Dread grips my heart with an iron claw, squeezing tighter with every passing second. I should never have allowed Aren to join me. I should have insisted Marcus take her home. The hallway is lined with rooms behind iron bars.

The first servant stops at one of the doors and opens it, the rusty hinges whining loudly in protest. Neither Aren nor I move. The skin on the back of my neck prickles, and every instinct screams that the plan to grab Aren and run was the correct one.

"When will we see the king?" Aren asks, her voice hollow in the dungeon's oppressive silence.

The servant doesn't answer. His eyes are flat, vacant. I can't tell if he didn't hear her or if he's simply ignoring her. Osian's men do not hide the glints of metal at their waists. I know we are in no position to resist. I take Aren's hand, squeezing it gently, and lead her into the cell. The servant closes and locks the door behind us, the thud echoing through the dark halls like a death knell. At least we're in the same cell.

Aren stands rigidly, staring at the locked door.

"Goddess damn it. So we're prisoners now?" she asks, her voice sharp with frustration.

"Sure looks that way," I mutter, my jaw tightening.

Aren throws her hands on top of her head and unleashes a truly creative string of curses. If I wasn't so on edge, I'd be impressed.

"Aren," I say, trying to sound calm even though I feel anything but. "If they wanted to kill us, they would have done it by now."

That doesn't seem to comfort her.

I glance around the cell, forcing myself to take stock of our surroundings. A single mattress on the floor for the happy couple. A single bucket as a chamber pot for the happy couple…and that's it. The perfect honeymoon.

"If I remember our way through that maze, I think we're somewhere below the throne room," I add, motioning to the vents above our heads. Light slices through the cell in sharp lines, barely illuminating the space. It's the only source of light other than the dim torches lining the hallway. The vents are high—too high to reach. Even if I let Aren stand on my shoulders, the openings behind the grills are too narrow to fit a fist through.

We're trapped.

"We just have to wait," I say, trying to temper the rising panic clawing at my chest. The Rings stir, their hum faint but insistent. They itch to be used, feeding off my frustration and anger. I dig my nails into my palms, and the sharp sting grounds me. If I use the Whisting to break us out, I could hurt Aren, and that's the last thing I want.

"You waiting for the king?" A voice comes from the cell diagonally across from ours. An older man leans against the bars, one arm dangling out casually, his wrist limp. I can just make out his white hair, but the rest of him is obscured in shadow.

"Yes," I answer truthfully, my voice tight.

"Good luck with that." The old man laughs a wheezy, rasping chuckle that grates against my nerves.

"How long have you been here?" Aren asks.

"Not that long. Couple of days, give or take. I'll probably get out soon, though. No one stays here for long."

Okay, that doesn't sound so bad. We can handle a few days.

"You seem to know a lot," Aren says, stepping closer to the bars, her voice laced with suspicion.

The old man coughs before replying. "Bah, everyone who lives in Engel knows what goes on here. Isn't a secret. People go missing all the time. Usually the ones who cause more trouble than they're worth to the crown."

"Is that what happened to you?" I ask.

"Yeah, I never know when to keep my mouth shut."

I don't like this. Not one bit. It's everything Katharine warned me about. Osian isn't a king—he's a tyrant.

Aren moves closer to the cell bars. "This happens a lot, huh?"

"All the time. Everyone here in Engel serves King Osian. Step so much as one toe out of line, and you'll wind up here. Beaten, bloody, broken… dead." He says it so nonchalantly, I almost don't believe him. "But the people are talking. If there's one thing the king can't take from us, it's our ideas."

I know this to be true. Ideas can turn into hope, and hope is more powerful than even the Whisting. Tyranny has no chance against ideas.

"You said you're getting out?" I ask, though I'm not sure I want to hear the answer.

"I said I was getting out in a few days. I never said I was getting out alive."

H ours pass, and there's nothing to do but wait. I have no way to determine what time of day it is. There's no sunlight in the dungeons, leaving us in the murky half-light seeping through the grills above.

I'm utterly exhausted. We've gotten little rest since we set foot in the desert, which feels like a lifetime ago. Aren dozes between bouts of pacing, but I refuse to sleep. If I have one of my nightmares, I'll lose control because I'm so agitated.

I keep myself awake by silently reciting all the essential trivia my father and tutors forced me to memorize. I stare at the slits of light above my head. I'm pretty sure night fell some time ago, but the throne room is still lit up with firelight.

A rhythmic pounding comes from above, followed by a shriek like an animal wailing. Occasionally, there are moans, then the cries again. No need to keep running infantry formations through my head; the unnerving, violent sounds are enough to keep me awake and alert.

Meanwhile, Aren paces the cell, holding herself stiffly. She shivers and rubs her arms as she walks, still dressed in her desert linens. Watching her is a good distraction from the noises coming from above.

"What do you think is happening up there?" she asks, eyes flicking up to the grates.

I roll onto my side, pressing my back against the cool wall. "Let's hope we never find out… Come here," I say, patting the space next to me on the mattress. "There's room."

She gives me a skeptical look.

"You're cold. Don't make this awkward."

"I'm not," she says crossly. She doesn't complain when she crawls onto the mattress and curls up with her back to me, keeping a slight distance. The space between us is excruciatingly close yet too far at the same time.

I yearn to close the gap, to pull her to me, but I hold myself back. There's still a hint of that orange blossom oil she brushes through her hair, making my mind fog in a pleasant haze. If I close my eyes, I can trick myself into believing we're somewhere else—somewhere beautiful, like her. Still shivering, she tucks her knees in tighter.

"Come closer," I say. "We'll keep each other warm."

Aren looks at me over her shoulder, and I give her an earnest nod. She shifts closer, resting her head on the crook of my arm. I throw my free arm around her, hugging her close to me.

At the beginning of our journey, she might have rolled her eyes and told me off, but things between us are different now.

It's the one good thing that's happened so far.

"This is not how I envisioned my adventures," she grumbles.

"Sorry to be such terrible company," I say, attempting a joke. "What *did* you envision?"

She hesitates.

"I honestly don't know," she admits. "Evandale was the only place I'd ever been. So, I didn't know what to expect beyond its borders. But I dreamed of more. I *needed* more."

"Aha! I knew it!" I declare. I squeeze her even closer to me. She wriggles as I hold her tighter. Her playful laugh is like a balm for my spirit.

"Is it so bad I want more out of life than a second-rate proposal from a drunk farmer?" she says, exasperated.

"No, not bad. Stubborn, maybe…and wise, and courageous. Plus, you got one from a prince instead." I can't help but smile and waggle my brows.

But she's not smiling with me. I can feel her sadness.

"But I didn't. Not really…"

I feel my heart sink. After all we've been through, she can't possibly think this is still all for show. She rolls over to look me in the eye, and my breath catches. Tears stain her cheeks, and I'm the cause. I take her hands in mine.

"Aren of Evandale, no proposal, no poem, no ode, no grand gesture is enough to express all you mean to me. You are more to me than I am to myself; to me, you are perfect. More importantly, you are perfect for me."

CHAPTER THIRTY-SIX

Aren

I take several deep breaths willing myself to believe his words.

I beam. I don't think I have ever smiled like this in my life. There's no wondering anymore. No constant questioning. And to think, we're coming to terms with our feelings just in time for us to die.

But there is still a little life left to live.

The dim light catches his beautiful eyes. They flicker like candles in the dark. Even in the murky gloom, I can see the shape of his strong, muscular body. It takes everything in me not to reach out and trace my finger over every ridge.

He doesn't look away. Neither of us says anything.

My heart is pounding so furiously that I'm sure he can feel it being this close.

It isn't the perfect time or place, but again, we may die soon. So, I gaze up at him, feeling safe cradled against his chest. He reaches out with a single finger and traces my lips. Tingles follow his gentle trail.

I let my desire to kiss him again overwhelm me.

"Kiss me, you idiot," I demand.

"As my lady commands."

He doesn't need to be told twice.

He rolls me under him. I revel in how good he feels…how *right*. I look up at him, and for a moment I'm lost in those eyes. He props himself up on his elbows, his mouth hovering just above mine, making me wait. Making us both wait.

Cheeky bastard.

He lowers his lips to mine and kisses me gently. He goes slow. I sigh as I bury my fingers in his luscious hair, scraping my nails across his scalp. I groan as he deepens the kiss, feeling him breathe into me. His tongue finds mine. He's melting my resolve like candle wax. I groan again, my entire body humming.

We're not pretending anymore. There are no more excuses.

Because this is real.

He's more delicious than anything I've ever tasted. I want to consume him, devour him. My desire deepens as his tongue slides and teases against mine. I can feel his growing need, hard and strong, against my softness.

I want to lose myself completely to the pleasure of Dietan finally holding me so completely in his arms, but I sense his hesitation. I know he's thinking about the Rings.

But there isn't a draft, not even a breeze—no sign that the Whisting is at bay.

He continues, growing more confident, placing soft kisses down my jaw, then down my neck. Finally, he pulls open my robe and unfastens the small hidden hooks. He slides the neckline wider, exposing me. My breath hitches. This is the first time a man has ever seen me in this state of undress. I start to nervously ramble, but Dietan places his finger lightly to my lips.

"Shh, you're beautiful." That same hand works its way down my upper body, lighting my skin like a sunrise over the horizon. Finally, he cups one of my breasts. A small gasp escapes my lips. He strokes the sensitive skin with gentle caresses, running the pad of his thumb over my nipple. I savor every brush, every twist. I whimper, pleasure radiating through my whole body.

I let my hands explore, too, removing his shirt, running them up and down his hard back, gripping him closer. Our kisses grow wilder, our breaths heavy. I reach down into his smallclothes and take him into my hand.

My eyes grow large with surprise. Dietan notices and roguishly smiles into our kiss.

I run my hand up and down his generous length. He shudders as a moan escapes his lips. I love that I can set his body on fire, just as he does mine.

His other hand starts to inch lower on my body, but then suddenly, his lips leave mine and he stands up.

"We can't… Not here," he says, his voice strangled.

But this feels so, so, so good.

"Why?" I rasp, reaching for him.

Dietan paces the small cell, taking deep gulps of air as he puts his shirt back on. I feel cold everywhere our bodies just touched. I watch him, confused, still flushed, my breathing ragged. Why did he stop?

He groans, rakes his fingers through his hair, and begins to pace again. What the hell is going on? Is this how I envisioned my first time? No. But did I want him to stop? Also, no.

He stops and turns to me, finally finding the words he's looking for.

"You deserve so much better than this. You deserve my four-poster bed, my window overlooking the sea. You deserve the world."

I don't know what this means. My mind races. He can't even look at me. He's staring at the grills high above us.

He takes a deep breath, then another. Then he finally lowers himself to sit beside me. "I'm sorry… I can't… I don't want our first time to be here, in a dungeon," he whispers.

He leans down and kisses me again—first my cheek, then my ear, then softly on my lips. I don't know what to make of this. I'm angry at our situation. I'm annoyed at his thoughtfulness. But mostly, I'm left wanting.

He pulls my robe back over my chest, fastening the hooks into place. I have to stare at the ceiling and ball my hands into fists to keep the tears at bay. I won't cry. We *will* get out of here alive.

For what feels like forever, we are silent.

"Fuck this dungeon," I finally mutter.

He snorts. "We can't fuck in this dungeon."

I can't help but laugh. He laughs right along with me.

That's better.

We lie back and snuggle side-by-side. Dietan kisses the top of my head. His presence is no longer an aggravation but a comfort.

We close our eyes and try to get some sleep. I cannot stop replaying every kiss, every touch, in my head. Has the prince become someone I can trust with my heart? My heart has never been this open, this vulnerable. I've never felt like I have a safe place to land.

I can't bear the thought of him walking out of my life if—when—we make it out of here.

I drift off to sleep thinking of Dietan and his four-poster bed.

When morning comes, I jolt awake at the sound of the cell door groaning open.

A guard in full regalia stands at attention, looking down at the two of us entwined on the mattress.

"King Osian will see you now."

CHAPTER THIRTY-SEVEN

Aren

It's a rude awakening, going from dreams about Dietan holding me in his arms to the shriek of the cell door opening.

"Come on," Dietan says as he helps me to my feet while a fully armored, gruff-faced guard waits impatiently.

I comb my hair with my fingers, trying to put it in some semblance of order, undoubtedly failing spectacularly. Once it's wound into a bun on the nape of my neck, I shake out the skirts of my desert linens and meet Dietan's gaze. He smiles, but I can see the shadows under his eyes. He didn't sleep a wink.

He takes my hand and links his fingers through mine. "Ready?"

I nod, and hand in hand, we follow the guard up and out of the dungeon.

The words of the prisoner across the hall last night still echo in my head. He's certain he's going to die, and my mouth goes dry as I wonder if we are walking to our end.

Dietan says nothing, his gaze steely and focused as we are led back through the golden palace. Then his eyes meet mine, and they brighten just slightly, making my heart rate quicken. His eyes are sea green today, like the ocean near his home that I so desperately want to see for myself.

My mind returns to last night—the taste of his kiss on my lips, the feel of him when I boldly reached into his smallclothes. He was so hot, so large. Just the thought of what could have happened if he hadn't stopped—if we hadn't been in the damned dungeon. What *could* happen once he persuades King Osian to help him with the Rings so he can finally live without fear of his own power.

It makes my knees weak.

He kissed me and meant it. And even in our shitty situation—imprisoned and now on our way to meet a king who could end our lives—my heart feels full because I know I've finally found a man worth waiting for all my life.

I never imagined it would happen.

In this moment, full of the promise of death, Dietan's love is worth all of the hardship. Whether he has said the words or not, he does love me. I know it. I know him. And to be honest, I probably fell in love with him the night he wandered into the Beak, thinking he could fool everyone into thinking he was a commoner. When he drank our strongest ale without complaint.

We arrive at a staircase that leads to the throne room.

"Shall we, my darling?" he asks, kissing the back of my hand. The way he says it feels different now than when he said the exact same words at every stop of the Wedding March.

"Yes, my prince," I reply, just as I did then, but I don't say it with my customary mocking tone. Instead, the words feel like ownership.

He is mine. *My* prince.

I slip my arm through his, and a handful of armed and armored guards lead us up a series of stairs.

The metallic clanking of the men's armor and the glint of sunlight off their halberds are stark reminders of why we're here and who we're going to see. My palms suddenly grow clammy. Dietan must feel it, too, because he puts a hand over mine and gives it a small, reassuring squeeze.

I focus on Dietan's confidence, absorbing some of it for myself. I pull my shoulders back and hold my head high, trying my best to imitate him, trying to feel worthy of him, of being a princess.

He watches me out of the corner of his eye as we reach the top of the stairs, and his lips quirk up into a small smile. "Everything is going to be okay," he says. "I promise."

I can only hope it's not an empty promise, but hope is all I have.

Hope and Dietan.

The throne room is a grand hall that looks to be made of solid gold. The nave is bordered on either side by gold columns holding up a ceiling so high, I wouldn't be surprised if a flock of birds could fly through it.

One by one, the guards escorting us take positions against the wall, standing at attention. They rest the butts of their gleaming halberds on the marble floor. I notice the grates at the outer border of the hall. The very same grates through which Dietan and I heard all manner of mysterious and unnerving sounds.

Before the great throne, a long table bisects the hall, resplendent with golden tableware and laden with so much food, I wonder who else might join us. As far as I can tell, we're the only people in attendance. I feel tired and rumpled in our unwashed desert clothes and would like nothing more than a hot bath and a chance to wash my hair—to look less common before this king.

"Welcome to the king's court," the liveried butler says, standing tall in front of the table.

My stomach rumbles at the sight of such a feast. The last full meal I had was at Katharine's house, and as welcome as her hospitality was after our ordeal in the desert, it doesn't compare to the spread before us.

There are platters laden with delicacies that couldn't have been easy to procure here. Roast pork and duck, grilled chicken and lamb, mountains of peeled and cut fruits, vegetables glistening in glazes, and soft bread shaped like animals line the center of the table. And even this far away from any ocean or lake, there are scaly fish and shelled oysters and other sea creatures in thick sauces.

I wonder for a moment if it's a magical mirage, like the glass city. It seems impossible that there'd be such variety and abundance in a barren place like the Great Waste.

Sparkling pitchers of water glimmer in the bright sunlight filtering through the open archways, and my mouth is suddenly parched.

"May I ask where the king is? We were told he was ready to see us," Dietan says.

"Yes, in due time," the butler answers. "His Majesty is occupied with other matters at present, but he will only be a moment. Please, help yourself to breakfast."

"Thank you," Dietan says politely. "I think the last time I had a good meal was in a tavern called the Raven's Beak."

He catches my eye, and a warm flush spreads across my face, putting me a little more at ease.

Dietan guides me to the far end of the table and pulls out my chair. After I'm settled, he takes the chair to my right, closest to the head of the table.

I feel awkward, sitting at a table in the king's court without the king present, but the butler doesn't seem bothered by it. He gestures to servants who come out of nowhere, like they've melted from the walls to start filling our plates. They set so much food in front of us that the decadence makes my stomach churn. I think of the desperate faces of the starving villagers we saw on our travels, like in Alba.

The butler, satisfied with the presentation, leaves. The servants move quickly, keeping their gazes down. I try to catch one of their eyes, but no one dares look up. They seem skittish, and my nerves remain on edge, every instinct telling me to get the hell out of here.

Dietan appears completely calm and begins to eat, so I follow suit, though my hands shake and the decadent meal tastes like ash in my mouth. My heart is pounding so hard, I can barely swallow.

Then the doors open again, and a familiar face walks in. "Good morning," the emissary says, his voice echoing around the nearly empty room. He pours each of us a crystal goblet full of water. I hesitate for a moment, wondering if it's safe. Then I notice the emissary takes a long sip of water from the same jug as he walks around to the head of the table. I glance at Dietan, who nods, and so I take a sip as well.

The emissary flops into the king's throne, settling in comfortably and cradling his goblet of water close to his chest, grinning. When no guards make any movement to stop him, I feel like I've been struck over the head with my own skillet. My ears ring. The emissary— He is actually—

Dietan raises his goblet to the emissary. "Hello again, uncle."

I goggle at him. *Uncle?*

"Hello, nephew. You're not as dumb as reported after all."

"Ha." Dietan smirks. "It's good to be underestimated, Uncle Namreth."

Uncle Namreth. I've heard that name before. Of course! It's the name of King Elgar of Alarice's younger brother—Dietan's granduncle. This is Prince Namreth, the one who disappeared, banished for some reason or other.

"I suppose Osian suits you better," Dietan says. "More ominous. Who'd fear someone called *Namreth*?" He says the name like it's an insult.

Dietan and Namreth stare at each other with open hostility, the tension radiating from both of them so thick, I'm certain they're going to come to blows. I eye the knife at my place setting, but before I'm forced to do something stupid, Namreth's shoulders relax. He leans against the back of the golden throne wearing a smug smirk. Dietan sits back in his seat as well, and I let out a discreet sigh.

And now I know why the emissary looks familiar. I can see the family resemblance. There are clear echoes of Dietan's face in his uncle's.

"The years have been kind to you, uncle," Dietan says. "Extremely kind. What is your secret?"

"Take a guess," Namreth says.

"The Whisting," Dietan answers.

I hold my breath. He stopped the sandstorm. Does that mean the Whisting can stop time as well?

Namreth arches an eyebrow. "Indeed."

So, the Whisting keeps him young, slowing down the aging process. Is that what will happen to Dietan if he doesn't get the Rings out of his body? He'll remain young forever, while I grow old?

My gaze lingers on Dietan's face in profile. He looks like he's been hewn from stone. I suppose that's why we're here after all—because Osian has knowledge of the Rings of Fate and can maybe help Dietan remove them. But why didn't he tell me he suspected Osian was his uncle? I stare at my plate, my already-meager appetite completely gone. *What else has Dietan kept from me?*

"Come now, nephew. Why so grim? Let's celebrate your engagement like family!" Namreth laughs.

Dietan doesn't.

"Cheers," Namreth says, raising his goblet. When neither of us toast, he doesn't seem to care. He shrugs and takes another sip.

"You were once a prince of Alarice, and now you are King of the Waste," Dietan says.

"I had no choice," Namreth answers. "When my brother passed me over in the line of succession to name you, his worthless grandson, heir to Alarice, I had to create my own destiny."

"You were banished for learning forbidden magic," Dietan says. "Grandfather didn't trust you with the kingdom."

"My brother is a coward. We could have used the Rings to make Alarice even stronger—to reshape the world—but what did he do with them? He gave them to your father, his son-in-law, to keep the kingdoms at peace. He entirely squandered such a precious resource, such an opportunity." His voice is level, as if he's discussing the weather, but I can tell by the way he grips the arms of the golden throne that his emotions are a storm ready to erupt.

"The Whisting is a gift to the land. It's never been about greed," Dietan says.

Namreth looks displeased to be interrupted. His lips curl into a sneer, and he leans forward. "Your mind is limited by your mortality. Such power must be wielded by those who are willing to use it."

On the table, Dietan's fist tightens, as if holding back the urge to use the Whisting on his granduncle.

Namreth leans back in his chair again, swirling his goblet casually. "The Rings of Fate are my birthright, and they were taken from me. So, I left, abandoned the home I wanted to protect, and sought power from the one place my brother would never turn to: Penrith."

Dietan scoffs. "We know you went to the Usurper. My father and grandfather kept track of you. Did you think you were free all this time because we didn't know where you were?"

Namreth looks a bit discomfited by that.

Touché, I think, proud of Dietan.

"So why are you here?" Namreth asks. Exactly what I want to know. I only know what Dietan's told me. He's surprised me many times on this journey by knowing of Veteria's existence, Katharine's name, and now Osian's true identity.

Who is Dietan of Loegria, really?

"If you're so smart, why don't you already know?" Dietan chides. "I've come to destroy you, obviously."

"Destroy me?" Namreth chuckles. "And how will you do that?"

Dietan shrugs.

"You think you're my doom, are you?"

Dietan sighs. "Okay, I'll admit I had other reasons for coming here at first. I thought you could be an ally. Even though you left Alarice behind to forge your own path, maybe you would see the value in joining us to protect your new kingdom and the people of Old Estyrion against the Usurper. I thought there might be good in you still. My mother said that growing up, you were the bravest of the Vindar knights, the shining hero of Alarice. Fighting men flocked to your banner, and the people threw flowers at your feet. I wanted to see for myself how you'd changed, whether you are that Vindar knight still. My father said it was a lost cause. My grandfather agreed. But I will be king someday, and I need everyone's help in this coming war against the Usurper. I thought I should at least try to get you on our side."

"Well, I'm sorry to disappoint you, nephew," says Namreth, not looking disappointed at all. "But I am loyal to those who are loyal to me."

"The Usurper of Penrith," says Dietan. "You would turn your back on your family to serve him?"

Namreth nods as he swirls the water in his goblet lazily. "I've chosen strength over weakness. You should, too."

"Loegria and Alarice are not weak, and our kings serve no one but their subjects."

Namreth looks thoughtful. If he's angered by Dietan's jab, he doesn't show it. "Aren't they, though? Our spies tell us that Loegria and Alarice *are* weakened. The treasure of the kingdoms, the Rings of Fate, are missing."

If Dietan is shocked to find his secret so plainly revealed, he doesn't show it. "Missing?" he asks with an eyebrow raised.

"Penrith has openly attacked the borders of Loegria, yet the king does nothing. Alarice is undefended; bandits and marauders control the Bandai Bridge. Both Donnel and Elgar appear in good health and of sound mind, so there can only be one explanation: your father no longer has the Rings of Fate.

"I know Donnel. He would never let his people suffer. If he hasn't used the Whisting by now, he doesn't have it," he continues.

The hairs on the back of my neck rise, but Dietan appears unrattled.

"The Rings are not to be used lightly—my father taught me that. The armies of Loegria and Alarice are more than capable of handling a few bandits and raiders. We were taken by surprise, it's true, but our kingdoms are mobilizing for the defense of our borders against the Usurper. You can depend upon that." Dietan radiates princely confidence, but I can't help wondering: Where are these promised armies? Why isn't King Elgar calling upon our farm boys and tradesmen's sons to serve?

"Your armies may have stopped him when he first took the throne, but the *disorder* in your border villages suggests they aren't ready this time. And Donnel would never permit such loss of life if he had the means to prevent it," Namreth says, echoing my uneasy train of thought.

"Then why hasn't the Usurper launched his attack?"

"Oh, we will, in good time. An army will rise from the desert and another from the ocean. Together, we will take all of Albion."

Dietan frowns. "But you can't—and you won't. Not until you know for sure that my father doesn't have the Rings. He can destroy you with a wave of his hand. Your power is nothing compared to the Great Rings of the Anemoi, forged by Skiron herself. You can raise a sandstorm but not a hurricane."

Namreth scowls, and I wonder if Dietan has gone too far in provoking him. "My scouts tell me there is a massive hole in the bridge between Loegria and Estyrion. Such destruction can only be caused by one who wields the Rings." He swirls the water in his goblet and gives Dietan a crafty smile. "And here you are, dear nephew."

"Here I am." Dietan's voice is calm and level, but he's gripping his knees under the table.

"Come to destroy me, have you?" Namreth chuckles again.

"Since you will not be an ally, you are my enemy and an enemy of Albion. I don't see that I have any other choice." Dietan shrugs as if he is merely observing the weather.

"Well, you are a fool. After I was passed over, Alarice means nothing to me."

"I suppose you have been my enemy for some time now," Dietan says thoughtfully. "I know that you sent your raiders after me and that you tried to kidnap and kill my bride. And that you're working with the Kilandrar."

The symbol Lydia drew in blood wasn't a mountain; it was Osian's crest. The very same that flies high on the flags above the castle. She was clever till the end.

Namreth smiles. His teeth look like fangs. "You will tell me where the Rings of Fate are, nephew."

"I will do no such thing. Ever."

My heart leaps in my throat as Dietan stands his ground.

Namreth's laugh echoes throughout the chamber. "You will give up the Rings of Fate, one way or another. I know you have them on your person. I can feel them on you. The Whisting calls to me."

Shit, shit, shit. This is bad. I ball the front of my skirt in my fists under the table and glance at the guards, who stand motionless but alert around the room.

Namreth narrows his eyes on Dietan. "Tell me, nephew, how does it feel, knowing you've come so far only to fail in your quest?" He takes another sip of his drink, waiting for an answer. "I think I shall enjoy watching you suffer. Slowly."

"Do what you will to me, but Aren has nothing to do with this. Let her go."

Namreth puts a hand to his heart. "Now, why would I want to separate you two lovebirds? By the goodness of my own heart, I allowed you to share quarters last night. Did you not enjoy it? Am I not merciful?"

"If you are merciful, let her go. Aren is as useless to you as the desert to a fish."

Here he goes, trying to get rid of me again, trying to keep me safe. But I won't let him. The Oracle told me to never leave his side for the good of Albion. Did he forget that already? I want to shout at him, tell him he doesn't speak for me, but Namreth shifts in the throne and leans forward, never taking his eyes off Dietan.

"Useless to me? I think not. She is very dear to you, isn't she, nephew? And that is *most* useful."

Dietan barks a laugh as if it is the most ludicrous thing he's heard at this most surreal luncheon. "Aren? She means nothing to me."

Excuse me?

I stare at him, body buzzing with alarm, and then slowly, I realize what he's doing. He's still trying to protect me. Trying to make Namreth believe a lie.

Right?

But Dietan doesn't even look at me. His gaze is firmly on Namreth.

"Nothing?" Namreth's smile is crafty. "A strange thing to say about your bride-to-be, isn't it?"

"Aren and I aren't really getting married. It was a cover so I could travel through the country without sparking suspicion. I don't love her. She's nothing to me. Just a country serving wench. I was just using her to get where I needed to go."

Well, that's harsh. He wants to protect me—that's why he's saying all this. Loveless marriages are common among royalty—just look at his own parents. But why would Dietan have admitted to the whole ruse?

I glance around the room at the servants. Surely, he knows it'd be disastrous for the truth to get out that the Wedding March was a lie from the start.

Hold on… Wait… My gaze flicks to the water in the goblet. So does Namreth's.

No, it can't be. But then I realize that my brain itches, just like it did in Katharine's home.

She's nothing to me. Just a country serving wench. I was just using her to get where I needed to go.

All three of us drank the henbane water.

Dietan is telling the truth. I'm nothing to him. He's finally admitted it. I can barely sit upright. It's like the world is toppling underneath me.

Everything he said to me last night was a lie.

I turn to Dietan, who sits rigidly in his chair. His face is solid, impassive, turned away.

I don't love her. She's nothing to me. I was just using her to get to where I needed to go.

So that's why he didn't want to make love last night. It had nothing to do with being in the dungeon. Sure, he was aroused, but he was just a man with a man's needs. That's all. That's why he kissed me. And he stopped himself because he didn't really want it. He doesn't really want *me*.

What a fucking bastard.

I grip the edge of the table so tightly, my fingers ache. I should have married one of the farmers who propositioned me back in Evandale.

Dear goddess, is this real? I can't breathe, can't move.

I don't love her. She's nothing to me. His words echo in my head, empty and flat.

I can't believe it. I thought I knew him. But I don't know everything, do I? It's now clear there are other reasons for his journey—reasons he didn't share with me, like looking for the Vindar. Even as he put my life in danger again and again—like *now*—he was lying to me.

A lie of omission is still a lie. He definitely drank the same henbane water that I did. I saw him do it. He can't help but tell the truth.

"Well, now *that* is a twist," Namreth says. "Your engagement was just a ruse to get here?" He looks at me, his smile only widening, as if the drama unfolding is too delicious to be true.

Dietan actually smiles back. "Could anyone ever really believe I fell for a woman like her? Does she *look* like a princess?"

Namreth beams and turns to me. "Did you know?"

My entire body is shaking as I vacillate between disbelief and anguish. "I knew we weren't really engaged, but…"

"Oh, no," Namreth says with false shock, then laughs. "My dear, you… You're in love with him, aren't you?"

The truth is there, right there, on my tongue. I grimace, trying to form a lie, trying keep it in, to protect myself, but the henbane is too strong. "Yes," I spit like it's a curse. The urge to cry burns at the back of my nose, but I hold it at bay, refusing to break down in front of these pricks.

Dietan remains impassive. He shrugs as if my feelings are inconsequential. I suppose they are. I suppose they've always been. How could I have been so fucking stupid?

I don't love her.

His words carve themselves into my bones, breaking me apart and reassembling me all wrong.

Last night, when he kissed me and pressed his body against mine, when he held me to keep me warm and I looked at his face, at his smile, his kind eyes, the gentle slope of his cheek against the dim dungeon light, I thought I knew him. I thought we'd become something more to each other than mere traveling partners, that our bond had grown deeper than the roots of a mountain.

But I was wrong.

So wrong.

I was right about one thing, though. From the moment I met him, I saw him for what he is. A liar. I should've remembered that. I should've known I couldn't trust a prince, a man, him.

The first time I saw Dietan in the Raven's Beak wearing that ludicrous disguise, I knew everything I needed to know about him, yet I was swept up in this grand fantasy. I'm not my sisters, who think the world is theirs. Only a dumbass fool would believe that someone like him could ever love someone like me.

All these years as a spinster should have prepared me for reality, but I foolishly threw all those hard-fought lessons away, falling for the very fairy tale I've always said was bullshit.

Against my will, a single tear rolls down my cheek, and I lower my head, unable to meet either man's eyes any longer.

"What's wrong, dear?" Namreth asks, his lips curling into a grin over the rim of his cup. "Is something the matter?"

"Yes," I say, because the damned poison is making me answer honestly. I want to say *no, nothing's the matter, I couldn't give a rat's ass*, but I can't.

"By now, you probably realize that what you've been drinking this whole time isn't water," Namreth says. "It's henbane. Delicious, isn't it?"

"Yes," I reply, because it's true.

"It's a local delicacy. Secrets are quite the currency in our quiet little kingdom. Do you like it?"

I try to force myself not to answer, but the longer I try to fight it, the worse the itch in my head becomes. I want to rip off the top of my skull and dig my fingers into my brain to stop myself from speaking, but instead I let out a ragged, "No, I don't like it one bit."

Namreth must enjoy the despair on my face, because his laughter fills the chamber. He tops up our cups again, relishing in his newfound victory. He watches the two of us like he's plucking the wings off some hapless insect. I'm helpless to stop it.

"This is so entertaining, truly. Family should visit more often." Namreth laughs.

"You know the truth now. Aren's of no use to anyone," Dietan says, lifting his goblet to his lips. "I do admit, though, she makes biscuits like a goddess."

"You don't say," drawls Namreth.

"Yes, the finest I've ever eaten."

I grit my teeth. The bastard.

Namreth seems giddy now. "Are you a good baker, girl?"

The truth is wrenched from my lips. "Yes."

Namreth looks pleased to hear it. "It just so happens there's a recent opening in the kitchens. Yes, you will serve nicely there, I think." He settles back in his throne. "I appreciate your candor, nephew. I can't wait to taste the biscuits myself. I always find a woman's touch in the kitchen is unparalleled."

A servant. I'm going to be chained to a kitchen, the exact place I've been trying to escape all these years. The pain inside warps me, twisting and turning and arching into my chest with barbs that explode outward. I remember Katharine's warning. I should have heeded it and ran back to Alba or died trying. This stupid, piece-of-shit prince is sending me to the kitchen for the rest of my miserable life, and I'm fucking furious. I'm rage personified.

I'm going to kill him.

I leap to my feet and lunge at Dietan, but guards rush in and grab me by the arms, holding me back.

Dietan barely moves and doesn't look at me.

"You lied to me!" This time, the truth feels so good coming out of my mouth. All the pressure in my head dissipates, the henbane loosening its vice grip on me as I shout, "I never should have trusted you!"

Dietan doesn't react.

"Look at me, you coward!"

He doesn't.

There is only one thing I can think to do.

I spit on him.

The glob lands squarely on the side of Dietan's face. Slowly, he reaches up and wipes it away. When he finally turns to me, his eyes are cold, his brows lowered. He gazes at me intensely. With a small shake of his head, he clenches his jaw but says nothing.

"Take her away," Namreth says.

The guards easily lift me off my feet, and I kick and scream, thrashing with every bit of strength inside of me as I'm carried like a child down the hall. Fury and anguish pour out of my soul, their guttural cry echoing around the room. They drag me out and slam the door to the throne room behind us. I'm still cursing Dietan's name when the guards lock me the kitchen pantry.

CHAPTER THIRTY-EIGHT

Dietan

The torture begins the moment Aren is hauled away, hopefully to the kitchens, where she'll be safe. Relief flickers briefly in my chest, but it's quickly snuffed out as Namreth's soldiers grab me from behind and throw me to the cold floor.

My knees hit the stone with a sickening crack, pain jolting up my legs. I bite the inside of my cheek to keep from crying out. I won't dare give him the satisfaction.

"Where are the Rings?" Namreth demands, his voice slicing through the air like a blade.

"You already have them. They're in your hands." My voice is steady, though my heart thunders in my chest. Every word scrapes my throat like sandpaper.

It's the truth. Namreth has me, so he has the Rings of Fate. He just doesn't know it. My stomach churns at the thought, bile threatening to rise. I fight to keep my face impassive, to give him nothing.

"I don't have time for riddles, boy!" he blusters, spittle landing on me as he yells.

I remain silent.

"I suppose you want to do this the hard way." Namreth sighs as if this were all some minor inconvenience.

The guards strip me to the waist and tie me to a post that had been brought into the throne room. A large mirror is carried in and positioned behind me — so Namreth can watch my whipping and my expression all at once.

Sick bastard.

I freeze as cold air brushes against my skin.

This is it.

My secret is going to be revealed. The scars the Rings have left on my back will give me away.

My breath comes in short, shallow bursts, and sweat prickles on my brow despite the coolness of the room. I clench my fists so tightly my nails bite into my palms.

But Namreth sees nothing. I twist to glimpse myself in the mirror, and all I see is smooth skin. The scars are gone. There's no mark on my spine. It's as if the Rings hid all trace of themselves.

The Whisting finds a way. It *chose* me, Veteria had said.

My secret is still safe for now. Relief surges through me, but it's short-lived.

The whip comes down hard.

The first strike is a lightning-crack of agony. My entire body seizes, my muscles locking up as fire streaks across my back. My breath hitches, and for a moment, I think I won't survive.

My mind goes blank. All thoughts are silenced in the snap of a second lash. I can't think, can't breathe, can't feel anything but the burning, searing pain.

They're going to kill me, I think dimly, the realization more horrifying than the pain itself. *It'll be Namreth who digs these Rings out of my corpse.*

Namreth's expression never wavers. He watches my face the entire time, his cold eyes boring into mine. I try to meet his gaze with defiance, try to hold on to some shred of dignity, but my resolve shatters by the seventh strike. By the eighth, I can't count anymore.

My screams turn into ragged, choked gasps, and blackness creeps in from the edges of my vision. My legs buckle, and I slump against the post, my wrists burning where they're bound above my head. I welcome the darkness when it finally claims me, my body limp and broken.

If I had some control over the Whisting, I might be able to fight back. I might be able to destroy my tormentors the way the kings of old buried entire armies, but my power fails me as it has so many times before. The Rings in my back remain silent, their power as still as the grave my captors want me in. Maybe the Rings want me dead, too.

—

I wake up in the cell I once shared with Aren, my back draped in moist rags that reek of the perfumed healing waters of the bath. When I shift slightly, I realize my back has healed entirely. Panic flood my veins as realization dawns. My stomach sinks like a stone. I know what's coming next.

I'm not surprised when they drag me from my cell the next evening and haul me back to the throne room. My legs tremble as I'm tied to the post again, the rough wood biting into my freshly healed skin. The first strike of the whip reopens the wounds that have just barely closed. I let out a strangled cry before I can stop myself. Again and again, until my back is raw and bleeding, until I'm a shaking, gasping mess. Then they heal me, only to start all over again.

This could go on for an eternity.

They want me to see death, but it simply reminds me that there's only Aren to live for.

CHAPTER THIRTY-NINE

Aren

I spend the night lying on a hard wooden pallet between sacks of potatoes and flour in the kitchen pantry.

I'm woken up by a large boot prodding me in the side. I blink up at a shadow looming in the doorway. I can make out the shape of an apron and a cotton cap. It's one of Namreth's kitchen servants.

The man doesn't say anything as he turns and leaves, which I take to mean it's time to get to work.

I sit up and rub my eyes, pressing the heels of my palms deep into my sockets. My eyes are still swollen and aching from crying most of the night. I don't remember falling asleep, but I do remember how Dietan looked at me as I was dragged away—the flatness, the indifference in those blue-green eyes.

He never cared about me.

He never felt anything for me.

He shook his head at me as if he was disgusted by my stupidity.

I should never have left Evandale.

Homesickness sweeps over me, an ache that pains me more than the soreness in my back from sleeping on the hard floor. It permeates my bones, sinks its claws deep into my soul, and shreds any last hope I hold about ever seeing my family again. From the wreckage, anger rises, propelling me to my feet. It fuels me. The blood pumping hard in my veins reminds me that I'm still alive.

I'm alive, and I hate Dietan.

I walk out of the pantry. It's still dark, and the only source of light in the room is the oven, where a scullery maid is tending to the fire. I'm used to rising before dawn when I open the Raven's Beak. So this scene, at least, is a familiar one.

The kitchen is occupied by five other servants—now six, including me. After they threw me in the pantry, they made me change out of my desert garb and into the simple smock and apron they all wear. I can't believe I've come all the way across Albion, only to end up right where I started. I retie my apron tightly with a knot at my hip to give my hands something to do, the motion as natural as breathing.

The cook who woke me up, a gruff older man with only one hand, is standing at a nearby station. "You," he says, pointing to the wooden counter next to his. It is clear and clean, save for jars of salt, flour, and yeast. Baking supplies.

So, this is where I'll be working until the day I die.

Wonderful.

Eternity stretches out in front of me, narrowing to a pinpoint that is absolute and inescapable.

No matter how hard I try not to think of the traitor prince, my mind returns to the same question over and over: is Dietan alive, or has his uncle killed him yet?

I have to stop thinking about him or I'll sink into despair. With a deep breath, I take my place at the counter and splay my hands on the well-used wood cutting board, stroking the grooves made by hundreds of knife cuts. I'm not the first baker to work at this station, and I won't be the last. "What happened to the baker before me?" I ask.

Someone shushes me.

I glance at the other workers milling about. The kitchen is filled with the sounds of hopping, pans clanging, water filling pots. No one meets my eyes. Everyone keeps their head down and works in silence.

The atmosphere is tense, with none of the camaraderie I'd grown accustomed to at the tavern. Even the men at the local blacksmith's in Evandale are more talkative, and I've only ever heard them say a handful of words at a time.

If only I was back at the Raven's Beak, surrounded by the sounds of laughter and clinking mugs and the bacon sizzling in a pan. This silence, compared to the cozy kitchen of my past, is like a knife to the heart.

"The baker's dead," the cook says, keeping his voice low. "The one before you." He's chopping a bunch of scallions with a knife in his right hand. The empty space where his left hand used to be is marked by shiny, red skin. It looks like it healed some time ago. He uses his knife to swiftly scoop the scallions into a nearby bowl. He moves so gracefully; it's clear he's been doing this job for a while.

I gulp and look around warily. No one else seems to be paying attention, but I keep my voice low anyway. "Osian?" I ask.

He doesn't answer, but then again, he doesn't have to. The fear, the silence—it's clear the mad king killed the cook. I wonder if he's killed Dietan, too. An ache blooms in my chest. No, I can't think of that liar right now. I won't let my mind go there.

"I'm Aren," I say loud enough for everyone to hear. "It's nice to meet you all."

No one looks up from their work or even acknowledges that I've spoken. Maybe the king mandates silence among the servants...or maybe it's better not to know anyone's name, so it's easier when they don't come back to work the next day.

Without another word, I prepare the biscuits Dietan claimed are my only talent. *Damn him*, I think as I measure out flour and milk. *Damn him and his cursed rings. Damn him and his lies.*

Did he ever even want to get those Rings out of his body?

My anger could fuel a thousand suns, and I pour all of it into baking.

I know this recipe by heart. I start to dice butter, adding a splash of vinegar and salt, all based on the feel of it between my fingers. These biscuits are a recipe passed down from my mother, and now I'm forced to make them for someone I despise. When I'm finished, I scowl at the shaggy dough on my cutting board and consider spitting in it. A secret rebellion.

No one will ever know.

"Don't," the cook beside me says. His scallions have turned into a small mountain in the silver bowl. "You'll just make it harder for us all," he adds.

Sighing, I leave the dough alone.

I bake the biscuits in the oven, and they come out perfectly golden brown, smelling of butter and richness. I plate them for the king's morning breakfast. Then I wait with the rest of the staff for the guards to unlock the kitchen door and let us into the main hall.

When it's time to serve the king, I carry my plate of biscuits to the throne room, flanked on either side by two armed guards. I try to appear impassive, even as I approach the king's throne, where he's seated before a table set for a feast for one. Fellow servants set down plates and pitchers full of food and drink, moving silently in the vast room.

There is no sign of Dietan. I'm surprised my heart sinks—irritated, even. I want to hate him for what he's done to me, the fate he's cursed me with, but I find it difficult. Even when he was wielding the Whisting on the bridge to the Waste, conjuring a terrible and terrifying storm as he levitated off the ground, I wasn't afraid of Dietan.

I was afraid *for* him.

And I'm afraid for him now, despicable liar or not. Surely some part of the man I treasured was real and not a lie.

A guard nudges me forward, and I bite my lip to stop it from trembling. I force my hands to stop shaking as I step up to the table, moving to set the plate of biscuits down on the far side of the buffet, but Namreth stops me. "Here." He gestures to an empty place near his hand.

I shudder. I don't want to get that close to him, but I can feel the guards' eyes on my back, so I move stiffly toward the king. I set the plate down and turn it, presenting him with the most appetizing view of the biscuits, which are still steaming from the oven. Golden biscuits in a golden castle.

He watches with that creepy smile of his. He's almost handsome, but there's something unnatural about him. Beyond his strange youth and his magic, he makes my skin crawl. I lower my eyes and step away, but Namreth stops me by grabbing my wrist, quick as a snake. His tight grip makes me wince.

"Don't you want me to tell you how they taste?" he asks. "Don't you want to know what's happened to that precious prince of yours?"

What I want to do is tell him to choke on the damn biscuits, but fear holds my tongue.

He doesn't let go of my wrist, even when he reaches out and selects a biscuit from the plate. He takes a large bite, groaning in apparent bliss as he tears it in half with his teeth. His eyes flutter closed, and he chews loudly, smacking his lips and savoring every morsel.

When he's done, he licks the crumbs off his fingers, his pink tongue flicking out like a lizard's. I feel trapped in his gaze as he runs his lips up and down his hand, softly moaning as he does.

Sick bastard.

He smiles when I can't mask my disgust. "Delicious," he says, eyes boring into mine. "My nephew was right about you. Too bad he'll never enjoy these again."

I might have fallen to my knees, if not for Namreth's hold on me.

Dietan is dead.

The prince is dead.

My prince is dead.

I want to scream or cry or shake the king's hand off my wrist, but I'm saved by the sound of a plate clattering to the floor.

An elderly servant, a man whose limbs tremble not just with fear but with sickness, kneels to pick up the silver platter he's dropped along with the grapes now scattered all over the floor. His bald head glistens with sweat, and he apologizes profusely, trying and failing to scoop up all of the grapes that roll out of his shaking hands and back onto the marble. The anticipation in the room buzzes like a hive, all the servants on edge.

Namreth sighs with annoyance and finally lets me go. I stumble back as he raises two fingers and points them toward the man.

Without so much as a sound, the man clutches at his throat, eyes bulging.

Namreth picks up another biscuit and eats it languidly while his fingers are still aimed at the serving man now thrashing on the floor, slowly succumbing to what must be the Unseen Death. I imagine an enemy of Dietan's meeting the same fate at his hand, and for the first time, I wonder if the prince would ever have been capable of such brutality. Maybe all kings and princes are.

I watch helplessly as the poor man chokes to death in front of us all. His back arches, he kicks his heels against the marble tile, he tries to crawl away—but nothing can prevent the air from leaving his lungs. Saliva drips out of the corners of his mouth as his lips move soundlessly, desperately. His face changes from pale white to red, to purple, to blue in a matter of seconds, like a horrendous sunset.

No servants come to his aid. No one tries to help him. No one can—unless we want to meet the same fate.

Eventually, the man falls limp, his face blue and frozen in a silent scream.

Namreth lowers his hand and reaches for his golden goblet. He takes a satisfied swig and continues to eat his breakfast. Guards enter the room and grab the man's body, dragging it across the marble floor and out of sight.

Like the rest of the servants, I just stand there, mute, horrified, and paralyzed.

Namreth can kill with a flick of his fingers.

His control of the Whisting is total.

My breath comes in quick, shallow pants as I stare at the spot where the man died. Dietan is truly dead, then. Dead like the baker before me. Dead like the old man they just dragged from the room. Dietan is dead and likely met the same gruesome end at his own relative's hand. I feel numb. My stomach is a pit of ice.

"Bring me more, just like this," Namreth orders, pointing to the empty plate of biscuits, his smile cold and his eyes colder.

—

The next several days are much the same. The cook wakes me up each morning from my sleeping pallet in the pantry, and I spend my days and nights laboring in the kitchen. I bake not only biscuits but honey cakes, fruit tarts, puddings, and date loaves. I live in the kitchen now. I eat all my meals there, I work there, I sleep there, and the only time I'm not in the kitchen is when I'm holding a tray of food to serve the king.

Ours is a grueling and monotonous existence. And every night, a thought echoes in my brain: *Dietan is dead, and I'm going to die here, too.*

Every day, I bake my mother's biscuits and deliver a plate to Namreth personally, and I'm forced to watch as he devours them, licking his fingers clean each time while never taking his eyes off me. He doesn't have to say anything. I can see what he wants to do to me as his slitted eyes rake over my body as if it's Loegrian territory he's of a mind to conquer. It's as if he'd like to devour me the way he's devouring the biscuits I'm forced to bake for him. He reminds me of the marquis, and it makes me want to vomit.

"A man could fall in love with a woman who made these," he leers. "Perhaps I will have a taste of what inspired my nephew to bring you all the way here, even if it was all a charade."

I remain silent, numb, showing no emotion that could be construed as an invitation or resistance, until he dismisses us all.

The only safe place I have left is deep inside my mind. I go there frequently, observing the world as if I'm watching it from someplace far away. I think of how I might find freedom again, and I dream about possible ways I can escape this hell.

Sometimes I even envision throwing myself out the window, but I'm too stubborn to follow through with it. If I kill myself, Namreth wins. I have to hold out hope that I'll make it home to Evandale one day. Hope is the only reason I can work in the kitchen day in and day out.

As for Dietan… I try not to think about him, and sometimes I'm successful.

One morning, my mind is back at the tavern. I can imagine it so clearly. I think about my regulars, even poor Shephard Belmis, and I hope that the war hasn't reached Alarice's borders.

But with Dietan dead and the Rings likely in Namreth's possession, Loegria and Alarice are defenseless. How long will it take for the smoke of war to descend on Evandale's pastoral fields? How long before the Usurper's army marches through our town and levels it to the ground? How long until the Kilandrar descend like tornadoes on our peaceful valley? If I ever get out of here, there may not even be an Evandale to return to, with everything and everyone I love burned to ash like that Loegrian village we passed through on our way here.

Then I snap out of my daydream, because I'm smelling smoke for real.

The air is full of it. I whirl around frantically. There's smoke billowing out of the oven. One of the scullery maids, a freckled girl with orange braids wrapped around the crown of her head, hasn't noticed it yet. She's restocking the firewood below, and flames start licking dangerously close to her hair.

I'm nearest to the oven, so I sprint around the worktable toward her. "Look out!" I cry.

The scullery maid jerks up, startled, not realizing what's happening. I launch myself into her, both of us collapsing on the floor just as the flames roar out of the oven mouth above us.

We both lie stunned for a moment until I push her away, shouting at her to get to the other side of the room, where the others have sought safety.

I crawl out of the path of the flames, heartbeat as frantic as my thoughts. The doors to the kitchen are locked from the outside, and the drop from the window is at least a dozen stories straight down.

We're trapped here with no means of escape.

Something is clogging the chimney, and a quickly thickening blanket of smoke is filling up the room. I have to stop the fire, or we're all going to die.

I stand and approach the oven again, pulling a dishcloth from the waist of my apron. The heat slams against me like a solid wall, and my eyes and lungs burn from the smoke. I cough violently as I grab the handle of the oven door with the towel and slam it shut. I pray it's enough to choke a fire this out of control.

I fall back, bracing myself on the central counter as wisps of smoke push their way out from around the edges of the iron oven door. Slowly, less and less smoke curls out from the seams, until eventually, the fire's out.

For long moments, the smoke-filled kitchen is completely silent except for our retching and coughing. The others are still in the corner, some of them holding wet rags to their noses, eyes watering and red-rimmed.

I cough again, panting hard, and take in their frightened faces. Everyone seems to be okay, but my heart still races. I put a hand to my chest, relieved, but say nothing as I fling the kitchen's single window as wide open as it will go and return to my station. We're going to have to wait until the guards unlock the door for the king's next mealtime for all the smoke to clear. For now, I need to get back to work.

I return to my biscuits and find that the butter melted too much during the ordeal. I'll need to start over. I throw out the ruined dough and begin again, measuring the flour and then the milk, when I feel eyes on me.

I look up, and one by one, the rest of the kitchen staff nod to me. I nod back.

The cook next to me resumes chopping vegetables, his designated job for the king's favorite stew. I can feel him glancing my way. I don't expect him to thank me, nor do I need to be thanked. I was just doing what anyone else would do. None of us want to die in here. But there's a definite shift in the air.

"Bing," he says.

After a moment, I realize he's told me his name.

Later that afternoon, the scullery maid I saved stops by my station. "More flour," she says, setting a bag down on the counter. It's the first time she's spoken to me.

I didn't ask for more flour, and I don't even get a chance to thank her before she scurries away, her red hair disappearing into the pantry.

But I don't need more flour right now. I'm done baking for the day.

I'm about to take the flour back to the pantry when Bing clears his throat and makes a furtive gesture at the bag.

Huh.

I set the bag of flour on the worktable and reach inside. Buried just under the surface is a small note on a piece of baking paper. It says:

Behind oven
Moonrise

I glance at the guard at the door and drop the note on the nearest open flame.

CHAPTER FORTY

Aren

I lie awake on my hard wooden pallet until the first rays of moonlight peek through the windows. Then silently, I creep on my soft-soled slippers out of the pantry and into the dark kitchen. I thought the scullery maid would be here at least, but the kitchen's empty.

I walk over to the cold, dark oven and look around. Yeah, no one's here. Maybe I'm being set up or it's some sort of test. But I'm determined not to give in just yet and examine the oven again, finding nothing out of the ordinary.

Behind oven, the note said. But there's nothing here.

I'm staring at the oversize, arched recess that houses the oven when I notice a slight discoloration in the mortar between some of the bricks. If I wasn't examining it closely, I would have missed it. Or I may have assumed the wall had been repaired. I run my fingers over the wall and stop when I encounter a loose brick. I test it with my finger, and it gives slightly, so I push it harder, until a click sounds deep in the wall behind the oven.

I gasp as a crack emerges in the brickwork, revealing a hidden door.

I quickly push the door open and slip inside, closing it quietly behind me. I test the interior handle, and the door swings open again easily.

Good.

At least I won't be trapped in here. When I pull the door shut again, I'm plunged into complete darkness. For a moment, I consider abandoning this whole endeavor, but instead, I lean back against the door until my heart rate settles and my eyes adjust.

Then I begin to shuffle forward over the rough-hewn wooden floor. It seems I'm in a cramped corridor barely wide enough to walk down without both my shoulders scraping against the walls. The darkness presses solidly all around, so I keep one hand on the wall and the other in front of my face.

Eventually, I hear soft voices in the distance, and the telltale glimmer of candlelight peers from around a corner several paces ahead.

Seven people stand in a cramped alcove in the tunnel, leaning over a single candle, the light capturing the worry in their faces as they turn to see who's joined them. It's clear that I've walked into a small meeting between some of the kitchen staff and a handful of servants I recognize from elsewhere in the castle.

The scullery maid is one of them, and so is Bing, the one-handed cook.

The maid breaks into a smile and reaches for me, pulling me into the alcove. I stumble on some toes and apologize. It's a tight squeeze.

"Thought you wouldn't come," she says. "We were just talking about you. I'm Siena, by the way. That's Tess, Lambert, Nelson from the stables, Arnfried, Rosamond. And of course, you know Bing by now."

"Hi," I say. They are of varying ages and skin colors, though all of them share the same wariness in their eyes. "Where are we?" I ask, keeping my whisper to the same hushed volume as the others.

"There are servant tunnels all over the castle," Siena says. Her voice is high, like a mouse. "Tons of them, everywhere, leading to the great halls and bedrooms, so we can appear in any room and tend to the king's every need. They forgot about this one or they'd have sealed it up to keep us trapped in the kitchen."

"Where are we, exactly? Will anyone hear us?"

"Not if we keep our voices down," says Siena. "We're just behind the east wing broom closet. No one else is in that corridor at this time of night."

I'm simultaneously relieved and surprised. So, the servants really did come out of the walls when we had that first meal with Namreth.

"What is this? Some kind of rebellion?" I ask, half joking. I realize that all this time, I've been wishing for something like this. I've secretly been hoping for a well-oiled resistance in this castle, waiting to strike and take down the mad king. This would be the kind of underdog story we hear about in legends and heroic songs.

I can't help my enthusiasm.

"Depends," says Bing, giving me a once-over. He scratches his unshaved chin with his wrist. "We don't know you." He has a haggard look about him, the air of a sellsword, like he's seen battle—or worse.

"I told you, we can trust her," Siena says to Bing. "She came in with that prince. She's a princess."

"I'm not," I tell them, shaking my head as an ache I've tried to bury these past days blooms in my chest. "I'm definitely not a princess and never will be."

Siena's eyes widen. "You're not? The Loegrian army isn't going to come rescue you?"

I would laugh if it weren't so sad. "No. No army. Me and the prince, we... Well, it's a long story." The others glance at one another, and I wonder if they know what's become of Dietan. Maybe one of them is assigned to cleaning the dungeons. I add, "No one's looking for me, I can assure you of that."

Siena's smile falls a little. "Oh." The girl isn't any older than fifteen, and her innocence is in full effect.

"Sorry," I say, a little disappointed myself.

"What are you, then?" Bing asks. "If you're not a princess?"

I shrug. "Just a barmaid with bad luck."

"A barmaid?" asks Tess. She's one of the servants who greeted us when we first came to Engel, a middle-aged woman with a world-weary air. "I saw you, hanging on the arm of that prince. What happened?"

"Like I said, long story."

"Do you think we have anywhere important to be?" Rosamond jokes. I don't recognize her, but based on the shiny burns on her fingers and up her forearms, she probably works with harsh salts in the laundry room. She turns to the guy next to her, who has been quiet the entire time. "We've got all the time in the world. Right, Arnfried?"

He grins. He's a little older than the scullery maid, maybe seventeen or so. "Whatever you are, you're one of us now."

It's a sweet gesture, and it makes me feel a little better, but it doesn't help our immediate situation. How the hell are we getting out of this damn castle?

Arnfried reminds me of someone, and I realize his name is familiar. "You're Katharine's son," I say, realization dawning. "I met his mothers. They're well, and they miss you." A shy smile graces his lips as he places his hand to heart in gratitude.

"How'd you end up here?" Tess asks. "And what's a Loegrian prince doing with an Alarician barmaid, anyway?"

Bing, who seems to be in charge, holds up his hand. "Enough. Let the lady be."

"Please, I'm not a lady," I assure them. I still can't get over how I almost believed that I could be. "Where are all of you from?" I ask, changing the subject.

"Some of us were born here," Bing says. "Siena is from western Loegria. Lambert, from the south. A few of us escaped Penrith when the Usurper took over. The rest of us wound up crossing Engel's borders one way or another, either by our own free will or otherwise."

Siena gives me a small, shy smile, as if she's embarrassed to ask. "Did you see Loegria?"

"Yes, we passed through parts of it on my way here." Then I turn to face all of them. "What do you want from me? Why did you call me to a secret meeting?"

"The way you handled that fire and the fact you found this tunnel with little instruction proves you're quick-witted. And you don't seem inclined to simply give up and accept your fate, which is a rarity around here," says Bing. "We meet like this to share information. The king forbids interaction between his servants, and we're kept intentionally isolated by our respective jobs, so this is the only way we can organize."

"Something's happening soon," Nelson says. "We think he's mobilizing his troops."

"Just because some prince arrived?" Bing asks.

"Who knows why? It's possible. But down in the stables, we got the order to fit all the horses with new shoes."

Bing shakes his head. "It's not enough of a sign. The king's whims are as fleeting as the wind."

"It's different this time," Nelson insists. He appears a little older than me and has a nervous energy about him.

Living under constant threat from an unpredictable tyrant will do that to a person.

"The day after you arrived—well, your prince arrived—there were rumors about the troops readying for deployment. The Loegrian prince showing up at our gates changed things around here. The army is going to march soon, mark my words," Nelson says.

"You know, I did notice there's been an order for more supplies," says Rosamond. "Tents, bedrolls, waterskins."

Nelson nods. "Conscripts, too. They've sent messengers to all the remaining villages, promising riches to any man or woman who'll sign up and threatening any villages who don't provide enough…'volunteers.'"

"That's been happening since I got here," says Bing. "It's all a lie. There are no riches to be had."

The group argues some more, trying to discern if there are any other clues to the king's intentions. They all have different pieces of the same puzzle, but there are gaps in everyone's knowledge. Their efforts are fractured, relegated to sporadic secret meetings in the wall just to know what someone else in a nearby room might be doing.

Siena keeps glancing nervously at me while the rest bicker. She looks just like my sisters, with that same bright-eyed wonder and innocence that makes me want to wrap her up with a blanket and tell her everything is going to be okay.

But everything isn't okay. I fear Nelson's right about Namreth's sinister plans, and with Dietan's arrival, it can't be mere coincidence. Maybe Namreth feels more confident moving to attack Loegria now that Dietan's been eliminated.

Murdered.

I close my eyes, pushing down my grief at the thought of not seeing him again. Never seeing his smile or hearing his laugh.

The liar.

"But why would the king want to send out his troops?" Tess asks skeptically.

"Well, there's a war going on out there," I tell them. They all gape at me. "You didn't know? Penrith has been on the attack for a few months now. War has already broken out along the Loegrian border," I say.

Everyone stares at one another.

"How long have you all been here? Trapped in the castle?" I ask.

Bing replies, "Too long. It was either this or join his army. I'll cut off my other hand before he can make me take lives for him." My stomach drops. He's desperate enough not to join Osian's army that he would do that to himself. "War has truly come to Albion, has it?"

I tell them everything I saw on the journey to Engel. The burnt village we came upon, the chaos on the bridges, the Kilandrar attacks. And I tell them as much of the truth of why I ended up here as I can, without mentioning the Rings. "Prince Dietan hired me to escort him across the kingdoms, posing as his bride, so we could stop the war before it began. But...maybe now it's too late."

Without Dietan, without the Rings, I fear I may be correct. I wrap my arms around myself as the grim realization settles over the group. Tess holds herself tightly, her gaze distant. "Many of us have family—husbands, children—conscripted into King Osian's army. We'll probably never see them again."

Lambert folds his arms over his chest. "You're lucky the king didn't believe you were really engaged to that prince, or you'd be with him right now in that dungeon, being starved and beaten, too."

My heart stops.

A strangled gasp escapes my lips, my hands flying to my mouth as my vision blurs with sudden, burning tears.

Dietan's alive? He's alive? He's *alive*.

A broken, breathless laugh bubbles up from my chest. "What did you just say? About the prince?"

"Yeah, the prince. Dietan, I think his name is? He's in the dungeon."

"You've really seen him?" I ask urgently.

"Blond hair, bluish green eyes, cheekbones? Pretty boy? Yes, I've seen him," Lambert says.

A ray of hope starts to bloom in my heart, even in this dark alcove. "He's alive?" I repeat.

"Are you not listening? I said he was. But only because Osian wants to play with him first," says Lambert with a scowl. "He likes to do that. He's a sadist of the worst kind."

"Torture?" My eyes burn with tears as I choke on the word. I take several deep breaths. Dietan isn't dead. He's being tortured and is in pain. But he's *alive*.

"Making the prince scream is Osian's new favorite pastime," Nelson says. "Happens almost every night. Sometimes he'll even have prisoners brought into the throne room and torture them sitting up there, instead of going all the way down to the dungeon."

So that's what we heard when we were in the dungeon. Torture. The screams from the king's victims above. Now Dietan is the one screaming. *Oh, Harvest Mother.* I place a hand on the stone wall for balance. I'd collapse if these walls weren't so close.

"I clean the dungeons. Clean the blood after," Lambert says. "Osian always makes a big ole mess of him."

Tears stream down my cheeks. I'm numb.

Dietan. Tortured. Screaming in pain.

"That's enough, Lambert," Bing says. "Spare the lady the details."

Bing asks Nelson for more information about the horses, but I don't hear the rest. I'm fighting to wrap my head around the fact that Dietan is still in the castle, still alive. My mind races with a million thoughts that overlap incomprehensibly with one another.

If Namreth had believed I was Dietan's bride-to-be, blessed by the Oracle and sealed with a treaty, I'd be down in the dungeons with him, just as Lambert said. A future queen of Loegria and Alarice would have been valuable to him, especially if he's planning to march on Loegria soon.

Did Dietan...save me somehow? By telling Namreth that he didn't love me, did he intentionally spare me from the torments he now faces?

No. That's impossible.

I saw him drink the henbane water. He could tell Namreth nothing but the truth: that I mean nothing to him.

I swallow as the voices of the others hum like a swarm of bees around me. But what if... What if Dietan found a way to lie even after drinking the henbane? Didn't I also watch Namreth drink the henbane? Surely that means the mad king has found a way to lie under the influence, which means it's possible...

My heart pricks with hope, even as I tell myself it's just wishful thinking. There's no way Dietan's as clever, as powerful as Namreth, is there?

He's just...a fool...right?

And above all, he's a liar...a skilled, convincing liar who has concealed the secret of the Rings from everyone, even his own mother, for a decade.

But I remember how brave he was, fighting the Kilandrar. And how he knew exactly who Katharine was—and probably even led us to her in the middle of the vast Waste. And that the other reason he is here in Estyrion was to persuade his uncle to be an ally. Dietan is more than a messy drunk who sneaks out at night. He's also more than the carefree, philandering prince he pretends to be.

RINGS OF FATE

I did know him. I believed in him. And I loved him.

Even if Dietan truly doesn't love me, how can I live with myself, languishing in the kitchen knowing he's being tortured? No matter how much he's hurt me, I've got to do something about it.

"How long until you think the king marches to war?" Bing asks.

"Why, so we can all escape?" Tess snorts. "Where would we go? The desert will kill us first."

"Arnfried swears there's a lost tribe in the desert, that his mother is some kind of queen who might shelter us, if we're discreet and can find them," says Bing. "But maybe the kid's just delusional." I don't know if I should confirm her existence. If one of them gets tortured next, I can't endanger Katherine's whole village.

I interrupt, catching Lambert's gaze. "Can you get me to him? To the prince?"

Lambert's eyes widen, fearful, his bravado gone. "I don't know. The king is keeping my family... If I get caught..." He brushes his hand nervously over his shorn head.

"All of us are risking everything by simply meeting here," says Bing.

"Your prince is as good as dead," Tess says. Siena shushes her.

I tamp down a sob in my throat. I can't cry. Not right now. Not when there's work to do.

Dietan's still alive, and as long as he's alive, there's hope of rescuing him. I may not have the looks of my sisters, or the skills of Lydia or Marcus, or the title of princess, but I have hope. Lots of it.

By morning, I'm back in the kitchen, folding layers into the biscuits, but my mind is deep in the dungeons of the castle. Dietan is down there somewhere, alone and hurting. I've had to restart the dough three times over because I'm so distracted.

I look up and notice Siena, the scullery maid, at her daily task of bringing a basket of fresh herbs to the pantry. I sidle up beside her, gently pulling her deeper inside.

"Something wrong?" Siena asks, startled. Her basket is full of herbs and edible flowers, a rainbow of colors and fragrances, all to be used for the king's meals.

"Nothing's wrong—I mean, yes, everything is wrong in this place. But I need to ask you something."

Siena looks fearfully at the door, and I pull it closed, leaving only a sliver of a gap so we can hear if a guard approaches.

"Ask me what? You're planning something, aren't you?" Siena asks.

I don't answer right away, as I wonder if what I'm planning is insane.

"You're planning to save your prince," Siena guesses.

Am I that obvious? But Siena's spirits are up. A fire lights in her eyes, and she's smiling. I can't help but smile back. My plan could get us all killed, but isn't it better to die trying to do the right thing than live the rest of our lives in terror, locked in this kitchen?

"It'll be risky," I warn.

"I want to help, but the guards are always watching us," Siena says.

"I know. You know your way around plants, don't you?"

"Yes," Siena says, gesturing to her basket. "My father taught me how to forage when I was young."

"And they let you pick them for the pantry?"

"Once a day, they let me into the gardens. The king keeps thousands, maybe hundreds of thousands, of varieties in his gardens. Why?"

"I need you to find one for me: a bell-shaped blue flower called devil's breath. It looks like this." On a scrap of baking parchment, using the nub of charcoal I keep in my pocket to write down recipes, I sketch the flower the marquis used on a night that feels like it was ages ago now. Another life. "It's often used as medicine."

Siena furrows her brow as she studies my sketch. "I might have seen it, but I'll have to check. What do you want to do with it?"

"Find me this flower, and I'll get us all out of here."

CHAPTER FORTY-ONE

Dietan

From the bottom of the pool, I stare up at the tiled ceiling, noticing how the ripples on the surface make the glittering tiles shift and shimmer like scales on a fish. It's almost hypnotic, the way the patterns writhe and dance with the movement of the water. Underneath, sound is a faraway hum, except for the heavy thrum of my heartbeat in my ears. Everything feels distant and removed, so peaceful that I think, maybe—gods willing—that now I can finally die. Maybe this time, they'll let me go. I can fall into sweet oblivion.

But no. The hand pressing on my chest yanks me upward by my shirt, dragging me out of the water just before I drown. I cough violently, my chest heaving as the perfumed healing water gushes out of my mouth in a desperate spray. The air burns my lungs as I suck it in.

Then a fist connects with the side of my face, sharp and brutal, breaking the skin inside my cheek. The copper tang of blood blooms across my tongue. I see stars. A cascade of white-hot light explodes behind my eyelids as my head snaps sideways. I reel, but the steady hands holding me up don't let me fall. My body tries to shield itself, instinctively jerking my hands up to protect my face, but they're bound behind my back.

Useless.

I groan, low and guttural, frustration and pain pooling into one sound.

Another blow. I don't see it coming. The crack of the strike sends pain radiating through my skull, so instant and hot it feels like I've been branded.

The guard holding me up digs his knuckles into my chest, fisting my shirt so tightly I hear the seams threatening to tear. I tense, flinching under the pressure, but there's nowhere for me to go.

"Again."

Namreth.

His voice echoes off the walls, cold and inescapable like the prison I'm trapped in. The sound slices through the dimness of the windowless room, through the pain. It feels burned into my bones.

I'm shoved underwater again. The healing waters rush over me, cool and tingling, washing away the bruises and swelling. My mouth, sore and swollen, heals in seconds. The split skin inside my cheek smooths over as if the wound never existed. It's almost comforting, almost serene—but I know it won't last.

My chest burns with the need for air as innumerable moments pass. I look up at the ceiling again, at the shimmering scalelike tiles, my thoughts drifting somewhere far away.

Home. If I were home, I'd be sitting in the library with a book, maybe listening to the waves crash outside the window. Or I'd be at one of those royal balls with Jared and Marcus—the ones I always found so intolerable and dull.

It's true that we never realize what we have until it's gone.

Home. Home was never peaceful. It was a lifetime of tension, my father and mother constantly sniping at each other when they weren't occupying separate wings of the palace, sending me back and forth between them. If I'm thinking of it now as a peaceful place, I know I'm losing my mind.

I take some small measure of comfort in the knowledge that I knew how precious Aren was when I had her. I didn't take for granted that she was the best thing that ever happened to me. That she'll never know the truth about my lies is my greatest regret.

The few minutes under the healing waters between torments are the only solace I have left. The moment I'm dragged out, the torture will start again.

It always does.

The pain I feel now, though, is nothing compared to the pain of seeing the look on Aren's face when she thought I betrayed her. When I spat out those hateful, calculated lies to Namreth, declaring she meant nothing to me.

And the evil bastard believed me because he didn't know I had a trick up my sleeve—and because I'm an excellent liar. I've practiced and perfected that skill, under my father's supervision, since I was ten years old.

The tiles above blur and come back into focus, as clear and vivid as the shock on Aren's face. The rage in her voice. The pain in her eyes. It's all burned into my memory.

But what haunts me most is the last look she gave me, right after she spit on me. When she glared at me with not just anger, but so much hurt and despair that I almost cracked and recanted my lies.

I did that to her. My betrayal—false as it was—broke her.

The thought feels like a blade lodged deep in my chest, twisting every time I breathe. It hurts more than the fists, more than the bruises, more than anything Namreth could ever do to me. I should never have brought her here. Her pain is my fault. And I don't know if I can ever forgive myself for it.

—

Tonight, I don't know how long I've been here... A week? A month? A year? Namreth studies me from the side of the healing pool. His expression is as detached as ever, like this is just another monotonous, tiresome task on his list.

"You can make this stop at any time, you know, nephew. Just tell me where the Rings are, and you'll be free. Where are they?" His voice is as smooth and cold as the stone under his feet. The malice in his voice belies his promise. He has no intention of ever letting me leave alive.

"Somewhere you will never guess," I say, truthfully enough, blinking the water out of my eyes. My jaw aches as I speak, but I manage to keep my voice steady. My chest, though, is tight, each word a struggle as the weight of my own resolve presses down on me.

Namreth tilts his head, the faintest flicker of annoyance crossing his unblemished face. "Everyone has a breaking point. We shall find yours."

He nods at the guard, and before the man can shove me beneath the surface again, a laugh, dry and hollow, scrapes at my throat like shards of glass. After what I've already done to Aren, little else can hurt me. My laughter is choked off as water fills my lungs, and the sour taste of guilt rises in my throat. I swallow hard, trying to shove the memory of Aren's anger and despair down, but it lingers, gnawing at me.

Before we left Katharine's village, the lost princess gave me a vial. An antidote. She said it was to help protect the thing I loved most, explaining that it would counter the effects of the truth-telling serum. There was only one dose, and I had to use it wisely.

I kept it on me, even finding a way to slip it into my boot when Namreth escorted us into the city. I knew he would serve us henbane, just as Katharine did. So, the morning of our audience with him, I slipped the serum into my mouth without Aren's knowledge.

She thought my words were the truth.

I don't love her. She's nothing to me.

Those words haunt me every single day, but it was better that I hurt her than let Namreth hurt her.

She'll survive my lie. She'll live because I betrayed her. It's all I can hold on to for now. At least I saved her from these torments. The more Namreth focuses on me alone, the safer Aren is. She needs to hate me to survive.

Just thinking of her is its own kind of torture—a pain even these healing waters can't soothe.

Why didn't I kiss her more? Why didn't I make use of the little time we had? My chest aches as I think about all the moments I held myself back, believing she wouldn't have welcomed my interest. How many times did I think about pulling her close, burying my face in her hair, feeling her body against mine, kissing the curve of her neck? How many times did I want to tell her how I truly felt and instead let my fear keep me silent?

She put up with me, my insufferable selfishness, for the people she loves. I'd give anything to see that quiet smile one more time, to hear her call me an idiot just once more.

I even miss the way she rolled her eyes at me.

I'm ripped out of my thoughts by the hands on my chest, yanking me upward out of the water by my ruined shirt. I gasp, coughing violently as the healing water gushes out of my lungs. My ribs ache with every heave, and my vision swims. For one brief, blissful moment, I was dreaming of Aren, and now I'm back here. The cruel reality crashes down on me like a hammer.

The guard standing in the pool with me pulls back and strikes the side of my head with a ham-sized fist, snapping my head back. Pain explodes across my skull and all the way down my spine. My vision goes blurry, white and blinding. I sway in the guard's grip.

Another blow lands on my nose this time—that's new. There's a sickening *crack*, and warm blood gushes over my lips, spilling into my mouth and coating my tongue with its metallic bite. I cough, spitting a crimson spray onto the guard's pristine uniform. My stomach heaves, but there's nothing left in me to throw up.

I brace myself for another blow, my muscles tensing in anticipation, but Namreth holds up his hand, staying the guard's fist. Relief flickers faintly in my chest, only to be extinguished by the next words out of his mouth.

"Show no mercy. Every strike you hold back is one more for your sister," Namreth says to the man, his voice dripping with venom.

Of course. That's how Namreth controls them. The guard looks horrified, his hands trembling as he washes the blood off in the pool's warm waters, but I know his qualms won't stop him. He's going to hit me harder now, and I don't even blame him.

I clench my teeth, forcing myself to stay upright, even as my body screams at me to collapse under the blows.

Namreth crouches at the edge of the pool, his knees drawn to his chest, like a child watching a show.

Without warning, he grabs a fistful of my hair and yanks my head up. Pain shoots through my scalp. My neck protests the angle, but I meet his gaze with as much defiance as I can muster. Blood dribbles from my mouth, curling into the water in thin red ribbons.

"You're holding back," Namreth says to the guard, his sneer deepening.

"N-No, Your Majesty," the terrified guard stammers.

Namreth releases my hair, and my head falls forward like dead weight. My chin smacks against my chest, and I bite back a groan. If this is holding back, I don't want to know what happens when the guard gives me his all.

The next blows are even more brutal, and I'm not sure how much more I can take. My nose throbs, my breath comes in sharp, shallow gasps through my bloodied mouth, and my head lolls to the side as the room tilts dangerously. My stomach feels heavy, and all I taste is blood. The sight of it swirling in the pool below me is hypnotizing and grotesque.

Namreth's voice breaks through my haze. "I'll say this one more time. This torture can end the moment you tell me where to find the Rings of Fate."

"I already told you where they are," I slur, my words thick, mangled by my broken nose.

"Dunk him."

The water washes away the blood and bruises, but it does nothing for the pain that lingers in my chest—the pain of knowing that I might not survive this, but even worse, that I've irrevocably hurt the one person who matters most.

Later, as the sun is just starting to rise, golden rays slant through the windows of the chamber that houses the healing waters—otherwise known as my own personal hell. Namreth tips his head to the side and studies me like a dog with a new toy. His cold blue eyes trace over my face, slow and deliberate, like he's sizing me up for some twisted purpose. The weight of his gaze is heavy and suffocating. Does this bastard ever sleep?

"You look so much like my brother," Namreth says, his voice low and smooth, almost thoughtful.

"So I've been told," I say, grinning through the blood in my teeth. My lips stretch painfully, and I taste copper. "Means a lot coming from you." My voice is hoarse, but I force myself to sound smug, refusing to show him how badly I'm hurting. "So glad we could have this talk, uncle."

Namreth doesn't react. He wipes his hand dry on his pristine robes as if I've dirtied him just by existing. The languid way he moves makes my skin crawl. I hate his unshakeable calm, like nothing could ever touch him. Idly, he waves the guard away, and the tension in my shoulders eases slightly as the man obeys. Namreth turns back to me, his expression unreadable.

"I hoped you'd come to your senses by now and start to see reason," he says. His tone is almost paternal. *Almost.* "You're only doing this to yourself."

I sniff. The blood on my upper lip is starting to itch. I want to swipe it away, but my hands are still bound, so I grit my teeth and let the irritation fuel me. "Why not just use the Unseen Death on me?" I ask, my voice laced with challenge. "You're so powerful. Why not kill me and get this over with?"

The moment the words leave my mouth, the truth hits me like an axe to the chest. "The Usurper," I say, more quietly now, tinged with dawning realization. "He knows I'm here. He'll kill you if you don't bring the Rings of Fate to him. Your life, your power, depends on my cooperation, doesn't it? His magic is stronger than yours. He can destroy you." A bitter laugh escapes me, though it feels more like a choke. "But I won't help you, dear uncle."

Namreth's eyes narrow, and a flicker of some new emotion—anger?—crosses his face. He doesn't like being called out. Good. I can't allow him the satisfaction of thinking he has all the power here, even if he does, while I'm bound and on my knees, the flagstones slick with my blood.

Everything I've said is the truth. I can't give Namreth the Rings. I don't know how to get them out of me. That's why I came to Engel in the first place. But the thought is little comfort now, as I feel the weight of Namreth's stare and the silent, suffocating threat it carries. My heart hammers, but I keep my face blank, keep my grin sharp, refusing to show how much fear coils in my gut.

Namreth considers me for a moment, scanning my face like he's weighing his next move. "Perhaps I've underestimated you. You're not as easy to break as I anticipated," he finally says, almost admiringly, though it's clearly meant to provoke.

I know this is just another ploy to get under my skin, so I shrug, forcing a grin even though my mouth aches and tastes of blood. "Could have just talked it out like normal families do," I snark.

Namreth's lip curls in disdain, the brief flicker of amusement gone as he stares down at me. His presence is suffocating. "Why do you let my guards hurt you?" he asks, voice sharp and calculated. "Why not show them what real power can do? Why not use the Whisting to stay their hands? I can feel it on you. You can command the winds."

My stomach churns as he speaks, every word digging into me like a blade. I'm grateful he never dosed me with henbane again after it failed to get him his answers at that first meal. Is this the moment *I* finally get some answers? My shoulders tense, but I manage to keep my voice steady. "I can't control the Whisting."

"Yet," Namreth says, soft but menacing, like he's been waiting for this moment.

My eyes narrow, my pulse quickening. Has this bastard been trying to force me to use my power the whole time? Torturing me to unleash the Whisting? My jaw tightens as anger bubbles under my skin.

If only I could. If only my rage could wake the Whisting as easily as my nightmares did. But the Whisting is silent—nothing rises within me, not even the whisper of a breeze. The Rings of Fate have been dormant since his torments began. They're as useless as I feel.

Namreth takes a slow step closer, his presence bearing down on me like a storm. "Tell me where the Rings are, and I will teach you how to use your power," he says, his voice like a serpent's hiss. "I have read all the ancient texts your gutless grandfather banned from Alarice; I can show you magic beyond his wildest dreams. You will learn that the Whisting is life itself. And with the power of life comes the power of death. If you learn to control it, you can control pain, you can control suffering, and you are beyond even the reaches of death."

His offer is the most tempting yet. My chest tightens at his words. But I force myself to sneer at him. "I don't care about the Whisting or controlling fate. I'm not like you." My voice falters for just a moment, and my thoughts drift to a simpler time. I just want to be by a fire at the Raven's Beak Tavern, eating a plate of biscuits with Aren fussing over me. I'd even help with the dishes afterward. She'd like that.

Namreth's frown deepens. "My boy, you are exactly like me," he says, his voice dripping with condescension. "You want the world to be better than it is. You want to exert control when every decision has been made for you your entire life. If you master the Unseen Death, you can finally take back your own destiny."

I sniff and spit blood onto the floor between us. My fists clench behind me, my nails digging into my palms so hard they threaten to break skin.

Namreth doesn't stop. He steps closer, and his words are low and commanding. "Everything you see here is a result of that power. I created this city out of nothing, just as the ancient kings did the capitals of Albion.

The sorceress Skiron wrote about how she raised the foundations of Lundenwic with her own magic, did you know that? I can teach you to achieve your fullest potential."

"Whatever it is you're trying to do, it won't work," I say, my shoulders trembling with defiance. "I'm never going to join forces with a traitor, and I'm never telling you where the Rings are. You'd best get back to torturing me, then."

The guards glance at each other, their hesitation palpable as they await Namreth's command. My heart hammers in my chest, my breathing shallow as I brace myself for whatever he'll do to me next. Namreth merely looks at me like I'm a disobedient child in need of discipline.

"Take care," he says, cold and sharp. "I am far kinder to you than the Usurper will ever be. You should relinquish the Rings to me now, rather than face Lord Boreas."

It's true, then: the Usurper really is Boreas returned. I shudder. My hands twitch against the ropes binding me, but I don't answer. I can't.

"Break his jaw," Namreth orders, like a death knell.

A hand grabs me from behind, jerking me roughly to my feet. My breath catches in my throat as the second guard walks around to face me, his hand forming a loose fist. My pulse pounds in my ears as I stare at the large fist as he raises his arm and draws it back. My stomach twists violently. I can't breathe. My shoulders tremble as I try to steel myself, but I feel small, helpless, cowering in the face of what's coming.

"Wait," Namreth says. The word slices through the tension like a blade. The guard stops mid-swing, but I flinch anyway, my body bracing for a blow that doesn't come. My chest heaves as I struggle to steady my breathing. There's a glint in Namreth's eyes, a cruel smirk tugging at the corners of his mouth.

"I've changed my mind," he says mockingly. "Untie him. Take him back to his cell."

I don't dare move, even as the guards step forward and untie my hands. My shoulders ache as the tension releases, and I roll them, testing their movement.

This lenience has to be some kind of trick. I hate how I flinch when Namreth claps his hands together, echoing like the crack of a whip.

"Better?" Namreth asks, almost teasing.

I glare at him, my jaw tight and my teeth clenched so hard it feels like they might shatter.

"You're relieved, aren't you? That he's not hitting you again?" Namreth presses, his voice dripping with false sympathy. "Remember this feeling. Enjoy it while it lasts. Consider my offer wisely, for I won't make it again."

The guards pull me to my feet, and my legs feel like lead as they drag me out of the room. I don't look back at Namreth, but his words cling to me like a shadow, wrapping around my chest and squeezing until it's hard to breathe.

CHAPTER FORTY-TWO

Dietan

Pain slows time to a crawl.

Since being dumped back in my cell, I've laid on my cot, unable to move. Namreth didn't let me back into the healing waters after this session, probably as some kind of twisted lesson. I'm a wreck, streaked with purple-and-blue splotches across my chest, my lip split, and a deep cut on my cheek. My face is hot, swollen, and I can barely open my right eye. Every joint is swollen, and my ribs crack painfully every time I breathe. One must have broken when the guards kicked me. It's happened so many times, I've lost track. My mind feels slow, like it's wrapped in thick cotton.

I want to sleep. My body begs for it, to escape this pain, but the dull, throbbing ache in every part of me denies even a moment's reprieve.

If Namreth expects me to beg for the healing waters, he's going to be disappointed. I won't give him the satisfaction.

I slip into a dream, or a hallucination.

It's hard to tell the difference anymore.

I envision biscuits dripping with butter and honey and a dark-haired maiden lying beside me.

Aren.

She's laughing, her voice like sunlight cutting through storm clouds. I see us together on a green pasture by the sea, the sky wide and blue overhead, the breeze scented with brine and orange blossoms. She presses her hand to my face, her fingers warm and soft. She scolds me for not bringing a blanket. The imagined sound of her teasing makes me chuckle out loud, a dry rasp that startles me out of the comforting picture.

If Aren were here right now, she'd kick my ass for being so pathetic. And gods, I'd thank her for it.

My eyes are still closed as I pull her image back into focus. Namreth might be trying to break my body and my mind, but he can't touch this. He can't erase her from my thoughts or my dreams. The memory of her laugh is enough to loosen the tightness of my muscles.

What wouldn't I give to go back to that day in the Raven's Beak and propose to her for real, with my mother's ring in front of all of Evandale? But even that wouldn't be good enough for my Aren. She deserves the world.

My chest aches—not from the bruises this time, but from something deeper.

Regret.

Her voice echoes in my head, so clear and sharp it sounds real.

"You must be kidding me. You're napping?"

I startle, my heart skipping a beat. The words are too vivid. Too close.

"I'm not napping," I murmur, my lips cracked and dry as I converse with a hallucination. "I'm simply resting my eyes."

"Looks like napping to me."

That tone—exasperated, teasing—is entirely Aren. It's even more real than my previous dreams. My mind playing tricks on me, pulling her voice into my fantasy. Still, I want to sink deeper into it, to let it sweep me away from the pain.

"Oh, sweet Aren," I whisper, my voice barely audible. "Sweet…"

A loud clang jolts me out of my reverie. My head snaps up, and I blink hard at the bars of my cell. A shadowy figure stands on the other side, hands gripping the cold metal door.

"You better not be dying on me, Prince Asshole. Now—get up."

RINGS OF FATE

I freeze, my breath hitching. My body protests, screaming in pain as I push myself up to my elbows, to see her more clearly. My heart hammers against my aching ribs, my pulse racing. "Aren?" Her name spills from my lips, disbelief lacing each syllable.

She's here.

She's really here, her face cloaked in shadow, but I'd recognize the curl of those lips anywhere. I stagger to my feet, every movement agony, and rush to the bars. "Aren!"

I grip her hands, and they're warm—too warm to be a dream, too solid to be a figment of my imagination. I struggle to catch my breath, the searing pain in my ribs be damned. I still can't believe what I'm seeing.

Her gaze sweeps over my face. I see the horror in her eyes, the way they shine with unshed tears as she takes in my injuries. Her fingers brush against my swollen cheek, and I flinch.

"Don't," I manage, taking her hand in mine again. My knuckles are raw, my wrists shredded, but her fingers laced with mine feels like a balm for wounds that no magical waters could ever heal.

Tears spill down her cheeks, glistening in the dim light. It takes all my strength to wipe the tears from her face with trembling fingers. "Don't cry," I whisper, my voice cracking. "I'm okay."

She knows I'm lying. I can see it in her eyes, in the way her lips press into a thin, trembling line. But she squeezes my hand, her grip firm and unyielding.

"I'm sorry," I choke out, the words tumbling over themselves. "I'm so, so sorry." For bringing her here. For every terrible ordeal she's endured for my sake. For everything. The weight of it all nearly drives me to my knees.

"Later," she whispers, urgent. "I need you to get your shit together, because I'm busting you out of here."

My heart skips a beat; hope and terror for her well-being war within me. "Aren, no. It's not safe for you—"

"Shut up!" she snaps. I do.

She glances over her shoulder, her eyes darting up and down the hall. "I only have so much time. I gave them a quarter of a dose, so they'll wake up soon."

"Pardon?" I ask in confusion. From the folds of her cloak, she produces a single buttery biscuit. The smell hits me instantly, and my stomach growls so loudly it almost echoes. My mouth waters as she presses it into my hand.

"I'll explain everything later," she says, quick and determined. "I promise. Just trust me. I've made quite a few friends in this castle, and we have a plan to get you out."

I stare at the biscuit, heavy in my palm, then at her. A painful smile pulls at my cracked lips. Even if this is all a fever dream, I don't care. I get to see her one last time.

"Just listen to my instructions very carefully," she says, her eyes locked on mine. "You only have to do one thing."

"What's that?" I rasp.

"Die."

PART FOUR

THE PRINCE IS DEAD

CHAPTER FORTY-THREE

Aren

"Die? But I'm already dead if you're here. You can't be real. I'm still dreaming," he murmurs.

"I'm real," I say, gripping his fingers until he winces. "Listen, this is going to kick you in the ass," I tell him, nodding at the poisoned biscuit in his hand. "I've put something in it that'll make it feel like you're dead… and look like it, too."

He glances skeptically at the biscuit, and I don't blame him. I also have my doubts. The plan is straightforward, but sometimes simple things are the hardest to execute.

I just have to hope I put in the correct dose. "This is our only option," I say. "If there were any other way…"

He nods. "I trust you." And then, without hesitation, he crams the whole thing in his mouth.

In a short while, when the guards wake, they'll find his lifeless body.

RINGS OF FATE

During Namreth's noon meal, my heart pounds so loudly I'm afraid others can hear it. My hands shake. I try to compose myself as best I can. At breakfast, the king devoured my biscuits, but now, he hardly eats. I know he's lost his appetite because he's just come from the morgue where he stood over Dietan's lifeless body, inspecting it before Arnfried sealed it up in a rough cloth sack with a needle and thread. Just like all the other bodies that come through, which he told me are numerous. Another bagged body of similar size and shape will be burned in its place in the morning.

I couldn't take the chance that Namreth might suspect the Rings were on his person as the king would surely order him dissected. So I gave Arnfried another herb that, when he applied it to Dietan's eyes and tongue, would make his body look diseased. It did the trick. Namreth hastily left the morgue as soon as he confirmed that Dietan was truly dead.

Namreth's face gives nothing away, but the way he picks at the biscuits sets me on edge. The seconds feel like hours. *Does he suspect anything amiss? Can he guess the part I played?* Maybe he's just angry about being deprived of his plaything.

Then, abruptly, he slams his fork down. He stands and strides out of the chamber. "Get back to work," he snaps, dismissing the servants.

As I make my way back to the kitchen, I envision the hidden chamber off the morgue where Arnfried hid Dietan's body. He rests there cold, alone, and unguarded. Dietan sleeps, mere inches from death, his heart beating so slowly that it can't be felt. His breaths are so minute that they can't be heard.

Harvest Mother, what if he's actually dead? What if the dose was too strong? What if he's dead and I find him pale and lifeless when I tear open the sack?

The terrible image runs through my head for hours as we go through the motions of our jobs, pretending it's just another monotonous day of servitude. This could easily be the day I've led all of us to our deaths, including Dietan. So far, the plan has gone perfectly, but the most dangerous part is still ahead.

When the moon is at its zenith and the castle is quiet, I sneak through the hidden door behind the oven to meet the others. Bing and Rosamond are handing out clothes Rosamond stole from her laundry shift. An assortment of muted, everyday garments, most taken from the numerous dead. They look nothing like the work uniforms the castle servants are forced to wear. They will blend in with the garb of the commoners outside the castle. They'll do well for what I've planned.

We dress in silence. We are all acutely aware of the risk. If any of us makes one mistake, we all die. As I look into the faces of these brave people I now consider friends, I wish we could turn back, achieve our ends some other, safer way. I wish I hadn't thrust them into danger.

Too late for that now. It's time to take our lives back. Time to get the hell out of this terrible place and take Dietan with me.

I cast aside my recognizable kitchen frock and apron and slip on a drab beige blouse and loose brown skirt that hangs well above the tops of my boots. It'll be easier to move and run. I tuck my hair under a cap that street vendors wear. Then I stuff clothes for Dietan into an empty flour sack as Bing goes over the plan one more time, mostly for my sake. They'd been plotting this escape for months before I arrived. Dietan and I are merely interlopers. Bing carefully lays out the details as he distributes hand-drawn maps to the group.

"Aren, Nelson will be waiting for you at the wall with the carriage. All you've got to do is get the prince there. You'll take some back streets to be certain that no one follows. Then you'll transfer to another conveyance, just in case someone notices the carriage leaving the castle grounds. You'll all meet up at the designated safehouse, then leave with the group. Once you make it outside the city gates, it's a day's walk southeast to the nearest village. Maybe two, depending on your pace. Stay off the trail and head directly east, toward the sun. Don't stop until you can't see the palace behind you. If something happens and you can't make it out of the city, look for the House of Healing. They are friends of the cause."

"Hold on. You're not coming with us?" I ask.

Everyone stares at him grimly, but Bing just smiles, eyes glassy. "I'll stay behind. Do whatever I can to make sure all of you get out safely."

"Bing, you can't—"

"We won't let you—"

Bing raises his hand to quell our protests. "Somebody needs to be here to set off the distraction we put together. This is part of the plan, and

RINGS OF FATE

I've made my decision. Go." He looks at each of us in turn. "Let me do this one last thing for all of you. I don't have family out there. Osian took everything from me. So let me do this. Go now. No more time to waste."

He's right. We're out of time. This is the moment we've all been waiting for—our escape. No one says a word. One by one, we each go our separate ways until it's just Bing and me.

"Here," he says. "We found this in the king's linens. I think it's your prince's."

I glance down and see that Bing is holding Dietan's royal knife in its well-worn sheath.

We lock eyes, mine becoming misty, and I take the knife from his hand. He wraps his fingers around mine. "I wish you speed and safety, Aren of Evandale."

"I…" I almost repeat his words back to him, but Bing will find no safety. A crushing ache settles in my heart, and I try to smile. "Thank you, Bing. You are a good man."

He gives my hand a squeeze before releasing it. I slip the knife into my shoulder bag as I watch him shuffle down the passage in the darkness back to the kitchen that he will never leave alive again.

It takes all my strength to yank open the door that leads from the servants' tunnel to the morgue's overflow chamber, where Dietan has been hidden in a secret room. I've studied the map that Arnfried drew for me, but now that I'm here, I feel woefully unprepared.

I lift my candle higher, widening its flickering circle of light. The chamber is dark and empty, save for the rows of bodies laid on stone shelves on either side, stitched into their bags.

Even with a kerchief tied over my nose and mouth, I gag. My eyes water at the rancid stench of death.

As I reach the center of the room, a chill crawls over my skin and my pulse pounds in my ears. It feels like the corpses are watching, waiting in the oppressive silence, as dread coils tight around my chest.

In the darkness, I can't see the latch for the hidden door depicted in Arnfried's drawing.

With one hand clutching the candle and the other over my mouth, I slink silently across the room in my soft-soled slippers until I reach the back wall and spot the iron hook protruding from the mortar between bricks. A drawstring sack hangs from the hook, full of sewing supplies for stitching the corpse bags, just like Arnfried indicated.

I pull down on the hook as instructed. Just like the door behind the oven, it reveals a passageway. For a moment, I hesitate, terrified of what I'll find.

Is he here? Is he even alive? Or did they find him when he woke up? There are a thousand ways this could have gone wrong, and I picture each of them as I stand frozen in the doorway.

Move! I tell myself.

I step inside the cramped, dark space, candle held high. Dietan's body lies on the floor, taking up the entire length of the chamber. The bag has fallen off his face, and his arms are limp across his body.

My stomach lurches. He looks truly dead. His face is swollen and purple, with more bruises since I saw him this morning. My heart beats frantically as I kneel at his side and place the candle on the floor next to me.

Every fiber of my being is shaking in agony, as I feel his wrist for a pulse. Panicked, I keep searching, but there's nothing. His skin is cold, and his face is gray.

Dear goddess, I've killed him.

I move my fingers over his neck, searching for a pulse probing the tendons and muscles, my palms clammy with perspiration. I feel...

Nothing...

Harvest Mother, forgive me, I didn't mean to—

Then I find it—the slightest hint of a pulse, slow yet steady. I sit back on my heels and huff out a breath. He lives.

Thank the goddess.

"Dietan," I whisper, pressing a hand to his cheek. His skin is so cold. How can it be so cold? "Dietan, wake up."

He doesn't move. I rummage around in my pocket for the vial of essence of hartshorn that Rosamond stole for me from the laundry chamber. I hold it to his nose.

I jerk the vial back when he startles violently. His face flushes, eyes wide as he sits bolt upright at the pungent odor that could wake the dead, which it appears to have done.

Batting my hand away, he groans the most miserable, profane utterances I've ever heard leave his lips.

"That's not very princely," I say primly.

Dietan curses once more. "I learned from the best," he mutters, and I shake my head.

"Get up. No time for jokes," I say, ripping the bag open and pulling it from around his legs. I grab him by the arm. "Move. We've got to get your ass up and out of here."

But Dietan doesn't move. He just groans, this time longer and louder, and his eyes slam shut, his body collapsing once again to the floor.

Oh, crap.

I knew this might happen, that it could take some time for the effects of the devil's breath to wear off. It might take a day or more for the poison to work its way out of his system. I'm no expert, no Veteria. It might take twice that, for all I know. But I'm certain about one thing: we can't remain here much longer or we'll both be sewn into bags.

"I need you to sit up. Can you do that?"

Dietan groans again. A flicker of light from the candle crosses his face, revealing an open eye. He looks at me, and I smile, trying my best not to sob at the sight of him, still bloody and broken.

"Hi there," I say softly.

"Hey," he replies, voice weak and scratchy.

His limbs sag like a rag doll's, and I struggle to slip the cloak over his shoulders. I steady his head and tug down his hood. Goddess, he's in terrible shape. His skin is lacerated and bruised like an old apple. He's not even going to be able to walk. But somehow, he must.

"I'm getting you out of here now, okay?" I say, leaning to put my face in front of his, to force him to look me in the eye. He manages to nod as I squat next to him, drape his arm across my shoulders, and wrap my arm around his waist.

Then I summon every bit of my strength to heave him up and onto his feet, all his weight bearing down on my back. He's heavier than I'd guessed, but I'll manage.

Though his head hangs limply and his legs threaten to collapse, I maneuver us through the hidden doorway and across the morgue without dropping him or retching. I close the door behind us, plunging us into darkness. I manage to take two steps into the servant's tunnel before I lose my balance, sending us both tumbling onto the flagstones.

"Sorry," I say. Not that he hears me. He's out cold.

Okay, let's try this again.

I sling his arm over my shoulder, but he seems heavier now that he's no longer awake. It takes twice the effort to get us both on our feet. Sweat drips down my face and my muscles are screaming, but I ignore the pain. After all, I'm used to back-breaking work, day in and day out. I'm reluctantly grateful for all those years of labor because, as they say at the Raven's Beak, I really do have the sturdiest back in all of Evandale. If old Shep could see me now...

We reach the end of the tunnel, and I run straight into the door. I nearly fall to the floor again, nose throbbing. I'm exhausted. Goddess damn it, I know I've said it before, but now I've really never been this tired in my entire life.

I throw our combined weight into the door, and it flies open, sending us stumbling out into the moonlight. Panting, I get my bearings. We're in an alley near the burn pit, and the acrid smoke from the day's fire fills my nose. I try not to linger, readjusting Dietan's weight, draping one of his arms over each shoulder so I'm wearing him like a cape.

An awkward, heavy cape that needs to wake the fuck up.

As Bing instructed, I head toward the castle wall, tripping over my feet as I drag Dietan along. There, I wait for the carriage that's supposed to meet us, for what feels like the longest few minutes of my life.

After what could be an eternity, I hear a clattering of hooves echoing in the distance and the groan of wheels turning. Nelson appears, sitting atop the plain, dark carriage. I want to faint with relief.

Wordlessly, Nelson climbs down from the driver's box. It takes our combined power to wrangle Dietan into the carriage, and I follow him inside, collapsing onto the interior bench. I hardly have strength enough to slam the carriage door closed as we ride off. Dietan is oblivious, face down on the carriage floor.

I would roll him over if I had any strength left, but I'm too exhausted to even form a thought. We won't be in here for long. I catch my breath as I wipe my sweaty brow with my sleeve. I peer out the carriage window searching for any signs of trouble. But the golden kingdom is quiet and glows an odd green in the blue moonlight.

For the first time since I came up with the idea of using devil's breath, I allow the slightest hint of a real smile on my face. The plan is working.

We might escape after all.

Nelson's carriage shudders to a halt beside a hay wagon.

Right on schedule.

RINGS OF FATE

I throw open the door and, with Nelson's help, haul Dietan onto the back of the wagon, covering him in hay, burying him so deep that not an inch of him is visible.

Lambert dresses the part of a farmer with a flaxen tunic and a broad-brimmed hat pulled low over his eyes. He even smells of manure.

He nods to both of us. "I'll drive him around a bit to make sure no one follows. Walk the block and meet me at that corner, by the butcher shop," he says. Then he's off. Nelson leaves, and I'm alone, circling the streets. I wonder suddenly if the plan might just be a bit too elaborate, too cautious.

I walk alone with only the moonlight as a guide. A pair of city guards turn the corner and walk my way, and my heart starts to pound.

There is no time to hide.

They've seen me, and any sudden movements would look suspicious. So I just lower my head and walk toward them, like I'm a simple fishmonger or baker rushing home to my family. The guards momentarily pause as I walk past them. They eye me but keep walking. Thankfully, they don't give me a second glance.

That was close. Too close.

On wobbly legs, I circle around the block and pass Lambert walking on the street. He nods to me before he disappears down the block, off to the meeting point.

A moment later, I find the wagon where Lambert left it. I run to it and push aside the hay, finding Dietan exactly where I hid him. Unlike him, I've never been a good liar, but I put on a little show for any prying eyes that might linger nearby. I roughly brush bits of hay off his shoulders, like I'm an angry wife who caught him where he wasn't supposed to be.

Dietan's revived a bit, sitting up on his own and scooting to the end of the wagon. I sling his arm over my shoulder, grateful that this time I don't have to drag him like a sack of flour. We move slowly, stumbling.

"Hold on, hold on, hold on, that hurts," Dietan says, losing his balance as I struggle to keep him upright.

"Shush," I snap, gritting my teeth. "I'm tired of you going to the tavern instead of coming home," I scold more loudly in case anyone is listening. I look around, checking alleyways and behind corners as I hurry us down the street as quickly as Dietan can tolerate. His head hangs low, covered by his hood, but at least I can hear him breathing.

Then a horn cuts through the night air. *Shit.* That's not part of the plan.

Something's wrong.

CHAPTER FORTY-FOUR

Dietan

"What in Albion did you put on me?" I mutter, holding the cloak hood to my nose. The stench is unbearable. "This thing reeks."

"*You* reek. Have you smelled yourself? You spent a day in the morgue," Aren snaps.

I don't bother to answer. She's right, I must smell like death itself. Hell, I probably look like it, too.

Maybe this beggar's costume is an upgrade.

I tug the hood back over my head, but my thoughts are spinning again, my head buzzing from the lingering effects of the poison. My eyes flutter open and closed. For a brief moment, I recall the poisoned biscuit and the long, dark sleep that followed. How long was I out? Hours? Days? I feel like I died and was dragged back to life—though that could well be the lingering effects of Namreth's torments.

Every step I take sends sharp spikes of pain through my legs and into my back. My ribs protest with every breath. Each movement reminds me that since our arrival, I've spent more time broken than whole.

Aren walks beside me, my arm slung over her shoulders, keeping me upright. Her grip on my waist is tight, steady. I lean against her as we move, step by glacial step, but I can barely keep my feet under me. If not for her, I'd have already collapsed face-first onto the street. I can feel her struggling under my weight, trying to keep me from swaying too much, from drawing attention.

She tries to be gentle—I can tell—but the effort costs her. I steal a glance at her, admiring the glow of her face in the moonlight. Even now, even after everything, she's still the most beautiful thing I've ever seen.

It must be a dream. That's the only explanation.

Maybe I never woke up at all. Maybe I'm still in that dark place between life and death, and my mind has conjured her here to give me peace before the end.

Then, without warning, Aren smacks me in the ear.

Pain explodes in my skull, my vision whites out for half a second, and my knees buckle. I stagger, too slow to catch myself, and land flat on my back in the gutter. Filthy water splatters everywhere—up my arms, across my chest, into my already filthy hair.

Definitely not a dream.

What the hell did she do that for?

"I told you, no more taverns," Aren scolds. "Just look at you. You can't even walk."

I am thoroughly confused—until I see the pair of guards hurrying toward us, spears in hand.

"You there—what are you doing?" one of the guards asks.

"I found my drunkard husband in the street. I'm taking him home," Aren says, still glaring at me.

I've had a lifetime to perfect the part of the drunkard, and now is my time to make a virtuoso performance. I sway, teetering as I struggle to sit upright. "It was just a few drinks, my love. Don't be like that," I say, voice slurring.

Aren wags a finger at me and opens her mouth, no doubt to chastise her drunken husband. But she's cut off when a group of five or six guards rushes past. "Come now! We're needed at the castle!"

The two guards standing over us acknowledge the urgency. Without giving us another look, they sprint off toward Castle Engel.

I track the guards from the corner of my eye, waiting for them to disappear. Aren watches them, too, fists clenched at her sides, breathing heavily.

I nod when they vanish from sight. The way ahead is once again clear, and she helps me to my feet.

"You're incredible," I tell her. "Quick as a fox."

She doesn't answer. There's no need to speak. We are alive and desperate to get the hell out of this terrible place. I don't know where she's taking us, and I don't care.

She leads me into a darkened alleyway, where I stumble over cobblestones. An alley cat hisses from the shadows. Aren catches me before I fall, pinning me to the side of a building. My head spins as the last effects of the drug work through my body. I want to kiss her but think better of it as my world starts to spin again.

"I can't… I can't…" I say.

"Can't what?"

"Walk. Or form a sentence. I can't think," I admit, leaning hard on the wall. "I have to rest."

I can tell from her expression that this is a terrible idea, but there's no choice. It's taken everything for me to get this far, and my legs give out. She catches me before I fall onto the dirty road. For a moment, we're both still, catching our breaths.

"We'll find a place to stop," she says, "but only for a minute."

I nod, and we hobble in the dark, stumbling down another alley behind some shops until we finally find an open door.

The stink of horse shit hits my nose.

"Hello?" Aren calls into the stable in a light voice. When no one answers, we slip inside and close the door behind us.

Aren kneels in the soft hay, helping me sit down, my back pressed against the wall. Moonlight melts through the windows, and a horse looks curiously at me, probably wondering why I'm sitting on his breakfast. I extend an open hand, and the horse sniffs at it.

"What are you doing?" Aren asks.

"Making a friend."

She snorts, rolling her eyes. "Of course."

I scratch the horse's comfortingly warm neck, which takes energy I should be conserving, until it wanders to a water barrel in the corner. Aren reaches over to brush some hair out of my eyes and gasps, then places a hand on my forehead. "You're burning up with fever." She clucks her tongue. "Albion's sake, how did I miss that?"

"Oh, I don't know. Maybe you were distracted because we've been running for our lives…with you carrying me most of the way, might I add."

She shrugs. "A good enough excuse, I suppose."

"I'll forgive you this one. I'll expect better care in the future," I say.

"Will you now?" It looks like she's contemplating if there will be a future.

Gods, I've missed this woman. After a moment, I ask, "We're free?"

"Not quite yet," Aren says, "and that fever you've got is going to make things more complicated."

"Sorry about that," I mumble, my thoughts fuzzy as the fever takes hold.

I reach for the softness of her cheek, but my arms won't cooperate. They scream with pain when I try to lift them. Maybe they're truly broken this time.

I can't help but steal another glance at her. She's beautiful, a vision from the dreams that kept me sane in the dungeon. With thick, dark hair, smooth skin, and shining eyes… I would do anything for that smile.

I'm still grinning as the world fades to black.

CHAPTER FORTY-FIVE

Aren

Dietan's head falls limply against my chest, and I curse under my breath.

He's passed out again.

The poor man is burning up with fever, and I can't leave him to find medicine or go to the safehouse to let the others know we're here. It's too dangerous.

Guards are patrolling the streets. Their boots echo against the cobblestones as they pass our hiding place. Farther off, bells at the castle ring loudly in the night, undoubtedly announcing our escape. I hadn't expected to be discovered missing until the morning, when we'd all be far away from here—all but Bing. But so much for that plan.

I gently lift Dietan's head from my chest, lay him down in the hay, and push myself to my feet, stifling a groan. Every muscle in my body aches from lugging this heavy prince around.

I hope the others all made it to the appointed meeting place. At least Dietan and I are safe for now, hidden in this quiet stable. The horses don't seem to mind our company, and they watch with interest as I scoop my hands into their water barrel and take a drink.

I tear a strip of cloth from the bottom of my shirt, dipping the torn scrap into the barrel to wet it. With the soaked rag in hand, I slide Dietan out of the tattered beggar's cloak and peel away his filthy shirt. It reeks of blood and grime, and I toss it to the far side of the stable. Tears well in my eyes at the sight of his naked chest, bruised and battered, with open wounds along his exposed ribs. No one tended to them, so they're angry and infected. It's no wonder he has a fever. It's lucky he isn't in worse shape.

That familiar ache returns to my chest. I know now that losing him for real would devastate me, and if I don't get his fever down, it might happen tonight. If we're caught and he's forced to face Namreth again, it most certainly will.

No, I can't think that way. I have to be strong for both of us now.

I place the cool rag on Dietan's forehead. He shifts restlessly, his moans barely audible over the relentless clanging of the castle bells.

He needs a healer and probably to sleep for a week, but we don't have that luxury. We can't stay in this barn, or we'll be captured. We have to join the others at the meeting point, if they're even still waiting for us, but I can't move him now. They'll just have to go on without us.

But if I can't get Dietan back on his feet, I'll have to walk the length of the desert with him slung over my back. I know it's sturdy, but not *that* sturdy.

"Aren..." he moans.

"It's okay, just rest," I say, placing the wet cloth back on his forehead.

He makes no effort to reply, so I assume he must be dreaming. It brings back memories of when I had the red fever as a child and I couldn't leave my bed for a week. I don't remember much, just the burning in my chest and forehead. I cried, afraid the fever would take me. Instead, it took Mother. Father sat at my bedside and told me everything was going to be fine. But when I woke up, Mother was dead.

I want to say something reassuring to Dietan but seeing him this way makes my eyes sting.

I'm sad and angry at the same time. After everything we did to get here, everything we've shared, I can't lose him now. "Don't die on me," I whisper. "Not here, not like this."

The night grows colder, and the minutes turn to hours. I soak the rag in the barrel again and again, placing it on his burning forehead, cheeks, and neck, trying to break the fever. He barely moves, lying against the hay bale like he's already dead. I try to clean his wounds, as best I can, but all I can do is wait for the fever to break and hope we're not discovered.

Every creak, every unexpected sound makes me jump, thinking we've been caught. Dietan shivers terribly, and I drape the beggar's cloak over him, only for him to start sweating and crying out again, forcing me to throw it aside. In the darkness, in my exhaustion, I lose all track of time. Dietan's teeth chatter, the fever threatening to overtake him.

"Aren?" he rasps.

"Yes, I'm still here."

"Not a dream," he sighs.

I stare at him in the dark. My body aches for sleep. Maybe just a small nap, just long enough to rest my eyes.

No.

What if I fall asleep and wake up and Dietan's dead?

Just like Mother.

I won't. Indignant anger bubbles up within me.

"We've come too far for you to die now, you bastard. Don't even think of dying. I broke my bloody back to get you out of that damned prison, and I never once complained. I think you can handle a little thing like a fever—right?"

He moans, and I tell myself he can hear me. "That's right, you lazy ass. It's time for you to share in the work. Fight the fever so we can get out of this hellhole."

He groans again, his chest rising and falling. Each breath he takes is another small victory, and I need all the victories I can get.

Gently, so as not to disturb him, I curl up against his side, making sure I'm not pressing on any of his wounds. I don't mean to fall asleep. I've been fighting it all night, but my eyelids are so heavy that, once I close them, there isn't a force in the world powerful enough to open them.

T he sound of the door banging open wakes me with a start. An old man in a cotton cap and a dirty tunic stands framed in the doorway by the morning sunlight behind him. "What are you— Who are you—?"

RINGS OF FATE

I leap to my feet before I'm even fully awake, hands up, ready to fight. But the man isn't dressed like a guard. He's a groom, or just some old man who has come to muck the stalls or feed the horses.

When I step back, I ram right into something solid and warm. To my surprise, Dietan is on his feet as well, though a bit unsteady. Thank the goddess, he's survived the night. I touch his forehead and find his fever is gone.

"How are you feeling?" I ask.

"Alive," he croaks, his face pale and his eyes distant.

The man hesitates at the door. He is old and feeble and looks just as frightened of us as we are of him. He cautiously backs away.

But Dietan pushes forward and holds out a hand in greeting. "Sorry to disturb you, sir. Obviously, we wandered into the wrong stable. Won't happen again," he says, voice radiating charm. Despite his broken nose and black eyes, his demeanor is regal, his voice filled with confidence and warmth. He tries to smile but winces at the effort.

The groom shakes his head. "Ye can't be here, y'know. And I don't wan' to know why y'are. So off you go. Get out of here'n don't come back. I've work to do. Leave, and if I find you've stolen anything, I'll call the guards."

My heart jumps at the mention of the guards, but Dietan takes it in stride. "Of course. We'll be on our way, thank you. No need to call anyone," he says as he picks up our things.

"We'll be going now," says Dietan, saluting as he passes the man. "Got turned around. Sorry. You won't see us again."

The groom just keeps shaking his head, and the two of us break into a run the moment we're out the door. But we don't make it far. When we turn the corner into a narrow alley, Dietan groans and slows to a limp, bending over and clutching his sides.

"Take it easy," I tell him, laying a gentle hand on his back.

"Any sign of guards?" he asks.

"Not yet. I don't think that man will call them. Knowing the guards here, they'd probably beat him for his trouble," I say.

But even if the old man doesn't report us, moving in daylight will be risky. At least the damn bells have stopped. I peek around the corner at the street and find it clear. We need another place to hide until I can figure out what to do next. We could be discovered any second, and I expect to hear the thunder of heavy boots running after us soon.

Dietan doesn't look like he can walk, let alone run. His color has briefly returned to his face, but it's already fading. He looks pale again, and sick. He gasps for breath and groans, holding his ribcage and wincing. "Don't mind me," he pants.

"Let's find another place where you can rest for a minute."

He waves me off, still breathless, dismissing me as usual. I roll my eyes and scan the street once again for soldiers.

"Where are we going, exactly?" he asks when he can talk again.

"Figuring that out," I say. "You had a fever, and you had to rest, so we couldn't meet the rest of the group in the meeting place on time."

"Oh, sorry about that." He sighs. "How truly inconvenient of me."

"Messing things up does seem to be your talent."

"I am the very best at that." He catches my eye and grins. Even with the grim situation we've found ourselves in, he still manages to keep his sense of humor.

I'm still worried for him. "You feeling any better?"

He coughs. "Not at all, but as you can see, my wit has returned."

"Darn. Was hoping you'd lose it."

"No such luck."

"Luck? We haven't had much of that."

"I don't know. I think we're doing quite well," he quips, looking like a carriage rolled over him, with his black eyes, bruised face, and limp.

"Shut up and put on your cloak," I say, throwing it over his shoulders, then pulling the hood forward to hide his bruised face.

There's no sign of the guards, but that doesn't mean trouble isn't just around a corner. We can't stay in the alley any longer. I support Dietan as he limps along like the drunken husband I claimed he was, barely able to match my pace.

Unlike when we arrived in Engel, these streets are filled with hawkers selling goods, which means we've found the market district. Tents are stacked with baskets full of fresh produce and salted meats. I hope we're not far from the city gates. As we make our way through the market, I keep us off the main streets, trying to make sure I'm not walking too fast for Dietan. I'm worried about him, but I'm frustrated, too, so I pick up the pace, dragging him along by the elbow.

"You're being awfully rough," he complains.

"I haven't slept."

"Remind me never to keep you up all night," he says as we round yet another corner. The city gates come into view at last. This would be good news, if it weren't for the battalion of guards barring the exit.

"Shit." I pull us back behind the corner and out of sight.

"Want to try to run for it?" Dietan asks, pinching his hood closed, covering his face.

"That's your plan, oh master tactician? Just run and hope they won't cut us down?"

Dietan shrugs.

"In your condition, I doubt you could even crawl."

"Now that you mention it, running probably isn't the best option." He sighs again. "What else can we do? Have you considered that they might not recognize us and just let us out?"

I crane my neck and study the activity at the gate. "That's not the issue. Our problem is that they've barred the gates. No one's getting in or out. At least, that's what it looks like."

I try to imagine some way to get past the guards, but neither of us can fight.

We have no choice but to double back down the alley to find another way around. Maybe there's a city gate that's not as heavily guarded? Some back entry for servants or merchants?

Each time we turn a corner, there are guards stationed in front of a door, or the telltale sound of boots marching, heading our way. We backtrack the opposite direction, but there's another battalion that way, too.

Finally, there is nowhere left to go.

There are no alleys or alcoves to hide in. We'll be caught, and I doubt our shoddy makeshift disguises will be of any use then. I try not to despair, when I turn another corner and find a golden temple flanked by towering columns and colorful banners billowing in the hot desert wind.

"*Psst!* Aren! Over here!" a veiled acolyte whispers from the doorway.

Dietan and I look at each other, surprised and skeptical.

How would a sister at this temple know my name? Then I remember: the House of Healing. I glance at the crude map Bing handed me.

This is our chance.

As we cross the street, a group of guards rounds the corner, and I shove Dietan the last several paces through the temple's open doorway. I rush in behind him as the veiled girl steps back into the entrance, her voluminous flowing robes hiding us from view.

I steal a look at the guards as they march by the temple, praying they won't linger by our door. Most of the men pass, but the last one stops.

"Sister," he says to the veiled acolyte as he riffles through his satchel, not five paces from where Dietan and I crouch behind the door.

I fear the worst, thinking he's going to produce a search warrant or an order from the king.

He walks up the temple steps, and my heart stutters.

Then he produces a handful of coins and places them in the veiled girl's hands. "For the work you do," he says.

"Sirona bless you," the temple sister says, pocketing the money.

He briskly marches off to join his company.

I stumble back deeper into the vestibule, relieved beyond words. My thundering heartbeat slows, and the glass tiles feel cool against my back. Dietan rests his weight on my shoulder, spent from our rushed escape along the city perimeter.

Inside the sanctuary of the temple, incense fills the air. Tinkling bells and running water echo from deeper within.

When the guards are gone, the sister turns around, lifting her veil and revealing her face. It's a welcome one.

"Siena!" The scullery maid is resplendent in her jeweled gown. Her fiery locks are brushed and gleaming with bangles chiming on her wrists. I must look a fright in comparison.

"Aren! We waited for you all night!" she says as we fall into a tight embrace. I don't think I've ever been happier to see a friend. "What happened?" she asks when she releases me. "Why didn't you make it to the meeting place?"

"I was…delayed," I say, giving Dietan a sideways glance. "He was in much worse shape than I thought…"

Dietan leans uneasily on the wall, twitching occasionally in pain. He's almost unrecognizable in his rags. The skin that isn't bruised and swollen is sickly and pallid.

"Oh, dear. Is that…?" she asks.

I nod.

Siena sinks into a deep bow. "Your Highness," she says. "I am at your service." I remember now that Siena is from Loegria.

Dietan winces as the two of us each take an arm and help him walk. He's still shaky, and he shudders each time he moves.

"Osian did this?" Siena whispers, looking aghast. "I knew he tortured his victims, but even the prince of Loegria…" She can't finish.

RINGS OF FATE

"He needs help," I say, gripping her hand urgently. "Good food and uninterrupted sleep and the best damned healer we can find. We need to get him on the road as quickly as we can." I sigh, thinking back on everything we've suffered, only to escape Namreth by the skin of our teeth, with the Rings still firmly embedded in Dietan's back.

"You're in the right place," Siena says. "We can help him here. Come on." She leads us deeper into the temple.

"What are you doing here?" I ask as we make our way down a long corridor bathed in the soft glow of copper braziers suspended from arched ceilings. "Why didn't you leave with the others from the meeting point?"

Her bangles jingle as she walks. "I told them to leave without me. I didn't want to go without you and the prince. This was the only place I could think to come when the alarm sounded. I was raised in the faith, and the temple is a safe haven."

"I'm so sorry. You shouldn't have waited for me," I say.

Siena looks me in the eye. "And leave my friend? You saved me once. We faithful do not rest until a kindness is returned."

We share a meaningful look. She is a loyal subject of Loegria, yes, but she waited for *me*.

Women—we look out for each other.

I'm beyond grateful, and I hope her decision doesn't lead to her death. "I'll get us all out of here, I swear."

"I know you will." Siena smiles cheekily. "It's the first time I've been outside the castle since I was sold into King Osian's service when I was ten years old."

My heart drops to my stomach. Ten years old. She was just a child. Who could do such a cruel thing, especially to someone so young? An even more fierce determination grows within me to escape. Siena deserves a life outside of these walls.

The heart of the temple is built of stones so massive they must have been assembled by giants. A handful of relics are displayed on plain pedestals, broken pieces of gold and marble from earlier epochs winking in the firelight. The main chamber is a veiled statue of a goddess with her arms raised. The gods here are not the ones who watch over us in Alarice, but in the presence of this ancient deity of old Estyrion, I feel welcomed. Harvest Mother would not be slighted that I give thanks to my savior today, her sister goddess.

Siena bows her head before the statue. "This is the temple of Sirona, goddess of health and healing," she explains. "The goddess without a face who welcomes all."

As we shuffle forward, holding up an unconscious Dietan between us, we lose ourselves amongst veiled acolytes dressed in the same robes as Siena. There are other weary travelers bowed in prayer.

No one pays us any mind.

I surmise this place is more than just a house of healing. I wonder how many others—escapees or otherwise—have come through these doors seeking sanctuary from the king's cruelty.

Siena leads us to a high-ceilinged chamber deep within the temple, where an older woman in flowing robes lights candles and incense. She turns when she hears us approach, her wrinkled face kind and welcoming. When she sees Dietan, she simply extends one hand toward the table, and we guide him to lie on it. He's completely unconscious, but he's breathing.

"Thank you, sister," Siena says, bowing with folded palms. I do the same.

The healer leans over Dietan, whispering some enchantment as she stuffs his mouth with herbs. She inspects his wounds with sure hands, rubbing them with ointments drawn from a series of tiny golden pots. I can see their faint glow from the other end of the table.

"Leave us," she orders. "This will take a while, and I don't want you to hear him in pain."

I can't bear the thought of Dietan suffering further, but I know too well from Veteria that many medicines require some measure of pain to do their work.

As I watch the healer tend to his wounds, my shoulders relax. The woman knows her craft. I can only hope that despite his many injuries, Dietan will be in a condition to leave soon, before we bring Namreth's forces to this temple's doorstep. He looks like death warmed over, and I pray the healer is endowed with all Sirona's blessings.

"Come on," says Siena. "You must be hungry." It's only then that I realize the air is ripe with the scent of seared meats, roasted vegetables, and fresh-baked bread.

Siena leads me to a dining hall and passes me a plate. She piles it high with all manner of hearty fare. We sit down next to each other at a long table with many others, including priests and priestesses in their imposing headdresses. I'm so hungry that I don't talk for a long time, focused on filling my mouth with the temple's bounty.

"Do you know what happened to the others?" I finally ask, when I've scraped my plate clean. "Did they get out?"

"I don't know. I imagine some of them did, but I could be wrong. I…" Siena's brow furrows with concern.

"The alarm—they figured out we escaped," I say.

"We can't be sure," says Siena hopefully. "But why else would they have sounded it?"

I nod. So much for my grand plan. I hope they all got to safety. I hope *we* can get to safety in time. I glance at the door, toward the room where we left Dietan with the healer.

Sienna pats my arm. "Don't worry. Sister Dosha is a true talent," she says with a note of pride. "She's from my home village, where they teach this art."

"Oh, I'm sure she's talented," I say. "But it's going to take a miracle to get Dietan on his feet before the king's men arrive."

CHAPTER FORTY-SIX

Dietan

"Please just kill me," I say.

But the healer tending to me only shakes her head and continues her work. Not one inch of my body has been left untouched by Namreth's brutality. Every injury screams in protest.

Still, I feel better than I did a day ago.

"Who are you? Where am I?" I ask, my voice scarcely more than a whisper.

"I am Sister Dosha," the healer says. "You are at the temple of Sirona."

The name rings a bell. Dosha was the name of a famed Loegrian healer who came to court at my father's invitation when I was a boy. Against all warnings, she decided to make the pilgrimage to Sirona's temple in the Waste, and we had little word of her since. We'd all thought she perished in the desert.

"I'm relieved to see you are alive," I say with some effort. "I remember you. You healed my leg when I was thrown from my first horse."

Dosha smiles. "It has been a long time since I set foot in Loegria.

RINGS OF FATE

I have learned much here, in Sirona's light. More than King Donnel's medicine men were able to teach me after three years at your father's court. But your father is a good king. May he bring the Rings of Fate to bear in the coming war and free us from the mad king's rule." My heart sinks as I watch her wipe her hands on a clean white cloth.

My mission into the Waste has been an utter disaster. As I drift in and out of consciousness, I wonder if this famed acolyte of Sirona might be able to remove the Rings from my body.

She produces a roll of clean white bandages and a golden pot of blessed ointment. "I'm sorry we no longer have the healing waters of Sirona to speed along your recovery," she says. "I understand you must return to Loegria urgently."

"Ah, those lovely healing waters. It will shock you hear that I'm not fond of them," I retort.

"Just one more thing Osian has claimed for himself," Sister Dosha says, irritation biting at her words.

She wraps a bandage around my hand as she continues. "The waters were claimed by King Osian years ago. Many of those who are sick or injured must now go to the king for aid. The royal healers are always happy to oblige, but their price is steep. Even the simplest healing must be repaid with a year's service to the king, sometimes two," Sister Dosha says, gently tying off another bandage. She shakes her head. "Without the blessed waters, our temple has returned to the old ways of healing. Our methods are slower than the waters, but as you can see, they still work. Now, rest, and let your body heal."

I close my eyes, and for once, no dreams come.

Several days later, I can walk.

Several more days after that, thanks to the healing salts, oils, and clay, I've come back to life and some semblance of normalcy. I no longer look like a corpse. I'm almost myself again.

I've been given a room on the top floor of the temple in which to recuperate. I have been denied any news that might disturb my recovery, and I haven't seen Aren since we arrived. The isolation is driving me mad. Unable to sleep, I step out onto the balcony to take in the cool night air. I can see Castle Engel in the distance, its spires reaching into the night sky like a clawed hand cupping the rising crescent moon.

Even though I'm safe and healed, there are many others who aren't. That castle is still filled with unwilling servants and prisoners in the dungeons. I wonder how many of them escaped when Aren and I did and how many remain. I promise myself that I won't abandon them, that I will find a way to free them all.

All of a sudden, a voice comes from behind me.

"You're supposed to be lying down, tough guy."

Aren. My heart leaps, and relief fills me from head to toe. I feel like I'm floating. She's finally come to see me.

Still gripping the balcony railing, I turn around slowly. Her face is in shadow, but her eyes are bright. I want to run to her, to take her in my arms, but instead, I fall into the familiar pattern between us and wave a hand nonchalantly.

"I'm tired of lying down. I needed some air—too much incense." My tone is teasing, but gratitude grips my heart like a vice.

Aren.

On painful nights at the temple, I imagined she abandoned me, that the healers were soothing me with lies when they told me she was still here.

"Maybe they want you gone. Ever think they're trying to smoke you out?" she asks with that sass I remember all too well.

"Maybe that's the temple's secret. They annoy the patients until they heal themselves and leave."

"Is it working?" she asks as she steps out onto the balcony and joins me at the railing.

I shrug. We stand in silence, the two of us looking toward Castle Engel looming in the distance.

I'm keenly aware of how close she is.

She's dressed in a sleeveless flowing gown of yellow silk. Her hair is twisted up into elegant braids, exposing the freckles along her shoulders. The airy fabric graces every curve of her body, every inhale. She looks like a princess. I fight the urge to touch her.

Aren appraises me, looking up and down my body. I'm relieved when she speaks first. "They must be doing something right. I was scared you'd never walk again."

"Scared? You were worried about me?" I ask, raising an eyebrow.

"It's a figure of speech," she says, smiling, her eyes drifting down to the bandages beneath my loose tunic. "Maybe we should see how well they did."

Then, with no warning, she smacks me in the arm.

"Gods, woman!" I recoil, rubbing at the sting. "What was that for?"

"You really have to ask?" She leans in close, fire in her eyes.

I don't dare answer the trick question. I just stay very, very still.

"Why did you send me to the kitchens? Why did you have to say anything at all?" she continues, pain blossoming across her beautiful face.

I hear the question she doesn't ask: *Why did you say you didn't love me?*

"Didn't you see me shake my head? I tried to tell you it was all a—"

"A lie?" she finishes for me.

"Well, yeah," I say.

"You're kidding, right?" she snaps. "I was supposed to know what a shake of the head meant? You really are daft."

It's like she stabbed me in the heart. "I thought you knew me."

"I do know you. I know you're a moron," she retorts, crossing her arms.

I bristle at that, my frustration rising. "Are you so thick-headed that you actually believed those things I said about you? I was obviously lying!"

"Uh huh, what else is new?" she says, turning to leave. I catch her wrist, holding it firm.

Our eyes meet, her breath hitches, and I feel the heat radiating off her skin. Her face flushes, her lips parting slightly, and something sharp and unspoken crackles in the air between us.

"I lied. About everything. All of it. If my uncle knew what you meant to me—" My throat tightens, the weight of my own words pressing down on me.

"But you didn't lie! You couldn't!" Aren hisses. "And you're lying to me now!" She tries to yank her wrist free, but I don't let go.

"I swear I'm not," I say, willing her to trust me again. Her eyes shine like glass, swimming with unshed tears.

I see the battle raging inside of her—the hurt, the anger, the disbelief. She's so damn stubborn.

That much I've always understood. "I promise you, I didn't mean a word I said to Namreth... Well, except that your biscuits are a godsend. I mean that quite literally now. They killed me to save my life."

Aren's gaze hardens, and it feels as if her eyes are burrowing into my soul, trying to see all the way to the very essence of my being. She sticks and angry finger right in my face. "Don't talk to me about biscuits."

I will never speak of biscuits again.

My usual wit is failing me, but then again, Aren is the one woman who was never impressed with my charm. I hurry to explain before I put my foot in my mouth again. "The henbane—"

"I saw you drink it, same as me," she says accusingly. In the moonlight, tears streak her reddened cheeks. "And then you said all those awful things—"

"Katharine gave me an antidote," I blurt out, gripping her hand more tightly.

Aren's eyes widen in surprise, but she says nothing. She inhales deeply, rubbing her eyes with her free hand. She lets out a wounded huff. The tears spill over, and she swipes angrily at her cheek.

"Why didn't you tell me before? Because you don't trust me?"

"No, of course not. It was just—it was too great a risk. Under the influence of the truth serum, without the antidote yourself, you might have unintentionally given it away. And Aren—your reaction had to be real."

Her demeanor softens. I loosen my grip but don't release her. Instead, I lower our joined hands between us. "You really thought I was dead?" I whisper.

Her lips tremble, and she yanks her hand away, turning her back on me. "Not just dead," she murmurs, gripping the balcony railing. "You… You… Harvest Mother, Dietan. I don't understand you."

I run a hand down my face, scratching at the stubble on my jaw. "I don't understand you, either, but I'm trying." A silent moment passes between us, but she doesn't turn around. "You thought everything I said to my uncle was true, yet you still saved me."

With her back still turned, she wraps her arms around her torso, shaking her head like she's scolding herself.

I step toward her, slow and deliberate. I can feel the heat of her body, the tension rippling through her shoulders as I near, and all I want is to pull her into my arms. Although even I know that would be a monumental mistake right now.

"I'm sorry," I say again. "I'm sorry, but you've got to understand, I had my reasons for lying to you, and it has nothing to do with trust. I had to protect you."

She scoffs.

"You really are stubborn," I say, clasping my hands in front of me to keep from reaching for her. "Are you saying I shouldn't have protected you? Should I have been honest? Told Namreth how much you mean to me? Do you know what he does to people in there? What he does to the wives of men who've dared strike out against him?"

Aren sighs, and her shoulders fall as she wipes away more tears.

I know we're both thinking of Lydia.

"If I hadn't lied, you would have been right there with me. Starved and tortured by the mad king himself. If Namreth had done to you what he did to me…" My voice cracks. "I wasn't going to let that happen. I would *never* let that happen. I would die before I let anyone hurt you, Aren. I thought you knew that."

"Everything you said was really…?"

"A lie. Aren, I'm so sorry." I would apologize a thousand times to take her hurt away.

I don't love her. She's nothing to me.

It's the furthest thing from the truth.

"War means having to make hard choices, and I chose to hide the truth from you to keep you alive and unharmed," I say.

Aren plants both fists on her hips and sighs. She turns to look at me, lips pressed together in a thin line, then rolls her eyes.

"Are we on the same page?" I ask tentatively.

"I don't know. Are we?"

I give her a speaking glance, my heart in my throat. "I hope so."

"And what page is that?" she asks.

"The one where we tell each other the truth."

Aren chews at her bottom lip. "You wanna know why I'm angry?"

"Is there just one reason? Because I assumed…" I trail off.

"I'm so damned angry with you because…" She clams up, suddenly tongue-tied. "For Albion's sake, Dietan, you're going to make me say it?"

This time, my heart skips a beat, hope shining like daylight through the rain. "Say what?"

Aren lowers her gaze, her cheeks flushed, chest heaving, and an overwhelming wave of longing wells up in me, burning me all over.

When she meets my eyes once more, she says, "I care about you so much it hurts. I hate it. I want to be rid of these feelings, but I can't seem to shake them. They're killing me."

Her words come fast, like water bursting through a dam, and I stare at her in wonder, afraid to even breathe, not wanting to stop their flow.

"I thought I'd lost you, not once, or twice, but three times. When they dragged me out of the throne room, I thought for sure they would kill you, and I couldn't do a damned thing about it. I...have never felt so helpless, and I hated you for it. But I also grieved for you. I was so angry at..." She gazes skyward. "Everything. Because I thought you didn't feel the same way that I felt about you, and then I was afraid I was never going to get to tell you. Especially when I couldn't find your pulse after the devil's breath. And then when you were burning up with fever, I didn't think you would survive the night."

I remain frozen, my heart hammering, blood racing. I broke her heart. So many times. And she's still here. I love how stubborn she is.

Growing up, I was told I would marry a princess someday. To myself, I vowed not to marry, because my parents were so miserable together. But now I realize I wasn't avoiding marriage, I just wasn't interested in any of the haughty, dainty women at court who decked themselves in jewels and gossip. I wanted someone made of grit and steel who'd demand better from the world and those around her—even princes.

And this woman, a barmaid from a little town in the middle of nowhere, with calluses on her hands, lush, dark hair, and striking eyes—not to mention the coarsest language and the sharpest mind in all of Albion—is exactly that.

She's more beautiful than any woman I've ever met.

"Aren," I whisper, and she doesn't shy away this time. This close, I savor every eyelash, every pore, every freckle. Even a fever dream in the depths of Namreth's dungeons couldn't make her this beautiful, this real.

Her warm breath fans across my skin, and something coils inside me, hot and ready.

Slowly, I reach out and tuck a piece of hair that has escaped its braid behind her ear. She doesn't flinch away from my touch this time.

"Aren Bellamore, you mean more to me than anyone else in this entire world," I say.

Then I close my eyes, lean in...and wait. I've been wanting to do this ever since she walked into the room. She rises onto her tiptoes to meet me.

The kiss is gentle, soft. Our lips barely brush, and it's over quickly, but it feels more intimate, more vulnerable than any of the earlier kisses we've shared. The warmth of her touch is as charming as a spell.

When I open my eyes, I find hers still closed, and I smile. For once, I forget about the Rings, and I'm just an ordinary man kissing an ordinary woman.

How strange, not to feel the chaos inside me as the taste of her fills my heart. Not to feel the Whisting, choking and savage, roiling within like a snake ready to strike.

I frame her face with my hands, brushing my thumbs over the arches of her cheekbones, and breathe her in. She smells of temple incense and of the healer's sweet oil. A soft sigh escapes her as my hand glides up her back, while her slender fingers send sparks across my skin wherever she touches. I deepen the kiss, caressing her cheek in my palm.

Aren's fingers curl into the fabric of my shirt as she pulls me closer. I slide my hand to her waist and draw her in, our bodies finally touching. I pull her tightly against me so that she can feel exactly how much I want her.

A low sound rumbles in my throat, and heat surges inside me like I have a fever all over again.

Without breaking the kiss, I guide us from the balcony, back inside, and lower her down onto the bed, her yellow dress spilling across the linens. For a moment all I can do is stare at her and wonder at my good fortune before I lie down beside her.

I meet her eyes as I peel down the strap of her dress, freeing her perfect, soft breast. I bring my lips to it, gently tugging, sucking her peaked nipple. Her breaths become ragged, filled with want. Seeing her cheeks flushed, eyelids heavy, makes me feel a desire I have never known before. I want to worship her just as the acolytes here worship Sirona.

I reach down to draw her skirt up, ready to stop if she shows any hesitance, but thank the gods, she doesn't. In fact, she grins, eyes wide as I move my hand up her leg, lingering on the smooth skin of her thigh, stroking until she squirms.

To my pleasant surprise, she's not wearing any smallclothes, so I slide my hand higher. She lets out a surprised gasp as my fingers skim through her slickness. She goes very still, body tensing, and I hold my breath, half expecting her to scold, or slap, or run screaming from the room. But instead, she smiles and arches her back as she luxuriates in my fingers making slow, tormenting circles. She runs her hands across my chest, leaving trails of heat as she strokes my abdomen. Her one hand starts to roam lower and lower still, until it covers my hardness.

"Gods," I murmur into the soft skin of her throat.

She strokes my length languidly, teasing me, making my insides coil in pleasure. She slides her hands back up my body and draws my face to meet hers once more. Breathing hard, heat rising inside me, I kiss her again, harder this time. She holds me close, her lips soft and warm, and the world melts away with another sigh.

There are temples to a variety of gods all over the world, but hers is the only one where I care to worship. I thank all the gods in all the heavens that I'm healed enough to enjoy this.

"Sometimes you make me forget to breathe when you kiss me like that," I murmur when we finally pull apart for a moment.

"Good," she says, her lip curling in a way that makes my blood roar. "Gives you more time to focus on what you do best."

"And what's that?"

"Kissing me back."

"Thank the gods this isn't a dungeon," I say, rising to my knees.

I sit back on my haunches and look upon Aren, beautifully mussed and rosy. I take the hem of her dress and slowly roll it up her body. She puts her arms up for me to pull the gown over her head. Then she sits before me, in radiant light, naked and perfect and mine.

"Think you're about to get lucky?" she teases.

For just a moment, my awareness shifts to the Rings, which have been quiet this whole time. They're still quiet.

I allow myself to hope.

"Oh, I know I am," I say with the biggest grin of my life.

CHAPTER FORTY-SEVEN

Aren

Dietan gazes at me so intently, I have to look away for fear of melting. I'm not wearing a stitch of clothing, and I reach for the sheet to cover myself, but he stops me. "I want to see you," he says, his eyes hungry.

"Well, fair is fair," I say, blood roaring in my ears and heating my face as I sit up and reach for the buttons of his shirt. My nimble fingers undo the buttons one-by-one, until his shirt flutters away from his torso, revealing several bandages. I reach out and run light fingers over the healing wounds. They're now a reminder of what he did to protect me.

I glide my hands down to his trousers. Like me, he's not wearing any smallclothes, and there's nothing small about this man. But I knew that already. I blush at my boldness, then smile. Of course, I took charge. I've never been one to just lie back and let things happen to me. Not in life, and evidently, not in the bedroom, either.

I unbutton his fly, and his trousers drop to his knees. Dietan, scars and all, is now completely vulnerable in front of me, as I am before him.

I *want* this man. I burn as my eyes roam his body. His broad chest, corded muscles, the fine golden hair leading to where it's apparent he wants me.

Then he pushes me back onto the bed. He lays beside me so I can feel the entire length of his body against mine, nothing between us. He groans at the contact, and I close my eyes, enjoying the feel of him. He's so warm, and his heart is beating as fast as mine.

I think he's going to kiss me again, but then he turns and hovers over me on his hands and knees, kissing a trail from my neck all the way down my stomach. Each kiss more stirring than the next.

He reaches my core, and with a gasp, I rise up onto my elbows to watch as he kisses that most tender part of me. His eyes meet mine, and I groan, flopping back in the bed. Never has anything felt this good. Never. He flutters his tongue across me, and I arch my back and shudder. His strokes are gentle, almost careful, but I want more.

"More?" he murmurs. "Did you say more?"

"Mmhhmm," I say, not realizing I spoke out loud, but now I can't even form words, because what he's doing with his mouth and tongue feels so good. No more tentative touches. He flicks his tongue as he sucks my sensitive bud between his perfect lips. But still, I want more—I *need* more. I squirm underneath him, something cresting, something hot and just out of reach.

Just when I'm sure I'll go out of my mind chasing a feeling I can't name, that remains stubbornly out of reach, Dietan slips a finger inside me. The added pressure on top of the exploration of his lips and tongue draw me closer to the elusive *something*. Like storm clouds darkening the horizon, the feeling bears down on me, relentless and inevitable. Just when I think the heavens might open, drowning me in sensation, Dietan… *stops*.

He rises up on his knees and looks down at me, poised at the juncture of my thighs. He's flushed, his face intent and eager. But now he's hesitant, a shadow of doubt flickering behind his eyes.

I grab his hand, lacing my fingers with his. "Dietan, please. I want this. I want *you*."

"As my lady commands." There's no sarcasm in his words this time. Only tenderness.

I squeeze his fingers, as we so often do, as my hips move under him of their own accord.

He takes a trembling breath, all desire again. "I'll go slow," he says.

"I know you won't hurt me." I beam up at him because I know that this time, it's true.

He hovers over me and uses his free hand to guide his tip against my entrance. I breathe heavily with anticipation as he barely pushes inside of me. He stops for a moment, and my heart is beating like a bird trapped in a cage.

"Are you okay?" he asks, meaning it in more ways than one. "I can stop."

I nod my head. I don't really know *what* I want, but I know it's *more*.

He pushes deeper, stretching me.

That. I want *that*.

"Yes," I plead, my voice almost a growl.

He grins, pushing in almost to the hilt. He withdraws slightly and then surges forward again, deeper this time. Goddess, he's huge. "All good?"

"Harvest mother, yes. I want you." I don't mean for the words to come out as a challenge, but they ignite a fire in Dietan's eyes.

He pulls out almost completely before thrusting all the way back in, and the feeling of fullness takes my breath away. Then he covers my mouth with his, kissing me as he sets a rhythm that makes my toes curl. I plant my feet on the mattress and tilt my pelvis to meet his thrusts, and he groans, increasing his pace to match my movements.

"Gods, Aren," he rasps. "You're going to kill me."

"Already tried," I say, gasping for air. "Failed."

Then he pushes up on straight arms, changing the angle of his body just enough to create friction on that most sensitive part of me where our bodies rub together.

I gasp, then whimper, squeezing my eyes shut as heat, white and furious, fills me and makes my ears buzz.

It feels so damn good. Too good. The way he fills me and… *Goddess*.

I grit my teeth and hold my breath as the storm inside me finally breaks, a tempest so total that everything in the world fades away except for this man and this moment.

I pulse around him again and again as pleasure shoots through me with the force of a lightning strike. I claw at his back, pulling him closer. I want this to go on forever, and at the same time, I need it to end before I'm swept away for good.

His gaze burns into mine, his body trembling.

When I scream his name, he falls right over the edge with me.

I open my eyes just as the first rays of dawn crest the horizon. I'm warm all over, and my body is still humming from last night. Honestly, I don't remember falling asleep, but when my eyes focus, I realize I'm not the only one awake.

"Morning," Dietan says. He's lying on his side facing me, cradling his head in his hand and grinning like the fool he is. His eyes are bright, slightly lined with weariness, and I wonder if he's slept since our second bout of lovemaking.

I rub the grit from my own eyes. "Were you watching me sleep? That's creepy, you know."

"I was waiting for you to wake up," he says.

"Were you now? I wonder why…" I tease as I notice the bulge under the sheets. "I see you're up. Been that way for some time?"

"Longer than I dreamed possible."

"That must have been hard."

"Harder than you might guess." He waggles his eyebrows.

"Really? I might have to investigate."

"By all means."

I snuggle closer to him, and my skin tingles all over, remembering the way his body moved with mine just a few hours before. It feels like a dream. But when he leans over me and tips my chin up to meet his. I know it's real. He smiles even wider and slips a hand between my legs once more, a finger stroking and then finding the white-hot center of my body, where I'm so ready for him.

"Looks like I'm not the only one who's eager," he says.

"Shut up."

"No, really. You must have been up all night to be this wet."

Well, he would know. "Stop or I'll kill you," I tease.

"No, you won't. We've already established that you're bad at that." He laughs as he adds another finger, slipping so easily inside. He strokes a little harder, and my breath hitches.

"Don't be so sure. Maybe I plan on using you until your heart gives out," I threaten, rolling on top of him.

He looks up at me, eyes shining. "Do it."

Last night, the first time we made love, it was urgent and frantic, as if making up for lost time. In the middle of the night, we reached for each other once more in the warm haze between dreaming and waking, a balm for the terrors that once filled Dietan's lonely nights. But now we take our time, exploring every inch of each other's bodies.

This morning, I want nothing more than to please him the way he's pleased me, and so I pull the sheet away, uncovering that glorious cock that's given me more pleasure than I ever imagined possible.

"Sweet goddess," I breathe, kneeling in front of him, thanking the Harvest Mother for blessing me with such a lover.

Dietan lies there with his arms folded under his head, and he cranes his neck to look down at me with a proud, lustful grin. "You look good from this angle," he says as his body trembles with anticipation.

I lean down and give it a long, slow stroke with my tongue, and he groans. His reaction pleases me—emboldens me.

I feel powerful.

So I hold his shaft in my hands, wrap my lips around the head, and take him all the way into my mouth. I love the taste of him, the smell of him, the sounds he makes as he arches his back in pleasure.

His hands slide through my hair, grasping and pulling as I suck his cock and work his length, savoring the salty, sweet taste of him. Every sigh and moan he makes drives me wild.

It feels satisfying to give Dietan pleasure. He's been through so much pain that making him feel good is a small victory.

"I need you," he cries as I take him deeper into my mouth. "Aren... please...I need to be inside you."

I stop and shake my head, a naughty smile on my lips. "We'll get to that later. Don't you worry," I say, then go back to sucking him.

But then he's tugging me up and away, and I let him. "Sorry, love, but I'm terrible at waiting."

"Is there anything you're good at?"

"This," he says, and in one powerful motion, he tosses me onto my back, shoving my legs apart with his knees.

"Oh—I..." I didn't expect that. He's so strong, and so demanding, it makes me melt and burn at the same time.

He kneels between my legs and pull my hips toward him so I'm perfectly aligned with his cock. He pauses for a heartbeat at my entrance.

"Don't make me wait," I warn.

And he doesn't.

CHAPTER FORTY-EIGHT

Aren

Breakfast is a temple-wide affair. Meals are sacred in the House of Healing, and everyone is invited to share in the bounty. Siena explained when I first came that all the food is free, gifts to honor the goddess and her healers from the faithful and the grateful among the city's denizens.

In the dining hall, platters piled high with warm bread, fresh dates, and ripe persimmons are laid out alongside carafes of wine and tea. Dietan and I peruse the selection. I decide on a piece of fruit. Before I can even reach for it, I hear a door slam open and stop short.

Siena rushes into the chamber, eyes wide and bangles jangling. Footfalls pound on the floorboards above us. She runs right up to us. "You need to hide. They're coming. Downstairs, now."

"Downstairs?" As far as I can tell, we're on the ground floor, and there's nothing below.

She ignores me, and without a word, breakfast is forgotten as acolytes and disciples shove tables and benches aside. Siena kneels and pulls back the rug underneath our feet, revealing a hidden door in the wooden floor.

"Help me," she says, and two of the nearest healers tug on the handle, prying it open to reveal a staircase. "Go!"

"What about you?" I ask.

"They aren't looking for me. I'm just a kitchen girl, a dime a dozen. They only care about you and the prince," she says with a shake of her head. "And my veils will keep me hidden." She pulls them forward, covering her face completely.

We don't need to be told twice. Dietan leads us downward into the darkness. Behind us, the hatch slams closed with a loud thud that echoes through the underground chamber. He finds my hand in the dark and squeezes it. I'm too terrified to even whisper, and for a moment there is no sound but our breathing.

Above us, we hear footfalls on the floorboards, some heading away, others drawing nearer. Then a thump, followed by a soft rolling sound that means the acolytes have rearranged the rug, then the scrape of chairs and tables sliding back into position. The chatter and clink of silverware sounds once more, as if nothing is amiss and no one is hidden beneath their feet.

I hold my breath.

Then we hear it: a door creaking open, raised voices, and heavy boots clomping into the dining hall. I strain to listen over my pulse pounding in my ears. Dietan gives my hand a reassuring squeeze. He leans down to whisper, "Don't worry. I'll protect you."

I squeeze back. But it's him who needs protection, I want to say. It's he who'll be killed—or worse, tortured and killed—if the king's men find us here.

My blood freezes when the heavy boots thump above our heads, raining dust on my face. I clamp a hand over my mouth to hold in a cough.

"We're looking for two fugitives," barks a stern voice. "A criminal who's escaped the dungeon and a cook from the kitchens who helped him."

So we were right, the alarms were because our ruse had been discovered.

"A criminal? Who is it?" asks one of the sisters with an innocent air.

"Some visitor who snuck into the palace and was caught. He faked his death. When guards went to retrieve his body for burning, he was gone. The king's beside himself with rage," the soldier says.

Dietan tightens his grip on my fingers while his other hand moves to the knife he's strapped to his hip. He's kept it close since I returned it to him this morning.

"This is a place of worship," we hear Sister Dosha say in her calm voice. "And you've interrupted our sacred meal."

The guard utters a muffled response I can't make out. I don't move. I don't breathe. My muscles are wound so tightly it feels like I might snap.

"You're certain you haven't taken in anyone injured? A badly beaten, light-haired, Loegrian man? A dark-haired Alarician woman would be accompanying him."

"No, no one of that description," says Sister Dosha, sounding unruffled and slightly annoyed to have to answer such questions.

"Lying to the kingsguard is treason," the soldier warns.

"I am aware, and you should be aware that we serve King Osian well here."

"You serve at the mercy of the king, and if it's discovered you have harbored fugitives, the king will raze this temple."

Sister Dosha wisely doesn't reply. Then there's the sound of boots circling the hidden door, raining dust on us once again. I pray to the goddess Sirona to keep me from sneezing.

I bow my head to keep the dirt out of my eyes and lean on Dietan, strong and silent next to me, focusing on him to keep the paralyzing fear at bay.

At last, the heavy footsteps recede. The clatter of breakfast resumes once again. Then, after what feels like forever, silence takes over as the room empties and acolytes and pilgrims go back to their tasks. We wait longer still, breathing more easily now, hoping the danger has passed. At last we hear the scraping of tables, chairs being pushed away, and the carpet being rolled back. The door springs open, and the light is painfully bright, stinging my eyes.

For an instant, I fear it's a guard.

But then I hear Siena's voice tell us, "They're gone." She reaches for my hand, helping me up the steps. Dietan follows with a steadying hand on my back.

We are back in the dining hall, which is empty not just of people but of food. My stomach growls. Thankfully, Siena hands us each a slice of date cake folded in a cloth napkin. "They're combing the city, looking for you," she says as we eat.

Dietan wolfs the cake down gratefully. I thought I was starving, but now I find my appetite is gone.

Namreth is looking for us.

He knows that Dietan is alive and I helped him. I hand my slice of cake to Dietan, who raises a questioning eyebrow before gulping it down, too.

"We can't stay here," Dietan says when he's finished eating. His jaw is set, his eyes hard and determined. "They'll be back," he adds, just as Sister Dosha returns to the room. She looks relieved to see us.

"Yes, they will. I don't think they believed me, but they can't move against the temple without proof." Worry creases her gentle face. "Are you sufficiently recovered?"

He stretches out his arms. Though I know he's sore from crouching in our cramped hiding spot, he is no longer in pain. "More than you know. You've done a magnificent job. Thank you, sister, for everything," says Dietan. "We need to get out of here today. We're putting everyone in this temple in danger."

The priestess nods. "We have use of a place near a grain storehouse that belongs to the temple," she tells us. "You can stay there as long as you need until you find a way to leave the city."

"I'm guessing we aren't the first people you've had to hide from Namreth?" he asks.

"No, and you won't be the last. The accommodations aren't as comfortable as here at the temple, but—"

Dietan nods sharply. "It will be more than sufficient. How do we get there without being discovered?"

"The wagon we usually use to transport supplies will be most inconspicuous. I've already called for it. It should be here before the next call to prayer. Siena can help you get ready."

I look at the former scullery maid. "Aren't you coming with us? We were all supposed to escape."

She shakes her head. "I've no home to go to, and I'm needed here. There are too many pilgrims who need help right now."

The king's wrath has been felt by too many of his subjects.

While I want to take her with us, I know it would only put her in more peril. She's safe here at the temple, for now. "Thank you for everything," I say with a sob in my throat as I pull her in for a close hug.

"No, thank *you* for getting me out of the castle," she says. "Be safe." To Dietan, she bows and says, "Sirona keep you, Your Highness, and may Loegria prevail against the Usurper."

We don't have much to pack.

I still have the satchel from the night of our escape. I give Dietan his royal knife back. The only things I brought from the castle are a change of clothes and a skillet I stole from the kitchen to replace my own. I ask Siena to replenish the casket of herbs Namreth took from me when I arrived. She does so happily.

She stuffs my satchel with dried meats and fruit while Dietan and I change out of our plain tunics into temple acolytes' robes, with hoods that hide half our faces when pulled up.

Siena leads us out the back, where a covered wagon waits. Dietan and I climb in to find that it's stacked to the canvas top with provisions. We squeeze between large woven baskets of grain, nestling beside two of the tallest. I hope they're big enough to hide us if the wagon gets stopped.

"It's going to make its usual rounds, but you should be in the safe house before nightfall," Siena says. "Here's a map. The wagon will drop you off a few streets away from the safe house. Good luck, and may Sirona heal your troubles." She hands us a scroll.

"May the Harvest Mother bless your bounty," I reply.

"As the gods will," says Dietan, who takes the map, and then we're off.

The sun beats down on the tarp, and the wagon shakes and rattles each time it finds some little divot in the road. Dietan jumps whenever we hit a rocky patch, his head bashing against the wooden frame holding up the tarp. "I thought you were used to riding in the back of carriages," I tease.

"Most definitely, but never with the produce." He draws an apple out of the nearest basket and takes a bite as the cart lurches to a halt.

"I think we're here," I say.

The driver opens the flap on the tarp. "Hurry. I can't stop long."

Dietan tosses the apple and lifts me out of the wagon, and then we scramble into the nearest alley. Without a goodbye, the driver is back at the reins. The wagon trundles down the street, leaving us with the crude map and only the slightest notion of how to find the safe house.

"Come on," says Dietan, squinting at the piece of paper. "I think it's this way."

In our hooded temple robes, we walk at a measured pace, trying not to look desperate and afraid.

"No—wait, it's this way," he says with a curse. "Sorry, I think I had it upside down."

I look over his shoulder at the scroll, searching for the landmarks as we walk through the city streets. I try to compare the crude charcoal lines to the actual streets of stone and brick.

"I think that's it," he says, stopping across from a building.

The safe house is an unassuming, cramped three-story structure, squeezed between two larger ones on either side. Dietan makes us circle the block once to make sure no one's following us before we walk up to the door.

He knocks, and the heavy door gives just a little. "It's unlocked," he whispers. Perhaps, like the temple, the safe house is open to all who need sanctuary. He pushes harder, and the door groans on its hinges as it swings open. We slip into a dark and windowless hallway, and once inside, without warning, someone slams the door shut behind us.

Before Dietan can reach into his robes for his knife, there's a flash of silver. Dietan launches himself toward the hooded man and slams him against the door. The stranger grunts at the impact, and the pair jostle for control of the knife, each gripping the pommel, but Dietan has the upper hand, forcing the blade slowly toward the man's throat.

The sharp edge nicks the stranger's skin. "Move a fucking inch, and I'll slice your throat," Dietan growls, and I've no doubt he means it.

I wrap my fingers around the handle of the skillet in my satchel.

"Please don't kill me...Your Highness," the stranger says.

Dietan hesitates.

I know that voice. Dietan knows it, too, and lowers his knife as I slowly put the satchel down. The stranger pulls down his hood.

"Marcus!" Dietan cries.

They wrap their arms around each other, clapping backs like long-lost brothers. After, Marcus holds him at arm's length, as if unable to believe his eyes. "Thank the gods you're alive!"

"Shouldn't you be in Loegria?" Dietan exclaims at the same time.

"You didn't really think I'd turn around and go home without you, did you? Can you imagine if I showed up in Lundenwic and told the king I'd lost you in the Waste?"

"He would not be pleased."

"He'd have my head. But it took longer than expected to sneak into Engel. And now I hear you've run into some trouble? No one could have foreseen *that*," he says sarcastically.

"Nothing I couldn't handle," Dietan demurs.

"Oh, that much is obvious, Your Highness. This is just a social call. We just trekked all the way through a fucking desert to say hello." Marcus laughs.

"We?" Dietan asks as footsteps descend the stairs. Jared peers down at him from halfway up, his expression morphing from confusion into joy. He's limping from a recent injury, but he doesn't let it slow him. He nearly slides down the stairs and collides with Dietan.

"Good gods, man!" Jared says. "What happened to you? You look like shit."

I haven't seen Dietan smile like this in a long time. "It's a long story…" he says.

It's then that Jared spots me. "Aren! You're still alive! Ophelia won't put me in an early grave after all!"

"I wouldn't be here if she wasn't," says Dietan.

Jared hugs me next and lifts me off my feet. "It's so good to see you!"

"You too," I say, my heart lightening at the sight of friendly faces. *How did they— When did they—* I have a thousand questions and can't decide which to ask first.

"Come, quickly, move away from the door," says Marcus, sliding a chair under the handle and ushering us deeper into the house. "I assume you're here for the uprising."

"Uprising?" asks Dietan, echoing my own confusion. "What uprising?"

Jared leads us up the stairs, leaning on the banister as he goes, grinning delightedly despite the effort.

"This uprising," says Marcus, beaming as he opens the door to a room off the landing. Because there they are—my people.

Arnfried, Lambert, and Tess are crowding around the map laid out on a small table. They look up in shock when we enter.

"Aren," exclaims Lambert, leaping up to hug me. "You all right?"

"Been better," I say as I greet Arnfried and Tess with hugs as well.

I can't help but notice that Rosamond, Nelson, and Bing are not among them.

And why are these three not gone from this wretched city by now, safe and free? *Arnfried was supposed to be back with his mothers by now.*

But they're here, and they deserve to meet the man they sacrificed so much to save. I step aside, revealing Dietan. "This is Prince Dietan of

Loegria. He was dead, but he's feeling much better now—right?"

"Right," says Dietan, drawing himself up with a measure of his usual, regal charm. "Hello, everyone. Thank you for your part in my escape."

Lambert gives him an elaborate bow, while Tess nods and greets him with a more subdued and respectful, "Your Highness." I'm reminded of how easy I feel with him now, after everything we've been through together.

"Have you eaten, Your Highness?" asks Tess. "Aren?"

"Just breakfast," I say. "And not much of it."

"Not much at all," Dietan laments. "We were about to enjoy a wonderful meal at Sirona's temple when it was rudely interrupted by guards intent on my death."

"Very rude," Marcus agrees.

Tess leaves the room, clucking to herself. I cross my arms and look at Dietan. "Didn't you eat both of the date cakes Siena gave us?"

"They were small."

Tess returns with a laden tray. "It's only bread, cheese, and tea, but it's filling. Please sit, Your Highness. Eat."

Arnfried and Lambert carefully pull the map and the figurines on top of it off to one side of the table. Marcus finds some plates and hands them to us. Jared pours tea.

"I understand this is a safehouse that the sisters of Sirona's temple have used of late. Who else knows of this place?" I ask, breaking off a heel of bread and looking around.

"One of the ladies of the court, a favorite of King Osian's, Señora DuVal. A devout and very rich lady who also just happens to want his head on a pike," says Tess. "He killed her husband and took her as a mistress."

I shudder and take a too-hot sip of tea.

"Yeah, he's one classy guy, that's for sure," Lambert says mirthlessly.

Dietan reaches for my hand underneath the table. I smile at him before turning back to my friends. "Tell me what we're working with. What happened the night we escaped? What was that alarm?"

"The king urgently wanted to see the prince and his possessions one more time before putting his body in the fire. They opened the sack and— well, you know. That wasn't no prince in that sack," Lambert says.

I shiver, imagining Namreth's fury at finding that Dietan—and the Rings—had slipped out of his hands. "All hell broke loose. Osian realized he'd been tricked and the prince had escaped. The guards sounded the alarm, and then he rampaged the kitchens personally, looking for you.

Bing tried to stall him and did a pretty good job of it…but…" He shakes his head.

My heart clenches in my chest. I knew Bing was going to do something like this, but it still hurts to hear about it.

"Osian snapped his fingers, and Bing died before he could fall," says Lambert. "I went back to look for him…" His voice wavers at the loss of his friend. "Anyway, Arnfried, Tess, and I barely got away and made it here."

"What about Nelson? Rosamond?"

"We think they made it out before the city went into lockdown," says Tess. "At least, that's what we hope, but… On Osian's orders, they were killing anyone who tried to leave the city." She shrugs helplessly. "It was a risk we all took."

Bing is dead. Nelson and Rosamond are likely lost as well. I swallow the lump in my throat. It isn't right. They had lives. Friends and family who'll miss them. Dietan is here right now because of their sacrifice.

Dietan clears his throat. He nods to the former servants who helped him escape, looking each of them in the eye, one after the other. "I'm in your debt. As Prince of Loegria, I promise you, if we live through all of this, I'll see that you are well compensated. You have my gratitude for the rest of my life."

"Appreciate that, Your Highness," says Lambert. Tess murmurs her thanks as well.

Arnfried extends his hand toward Dietan. "Thank you, cousin."

Dietan takes a closer look at Arnfried. He grips his hand, a smile blooming across his face. "You're Katharine's son," he says and pulls Arnfried into an embrace. "Your mothers will be so relieved to know you're alive."

There is a solemn silence, and then Dietan lets Arnfried go and turns to his friends, who've been quiet during the reunion. "And how'd you two jokers link up with this crew?"

Marcus laughs, leaning against the doorframe, while Jared throws himself down on a stool, his leg extended awkwardly as he reaches for a mug of tea. "This fellow," he says, pointing to Marcus, "sent a messenger to Evandale, and I met up with him at the Sarindale Outpost. We weren't there a day before we were attacked. Raiders—likely backed by the Usurper, again. They no longer fear the kingsguard. I took a spear in the leg"—he gestures to the wounded limb—"and it hurt like a bastard. Good thing we found a healer in town, or I might have lost it at the knee. Marcus feared I'd need a month to mend and threatened to leave me there while he went searching for the two of you. I refused. A bum leg wasn't going to slow me down."

"Still, it took us ages to get here," says Marcus. "Sorry. I had to leave soldiers in Evandale and at court in Loegria, where your family are now," he says to me. "Jared escorted them there before meeting me."

"Ophelia didn't want me to leave, I'll tell you that," says Jared. "But I wasn't going to stay at court while you were lost in the Waste." He turns to Dietan. "What the hell were you thinking, man?" He shakes his head. "Anyway, nearly as soon as we crossed into this wretched kingdom—which, by the way, totally deserves its name—we were met by Princess Katharine's people, who were expecting us."

Arnfried stands a little straighter at that. "Your mother is a formidable woman," says Jared. "A handful of her warriors saw us most of the way here, before we did the rest on foot. The princess didn't think much of your mission, either," he adds, glancing meaningfully at Dietan.

"It wasn't much of a success," Dietan admits nonchalantly. He turns to Marcus. "I can't believe you let Jared walk the rest of the way to Engel on that leg."

Marcus snorts. "Once we got close enough, we hitched a ride with a wagon train bringing supplies to Engel. We assumed they were merchants, but in truth, they worked for this Osian fellow—apparently everyone here does. Got us into the city, at least. We were delayed a few days, since they had the unfortunate idea to take us captive once we arrived."

"They like to do that," I chime in.

"Should I ask how you escaped?" Dietan drawls.

"Let's just say they shouldn't have bound Marcus's hands so loosely."

Marcus grins.

"After we escaped, we asked around near Castle Engel if anyone knew what happened to the Loegrian prince and his bride, and we were lucky enough to run into Lambert here not two days ago," says Jared. "He brought us to this house."

"We were waiting for you," Lambert says to me. "We went to Sirona's temple looking for a place to hide because we knew Siena would be there, and a priest in a fancy robe like the ones you and Aren are wearing told us we could stay here," Lambert said.

"The temple didn't tell us they were hiding you, and I don't blame them," Marcus adds.

"They didn't tell us they were hiding you, either! We thought the safe house would be empty," says Dietan.

"Seems like it's not their first time smuggling important refugees," Jared remarks. "We were just about to scour the city when you arrived."

"They've sealed the whole place. Doubled the guards at every gate, patrols half a day's ride in all directions. No one goes in or out," Marcus continues.

"Fine with me," says Dietan. "Nowhere else I need to be."

Jared sighs. "There's a time for humor, my friend, and now is not the time. Princess Katharine's people won't be able to get close enough to retrieve us, which was the original plan. They've never had the numbers to take on Osian, and certainly don't now, with Estyrion arming for war. We're well and truly fucked. Your father's actually going to have our heads for this—that is, if we get out alive."

But Dietan is unmoved. "I came to Estyrion for a reason," he says. "That reason, ultimately, was to win a war. The original plan may have been a bust, but now that we're here and we know that Osian—Namreth—is in league with the Usurper, and the best way we can help my father and grandfather defeat Penrith is to remove this false king from his tacky golden throne."

"And how exactly do you plan to do that?" asks Jared.

"I'm going to do what my grandfather should have done all along. Destroy him."

CHAPTER FORTY-NINE

Aren

I'm lying on a narrow cot in the safe house just inches from Dietan's, but the gap between us might as well be as wide as a bridge between two kingdoms. I toss and turn, unable to sleep ahead of the dangerous mission ahead.

My mind swirls with too many thoughts—hoping my sisters and my father are safe, and grieving the loss of Bing, who sacrificed himself to help us escape. I'm immeasurably grateful for my new friends sleeping beside me. They risked so much to get Dietan and me out of the castle alive.

If Mother could see me now, I wonder if she'd be proud that her sensible eldest daughter grew up to plot assassinations with a handsome foreign prince.

My thoughts turn to the night in the stable when I thought Dietan would die of fever. Then the magical night when Dietan and I woke up together from a haze of finally, *finally* acknowledging what we meant to each other. Was that just this morning? I thought we would have more time. More time to kiss and heal in the temple. As if he can sense what I'm thinking, Dietan throws his arm over me, bridging the gap. With his hand in mine, I'm finally able to sleep.

In the morning, Dietan confers with the team, bustling about the table, drawing lines on the map, moving tiny figurines. They propose strategies, then tear them apart, debating how they might fail or succeed. Dietan leads the discussion, his tone confident and commanding—like a prince. No, like a future king.

"Marcus, if you please." He motions to the map on the table as everyone in the house gathers around him.

The general nods, standing. "Based on the information we've gathered, Namreth will soon march on Loegria. We have days to prevent this, maybe less. As you know, he's closed off the city gates, and no one is allowed to leave, but we've learned that people are still allowed to enter at a single, heavily fortified point." He turns to Arnfried. "You scouted the eastern gate?"

Arnfried nods. "Entire caravans are being let inside the city, and we think we know why. The king is throwing a banquet."

"How can you be certain?" I ask.

"He's done it before to mark the start of a campaign. He throws a banquet to rally his troops and honor his generals," Arnfried explains.

"More like scare the shit out of his generals," Lambert says knowingly. "They know it'll be their last meal, if they fail."

Intel starts to flow more freely from Arnfried. "According to the castle staff, this is the biggest banquet he's ever planned. Guards are bringing people from all over Estyrion to augment the existing staff. Especially in the kitchen and banquet hall." He gives me a meaningful look. I'm glad we spoiled the mad king's plans with our kitchen jailbreak.

"It's going to be huge," Lambert adds. "Big drunken orgy, no doubt. Lots of wine, lots of food. The king and his high-ranking officers will be occupied."

"Then it's the perfect time to strike," says Marcus. "They won't suspect a thing."

"Exactly." Dietan nods. "We'll plan to attack in the middle of the raging party after he and all his most loyal supporters have eaten and drunk their fill. They won't be prepared for an attack. We can eliminate many enemies at once."

"According to our information, most of his allies are only loyal to him because of the threat to their families if they don't. In fact, we know that many of his generals and administrators' wives are courtiers at Castle Engel, to insure their good behavior," Arnfried confirms.

"Hostages," Tess spits.

"Exactly. If we act swiftly enough, it's unlikely that anyone will pick up a sword in retaliation," says Marcus.

Tess adds, "Security in the castle will be tight. Namreth is confident that no one can match the Unseen Death, but even so, he doesn't allow weapons in the castle except for those his guards carry."

Jared bites his lip, unconvinced. "Just so we're clear. We're thinking of storming a *very* well-guarded castle and killing a king who has control of the Whisting." His eyes dart to Dietan briefly before he continues. "…With nothing more than our fists. And on top of all that, you expect us to simply walk in?"

"Like it's hard?" Dietan laughs wryly.

"If we don't strike him at the banquet, then when? When he marches with his army? With thousands of soldiers at his side? When he meets up with the Usurper and doubles their strength?" Marcus asks. "Much easier to do it now when he least expects it."

Jared sits hunched over the table, biting his thumb till the skin turns white. "It sounds impossible," he says. "I'm all for bravely facing down impossible odds like the heroes of the First Epoch, but it doesn't help your father and grandfather at all if their heir meets an avoidable end on the floor of Namreth's banquet hall. This is suicide."

"Technically, it's homicide," Dietan says cheerfully.

"Apologies, Your Highness, but you still look like shit, and so do I," says Jared. "Even if we manage to sneak in undetected, without weapons, what are we going to do when we get there? Insult his taste in interior design?"

Lambert laughs. "Oooh, good one."

But the rest of the table looks to Dietan. I can tell that Marcus, at least, hopes that after his display on the bridge, Dietan can unleash the Whisting and challenge Namreth. Because without magic—without an army—the plan is clearly preposterous.

"We'll figure out how to get weapons somehow, but the main thing is to get inside the castle." Dietan sighs, serious now. He bows his head and closes his eyes. When he opens them, he is looking straight at me. "What do you think of the plan?"

I blink in surprise. "Me?"

"We escaped because of you the first time. Any thoughts?"

Everyone turns to me, but my mind goes completely blank. I'm entirely underqualified to participate in anything like this, let alone to advise on military strategy. I'm not a soldier or a general and definitely not an assassin. My skills are confined to the kitchen and the sewing bench. Not here on the cusp of an impossible assassination attempt. I feel like I'm watching the last grains of sand slip through an hourglass.

The warmth in Dietan's eyes is more comforting than honey porridge on a cold morning and makes me wish I could summon an army, or Veteria, or Sirona herself to ease his great burden. But I'm just a barmaid from a small town in Alarice, a long way from home, and I'm not even the princess they all believe I am.

"Can you all give us a moment?" he asks the group. Gently, he leads us away from the table.

In the quiet of the hall, Dietan rests his back against the wall, his long arms folded across his chest. I lean against the opposite wall, propping myself up as the weight of the world presses down on my shoulders.

"You okay?" he asks, voice low.

"Not really."

Dietan waits quietly, without judgment on his face.

"If you tell me this is a bad idea, I'll listen," he says. "We can scrub this whole mission. Forget taking down Namreth. Plan our escape instead. Get ahead of his army and rally Loegria to meet them on the battlefield. Say the word, and I'll follow."

To think—a prince taking advice from a common barmaid. If I could go back in time and tell my past self that this would happen, that Aren would laugh herself silly. But back then, I didn't think a prince would ever look twice at a girl like me.

"I just... I don't know... I'm not *this*." I gesture to him and beyond to the group waiting in the room. If I make the wrong decision, I could be putting everyone's lives at risk once more. And I've lost too many already.

Dietan seems to understand what I'm thinking, even if I can't put it into words. "It's my job to put my life on the line for my kingdom," he says, taking my hand. "That's why princes are raised to ride into battle. My father first put a sword in my hand—this royal knife, actually—when I was five years old. But it's not your job. And other than Marcus, it's not really any of their jobs, either."

But Dietan is looking at me so intensely. I can't look away. Nor do I want to let him down. He's a fixed point in the chaos.

I think about the twins, and my father, and everyone in Evandale who might die if the Usurper invades. The look in Dietan's eyes is all I need to know. If we don't stand up to Namreth now, it might be too late. I take a deep breath. "I told you I wouldn't let you do this by yourself. Let's give that mad king hell."

Dietan stares at me like he would take me to bed right this moment, if not for the friends and allies waiting in the next room. Instead, he lifts my hand to his lips, bows, and kisses it, like I'm a real princess.

When he straightens, he looks every inch a royal prince. He says, "It was your idea to fake my death to break me out of there in the first place. How would you break me back in?"

We're partners in every way, I realize. I trust him, and he trusts me. He respects my judgment and asks my opinion the way he would Marcus, or any of his royal advisors. He wants to know what I think. And what do I think? I think…I think…

"Aren?" he asks.

"Okay, so maybe I have an idea."

His smile widens. "That's my girl."

CHAPTER FIFTY

Dietan

Breaking me out of the castle was one thing. Breaking me in is another one entirely.

The plan is simple yet intricately layered. Each step must be executed as perfectly as possible to get us in the door.

I slowly dress in commoner's clothes, making sure they look plain and nondescript. I will need to be unassuming, forgettable, invisible.

I pick up the little dish of ground leaves that Aren set on the table for me. I start combing the paste through my hair with my fingers, until my golden waves are convincingly chestnut brown. Pulling a hood over my head, I tuck it low over my brow to obscure most of my face. Hopefully, no one will be looking too closely at peasants' faces, especially the faces of those who might be undead princes.

Over my shoulder, I catch sight of Aren as she finishes dressing, and I'm drawn toward her like she's tangled up my heartstrings. She notices me watching and gives me a small smile. "Are you ready?" she asks.

"With you, my love, for anything."

"Really?" Aren quirks an eyebrow. "The whole 'my love' thing? Still?"

"Well, aren't you?"

She twists her hair back into a simple bun, securing it at the base of her neck. "But you only used to call me that because we were pretending to be engaged. You didn't really mean it, so it feels weird now."

"I see. What would you prefer?"

"I don't know."

"Then why are you complaining?"

Aren smirks. "I just assumed you'd come up with something more creative."

I swagger over to her. "What about my sweetheart, my Aren?"

"Hmmm. That sounds like you own me."

Placing my hands on her arms, I pull her close and gaze deeply into her eyes. "You have it entirely backward. You own me, body and soul."

I love how I can fluster her so. I like the way she blushes and goes speechless. She rolls her eyes, but I know I have her where I want her…and I want her very badly. "We'll work on it later," I murmur as I take her in my arms.

"But—the others?"

"The door's locked," I say. "And everyone's already outside."

"Won't they wonder where we are?" she asks, looking over her shoulder to the window.

"Nah," I say, lifting her skirt and maneuvering us so her back is pressed against the wall, away from the window.

"We'll have to be quiet," she whispers, even as she slides her hand down my trousers. "And fast."

I grin, body heating like it does every time I'm with her. "As my lady commands."

There's no turning back now.

The eastern gate to the castle grounds stands wide, the portcullis raised, crowded with people. Since arriving, it's seemed to me that there were very few residents living in the city, other than the soldiers housed in the enormous barracks behind the castle. So, it's surprising to see hundreds of commoners file through the castle gates, carrying sacks of flour or pulling wagons full of spices and sweets under the watchful eyes of soldiers. Clearly, they've been here all along. Existing just out of sight, undoubtedly, to avoid their king's notice. I assume most of these poor souls are family and friends of Namreth's soldiers, lured to the middle of the desert by the promise of safety and prosperity.

Aren and I shuffle along with the crowd, keeping our heads low. At the southern gate, Marcus, Jared, and the others are doing the same, making their way into the grounds dressed in commoner's clothes, trying to blend in, hoping no one will take notice of them.

I lower my gaze as we approach the guards. A tall fellow with an even taller spear grips the shaft when he catches my eye. His fingers tense, turning white. "You there!"

Fuck. I clench my fist as he pounds the butt of the spear hard on the bare earth and thrusts it forward to halt progress. But the shaft comes down behind me, not in front.

Quickly, the guard pulls the poor fellow at my back from the crowd as he cries out. "What did I do?"

"Traitor," the guard accuses, then spears the man right through the gut in front of everyone waiting to be allowed inside the castle. The man dies at our feet, blood pooling from his chest, and the guard scowls at the crowd before declaring, "Let that be a warning to you all."

The man was chosen randomly. My veins are ice cold with fury at the cruelty. But by chance, I live, and by some twist of fate, our plan continues.

Without even looking at Aren for fear of bringing attention to her, I begin shuffling along with the crowd again. I wait with dread for the Rings to call out to me, vibrating to be used like they have in moments of danger in the past, but they remain quiet, marking their presence with just the faintest, steady hum. I haven't felt their heat under my skin since Aren and I were first imprisoned in that dark cell.

Each step toward the castle feels like I'm walking deeper into freezing water. I know what lies in those dungeons, what terrors are hidden behind the golden walls.

As we approach, guards stand at the ready, surveying the crowds. One man cracks a whip, and I flinch, ducking my head. I breathe deeply, evenly, to calm myself.

The soldier strikes a commoner, who falls to her knees. He cracks the whip once more in the air. A threat to anyone who steps out of line or moves too slowly. No one dares so much as to look at him.

My eyes burn with fury, but I keep my head down. This misery must end. Tonight.

RINGS OF FATE

I feel Aren tremble at my side. "It's okay," I whisper. "Almost there."

A few paces ahead, the castle doors are a welcome sight, despite the cruelties I know lie within. I again notice the strange magic shimmering off them that seemingly only I can see.

One by one, guards inspect and admit the new hires, permitting them entry. It's a slow process under a hot sun. One girl is admitted, the next denied. Twenty are ushered inside while two others are sent packing.

When it's our turn, the guards look us up and down. The soldier in charge, a hard-faced woman, chews at something awful and brown, then spits it out onto my feet, watching carefully to see how I'll react.

Every muscle in my body tenses. Every bit of breeding I have tells me to put this guard in her place, but I tamp down the feeling, holding it in check.

"You got a problem?" she asks when she sees my fingers move, a drop of perspiration on my brow.

"No problem," Aren says, taking me by the arm. "Just a bit tired."

"Then go on. Keep moving," the guard says, already bored with us. She turns to whoever is next in line.

The next set of guards is more thorough. "Security check," says a guard in black leather armor, sword hanging in a scabbard from his belt.

I press my palms against the cold stone wall.

The guard pats me down roughly. I keep my face neutral, and my head bowed low.

Another guard pats Aren down, and she makes no protest, even when his hands linger too long on her chest. "Should we send this one to the harem?" The guard laughs.

The other guard snorts.

Rage fills my chest, blood roaring in my ears, but I can't do anything about it. Not yet.

"All right, clear," the guard declares.

They've found no weapons on us. My royal knife is safe for now. With a wave of his hand, he lets us enter, but not before smacking Aren roughly on the behind.

Aren catches my eye, pleading with me not to react, and it takes all my will to hold my temper. My vision tunnels, my hands shake at the effort, and I can feel the power of the Rings trickling through my veins like molten gold.

"Hey, I'm okay," Aren says, keeping her voice low.

I clench my jaw. "That doesn't make it right."

"No, it does not, but this is also not the time or place for chivalry."

I hate that she has a point. "I'm going to burn this place to the ground when we're done here."

"I'll bring the matches," she says.

The castle is loud and crowded when we enter through the servants' doors. My every nerve is on edge as I expect someone to shout an alarm, to stop us, but most of the soldiers inside have already begun partaking in the festivities. Despite the early hour, wine flows from fountains in the atrium, smoke fills the high-ceilinged halls, and laughter and singing float through the air.

There is no sign of Namreth yet, but he is here somewhere, preparing to make a grand entrance when the banquet begins.

Lambert, Tess, and Arnfried arrived several hours earlier to disseminate the plan amongst the castle servants that they and Aren can vouch for. Aren raises her hand to her ear in a gesture that means she recognizes the frazzled butler who supervises the new hires as one of them. The butler nods, recognizing me despite my hair. "You two are assigned to the kitchens and later to serve at the banquet, but first, you have to change," he tells us as a guard watches on.

We are given fine servant's clothes, embroidered silks, and masks that look like animal faces. Aren is given a fox mask, and I am handed a white wolf.

It's a coincidence, surely, but the wolf is the sigil of the royal house of Alarice. The symbol is stitched onto every banner my grandfather will send into battle against the Usurper. Wearing it will give me strength. I tie it tightly around my head. I will not fail him.

We change in the servants' quarters, and we now don our new clothes. Aren secures the mask over her face, leaving only her eyes visible. The animal masks are undoubtedly intended to remind us that to Namreth, servants are less than human. My stomach churns when I remember that Namreth is my blood, and I once more struggle to quell the Rings.

Not yet, I think, and their agitation abates to a quiet hum.

Aren knows where she's going, so I follow her, keeping an eye out for trouble. Most everyone we run into is too deep into their wine or their conversation, so we slip easily into the kitchens.

The smells of roast meat, butter, and spices are overwhelming. Namreth hasn't lost his taste for Alarician delicacies even in this parched desert.

The kitchen is the most packed area I've seen yet, and the most silent. No one speaks. Everyone moves as if they are puppets on strings, revolving around one another in a coordinated dance. No one looks at us as we enter.

How many of them are in on the plan?

Aren guides me to the pantry, where she fetches her supplies—including the special seasoning she requested. My eyes go to the knives in woodblocks on the counters. I count six right there. But I must be patient.

By this time, the others will have made their way to their positions, too. All I can do is focus on my assigned tasks and think about how I will kill the king when the time comes.

Aren does most of the work making the pies, while I act as her assistant, handing her anything she asks for. She macerates the fruit, folds the crusts, cuts the pastry. It's a delicate process, and in any other circumstance, I would have loved to watch her work.

"Hey," she whispers, quiet enough to not be heard over the clanging of pots. I look at her. She tips her head toward a knife that's just been cleaned, sitting on the edge of the sink. It's a carving knife, the blade hardly wider than two fingers, but it's sharp.

I turn so my back is to the knife. I grab the handle and hand it off to her, swift and silent. She tucks in her waistband. No one notices. If they do, no one says a word.

One down. Many more to go.

When I pull the last pie out of the oven, time is up.

The sun set hours ago, and the party in the grand ballroom of the castle is in full swing. There is a constant rotation of servants moving food out of the kitchen, and it hardly lets up, even now. All in all, Aren has armed the entire kitchen staff plus some designated servers who have passed through to bring food to the ballroom. The special pies are stacked on a large cart, still steaming and ready to be served, but some guards stationed in the kitchen are growing impatient to get on with it.

"You there. Bring that here!" a guard shouts at me. He is already rosy-cheeked from wine and glares at me with beady eyes.

The perfect combination: drunk and mean.

I stare, baffled that anyone would talk to me. I glance in Aren's direction, and she nods. I bring the pie toward the guard.

"Set it down," the guard orders.

I do as I'm told, placing the still-hot pie on the counter. I step away, hands tucked behind my back like I've seen so many other servants do at my father's table.

Unceremoniously, the guard sticks his finger into the pie. "What's this?" the guard asks, his voice low and teasing.

He watches me expectantly, waiting for an answer with his finger still deep in the pie's crust. It must be hot, but the guard just stares at me with a wide, hungry smile.

"Rhubarb," Aren says, coming up to my side, and then adds, "sir."

The guard's eyes turn hungry as he looks at Aren, and I bristle. The guard slowly pulls his finger out of the pie and licks it clean.

"Delicious," he says, leering at Aren.

"Thank you, sir," Aren says. "May we deliver it to the king now?"

The guard waves her on, and I set the pie on the cart with the others. Together, we push it into the hall and toward the throne room, all while the guard watches Aren with a salacious smile.

The desire for revenge boils inside me, waking the Rings.

The Rings have been quiet for so long. They grow more agitated with every step I take, their familiar hum coming to life. *Not yet, not yet*, I think, hoping to control them. Blood rushes in my ears, making it difficult to hear anything as we walk. The closer we get to the throne room, the worse it gets.

The throne room is the heart of the party. The music is loud, the roar of voices even louder. Guests are sprawled all over the hall on pillows and couches, slowing our progress as we navigate the cart to the table.

Everywhere, there are people gulping bottles of wine and soldiers having their way with masked, half-naked men and women. It is a last night of debauchery before they march off across the Waste.

I hear the cracking of whips, cries of pleasure or pain indistinguishable from one another, the sound of flesh pounding flesh. Bodies are draped across the floor, some so still it's hard to tell if they are alive. All I want to do is cover my ears and close my eyes.

Suddenly I'm back in the dungeon. *Cold, alone, hurt.* The world closes in on me, and I fold into myself again, feeling small and helpless and weak—

Aren grips my hand, and I jolt back to the moment. I'd forgotten where I was, but her touch brings me back to myself. She lets go and looks at me from behind her fox mask, her eyes glittering with sympathy.

I can't break now. I just need to survive a few more minutes.

We are almost there.

Servants are already tending to the table, laying out more of the cakes and pastries Aren had made, which the guests pounce on like ravenous dogs. Good.

Namreth watches this all from his golden throne at the end of the table, his hands folded in front of him, smiling at the scene around him. The table is piled high with food and drink, with more and more coming.

Servants swarm the throne room, darting in and out. I spot a cat-masked servant with a limp. Jared. My blood roars louder. Marcus must be close by even though I can't see him. It won't be long now.

My heart stops when Namreth calls to Aren, "You! Bring me one of those!"

Stay away from her, you prick. Don't you fucking dare—

Aren sets down one of the special pies, but Namreth pays her no attention. He's busy laughing at one of his generals dancing with a drunk girl in his arms.

Aren slips away, giving me one final look before disappearing into the sea of bodies.

Cackling laughter splits the air somewhere to my right. There's a groan of pleasure from the back of the room. In my ears, my heartbeat thunders as I push the pie cart toward Namreth.

This will never end.

Namreth will never stop. He will keep hurting people, bleeding Estyrion dry, and haunting me forever. I can never rest again. Not unless I kill him.

Right now.

I slip my hand into the back of my waistband, feel the handle of the knife, and grip it—

The drunken general spots the pie on the table and drops his now-unconscious dance partner to the floor. He digs his grubby hands into it, thrusting fistfuls of crust and filling into his mouth. After several gulps, he stops, dead in his tracks. He breath falters, eyes bulging.

Well, good to know the poison works. Except everyone was supposed to have some, and it wasn't supposed to work this quickly.

The general drops to the floor next to his dance partner, convulsing and foaming from the mouth. As the behemoth goes down, he knocks over a servant with another dessert cart. Plates and glass shatter, bringing all music in the throne room to a whining stop.

A lone cleaver skitters from the waistband of the servant's uniform— all eyes on the knife.

We're fucked.

CHAPTER FIFTY-ONE

Aren

No one moves. No one breathes.

All eyes are locked on the glistening blade as it slides to a halt. Then to the dead general. I catch Dietan's eye, holding his gaze for the length of a heartbeat.

Crap.

Now more people are retching, especially those who've had some of the special desserts. Then the room erupts into chaos.

"Guards," says Namreth, his voice calm, controlled.

They sound the alarm, and down another hallway, a horn blows. Heavy boots echo in the corridors, growing louder as they near. The clank of armor fills the air.

Shit. So much for hoping a majority of the soldiers would be unconscious when we struck. Or looking at the general on the floor, dead apparently. I wasn't counting on someone eating that much. At least the commanders attending the party seem to be very drunk.

Men with shiny medals pinned to their chests stagger and gape as panicked ladies in silk gowns and jewels shove their way toward the doors only to find them blocked by the approaching guards.

One after another, guards spill into the room, spears and swords at the ready. They grunt and shout, eager for battle—too eager. Maybe they were celebrating in the barracks after all.

The show of force sends the guests scrambling yet again, while the masked rebels scramble to reach their weapons. In an instant, everyone's running, the chamber's jammed with people, and Harvest Mother, I can't find Dietan.

I hurry toward the place where I last saw him, but he's gone. Lost. I nearly trip over a bejeweled woman who's stumbled and fallen in the panic. I look for any sign of Dietan's white wolf mask. Any sound of his voice.

Nothing.

The screams of the crowd compete with the soldiers' war chants and the shouts of the rebel servants, who fumble with their humble knives. The guards take notice, and both sides clamber for the blades.

A rebel reaches for a knife on the floor, only to have his hand cut off at the wrist by a guard. A servant bares her knife, her grin triumphant. But she's slow to act, and a guard slits her throat from behind. My stomach sinks. I should have known that our brave band of castle servants never stood a chance against the mad king's battle-ready soldiers.

The soldiers are all red in the face, eyes filled with fury, or maybe just drink. Regardless of the cause, they are bloodthirsty.

In the middle of this chaos, the king sits calmly on his throne, a gust of wind swirling around his feet. He scans the room, quietly taking stock. His striking blue eyes turn to the sickened guests near the poisoned tray of treats, then to the growing number of armed servants. He realizes what is happening, and his vengeance is swift. He holds up his hand to the nearest servant girl and snaps his fingers, ripping the mask off her face with a gust of wind. She isn't one of the servants we recruited to our cause, but that doesn't matter.

Namreth stands. He clutches her chin, and the blood drains from her face. He lets go, and the girl falls, trembling, from his grasp. Then I witness the most terrible thing I've ever seen in my whole life, an image that'll be scorched into my memory for the rest of my days.

The king snaps his fingers, and with a crack, the girl's chest collapses, her rib bones snapping like twigs, her sternum folding in on itself. Her whole body convulses as a steady stream of red dribbles first from her mouth, then her nose and eyes. She's dead before her head hits the marble tile.

Everyone is screaming. Good goddess, every soul in the room is running wild.

A soldier tackles a servant who tries to run away, ripping off her mask and pummeling her into the floor with his fists until she no longer moves and blood pools around her body. A rebel jumps on his back to retaliate, but a second soldier spears him with his sword, driving the blade into his open mouth.

Two more servants fall to the ground beside each other. A third, thin as bones, drops down over the others, while a fourth, a boy of no more than twelve, falls to his knees beside them, sobbing. Some try to run, but the doors are all closed, the exits blocked.

"Where are you?" I yell, but Dietan's still nowhere to be seen. We're losing, and losing badly. I try to find Marcus, Jared, anyone, but a gauntleted hand crushes my wrist, and a steady stream of my own blood dribbles down my arm. With his other hand, the soldier rips the mask from my face. It catches on my hair, tearing a clump from my scalp, but I don't scream in pain. I won't give the bastard the satisfaction.

I twist and turn, straining against his fist. "Dietan," I cry out once again as the soldier forces me to my knees, my arm going numb, my head wound throbbing, the pain growing sharper.

The rebellion is a complete disaster, and Dietan is still nowhere to be found. I fear the worst, that he's been killed in the chaos, that he lies dead and overlooked beneath our feet.

Namreth is another matter.

Across the chamber, he's watching the scene with a bored look on his cold, handsome face, so like and unlike Dietan's. He stands up from his throne, and a wild wind stirs around him as he stalks the room, killing masked servants, one after the other, stealing their breath with a twirl of his finger.

Slowly, Namreth makes his way through the party, a nightmare come to life. Blood stains the floor. Servants are snapped like twigs.

Tess tried to warn us.

We're not faster or stronger than the wind. We cannot beat the Unseen Death.

Tears blur my vision. This was a mistake. We should have fled the city. We should have run far away during this banquet, rather than return to the site of so much suffering.

Namreth stops to lift the mask from the face of a slender girl of maybe sixteen. She trembles as he shakes his head, sighing. "Did you really think you could win against me? Have I not done my best to make you all understand? Have I not crushed every breath of dissent all these years? All of you live only because of my mercy."

Then with a snap of his fingers, she falls to the floor, dead, the breath stolen right out of her.

He stalks through the hall, death walking—emotionless, pale, precise. He rips through bodies, breaking them to pieces.

It's sick. He's sick.

Even the soldier who's holding me is stunned by the king's cruelty. He loosens his grip, and I pull free.

I roll out of his reach even though he makes no attempt to follow me. Like the rest of those assembled, he's transfixed by Namreth's rampage of destruction. The soldiers, the guests, the servants—everyone is paralyzed. I creep away and resume looking for Dietan.

Oh, goddess, don't let him be dead.

I elbow through the crowd, past rebels and loyalists alike, shoving past the last of the guests who are still pressing toward the doors to flee the banquet, desperate to be free of the slaughter.

I duck between two guards, nearly colliding with a fellow servant—and then I see him. He's alive but surrounded by a handful of dead bodies and a phalanx of soldiers, leveling spears and swords at him. There are so many of them. Too many.

His wolf mask is torn off, and he's bleeding from a cut on his forehead. He doesn't have a chance, he only has his knife not his sword, but that doesn't stop him. He is brave and fierce, but if we don't find a way to turn the tide, he'll soon be dead.

"Dietan," I call, running up behind him.

"Aren," he breathes when he sees me. My heart thunders with joy that he's alive.

We stand back-to-back, just the two of us against the whole damn world. And hell, it might have been easier to fight the rest of the world, because at that very moment, Namreth sees us.

He twitches, and a glint of recognition crosses his face. "The prince and the barmaid," he says as he strolls through a wave of people who fall dead, one after another, in his path.

I kneel to grab a knife at my feet. It feels too small in my hand, much smaller than a frying pan. It's useless against Namreth, but I hold it up anyway, Dietan at my side. How did we ever think we'd best Namreth?

The mad king's cold eyes bore into mine.

Namreth raises his hand...

The sensation starts with a tingling in my throat. Then a tightness in my chest. Then... *Harvest Mother*, I think as the air rushes out of my lungs like a bellows being squeezed. My head spins and I choke. I'm going to die.

So, this is the Unseen Death.

Namreth stands so nonchalantly, as if he's enjoying watching me suffer. Maybe he's killing me twice as slowly as any of the others. Or maybe I've lost all sense of time. But I won't give him the satisfaction of my pain. Even though I'm on my hands and knees, I won't beg.

"Fuck you," I say with my last breath.

He doesn't flinch. His eyes are fixed on me. His face is steel and iron, malice and hatred.

I'm going to die. I can feel it. The world goes black at the edges, and my head—my whole body—is on fire, like I'm going to explode.

So, this is the end. Maybe Namreth feels it, too, because he's grinning a madman's grin, relishing my death, dragging it out.

I clutch my throat.

We failed.

This madman will steal my life, then Dietan's, and then join the Usurper in marching on our homelands. A tear rolls down my cheek.

I'm sorry, Dietan.

We didn't have enough time. I didn't even get to tell him how I truly felt. How I'd rather die here having loved him than live never having met him.

The room grows colder, as if wind is circling me. My fingers are numb, and the candles flicker, dimming in the corners of my vision.

And still the winds rise.

Then Namreth stumbles. He suddenly falls to the floor, and a gust of wind hits my face.

I turn to Dietan in wonder as the air rushes back into my lungs. I can *actually* draw another breath, then another and another. I never knew that air could taste this good.

My head begins to clear, and I rise to my feet as Namreth skids across the marble floor, skittering over the tiles like a pebble being skipped on the surface of a pond. He rams into an oak table with a loud *crack*, the wood nearly splitting.

For an instant, the battle pauses.

A moment ago, Namreth seemed invincible, but now he's on his ass, face red, teeth clenched in pain. His unnaturally youthful features look older, undoubtedly rattled by the realization that he might not be the only power in the room.

"Dietan? *Goddess above*, Dietan. You did that?" I'm amazed, and proud.

Dietan doesn't reply. He's oddly…calm.

No, he isn't calm. He's focused.

His hands are raised toward Namreth. The winds whip around him, swirling upward from the floor and churning debris around him like a hurricane. The growing storm flutters his hair. It slices at my clothes and face, tears tapestries from walls, roaring around the hall like a living thing.

The Whisting has returned to him.

CHAPTER FIFTY-TWO

Dietan

I feel alive.

Gods, I've never felt so alive. Power pulses through my body, matching the rhythm of my heartbeat. The Whisting wipes away all doubt and fear. Everything spins as the Whisting unfurls at my feet, the Rings thrumming with untapped power.

They want to be used. They *need* to be used—risks be damned.

The Whisting came back to me when I saw Aren fall to her knees, when I saw her light start to dim. As she faded, the Rings roared to life, unrestrained, for the first time since we arrived at this castle, which feels like lifetimes ago.

The power rose so unexpectedly, I didn't have time to think or plan, or to hold it back with breath and will. I just acted. I called the wind to me, and the Rings answered, throwing Namreth across the chamber.

The mad king is still lying there, sprawled on his back, and his guards all stare at me. They seem unsure of what to do next, their mouths hanging open like fools as they realize I hold the same great power as Namreth.

RINGS OF FATE

They silently weigh their options, exchanging glances, asking themselves if they should run or fight. I bet they're all wondering how I came back from the dead. Half of them gawk at me like they've seen a ghost.

But I'm not a ghost. I'm a nightmare, a vengeful one.

At my feet, Aren looks up at me, eyes wide with fear and wonder.

She's alive.

I want to call to her, but I can't. I can barely form a thought. The power inside me is like lightning, like a thunderstorm under my skin that must be set free.

On the far side of the chamber, Namreth stirs.

He pushes himself shakily back to his feet. His hair is disheveled, eyes bulging. I hoped he was finished. I hoped the man's back was broken, and his spirit, too. It was a fool's hope, of course, but I've always been a hopeful fool. Aren reminds me often.

"Nephew," Namreth says without evincing too much surprise. "Still alive," he sneers. "Still foolish." Namreth throws back his hair, wiping dirt and a dash of blood from his brow.

I close my eyes as the storm in my chest shudders and jolts, thrashing against my thoughts. Another wave of energy rolls out from me, but it's unfocused, and I fear I'll lose control like I have in the past. I fear I'm not strong enough, that I'll devour my very breath at my own hand. I fear that my father was right all those years ago. I had no business touching those rings when I was ten, and I have no business with them now.

Yet here I am.

"This is your doing?" Namreth asks, taking a step toward me and holding his hands wide, to encompass the broken bodies strewn around his enormous golden hall. "This ridiculous uprising? This pathetic rebellion?"

I don't speak. Sweat blooms on my forehead as I try to control my power, but it's whipped away in the gale. Aren covers her eyes as shards of glass and porcelain swirl around her. The tempest around me is growing, its power unchecked.

Stop, I order the Rings. *Stop, stop—*

I've let the storm run wild, and I still don't know how to bend it to my will. I try to breathe as I was taught, counting my heartbeats, straining to take control of the winds.

"Alas, you don't know how to wield it, do you?" says Namreth. "You hold so much power within you, and you don't even know where to start. But I do."

Around him, a second tempest rises. It expands, encircling him in an eddying vortex that picks up the debris from the battle tossed on the floor. Every fractured shard of wood and stone is swept up in the gyre.

Namreth advances, and the whirlwind carves deep grooves in the marble tile. It cuts through chairs and tables, sending splinters hurtling in every direction. He cleaves a path through the bodies in his throne room, moving slowly, one deliberate step at a time, so that all who still live might know his power and choose a side.

Once, in an age long past, the Whisting carved mountains and valleys. Now, Namreth cuts through the storm I raised. The air thrums like the inside of a war drum as the cyclones batter each other.

"Think you can match me, nephew?" Namreth shouts over the howling wind. His guards step forward, locking shields, spears held ready in my direction.

There are dozens of them forming into crisp lines, one row in front of the next. More approach in the distance, marching through the halls, ready to take the place of any man or woman who falls.

I stand in the heart of the enemy's castle. The rebels are outnumbered a hundred to one, maybe more. I don't know if I can stand up to Namreth. I can't even control my own power. The man is smiling, grinning like a cat lapping cream as he watches me struggle.

A moment later, Namreth's storm strikes. Splinters tear at my skin, and on the floor, those same slivers tear at Aren's dress and skin. The vortex of wind around him expands to fill the whole hall, devastating everything in its path. He does not distinguish between friend and foe. Guards and rebels alike fall to their knees. A shard of wood spears a portly man in the temple; a knife lodges in one boy's chest, another in an eye. His guards bear the brunt of it, but soon the full fury of Namreth's tempest will descend on me.

For a brief moment, the wall of soldiers sent to threaten me shields me instead. In this moment of calm, my thoughts clear.

I glance down at Aren, and in her eyes, I see faith. I see someone who believes in me even when my own faith is gone. She looks so small, so frail in the face of the power overtaking me, but she's neither of those things. There's fire in her eyes, and it reaches into my soul. Her unwavering strength gives me confidence. I cannot let Namreth take her.

For Aren, I can do this. For her, I will defeat him.

I call the Rings, and they answer. Fire blooms under my skin, flashing like bolts of lightning. It feels like euphoria, ecstasy. It feels magnificent.

RINGS OF FATE

The tempest around me expands, cutting into the torrents raised by Namreth. Unlike my uncle, I have no precision or finesse. Just raw power that makes a mess out of everything, sending tables and chairs careening into one another, plates slicing through pots, forcing the guards to retreat, to hide behind their tall shields and wait out the storm.

I focus on beating back Namreth's power. I clench my fists, my power feeling too big for my body. The air in the throne room darkens, storm clouds gathering at my command.

Then reality shifts. And realigns. And I'm transported into a dream.

The battlefield.

And the bodies.

A kingdom in shadow.

Dark winds churn around me—a gathering storm.

Then a voice. Her voice.

"Dietan!"

My chest heaves. Grief hits me like a hammer. Again, I hear Aren's voice cutting through the roar of the winds.

The truth slams into me. I've gotten it all wrong.

My visions aren't about Loegria. They're about Namreth. They're about this fallen kingdom, this golden city. This is where it will all end.

Am I the weapon that will bring about his fall?

The Rings of Fate will take my life, but first, I will end Namreth's.

Looking at Aren, I understand now. I will never survive channeling the full power of the Rings. I've barely survived in the past, using only a fraction of their strength. I was doomed from the start, from the moment the Rings chose me at ten years old.

This is how it ends.

I must sacrifice myself to destroy Namreth.

There is no other way.

Aren stares at me, realization dawning on her face. A hint of anger, even. It's a look that says, *Don't leave me. Don't die, you bastard.* But there's no other choice. I have to sacrifice myself for my people.

More importantly…I'll do it for the one person who matters most. I smile at the thought that she'll be so mad that I chose to save her rather than myself.

The Rings are alive, their power unleashed, filling every part of me, tearing at my body from the inside.

I *feel* it.

I hold a power that even Namreth cannot match...a power that will claim his life and mine.

I meet Aren's horrified gaze. "Return the Rings to my father," I say, willing the Whisting carry my voice through the wind just for her. I know she hears me because she covers her mouth, and a tear rolls down her beautiful face. "I love you, Aren."

Then, calling the Rings, I turn to face my kin, the mad king of the Waste.

CHAPTER FIFTY-THREE

Dietan

I bear the Rings of Fate.
I am the Anemoi unleashed, wielding the power of wind and air, cyclone and hurricane. The Whisting roars inside of me.

Namreth raises his arms. Our magic collides, like two stags locking horns.

Someone rushes in, grabbing Aren. *Marcus? Good.* She's safe, and I can turn myself over to the Rings. My thoughts swirl like I'm underwater again. Distantly, I hear other voices. A familiar one. Jared? Is that his name? My memories slip from my mind like raindrops. The Rings demand everything from me, and I lose myself in their power.

A woman calls to me, but her voice is swept away in the gale.

Servants and soldiers scream, cowering as the tempest grows. A moment ago, Namreth's power was hurling plates and chairs, but now it's throwing men and women. It tosses them in the air, slams them into walls if they're lucky, impaling them on spears if they're not.

Namreth's power will take down every guard and rebel alike. It will tear apart every soul in this hall if it's allowed to continue. I *know* if he's not stopped, Namreth will bring down the castle itself.

I counter Namreth's gale with a black and swirling thunderstorm, my smile wide and wicked. This is what the Rings want of me, what they've been waiting for all these years.

I bring my arms together, and the beams in the ceiling bend. The floor beneath me bows, threatening to crack open. Columns buckle, and the arched roof sags dangerously. The room itself is breaking apart, and fragments of the walls and ceiling are swept up in the tempest. The cyclone surrounds me, and I'm in control.

I *command* the tornado.

The guards retreat. Every surviving person in the hall retreats. This is no longer a battle between mortals.

It is Anemoi against Kilandrar, its dark mirror.

I direct my storm to the center of the room, to spare innocent lives, focusing only on Namreth.

The King of the Waste stands before me, unnaturally calm. The tempest doesn't lift the smallest hair on his head. He's the master of the Unseen Death, and I wonder again if I've been fooling myself. In answer, the power surges in me hot and sharp, as if answering.

I throw all of my newfound power at Namreth. I bare my teeth, commanding the Rings to my will, but Namreth is faster. Better.

His storm carves through my gale as I gasp for air. My chest tightens of its own accord, and my hands and feet go numb where I stand. A sudden pressure builds behind my eyes. I'm suffocating. I'm choking, and in a moment, I will pass out. My vision will fade to black, and that'll be the end. My throat closes tighter with each passing moment. I grasp in the dark for the Rings' power, but just as easily as it surged in me, it's lost.

Gone.

There is no air left in me.

Namreth's hold on me is absolute.

"Dietan!" *Aren?*

No. Get back. Her voice is too close.

I thought she was safe, but she's right here. I need her to be safe.

I search one last time for the power of the Rings. I find only a fragment, enough to draw one final breath before Namreth can steal it away. I take one more step toward him…

I inhale, but the air I summoned is all gone. The walls close in on me.

Still, I struggle against the darkness and the winds that threaten to tear me to pieces.

If only I could breathe. *Just one more breath.*

But the air is gone from my lungs. My chest is on fire, and I feel my ribs start to compress, the bones strained to the point of breaking. Something cracks in my chest. I fear my death will be just like the others, just as terrible.

Namreth takes a step forward, then another. His voice cuts through the storm. "You really think you can match me? You can't even breathe!"

He's right. No cut on my palm or smack in the head with a skillet will pull me out of this. The air is gone, and there is only pain left in its wake. Pain in my chest and in my head, a crushing, lancing torment that threatens to overcome me.

"You're so afraid of this power. But I've spent years embracing it, learning all there is to know, all the magic that your precious grandfather forbade you. And look where you are now!"

I fall, one knee hitting the floor, then the other. Black spots bloom across my vision.

Of course it frightens me. I'm not like Namreth. I don't want this destructive power. I never chose this.

It chose me.

"Dietan!"

My name echoes dully in my head, cleaving through the pounding of my heartbeat in my ears, through the pain in my chest. Then I realize—Aren is calling to me. She's on the edge of the storm, thrashing against Marcus's hold on her. How stubborn she is...

"Focus! Breathe!" Aren cries.

I can't. I don't have the strength left to take a step. To lift a finger. To inhale.

My chest is collapsing under the inexorable grip of the Unseen Death.

Somewhere in the distance, Aren breaks out of Marcus's arms and runs into the storm.

I don't know what she's thinking, but one thing is for sure—men have always underestimated her.

She shields her face as she pushes through the storm. I see it at a distance, as if I'm watching a play on a faraway stage. The wind shreds her exposed skin as I watch, engulfed in Namreth's vortex, unable to act. She bleeds as she calls my name, and I wish I could shield her, but I'm too weak.

She fights through the storm until she reaches me, wraps her arms around me, and holds me so I can't fall. I'm almost gone, and her face is the only bright thing in the dark.

What are you doing? I think.

I can't speak. I can't breathe. *Get out of here.* But of course, she can't hear me and wouldn't listen if she could.

"You're strong, you're amazing, and most importantly…" Aren whispers, holding my head in her hands. "Remember what you said? When we're together, you don't need to breathe."

She takes my face in her hands and covers my mouth with hers, breathing into me.

Breathing *for* me.

Her sweet life force surges within me, mingling with the Whisting trapped under my skin, bursting through the vice grip on my lungs—and releasing me from Namreth's hold.

I kiss her back, and the storm raging inside of me settles. It goes completely quiet. My world shrinks to the feel of her soft lips on mine, her warm hands on my cold face, her breath on my cheek. Her breath curls gently across my skin, flowing into me, through me.

The darkness recedes. Her face, an inch from mine, is the only thing I see. Gods, she truly is the most beautiful woman in the world. Nothing else matters, nothing else but her.

The Rings call, surging just under the surface of my skin, and I command them to remain calm.

The Rings may have chosen me, but they don't control me. Not anymore.

At last, I understand how to manage their power. There are two of them and two of us, a matched pair. Together, and only together, we control them.

Lips still on Aren's, I call a narrow but powerful cone of wind. It crashes down on Namreth with a force that could level a mountain. With the intensity that once turned the peaks of old Albion into valleys, I strike at the mad king. I don't have to open my eyes to see it. The Rings within me see it, as if I'm watching from atop one of the golden chandeliers.

Namreth wields a piece of this great power, but I can block him with the full force of the Whisting. He fights against it, drawing even more of his dark power, summoning the ancient and forbidden magics he has studied all these years. But every gale and storm he conjures falters beneath the strength of the Rings I wield.

Namreth is pricked a thousand times by sharp glass and steel and wood; the whirlwind around him turns red with droplets of his own blood. The winds howl louder than his screams.

He has nothing and no one to help him.

He's alone…and because he is alone, he is weak.

From the rafters, the Whisting looks down on myself and Aren as we cling to each other, still kissing. It's like watching a dream, as the Rings rise from my back through my tattered, bloody shirt. It's been decades since I've seen them, and they look different to my adult eyes. They glow and hum, made of magic itself, rising above our heads, gold and silver, thrumming with power. The two linked rings grow larger and larger, hovering at the center of the storm, power rolling from them like thunder.

They twist to lie one atop the other, hovering above Namreth, then fall, dropping over his head and past his shoulders, encircling him.

The Rings glow bright, tightening around Namreth's arms and torso. He thrashes against them, teeth gritted. Then his eyes dart to Aren's mouth on mine, the breath we share, and I can see in his face that he knows. He knows that together, Aren and I can control my power. We've won.

He tenses, body rigid with pain, trembling and jerking. And just like that, it's over.

His body falls limp and motionless to the floor.

The Rings have taken his power from him.

Aren's lips are still on mine, but I'm no longer just watching from above. I see through the Rings, and beyond them. I'm the storm and the wind and the sea and the earth. And I feel everything. The wind ebbing, the rain stopping, and Aren in my arms.

With a tearing pain, the scar on my back burns like I've been branded. The familiar sensation of the Whisting humming just under the surface returns. But then the Rings fall into my palm, warm and solid and familiar. One gold and one silver. And like water poured into a bucket, I come back to myself. I'm once again just a man. A man who is alive and holding his love.

Aren pulls away and regards me with tears in her eyes, and all I can do is stare. She survived. I survived—because of her.

Namreth moans. He's alive, but the Rings have stripped his power. Instead of an intimidating, youthful king, he's a frail old man, with thinning gray hair, his face deeply etched with a lifetime of bitterness. His head lolls at a painful angle as he stares at us from the floor, his mouth open in shock. With one last rasping breath, the wretched bastard finally dies.

The battle is over.

The king is dead.

Everything is quiet and still, as if the world itself has forgotten how to breathe.

From the rubble lining the chamber, faces appear, people covered in dust. They almost look as if they're part of the wreckage—bleeding, their clothes shredded.

The enormous golden hall is ruined. Namreth's throne is nothing but dust. There isn't a table standing or a column that isn't cracked and halfway collapsed. Light shines down through gaps in the ceiling. There are people who need help, and there will be time to help them.

For now, I care only for Aren. Pulling her close again, I revel in her warmth and close my eyes. She wraps her arms around me and whispers, "Brave idiot."

A cheer rings out in the distance, then another.

Aren grins up at me as the hall breaks out in hollers and whoops of relief and gratitude and joy.

"Well, that was one hell of a kiss," I say.

Then she kisses me again. Because yes, it was.

CHAPTER FIFTY-FOUR

Aren

Dietan has called the surviving fighters of Namreth's army to assemble. They trickle into the remains of the great hall and spill out into the courtyard and out onto the castle grounds. Their armor is tattered, their faces caked in dried blood. Some tremble from shock. Others assist the wounded.

A stout fellow with only one gold epaulet intact draws a sword and calls to the others, ordering those who can stand into lines, but there is no fight left in these soldiers. Many are too frightened to join the ranks, and some drop their blades when Dietan stands before them.

There is no malice in his eyes. These fighting men and women were probably just following orders, coerced into obedience just as the castle servants were. Dietan reaches for my hand, and I join him, knowing what he's feeling. He doesn't want there to be any more violence.

"I'm not Namreth—Osian—as you have probably guessed," he says, shaking his head, still dazed. "I am Prince Dietan of Loegria, and I have liberated Castle Engel. This fight is over. Of that, I can assure you. Throw down your blades and walk away. Go back to your homes, back to your families and loved ones. Be done with this evil place."

For most, his words are welcome. I doubt there are many who want a fight, but one or two are unmoved. Maybe they have nowhere to go. Maybe they just don't know when to stop. I wait for one of them to strike, but no one does.

"You heard His Highness," says Marcus. "Begone, you fools. The fight's over unless you're looking to start it up again. Eager to tangle with the Rings?"

At that, the last of the guards throw down their blades. One man simply falls to his knees and sobs. But soldiers aren't the only people in the room. I look among at the faces around us and spot my friends.

Our little band of rebels made it out alive. They stare in blank-faced shock. They didn't know Dietan had the power of the Whisting. Or maybe they're just surprised to be alive. Lambert, Arnfried, and Tess stand together, clothes ragged, nursing their injuries. No one walked away from that tempest unscathed.

Their bodies will mend, but the scars will remain.

None of us will forget what happened today.

The people of Engel lived with the power of the Unseen Death, under Namreth's terrible reign, for years. The fear in their eyes remains. Will any of them ever trust Dietan now that they know he holds the same power?

Marcus and Jared watch the people, too, silently waiting for their reaction.

I decide I must make the first move, to assure them that Dietan is not like the king he just vanquished. I let go of Dietan's hand and step in front of him, addressing everyone—those who remember me, and those who don't.

"Prince Dietan of Loegria unseated King Osian. Who, in truth, was his granduncle, Prince Namreth of Alarice, and no true heir to Estyrion." I point to the body on the ground, and a flurry of murmurs breaks out around the hall. His identity hadn't been common knowledge until now. "The bastard's dead, and no one's going to force you to march on Loegria. You're not enslaved to a monster anymore. You're free. Prince Dietan has freed you all, and all of Engel and Estyrion."

A buzz of confused, excited chatter arises from the crowd.

"Hail, Prince Dietan, Liberator of Estyrion!" declares Jared, raising a sword. Marcus raises his in perfect unison.

RINGS OF FATE

Then one man kneels, and the girl at his side does, too. One by one, others follow. They drop whatever they are holding and fall to their knees, and the clang of their weapons on the marble ring out like bells all around us.

"Prince Dietan," Lambert cries, then slowly lowers himself to one knee. He bows his head. The rest of the hall does the same, taking a knee in fealty.

Relief melts across Dietan's face. He might not feel ready to be a king, but "liberator" suits him. He earned it.

"I guess it's only appropriate…" I say. I lower myself to my knees before Dietan, my skirt flaring out around me.

"Aren, please. Don't…"

"Your Highness," I protest. "It is only proper."

But Dietan grips my elbow and brings me back to my feet. When he does, he drops to his knees instead. He looks up at me, eyes shining, and a flash of memory from a simpler time comes back to me. A prince kneeling at the feet of a backcountry barmaid.

He's the prince of Loegria, the liberator of Engel, the savior of Estyrion. And he's on his knees in front of everyone. I don't know what to do. Everyone else is still bowing. When he smiles at me, Dietan's eyes are full of unshed tears.

My own tears fill my eyes. I've been so scared of losing him, and I almost did, again. But I saved him. And he's saved everyone.

"Stop being silly. Honestly, get up before they start laughing."

Dietan presses his lips to the back of my hand and slides a familiar gold band, that moments ago had been a part of him, onto my ring finger. He wears the silver one. Silver for the ores of Loegria and gold for the wheat fields of Alarice. The Rings of Fate. "Aren my love, will you do me the greatest honor of becoming my wife?"

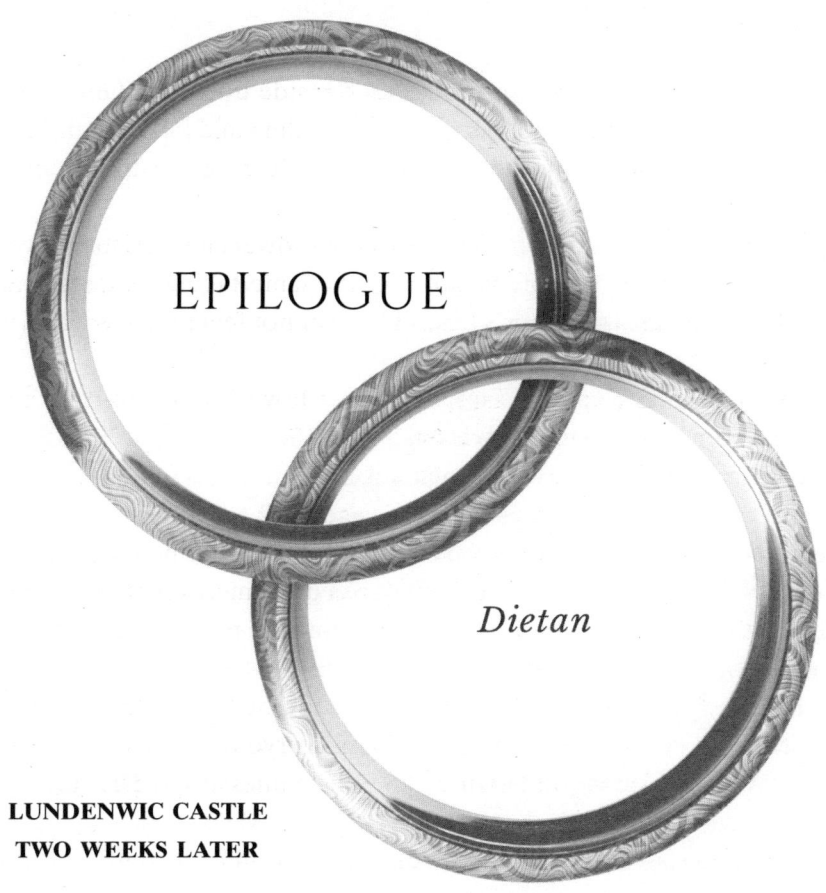

EPILOGUE

Dietan

**LUNDENWIC CASTLE
TWO WEEKS LATER**

"You have to tell us everything!" Sonja says, taking Aren's hands. "Everything!"

"Did you actually go to the Great Waste?" asks Ophelia.

"Hold on! Let me take my cloak off first!" Aren laughs, slipping it off before being hugged vigorously by her sisters, one on each side.

I watch, amused, as Aren struggles to free herself from the twins. Marcus and Jared are waiting in the hallway, and they don't bother breaking them up, either, even if neither of them has seen the girls for weeks. Not to mention that Jared and Ophelia have a wedding to plan. Still, no one so much as lifts a finger or dares break up the reunion.

No man is brave enough for that.

"We missed you so much!" Ophelia says, smothering Aren's cheek in kisses.

"We were so worried!" Sonja adds.

Aren smiles. "Nothing to worry about. And by the way, look who I brought with me," she says, gesturing for Marcus and Jared to join us. They enter the room, all grins. Sonja scrambles to her feet while Ophelia squeals and leaps for Jared, who catches her midair and spins her around.

Sonja and Marcus stand awkwardly in front of each other, and Marcus wrings his cap in his hands. "Did you get my letters?" he asks.

"I did," she says, blushing. "They were lovely."

Marcus catches Aren's eye, offering a relieved smile. Aren winks at him and then comes to my side. She reaches for my hand, leaving the two couples to reunite in peace.

"This is your home?" she asks.

"Our home," I correct, walking her into the castle yard. No one was home when I arrived, the twins explained, as my father is out on the border towns and my mother and sister had already left for the summer palace. The sisters were to join them today, until we arrived.

I'm glad I have this moment with Aren before my family is reunited. We stroll through the gardens, ambling down winding trails, stopping at my favorite ancient tree so I can brag about how rare it is before we move on.

I take her to the library, where we kiss among dark stacks of ancient tomes. We walk slowly through the hall of tapestries, then a bit more quickly through a corridor flanked by historic suits of armor before racing past the statues of the kings and queens of Loegria.

"I'm boring you," I say. "Would you like to see the kitchens?"

"I think I've seen enough kitchens for one lifetime. Does the prince have a bedroom?"

"Several."

"Several? Interesting. Care to take me to one?" she asks, and I'm a fool because it's only then that I realize it's really been quite a long journey to Lundenwic, during which we were never truly alone.

"Posthaste," she orders.

"As my lady commands." I don't waste another minute, and the moment we enter my private quarters, I slam the door behind us.

Hours later, Aren is on her back in our bed, out of breath and smiling up at the painted ceiling depicting the ocean gods and their endless battles. The way she looks at it, I know she finds it breathtaking.

This bedroom is the best in the castle—especially from this angle. Especially when Aren's lying naked next to me. But I don't care about the ceiling. I have better things to look at than art.

Crawling up her body, I prop myself on my elbows and look down at her, blocking her view of the mural. She sighs and gives me a dreamy smile, and I know she's still feeling the high of our lovemaking.

"So, you've had two weeks to consider," I say. "Will you marry me, for real?"

She huffs out a breathless laugh. "Of course, you're only asking now after…" She gestures to our naked, sweat-slicked bodies.

"You know you want to," I say, smirking. "But for whatever reason, you're too stubborn to admit it."

"Only because I've become enamored of the luxuries of royal life, thank you very much," she says. "I've had enough of cooking and cleaning for the rest of my existence."

I laugh and bury my face between her breasts, breathing her in. I love the heat of her, the scent of her, the feel of her.

She reaches out, idly tracing the ring-shaped scars on my back, which still haven't fully healed, despite the rings now adorning both of our hands. I glance at her, a small smile tugging at my lips.

"Does it hurt?" she asks.

"No," I murmur. "Hasn't for a while."

We don't say anything after that. We just listen to the waves crashing in the distance, the sound echoing through the open window. The rhythm is steady, soothing, like the beat of her heart beneath my ear.

After a while, her voice comes, soft with sleep. "Dietan, do you really want to marry me?"

I crack an eyelid open. "You really have to ask, Aren of Evandale?"

She shifts, and I roll onto my back beside her, tucking her against my side, her head beneath my chin. I wrap an arm around her, holding her tight.

"I'm not Aren of Evandale anymore. At least not the same Aren who left Evandale. That Aren of Evandale never thought herself worthy of a prince," she says.

I plant a soft kiss on her nose and say, "Well, that Aren of Evandale was wrong."

She stares deep into my eyes and says the words I've been waiting to hear for so long. "Okay."

"Okay?"

"Yeah," she smiles. "I'll marry you."

Joy fills me from head to toe, but it's compounded by the words she says next.

"I love you Dietan," she says, with a serious look on her face. And she doesn't add a joke, or laugh, or call me your worship or a dumbass.

"I love you too," I say, even though she already knows that. I'll say it again and again for the rest of my life.

She drifts to sleep and so do I, the two of us entangled in each other.

My heart settles into an easy, steady rhythm, forever beside my future wife.

ACKNOWLEDGMENTS

A huge double ring of medals to the incredible, strong, amazing, and hilarious women at Entangled. You guys are WAY too much fun! First off, Liz Pelletier, goddess, thank you for buying this book on a one-line pitch and for believing in us! Thank you to the entire editorial team: Mary Lindsey, Sarah Guan, Justine Bylo, Becca Heyman, *in lumine Tuo videbimus lumen*—in thy light shall we see light. Thank you for lighting the way. Thank you to everyone in marketing, publicity, design, and communications—Britt M, Curtis, Rae, Hannah L, Justine, Stacy, Melanie, Heather, Victoria, Cai, Riki, Hannah LP, Britt Z, and so many others—and to LJ Anderson and Bree Archer for the gorgeous cover design.

Thank you to Richard Abate and Hannah Carrende at 3Arts, who have never failed me. Thank you to all my friends and family. Thank you to Mike, my partner in crime and partner for life. Thank you, Mattie, for being the light in our lives. Thank you to all my amazing readers who have grown up reading my books and buying them for their kids.

APPENDIX

THE HISTORY OF THE LANDS OF ALBION

The Time before Memory

The land of Albion was once desolate. Swept by wild, impossible winds, the continent was stark and rocky, filled with high cliffs and barren plains. Few chose to live in this desolate place. Those who did were a nomadic folk, sheltering in caves, hunting but seldom finding anything worth gathering. The people worshiped the winds, calling them Anemoi, winds so powerful they were imbued with a magical force called Eurus.

The First Epoch

Monks in the high caves of Albion revered the Anemoi in the time before memory, but there was one named Skiron who believed the Anemoi were not gods but were instead an elemental force that could be tamed. She learned to control that force. Wielding its power, she tamed the savage winds, forging a new discipline she called the Whisting. In her monastery, she trained a group of four acolytes with its power, and together they used the Whisting to level mountains and fill valleys, diverting rivers and forging lakes. They made the deserted, mountainous country suitable for living and farming. Thus, the first epoch of Albion came into being. The four kept the peace, and in this time of calm and prosperity, four kingdoms were born: Penrith, Loegria, Alarice, and Estyrion.

The Second Epoch

After five centuries of peace, there came one who was named Boreas, a descendant of one of the four, and on the Night of Silence, he discovered a dark force to the Whisting and used this new power for something unheard of: violence. In a single night, with his band of Kilandrar, corrupted Anemoi, he destroyed the order of the four, killing the other three in their sleep. This new dark magic was called the Unseen Death, for the way he silently killed the others.

In this new age, Boreas alone wielded the Unseen Death and used it to reshape the land once more. He conquered leaders and crushed armies, unifying the four kingdoms under his rule. He built a castle and ruled from the land of Estyrion. For centuries, the successors of Boreas ruled the four lands until the Night of Stillness, when the sons and daughters of those three who were once kings and queens murdered the strangely long-lived Boreas at his own banquet, ending his reign and the epoch. At the moment of his dying, Boreas laid waste to all of Estyrion, and it has been a barren, empty place ever since, just as it was in the time before memory.

The Third Epoch

Boreas the Unbeliever was defeated by the Vindar knights and the Rings of Fate, rings that contained the pure, elemental power of the Whisting, blessed by the Anemoi. The three kings and queens who took Boreas's life resettled the old kingdoms of Loegria, Alarice, and Penrith, forging new dynasties. They agreed that all knowledge and writings related to the dark force of the Whisting should be destroyed and use of the Unseen Death would die with Boreas.

For centuries, the Rings of Fate kept peace throughout the land. But now the world is changing...the wind knights are no more, something new rises in the Great Waste of the former kingdom of Estyrion, and the kingdom of Penrith has fallen to the Usurper. Rumors abound that he is none other than Boreas returned and that the fearsome Kilandrar have once again taken to the air.

AN ASSASSIN, A BAKER, AND AN EVIL SORCERER WALK INTO A TAVERN...

EXPECT SOME CHAOS.